DOUBLE TAKE

Brenda Joyce

St. Martin's Paperbacks

Extraordinary praise for the novels of Brenda Joyce

DOUBLE TAKE

"Sizzles with intrigue and suspense."

—*Romantic Times*

"A fantastic tale of passion and intrigue with lots of twists and turns."

—*Old Book Barn Gazette*

THE CHASE

"Well-written . . . the plot has so many twists and turns and surprises you won't be able to put it down until the last page . . . a very enjoyable suspense novel."

—*Sullivan County Democrat*

"Joyce skillfully weaves together past and present to create an amazing story of intrigue, wartime passion, and thrilling twists and turns."

—*Publishers Weekly*

"Fast pacing and dual plot lines from the past and the present make this thriller a riveting read. Powerful and dynamic, this is a book not to be missed."

—*Romantic Times*

"Non-stop . . . filled with action, mysteries, romance, and an awesome ending!"

—*Huntress Reviews*

MORE . . .

HOUSE OF DREAMS

THE THIRD HEIRESS

"Sexual intrigue, betrayals, and century-old cover-ups . . . this genealogical thriller is a page-turner and could perhaps prove to be her breakout novel."

—Publishers Weekly

"Real suspense!"

—Kirkus Reviews

"Exciting!"

—Booklist

"Taut suspense, deep character analysis, intricate plotting, and superb writing technique characterize Brenda Joyce's new novel and offer her fans another book for their keeper shelves. Combined with nail-biting suspense, *The Third Heiress* kept me reading long into the night; it is Ms. Joyce at her best."

—Under the Covers Book Reviews

"Bestselling author Brenda Joyce mixes intrigue and romance into a page-turning tale you'll be loath to put down."

—Playgirl

"A tense and atmospheric thriller. *The Third Heiress* adds gothic and ghostly overtones to a story of one woman's obsessive quest for truth and justice."

—Romantic Times

This book is dedicated to Elie, again.

Life is so full of surprises . . . Thank you for always being there.

PROLOGUE

The phone call came at one in the morning.

It would change her life.

She hung up the receiver, stunned. And for one moment, Kait was simply paralyzed. After all these years—how many had it been?—Lana had walked right back into her life.

Kait fought to breathe, fought to think. Lana had sounded frightened and tense, which was completely uncharacteristic for her. What did she want? All she had said was that they had to meet, and now, and that there was no time. Oh, God. Something had to be terribly wrong for her sister to so suddenly reappear in her life this way.

Kait leapt from the bed, sweating, even though it was a pleasant autumn night. Memories of the past began to dance around her, taunting, teasing, tearful—expectant. She was afraid—but she was also hopeful.

How many nights had she lain in bed, her mind straying to the twin sister who had chosen to walk away from their relationship, who had almost completely disappeared? How often had she thought of hiring an investigator to find out where Lana was and if she was all right? But just when she was a heartbeat away from doing so, Lana would call, telling her that she was in Paris or Rio, asking how she was, reassuring Kait that all was well. Those calls were few and far between. They lacked detail and substance. But they had always given Kait hope, which she had clung to.

And now Lana was here, in Manhattan, insisting that they meet.

Kait dashed to the closet, grabbing jeans. She *had* to go. It never even crossed her mind to say no, because this telephone call, unlike the others, signaled that something was terribly wrong.

Five minutes later, she was hurrying down Central Park West, past several doormen, who regarded her with bleary eyes from behind the locked front doors of the buildings they kept. She veered left, fully alert and no longer dazed, but tense now with worry. Possibilities flooded her mind. What did Lana want? When had she last spoken to her? The phone call, coming like this, felt like an emotional mugging. Kait not only didn't know what to think, she didn't know how to feel. She was frightened, but, dear God, this time, Lana wasn't going to walk out of her life again.

In spite of the tears that burned the backs of her eyelids, Kait was determined. Somehow, this phone call would be a new beginning for them.

The coffee shop on Columbus Avenue was brightly lit and surprisingly busy. Her steps slowed as she approached, her heart lurching and then racing with overwrought nerves. Fear of rejection made her want to turn around and run away, but Kait pushed open the door firmly instead. If Lana wanted to resume their relationship, she would not be calling in the middle of the night. Clearly she wanted something else. Whatever it was, Kait intended to deliver, for that might bring them together. But their estrangement had begun so many years ago, in late childhood and early adolescence. And Kait had never understood *why*.

She inhaled harshly, stepping through the glass door and into the illumination of the too-bright interior lights. As she did she caught a glimpse of her frighteningly pale reflection in the mirror on one wall—she had never been this starkly white, the contrast almost gruesome with her short, dark hair. And even from a short distance, there was no mistaking the trepidation in her blue eyes.

What *could* Lana want? What *had* happened?

And why couldn't this have been a simple reunion, in the light of day?

She turned, her gaze swinging out over the crowd in the coffee shop. Most of the patrons were in their twenties, having had that one extra drink and now eating off the effects. The atmosphere was oddly festive and extremely noisy, a glaring contrast to her own nerves and state of mind.

Lana stood up from a booth where she had been sitting alone.

Kait saw her and froze.

And the words rang in her head, so loudly, she expected the diners in the café to turn and look at her. *Please let me have a sister now.*

She told herself that people did change, and even if Lana hadn't, maybe she needed her only family now as much as Kait did.

Lana was her sister, her twin, and she had never stopped loving her, even if the hurt had been so insidious, an inflicted wound so tiny and microscopic at first that it had been years and years before she had ever recognized its terrible presence.

Tears blurred her vision. But she was there; she was really there.

"Kait," Lana whispered. "Kaitlin!"

She swallowed and somehow pulled herself together, moving toward the stunning brunette who could have been herself. "Hello, Lana." She paused at the edge of the table within the booth.

Lana stepped swiftly out—her restless energy had hardly dimmed, Kaitlin thought. Nor had she really aged—she appeared to be in her late twenties, and their last encounter had been about seven years ago, when they were twenty-five.

Lana was five foot five, her face a perfect oval, her complexion naturally fair, but brushed now with the slight bronze glow of one who lived a healthy, outdoors life. Her dark hair was cut in a bob that was just above her shoulders, and she remained a perfect size six with Susan Lucci curves. Kaitlin was thinner, and she had had her hair cut gamineshort with flirty layers and trendy little wisps that poked about however they pleased. She realized that Lana was also surveying her.

"You look like a kid in that cut," Lana said with a sudden, strained smile.

"You're still gorgeous," Kaitlin heard herself reply. Now was not the time to cry.

"Do you hate me?" Lana's eyes met Kaitlin's, pointed and direct.

"I never hated you," Kaitlin cried, the truth. "I'm so happy to see you!"

Lana's tension visibly decreased. She smiled, and went from gorgeous to breathtaking. "I miss you, Kait."

The hope flared. It became consuming, full-blown. "I miss you, too." There was so much Kait wanted to ask, but words failed her now. Where did Lana live? What was she doing for a living now? But, mostly, she wanted to know why they weren't real sisters, why they weren't friends. Their mother had died of cancer when they were children, but several years ago their father had died as well, and Lana was the only family Kait had.

"Kait? Let's sit down. I don't have a lot of time."

Kait didn't move. "But—you only just got here," she began.

Lana gripped her hands. "I'm in terrible trouble. I need your help. I know I've been a rotten sister, but that's going to change now, Kait, really. I need your help, just for a couple of days." Suddenly she released her hands, withdrawing a sealed envelope from her handbag. "This letter will explain everything."

Kait was reeling. "What do you mean you're in trouble? What's wrong? And of course I'll help, you know I'd always help you, Lana, always!" But even as she spoke, meaning her every word, she was sick, because Lana was clearly leaving her again, and it was too soon, too much; Kait simply couldn't digest what was happening.

"I need you to take my place for two days, Kait," Lana said tersely.

Kait gasped. "What?"

"You need to cover for me. The way we did when we were little kids. It's all in the letter, Kait." Her blue gaze was searing. "I *have* to go!"

Kait gripped her arm. "You want to switch places? For two days? I don't understand!"

"Will you help me?" Lana demanded.

Kait looked into her eyes and saw steely desperation. "Of course I'll help you," she began.

"Good!" Lana slid Kait's purse off her shoulder, handing her own Gucci handbag to her. Then she took a garment bag from the booth and shoved it into her arms. "Tell everyone I cut my hair," she said tersely. "Here in the city, at Bergdorf's."

"Wait!" Kait grabbed her wrist, realizing she was about to leave. "I need to know what's going on. I need to know when I'll see you again!" Panic claimed her, and it had less to do with trading places than it did with losing her twin sister all over again.

"Two days from tomorrow," Lana said with a brief, reassuring smile. "It's all in the letter, Kait. I have to go. I have a car waiting. There's no time."

With Kait's bag on her shoulder, Lana hugged her hard and started through the coffee shop for the door. Kait came to life and ran after her. This could not be happening this way! And the severity of the trouble her sister was in struck her now. Something terrible had to be happening, otherwise Lana would not have called as she had, and she would not be rushing away like this.

"What kind of trouble are you in?" she cried, chasing her out the door and into the cool New York City night.

A Lincoln Town Car with a driver was idling at the curb. Lana swung open the door and turned. "The killing kind," she said.

ONE

Kait had been driving on a winding country road with no line dividing it for some time now. She had left the small quaint town of Three Falls, Virginia, about twelve miles behind. It was the following afternoon, a mere twelve hours since Lana's telephone call, and she was tense with anxiety and even fear. That tension had been present ever since she had promised Lana that she would switch places with her. It had increased and turned into dread when she had read and then reread Lana's letter last night. Her grip on the leather-bound steering wheel tightened. *Was she really doing this?*

Could she really do this?

Abruptly, Kait swerved off the road and parked Lana's Porsche. The rolling hills of the Virginia countryside were breathtaking and had been so for some time; it was early autumn and the land was alive with a brilliant kaleidoscope of flaming color. Kait found herself turning off the ignition and climbing out of the small silver sports car. The fields in front of her were bordered with pristine white fences. Horses grazed not far from where she stood, and in the distance she saw several white barns and outbuildings, trimmed vividly with evergreen, and beyond them a colonial house on a hill. There was a lump in her chest and she couldn't seem to breathe. Tears came to her eyes.

This was Fox Hollow. This was Lana's home. It was storybook perfection.

Kait clung to the top rail of the fence trying to calm and compose herself, as she was expected at Fox Hollow at any moment. She had obeyed the instructions in Lana's letter exactly. She had called the housekeeper, Elizabeth Dorentz, to let her know she would be arriving around one in the afternoon. She had taken the eleven A.M. shuttle from La Guardia and picked up Lana's Porsche at Reagan National in longterm parking. She was wearing Lana's clothes, makeup, and jewelry—a pale tan Armani pantsuit with high heels, her red lipstick, her beautiful Chopard watch with its diamond bezel, her rings and earrings, just as she was carrying Lana's Gucci bag, her wallet, her driver's license, and her cell phone. And she had called in sick at work, explaining that she would be out for a few days—Kait was a VP at a small PR firm on Madison Avenue. Yes, she was really switching places with her sister; she was really participating in a monstrous deception.

But there was no choice, because Lana was in trouble, and she hadn't exaggerated when she had said it was the killing kind.

Kait inhaled deeply but could not stop shaking. Lana's letter had been a bombshell. No, it had been a nuclear explosion, and she still didn't know how she could manage it, how she could survive its contents. *Lana was married. And Lana had a daughter, a four-year-old little girl named Marni.*

The flaming orange trees and fading green fields blurred in her vision. And Lana wasn't only married, she had been married for six years. Six years ago, she had gotten married, without telling Kait, without calling her, without writing her, without inviting her to the wedding.

Why?

The betrayal was acute, overwhelming. All these years, Lana had been living a short shuttle flight away. All these years, she had been the mistress of an old moneyed horse farm and the wife of the Virginian, Trev Coleman. Kait didn't think she would ever recover from the fact that she had been so thoroughly excluded from Lana's life. The question of why would haunt her forever.

They had never been close like other sisters, not even as small children. As an adult, Kait had rationalized that because they were so different, they had merely had different friends, interests, and activities, and thus their estrangement. Lana had been the tomboy as a child, Kait had been a bookworm. Lana had enjoyed and excelled at gym and sports, Kait had dreaded every time she got up to bat, every time they chose teams for a game. In many ways, Lana had been the extroverted one, Kait the reclusive one.

Their parents had been solidly middle class, and the sisters had grown up in Darien, Connecticut. They'd both fallen wildly for horses, and had worked at a local stable for lessons. When their mother had died of cancer the twins had been turning thirteen; Lana's tomboy nature had been changing, and suddenly lip gloss and tight tank tops appeared with her low riding jeans. Kait had become a serious student, earning straight A's on every report card. The jocks began looking at her sister; Kait's best friend was another A student and her neighbor, Tom, a geeky type who was already creating computer games and programs. Other girls began to look to Lana as a role model. Miniskirts appeared. She pierced her ears, cut her hair. Kait went to the stables less, Lana went more. She had her first boyfriend just after their mother died. She told Kait she wouldn't go all the way until she was sixteen.

Their mother's death should have brought the two sisters closer together. But it did not; the reverse was true. For Lana, there were more boys, and there were late parties and the small lies needed to cover them up. For Kait, there was confusion, anguish, and bewilderment. School became even more important to her—she didn't have her first date until she was a freshman at college. And it was no surprise to Kait that Lana would choose to go to a different college entirely, and it was even less of a surprise when she dropped out her junior year. Their father, who had hung on to their life the best that he could after the death of his wife, had given up attempting to control or even guide Lana for years. She didn't tell anyone she was quitting school, and it was a year or so later before Kait learned that her sister was in New York City, working as a waitress while taking acting lessons.

Kait knew that they had never been close because they were so very different by nature; but other sisters were different too, and they were still as close as best friends. Lana's indifference had always, secretly, hurt. Kait didn't know when the wound had first been inflicted, but it felt as if it had been within her forever.

Now there was the fact of her sister's marriage, her sister's child. The pain was acute. But with it, there was the oddest joy. *Kait had a niece.* And in a few moments, Kait would meet Marni. She simply could not wait.

But she had to compose herself now, and quickly. She closed her eyes tightly. Squeezing them shut. Trying to breathe. It was impossible, because in a few minutes she was going to have to walk through Coleman's front door. He was out of town on business, but she was as afraid of discovery as she was of successfully deceiving his family and friends now.

It was an amazing twist of fate, Lana's marrying Trev Coleman. A few years ago Kait had contacted him about using his estate for a charity event sponsored by one of her largest corporate clients. She'd actually seen his photo in *Town & Country* once, on a society page for a local Virginia event, and he'd caught her eye, because he was a tall, handsome man with an unusual complexion—he seemed swarthy, but he had brown hair heavily sun-streaked with gold. In his tuxedo, he'd been at once elegant and virile, another unusual combination. A co-worker had then suggested his name some time later when they'd been given the account for the charity event. Oddly, Kait had been filled with excitement at the idea of contacting Coleman. She did her homework and learned he had been recently widowed. And he had seemed amenable to the idea over the phone; in fact, the conversation had turned friendly and almost personal in the end, leaving Kait foolishly breathless. She had anticipated their business meeting, speculating about what he might be like in person, and as foolishly had taken hours to decide the night before what to wear, but in the end, they had never made a deal. He hadn't shown up for their lunch meeting. She had waited for him at Le Cirque for well over an hour in her brand-new Sergio Rossi mules and a simple black sheath. He hadn't even bothered to cancel. Kait had been annoyed. She had also been slightly humiliated, sitting there at the five-star restaurant sipping Perrier like a jilted girlfriend, not like a publicist wasting her valuable time.

She had wound up using a smaller but very picturesque estate on the Hudson River instead.

And now Lana was his wife. And she, Kait, was on the verge of walking into her sister's life in order to pretend to be Coleman's wife and Marni's mother. It was wrong in every possible way, and Kait's very nature rebelled against what she was about to do, but there was simply no choice.

Kait dug into the pocket of her pale beige wool trousers, extracting Lana's letter. She unfolded the crumpled pages and read it again, the words blurring and fading before her eyes.

> *Dear Kait,*
> *I have so many regrets, and the biggest one is my failure to be the sister you have always wanted and deserved. Yes, Kait, I know you as well as you know yourself, and I know you have always wanted my love, and deliberately I have withheld it from you. You see, Kait, I have always been jealous of you, because you were the perfect student and the perfect daughter, because Mom and Dad always loved you the most. But no more. Kait, I swear to you, that when this is over, I am going to make up for every single moment we have lost. When this is over, we are going to finally have the chance to be real sisters and best friends.*

Kait blinked back hot tears, still stunned to learn that Lana—whom she had always admired so, who'd had all the boys, who had always been one of the most popular girls in school—had been jealous of her, and read on.

> *I'm in trouble, Kait. Serious, deadly trouble. I borrowed a tremendous amount of money behind my husband's back in order to stave off his creditors and to prevent foreclosure on Fox Hollow, our country estate. While that was accomplished, it seems that I went to the wrong people and now Paul Corelli has threatened not just my life but that of my daughter's if I don't pay him back by the end of this week. There is someone who I haven't seen in years, someone I was once close to, who I believe will help me out of the dilemma I now face. I only need two days for you to cover for me. It will work because I haven't told anyone about you. No one knows I have an identical twin, so no one will ever suspect the switch. And when I return, when I pay off Corelli, I will introduce you to my family and we can start over—if you will allow that.*

Kait hung on to the fence, the wrinkled letter in her hand, still trembling. As far as she could see, fading green hills rolled and spilled away, framed by the flaming orange and yellows of the turning oaks and elm trees of fall. In the distance and to her right was a dark blue lake, a bevy of ducks flying above it; several broodmares that were clearly in foal were grazing by the lake. The sky above her was brilliantly blue, making it a picture-perfect day.

Not only was Lana's life in danger, but so was Marni's. Kait was terrified for them both.

Which meant she was doing as Lana had asked, because there simply was no other choice.

And did Lana really mean that she regretted their past? Did she really intend to start over with Kait, and forge the friendship they had never had? After all of these years, did she finally realize that she needed and wanted her sister in her life? Kait was filled with hope. But so many years had gone by that there was doubt too. Kait *wanted* to believe that her sister was sincere. Maybe, having faced threats from this Corelli person, Lana had realized that it was time to finally include her sister in her life. Maybe she finally realized the importance of family.

But how much money did she owe? And who cared so much for her now that he or she would lend or give it to her? Kait didn't like the sound of any of that. It was odd.

Lana had her cell phone. Kait intended to call her the moment she had the chance—which meant that once she was settled in and no one suspected who she really was, once she had a truly private moment, she would call and try to find out more details about the problems Lana faced. Lana hadn't given her, Kait, a chance to help in any way other than to cover for her—clearly she didn't want her husband to know about the trouble she was in—but Kait knew that where there was a will there was a way, and, surely, she could help Lana raise the money to get this Paul Corelli off her back. And then there were the police. Kait couldn't understand why her sister hadn't gone to the authorities. That in itself made absolutely no sense.

Kait pulled a lighter out of her pocket and burned the letter. Then she rearranged her expression, which she knew had to be a worried one, and with a slight smile fixed on her face, she returned to Lana's small sports car. The flamboyant and expensive Porsche was a convertible, but Kait did not have the top down. She slid into the driver's low-lying bucket seat and turned the ignition back on, then pulled down the mirror on the sun visor to check her red lipstick. It hadn't smeared or run. For one moment, Kait stared at her eyes, contoured now with Lana's almond brown eye shadow. Kait favored nude glosses and mascara but rarely wore any more makeup, not even to work; and out of the office, it was strictly blue jeans and T-shirts. She was far more than chic now, she was incredibly glamorous, and that, coupled with the lie she was about to commit, meant that she felt unbearably uncomfortable—as if she had somehow stepped out of her own skin and into someone else's—which she had. Lana had always been the fashionable one, the chic one, and Kait looked so much like her sister now that it was surreal.

A huge ball of fear sickened her stomach now.

Could she really do this? How could she not *do this?*

Kait put the Porsche into gear and slipped back on the road. She also failed to understand why Lana hadn't shared her burden with her husband. If she were Lana, she would confess everything to her husband, and somehow, with his support, find a way to raise the cash and get out of the mess she was in.

Kait wished that she'd had a chance to reason with her sister. Even knowing how opinionated and determined Lana could be, if Kait had had her way, she would have talked Lana out of this deception, convincing her to go to the police and her husband.

The road turned. And suddenly Kait was face-to-face with a pair of brick pillars, each one with a brass plaque. One gave the number of the estate—1296 NORTHWOODS ROAD. The other merely read FOX HOLLOW.

Kait was one second away from whipping the Porsche into a U-turn and fleeing. Instead, the last lines of Lana's letter resounded in her mind.

> *Kait, I am desperate. I would never ask this of you if I weren't. You're my sister, my twin, and even after all of these years, I know that bond can't be severed. I know I can count on you.*

Lana was never desperate. Lana was always cool and calm, always smiling, always filled with confidence. But she was none of those things now. Now, she was scared.

And from the sound of things, rightly so.

Kait drove between the two brick pillars.

Summoning up her courage, absolutely willing her nerves to be steady—and reminding herself that no one could possibly suspect the switch, at least, not yet—Kait drove slowly up a long gravel driveway lined with more sparkling white paddocks and a succession of stately oak trees. *Could she deceive everyone?* Wouldn't someone be able to see through her superficial disguise? After all, she and Lana were nothing alike!

Kait wanted to retch. But she hadn't been able to eat all day, so she knew it was only her overwrought nerves. She had to be more like her sister now. She had to be charming, extremely confident, naturally sexy.

But surely Lana's own child would be able to tell the difference between her aunt and her mother, even if they did look alike. But Lana had felt certain that Marni would not know and she had said so in her letter. She had also written that Coleman had a teenaged daughter from his first marriage, Samantha, and she had left a description of the house, the housekeeper, and the staff. Kait wanted to believe as Lana did that they could pull off this deception; she wanted to turn the car around and drive away. *No matter the trouble Lana was in, everything that they were doing was so terribly wrong.*

But Kait couldn't take a chance on Corelli hurting either her sister or her niece and it was as simple as that.

Suddenly a band of long, lanky yearlings raced by on her left. Surprised, Kait started, but then she slowed, and before she even knew it she was watching the beautiful young Thoroughbreds playing gracefully in the adjacent paddock, distracted. The band of yearlings, all chestnuts and one black, turned and galloped away, tails high, manes flying, and Kait felt herself smile. She simply had to watch them until they disappeared from sight. Lana had to be the luckiest woman in the world, to have a man like Trev Coleman fall in love with her, to have a daughter—a family—and a fairy-tale home like Fox Hollow.

Kait started the Porsche down the drive again. She had her window wide open, and now she sniffed the crisp, fresh country air with a deep appreciation. And as she drove past an outdoor riding ring and six state-of-the-art whitewashed barns, one of which was probably a huge indoor arena, her heart quickened, this time with anticipation. A part of her could not wait to walk through the front door and get settled in.

Kait quickly had to remind herself of what she was doing and that this was not her home. But on the other hand, a few days from now, she would be a legitimate family member and undoubtedly from that point on a frequent guest. Then she saw the house.

It was a brick colonial, built in the late eighteenth century, with a high temple pediment and six huge white columns supporting it. The beautiful residence sat above the rest of the estate on a hill. As she drove up the drive toward it, her anxiety returned. A dusty black Land Rover and a big, brand-new cobalt blue pickup truck sat off to the side of the house, in front of a garage that was so beautifully designed that it looked like a residential wing. The hood of the Land Rover was up. Her heart skipped as she braked and turned off the ignition; a man slammed down the hood and looked at her.

This was it.

The point of no return.

She had parked beneath a huge oak tree, out of the sun; now, she lifted her gaze with real trepidation and met an intense blue stare. Kait relaxed, because for one instant she had feared the worst—that Coleman had changed his plans and was at home. But this was not Trevor Coleman. Trev was darkly blond and tanned, and Kait knew he was in his mid-thirties. This man was in his early forties and he had dark, short hair. He wasn't short, but he wasn't tall and he had the physique of a boxer or a weightlifter; Coleman was tall and his build was average. Besides, this man was wearing a very worn and faded pale blue T-shirt (which revealed bulging biceps and rock-hard abs) and rather stained jeans with a pair of work boots. Kait felt certain Coleman ran his estate in tan breeches and knee-high riding boots. This was not, thank God, Lana's husband.

Kait felt certain that this was a recently hired employee, Max Zara, part handyman, part stable boy. Kait realized she was gripping the wheel. She took a deep breath, forced a smile, and grabbed her purse, stepping out of the car. She stumbled in Lana's high heels and winced.

She realized that posing as Lana even for two days might have technical problems—like the three- and four-inch heels her sister favored. Hoping Zara had not seen her little faux pas, Kait slung Lana's Gucci bag over her shoulder and went carefully to the back of the car. She flipped up the Porsche's tiny trunk lid.

The back of her neck began to prickle. Kait had the awful feeling of being watched; she stiffened automatically and turned with dread and a lurching sensation in her stomach. Max Zara was staring at her. His regard was so fixed that Kait flinched. Had she just remarked hostility in his eyes?

Perhaps this wasn't Zara after all.

His brilliant blue eyes slipped over her coolly. "Pleasant trip, Mrs. Coleman?" he asked with an accent that had to be Brooklyn or Queens. He was certainly no native Virginian. He did not smile, not even slightly, and his eyes were ice cold.

Kait had not mistaken his hostility—he reeked with it. She pulled herself together, bewildered and taken aback. "It was wonderful," she said as warmly as possible.

He continued to stare.

Kait hesitated, as he offered no reply. What was going on? She knew she was missing something—because she saw speculation as well as enmity in his eyes. Why hadn't Lana mentioned that they were at odds? Were he and her sister at odds? And, if so, why? He was only a hired hand—how much could Lana have to do with him? She forced a smile. Lana had told her husband she was going to New York to do some shopping. "I found a lot of sales," she said brightly. God, she sounded as panicked as she felt! She had to get a grip.

He sauntered over, his gaze never wavering, and the closer he came, the more she tensed. "Not a lot of bags for a shopping spree," he remarked, finally glancing away from her and into the trunk where she had Lana's single garment bag and one shopping bag from FAO Schwarz.

His eyes were so pale that they were unnerving—especially when they settled coolly on her again. "I'm having everything sent," she said, turning. She felt shaken, but she had just been caught in her lie. She reached into the trunk and hefted out the garment bag.

Instantly, his hand brushed hers, closing on the bag as he took it from her. "Now why would you go taking your own bags from the car?" he asked, eyes narrowing.

Their gazes smacked into one another. Kait could hardly think, much less respond, and then it hit her—she was a wealthy woman, she was waited upon. She had a role to play, and she had better start playing it now.

Zara's pale blue gaze pinned her; he did not reach for the shopping bag, and he waited patiently for her answer.

But what answer could she possibly give? "My feet are killing me and I am desperate to change my shoes," she said quickly, managing a smile and feeling a flush, but actually, it was the truth.

He was unmoved. "I'll bring your bags right up, Mrs. Coleman," he said, and his eyes slid over her again, this time in a sexually disparaging manner.

Kait was so stunned by his rudeness that she turned and fled toward the house, tripping again in Lana's high-heeled boots. She heard the trunk of the Porsche slamming. She wanted to throttle her sister for not warning her that there was some kind of intense conflict going on with one of the estate's employees. But was it a conflict or something else? That man had undressed her with his eyes, and of that she had no doubt.

She reminded herself that her sexy sister often provoked such reaction in men. Lana had begun flirting as a child—as a teen, she'd had boys begging for her attentions. She had always been naturally coy; without any effort, she had always attracted men. While Kait recalled all this in a flash, now her own mental excuses for her sister felt feeble.

Hopefully Lana had not been flirting with Max Zara right beneath her husband's nose.

Kait composed herself, finding her balance and looking

up. Someone was standing on the porch, framed by the massive columns holding up the temple pediment of the house. As Kait approached, she saw a tall, shapely older woman clad in riding breeches, paddock boots, and a crisp white shirt with a navy blue sweater draped over her shoulders. For a woman dressed to be in the stables, she had not a speck of dirt upon her. Very serious, square tortoiseshell glasses framed a square face with high cheekbones and some interesting lines; her graying blond hair was pulled tightly back into a chignon. Kaitlin knew this was the housekeeper, Elizabeth Dorentz. She was smiling politely, impersonally, at her.

Kait smiled back, her heart racing with fear, and began up the wide, steep stone steps to the porch of the house. "Mrs. Dorentz," she began. "Am I glad to be . . . home." She tripped over the last word.

Elizabeth nodded. "How was your trip? I have lunch waiting." Her eyes narrowed and slid over Kaitlin. "You cut your hair."

Kait wet her lips, running her hand through the Meg Ryan layers. "I did. At Bergdorf's. It was time for a change."

Elizabeth didn't respond. She turned and walked into the house.

Kait blinked, once again thoroughly taken aback. Had she just been rebuffed? But what had she done? Lana had said that Elizabeth had been with the family for decades—ever since Trev Coleman was a little boy. Surely she had imagined the other woman's rudeness. Maybe she was curt and brusque by nature. And then Kait felt eyes on her back, right in the center of her rigid shoulder blades. She glanced back. Max Zara's stare was as cool and unflinching as earlier. Kait simply could not bear the tension—she hurried into the house after Elizabeth Dorentz, perspiring.

And the moment she stepped over the threshold, she entered another world, another time, another place.

Kait halted, breathing deeply, the scent of pine and lilac strong.

She stood in a spacious foyer. Smooth oak floors were underfoot, pine beams overhead, and a wide staircase led to the upper floors of the house. Kait was certain that the house had been built in colonial times, which meant that the interior had been completely renovated in the recent past. Directly ahead was a huge living room—clearly several walls had been knocked out to accommodate the designer's aims. The décor was old-world elegance: antiques vied with tweeds and leather, nineteenth-century paintings hung on the walls in old and faded gilded frames. As Mrs. Dorentz had disappeared, Kait found herself walking into the living room, where a wall of huge windows looked out on the pastures and horses below, with rolling blue hills framing the horizon.

Her chest was tight. It was so beautiful—the view, this room, the house—and she could imagine being curled up in that huge stuffed tan suede chair at night, the one not far from the massive stone fireplace, her feet on the matching ottoman, the brown-and-green paisley throw on her lap, a book in hand, a glass of wine at her elbow. Because, while this room was clearly for entertaining, it was as clearly designed for family comfort. She smiled when she saw a small horse model peeking out from the sofa's plush throw pillows. A tiny rider doll was on the horse's back.

Marni would be at pre-K now.

Kait had to close her eyes and pinch herself.

Lana's life was like a dream come true.

The rich, deep timbre of a man's voice drifted through the house, reaching her. It was a voice she had heard only once and years ago, but it was a voice that she would never forget. Kait stiffened impossibly, stunned, her eyes flying open, her heart racing with alarm. The unseen man now approaching in the hall was Lana's husband, Trev Coleman, and Kait simply knew it.

Her throat went dry. Her worst fear had just been realized. She became paralyzed.

He would take one look at her and demand to know who the hell she was and just where the hell his real wife was.

His words became distinct. "I mean it. . . . Couldn't have

done it without you . . . If ever I can . . . Yeah . . . Thanks again. Great job." His voice was a bit scratchy, very distinctive, and completely sensual.

And as his voice became clearer, as his footsteps sounded, she felt herself turn into a block of ice. Trev Coleman had changed his plans. He was there, at Fox Hollow, in the house. They would meet at any moment. Oh, God, what should she do now?

An image of Lana assailed her. Her blue eyes were filled with fear.

His footsteps halted. Kait knew he stood behind her, on the threshold of the living room and foyer. Kait didn't move—because she could not. Lana and Marni were in danger. She had to go through with this. And slowly, her mind turning oddly blank, hardly able to draw a decent breath, Kait turned.

He was backlit by the sun. For one moment, Kait only saw a tall, broad-shouldered silhouette. For one moment, she prepared to blurt out the truth. For one moment, she felt the way she had at Le Cirque, sitting there in her best black dress, in brand-new sexy shoes, waiting for him to appear, to smile at her. Then he took another step, from sunshine into shadow, and she saw his face. He saw her and halted in mid-stride, as if surprised.

Their eyes met.

His were green.

Kait forgot to breathe. The two photographs she had seen years and years ago hadn't done justice to this man. Oh, no, he was drop-dead good-looking, with movie-star sex appeal.

Trev Coleman didn't move. Neither did Kait. They simply stared unblinkingly at one another, and Kait felt that her expression had become as unreadable as his.

And in spite of the danger Lana was in, Kait almost prayed that he would look at her and see that she was not Lana instantly. Because then he would be told the truth he deserved to know, and then he and Lana could work this out together, as a husband and wife should.

His eyes weren't merely green, they were the green of Ireland in the spring, and they were framed by thick, black sooty lashes. Kait knew she was staring, but she could not stop. His face was oval, a face with a slightly crooked and oh so interesting nose and high, high cheekbones. His mouth was full. He was lightly tanned. His brownish-blond hair was wildly sun-streaked, clearly an act of nature, clearly indicating a lifetime spent outdoors. He wore faded jeans, not fancy riding breeches. Kait guessed that he was about six foot two inches tall, and his legs were so muscular from a lifetime of riding that his thighs strained the worn denim there. A beautiful V-necked teal cashmere sweater clung to his broad shoulders and the firm planes of his chest. He wore faded brown lug-soled paddock boots. Something gold glinted from one wrist—a hefty, expensive watch. It was the only jewelry he wore—he didn't even wear a belt.

Kait felt as if she had just been struck by a runaway locomotive.

Somehow, deep within herself, she sensed that she would never be the same.

Lana was so lucky.

"You're staring," he said flatly, his green gaze narrowing.

She came to life. And horrified, she felt her cheeks flame. Worse, she could not get a word out—in fact, an appropriate greeting failed her completely, as if her tongue were actually tied in knots.

He jammed the cell phone into his back pocket and then looked up at her again. Never had she been so mesmerized by a pair of eyes. "You're back," he added as flatly. "You cut your hair." Both sentences were uttered dispassionately.

It hit Kait then. This man was Lana's husband. What kind of greeting was this? Where was the hug, the smile, the kiss? He didn't look very happy to see her. In fact, he didn't look happy at all. She managed to stretch her lips into a taut smile, her heart pounding so hard now that she felt faint. Somehow, she said, "Yes, I'm back. I cut my hair. Do you like it?" And she could hear how her own words sounded, tremulous and tentative and frightened.

He gave her an incredulous look and walked back the way he had come.

She was stunned. And as it hit her that he had just rudely turned his back on her, she began to tremble. *Oh, my God. What was this?* Had she been mistaken—or had she seen anger in Lana's husband's eyes?

Kaitlin was afraid she had seen far worse.

Had she seen disgust in Trev Coleman's eyes?

She fought for her composure. Wouldn't Lana have warned her if something were amiss in her marriage?

But there had only been Lana's letter, most of which contained instructions for Kait. And why would Lana have mentioned anything in regards to her marriage when she had expected Coleman to be away during Kait's charade? Kait inhaled, hard. Surely they were merely fighting—married couples had their ups and downs. But there was no sense of relief, and she simply refused to think of how cold Trevor Coleman had just been.

Suddenly he was in the foyer again. He thrust an envelope at her. "This is yours."

She met his green eyes and was stabbed with breathlessness again. For a moment, looking at him, she simply could not speak. His sheer masculinity made her feel tiny and petite, small and utterly feminine, porcelain and doll-like, when in actuality she was five foot five, healthy and strong, lanky but lean and fit.

"Sorry about the timing," he said, not looking sorry at all. He looked anything but sorry—he looked annoyed, smug . . . pissed.

She came to her senses and realized she held a large manila envelope in her hand. "What is this?" she said.

"Divorce papers," he said.

And, finally, he smiled.

TWO

Had a bomb exploded in the room, Kait could not have been more shocked.

Coleman turned away.

"What?" she managed, realizing that her mouth was hanging open. And her mind began to race. *Lana's marriage was not what she had believed it to be; Lana's husband wanted a divorce.*

Trev Coleman did not even look at her now. "You heard me," he said.

Kait could only stare speechlessly at his back as he walked away.

"I'll take your bags up now."

Kaitlin turned to meet the cold and far too speculative blue eyes of Max Zara. Clearly he hadn't missed the exchange with Trev Coleman. "Yes, please," she whispered, still stunned. "I . . . need to change."

Zara was startled. He looked at her with surprise, his eyes no longer hard, but the speculation remained, intensifying.

Kait bit her lip. She knew she was acting like a frightened mouse, and her sister was anything but that. She managed to clear her throat. She sent him a grateful smile. "Thank you," she said more firmly.

Suspicion filled his gaze. He regarded her for a moment and suddenly Kait felt certain that he sensed she was an impostor.

He turned abruptly. More dismay filling her, Kait watched him heft her two bags as easily as if they were a pair of books and he started toward the stairs.

Kait shifted away, leaning against the wall, rubbing her temples. Oh, God. What was she going to do now? *Why hadn't Lana told her that her marriage was in serious trouble?*

Suddenly a new thought struck her. *Had Lana even known that Trev Coleman wanted a divorce?*

With real trepidation, she glanced over her shoulder and glimpsed Trev Coleman at his desk in a study—he had left the door ajar. He was searching for something on the desktop, apparently without success, his handsome face taut with tension, a piece of gold hair falling over his brow. Her heart lurched hard. How was she going to handle this . . . him?

First things first. She must regroup immediately, before her charade was discovered. And for one thing, Lana was not vulnerable or anxious; she was very confident, very charming. She also had a temper, and she knew how to do battle. Kait had to become that way, too, and immediately.

Except it wasn't in her nature to lash out, and she had a dilemma on her hands. How should she handle Trev's declaration?

Mrs. Dorentz appeared, a tray in her hands. On it was a beautifully prepared and presented chef's salad and a cup of coffee, creamer, and sugar bowl, the last two items sterling silver. "Max, when you come down, can you take a look at the washer? I meant to tell you earlier that it is making an odd noise."

Kait watched Max nod at the housekeeper, his expression now perfectly agreeable. "No problem," he said. He sent Elizabeth Dorentz a smile, one which made him an interesting and appealing man—he had a cleft chin and dimples— and then he left them standing there to trot upstairs with her bags.

Elizabeth Dorentz gave her a reproving look. Kait realized she had been staring at Zara. She felt herself flush, and hoped that Elizabeth had not misinterpreted her look. "Boy, is it great to be back," she said, attempting a smile. Was the salad for her? Somehow, she did not think so.

Elizabeth did not respond.

"I've been under the weather," Kait added quickly. "I had a terrible flu. I spent two days in bed in New York. What a waste! I'm still not feeling all that great." It was time to establish her story. She was a size smaller than her sister and the difference had to be explained.

"I'm sorry you were ill," Elizabeth said politely. "I'm going to be late. I just called the school to tell them. I put lunch out for you. On the table," she added, as if that point needed clarification. "Trev, may I come in?"

Trev looked up. Kait's gaze went to him as if he were a huge magnet, and as he nodded at the housekeeper, his gaze swerved to her, as well. Their eyes met briefly before he looked away. "Thank you, Elizabeth," he said pleasantly.

She set the tray down. "I'm off to get Marni," Elizabeth replied, her tone completely different now. It was unguarded, friendly. "Do you need anything from town?"

"No, thanks." Trev smiled at her.

Kait's heart seemed to stop. Elizabeth was going to pick Marni up at school. Marni—her niece. Lana hadn't left any instructions regarding her care or even her routine, which now seemed glaring and odd. "I'll go," Kait cried impulsively, excitement sweeping her. She rushed to the door of the study; she couldn't wait to meet her niece.

Elizabeth whirled. "What?"

Kait saw the absolute surprise on her face, which she could not understand. And she saw Trev's wide eyes riveted on her as well. She hardly understood what she had done to surprise them both, but too late she realized she had no idea where Marni's school was. Why hadn't Lana written all the pertinent information down?

Disappointment seared her. "I . . . uh . . . I really miss her. But I'm exhausted from the trip," she continued lamely. The trip had been a forty-minute shuttle flight and an hour's drive from D.C. "And that flu has sapped my strength. I, uh, had better let you go."

Elizabeth Dorentz simply stared. "You don't pick her up. I pick her up. I pick her up and I take her to school every single day."

Kait stared back. Was Elizabeth being territorial as far as Marni was concerned? But at least she now knew a bit of Marni's routine. She also didn't believe that the housekeeper picked up Marni every single day—surely, now and then, Lana took her daughter to and from school. It was becoming very clear that Elizabeth had a chip on her shoulder. "You know what? I had better grab a bite to eat and go to my room. I'm going to take a nap. But I will pick her up tomorrow," Kait added very firmly.

Elizabeth nodded tightly, her brows furrowed above her tortoiseshell glasses. Then she left the house, her stride long and athletic, the door closing behind her.

Kait hesitated, torn between the urge to confront Trev Coleman for her sister's sake, and to flee as far from him as she could. She was still reeling from the shock of his handing her divorce papers—and from his being cold and nasty about it. *Lana hadn't said a thing.* Could she have been oblivious to her husband's feelings?

Kait found it hard to believe that she would be ignorant of the state of her marriage. But she would not be the first woman to be told by a spouse that he wanted a divorce. Sometimes, one simply refused to see the writing on the wall.

A chair slid back. Kait flinched and looked at Trev Coleman as he stood up. "You never pick up Marni," he said.

"*Never* is a very strong word," she returned nervously.

"So the games begin," he murmured, not pleasantly.

Fear slid up and down her spine. She backed up. She needed help here, she realized, and anger flashed within her. She had walked into Lana's life, assuming it to be a pleasant one, never dreaming that she was entering a war zone. Kait realized that she had to speak with her sister immediately. Lana had said in her letter that she would call her in two days when she was on her way back to Fox Hollow. That had implied that she would be out of touch until then. But Kait wasn't going to wait two days to speak with her sister—if Lana didn't know about the divorce, she needed to know immediately. And, even more important, Kait needed advice on how to deal with Trev Coleman.

Kait swallowed hard. "I don't know what you're talking about."

He made a sound of disgust.

Kait fled. She quickly moved into the foyer and paused beside a window, watching the housekeeper driving away in the dusty Land Rover. Her temples throbbed. Was Lana still carrying Kait's purse with her cell phone? Would she pick up? God, Coleman was so hateful—her sister had to have known what was coming.

How had their storybook marriage come to this?

Then she heard his footsteps approaching in the corridor and any relief at being briefly alone vanished. Kait tensed instinctively and looked up. Trev was walking toward her. He didn't look at her, but she was helpless and she watched him as he stepped right past her and went outside without a single word. A moment later she watched him climbing into the big blue Dodge pickup parked there.

Her heart lurched as she turned away from the window while he drove off. And finally she was truly alone.

What was going on? Did everyone dislike her sister? Was it possible? After all, Fox Hollow was her home, too. But that awful worker, Max, clearly had an ax to grind, and so did the housekeeper. And as for Trev Coleman, he was not the first husband to want a divorce, but he seemed to be furiously angry with her sister and just barely containing himself. Why?

And Kait was angry, too. Lana should have warned her about the issues she would face when trading places with her. She should have warned her just in case Coleman did exactly as he had—in case he changed his plans and appeared unexpectedly at Fox Hollow. But the truth was, even as children, Lana had always known when to omit the truth in order to get what she wanted. However, they weren't children anymore, and what they were doing was immoral and terribly wrong. Lana should have been more honest with her.

Kait took a deep breath and calmed down. Her sister did have a good excuse for her behavior—she was being threatened by that Paul Corelli, and so was her daughter. That might make anyone distracted, thoughtless, and selfishly determined to do whatever had to be done.

At least she had passed the first series of tests—no one knew she was covering for her sister. Somehow, she had pulled it off when they were as opposite as night and day.

The next big test would be Marni.

But she was really alone now. As she realized that, the last of the terrible tension she had been afflicted with drained away. This would be a good time to explore the house. Lana had drawn a map for her, but she should inspect each room anyway. However, even knowing that, Kait turned slowly back around. Trevor Coleman had left his study door wide open.

Kait didn't hesitate. She dropped her bag on the windowsill and walked into the room.

And the moment she stepped inside the wood-paneled room, she knew she was entering Trev Coleman's inner sanctum. The room reeked of his masculinity. Here, the floors were stained the color of cognac and darker antique beams finished the ceiling. A large cherrywood desk covered with files and folders faced a stone fireplace, upon which were many framed photographs. The windows behind it looked out over the first of the six barns and several paddocks where his horses grazed. A beautiful rug covered the floor, mostly beige and blue and green; the sofa was dark, emerald green leather, and the rest of the furniture was upholstered in masculine tweeds. Kait realized she had become immobilized. She could almost feel Trev Coleman's presence, even though he was gone.

Kait glanced at the fireplace; a painting hung over the mantel, the portrait of a magnificent, eagle-eyed chestnut horse. There was an open newspaper on the floor by the sofa, an empty scotch glass on the side table. She noticed a stack of horse magazines on the coffee table, two of which were also open. She hugged herself. Had he spent last night in here, alone with his papers and magazines? Did he despise his wife? Did he really want a divorce? Maybe he was only angry with her, but if so, why? What could Lana have possibly done to make him so mad, or was it a terrible misunderstanding?

Kait prayed the last was true.

She hurried to the desk. It was a mess. There were so many files, folders, pads, and notes she doubted he knew where anything was. She was reaching for the phone when she saw the photographs of Marni.

Abruptly she sat down in his chair. Her heart had gone wild. She lifted the portrait of the prettiest little girl she had ever seen. Her hair was dark like Lana's and her own, but riotously curly, and her eyes were green and her complexion olive, undoubtedly the same as her father's would be, should he forgo his tan. She was smiling shyly at the camera, and tears filled Kait's eyes, love swelling within her chest.

Was this what her own daughter would one day be like?

She could barely wait to meet her niece and take her into her arms.

There were other photos of Marni on a snow-white pony that Kait felt certain was far too large for a four-year-old. In one of the photos she was actually going over a tiny jump in a riding habit at a horse show.

Kait lifted another photo, this one clearly of Trevor's daughter from his previous marriage. In her letter Lana had mentioned that Sam was now sixteen, but in the two photos on his desk she appeared a bit younger. She was a beautiful blonde with a sunny smile and hazel eyes, but both photos were portraits, and there were no shots of her on horseback. Kait wondered at that.

And where were the photographs of Lana?

Kait suddenly turned. A bookcase was catty-corner to the wall of windows behind the desk, and sure enough, there on one shelf was a wedding photo of the bride and groom, both wreathed in smiles and looking like candidates for Mr. and Mrs. America. There were other photos of the once happy couple, including one of Trevor in a tuxedo, looking incredibly elegant and virile, with Lana in a daring evening gown that dripped over her every curve. His arm was around her, he was smiling and content, while she was laughing, undoubtedly at something he had said. What a perfect couple they made—in appearance, anyway.

Surely they could work things out.

If they had been that happy once, surely they could find that happiness again.

Kait swallowed, having to turn away from the photos of her sister and her husband when they had been so enamored of one another. She glanced briefly at a half a dozen photos of Lana astride at horse shows.

They brought back so many memories. Lana was a natural athlete, and a very competitive one. While they had both worked at a local stable in return for riding lessons, Lana had started winning top ribbons at the local shows from her very first time out when they were seven and in second grade. Kait had hated showing—she'd only done so once or twice and found the pressure of being the center of attention far too much. When their mother had passed away they had been thirteen, and their father had bought them both large ponies, and Kait now knew he had been hoping to distract them from their loss. Lana had continued to show, successfully; Kait had ridden for pleasure. Kait still rode on the weekends in Central Park or sometimes in Westchester, but she hadn't had a clue that Lana had become so deeply involved in the horse world. That fact only added to the argument that Lana was eminently suited to be Trev Coleman's wife.

Kait brushed her eyes. There was no denying the sadness in her heart now, but she was aware too of the emotion being much more complicated than it had any right to be, and she refused to analyze it or herself.

Kait turned her back to her sister's photos and lifted the phone, her intention to try to reach her sister. She quickly dialed her own number, and as she waited for Lana to pick up, it crossed her mind that it might not be fair to tell Lana that Trev wanted a divorce, not when she was incapable of doing anything about it, not when she would be back in two days. Then she thought about how unfair it was for her to have been put in this position. She desperately needed Lana's advice.

But Lana did not pick up. Instead, Kait's voice mail came on.

As Kait hadn't been given the opportunity to give her sister her PIN code for retrieving voice mail, she hung up with a terrible sinking sensation. She might not reach Lana at all; she might not be able to speak with her until she actually returned home to Fox Hollow in two days. And that meant that she would have to manage the divorce and Trev Coleman all alone.

She shuddered.

Kait hated the idea of facing Trev Coleman before she had a chance to speak with her sister; nevertheless, she had better think through the best way to deal with the current situation. Could she somehow help Lana salvage her marriage? That seemed to be the only possible course of action.

She took one last look around the study, but had no excuse now to be lingering there. And, frankly, something about Trev Coleman had unnerved her—she had no wish to be caught in his office, or to be accused of prying or anything else. She walked back into the hall. Her purse was gone.

She stared at the empty windowsill. She had set the Gucci bag down there—hadn't she?

Kait felt certain that she had. Panic rose. Kait tried to recall if there was anything incriminating in her bag—she simply did not think so, but the panic did not abate. Kait hurried into the living room, but her bag was not in sight.

She could not have misplaced it. But she was alone in the house. Wasn't she? Elizabeth had left to fetch Marni, and she had also seen Trevor driving off.

But Max Zara was upstairs. Kait realized now that she hadn't seen him come down, and if he had, it had been by a back stairs or when she was engrossed in the study. He was odd and suspicious to begin with. He seemed to really dislike her sister. He seemed to have an ax to grind. But why the hell would he lift her bag?

Kait glanced at the stairs, calling, "Max?" There was no answer. She found her way to the kitchen easily enough—beyond the living room was the dining room and through that the kitchen. She ignored the spacious room with its sunny breakfast area and stainless-steel refrigerators, hearing a noise from another room. She passed a pantry and then stepped into the room with the washer, dryer, and a spare utilitarian sink.

Max was on his knees, tools on the floor beside him, the washer pulled out from the wall. He did not look at her.

Her heart pounded. Did she dare ask him if he'd taken her bag? Did she dare be that direct?

He said, "You want something, Mrs. Coleman?" But he did not look up.

His tone insinuated something dirty and Kait recoiled. "I seem to have misplaced my handbag," she said carefully.

"Maybe you left it in the car," he said, finally settling back on his haunches and gazing at her. Again she noticed his huge, bulging biceps and thick, powerful hands. And the worn undershirt revealed his washboard abs. He could probably snap a watermelon in two with his bare hands, Kait thought uneasily. He had probably been in the marines as a youth.

She didn't like the way he was looking at her—she said, breathlessly, "I took it with me. I guess it just walked off on its own accord."

He made a disparaging sound.

Kait turned and hurried across the kitchen, past a wood center isle and a stainless-steel stove. She swept through the dining room, where Elizabeth had left a set table, with a salad in a glass bowl and a platter of seared tuna steaks. Kait continued through the house and up the stairs.

Max had to have taken her bag. But why?

Just then, it was very hard to think clearly.

Kait rushed up the stairs, passing four bedroom doors and entering the last room on the floor. She quickly stepped inside, closing the door behind her. She leaned against it, aware suddenly of extreme exhaustion.

It competed with her frayed nerves for her attention. *Calm down,* she told herself. There had to be other people employed at Fox Hollow—a housemaid, grooms, who knows? Someone might have taken the bag simply because it was a valuable item in itself. The bag's disappearance did not mean that someone was on to her.

She fought to relax, an impossible feat. She told herself that even if Max had taken it, he wasn't going to realize that Kait was a fraud. Lana had written in her letter that no one knew she had a twin, so no one would ever suspect their deception.

She wasn't relieved. But she started to look around, incapable of tamping down her curiosity.

She stared at the king-sized bed in the center of the room.

The bed had a massive dark oak headboard and footboard, and a paisley quilt spread in black, red, and gold covered it. Three sets of pillows in contrasting hues and fabrics made the bed luxurious and inviting. A dark red Oriental rug covered the oak floors, an orangey tweed sofa was in front of the fireplace, and various antiques filled the room. *How was she going to share a bed with Trev Coleman?*

And Kait was suddenly furious for being put in the position she was now in. What was she supposed to do, lie there sleeplessly all night, right beside him? Surely he wouldn't become amorous—after all, he wanted a divorce. But if he did, was she supposed to claim a headache? And that didn't solve the real issue—there was simply no way she could share his bed even if he never tried to touch her, not even once.

It was absolutely impossible.

And Kait refused to even consider why.

Kait backed away. She didn't even want to share this bedroom. But she wanted to smooth over his anger now, for her sister's sake, so suggesting separate bedrooms was not the right tack to take. Kait felt as if she were stuck between a rock and a hard place—worse, she felt as if she were slowly but surely drowning. In that moment, she felt like throttling her sister.

She reminded herself that Lana's life was in danger, and so, maybe, was Marni's. And if she had to share the bed, so be it, she'd keep a pillow between them. It was only for two nights, and a small price to pay if Lana paid off Corelli and got herself out of the mess she was in.

Kait couldn't quite recover her composure.

And as Kait hurried from the bedroom, entering a huge walk-in closet the size of most people's bedrooms, she realized that the master bedroom completely lacked her sister's touch. It was almost as if she didn't live there.

Perplexed, Kait paused in the walk-in, which was evenly divided, with Trev's clothes hanging and folded up on shelves on one side, Lana's on the other. Kait stared at a row of exquisite suits, then at piles of jeans and sweaters. She glanced down at several pairs of designer loafers side by side with high show boots and running sneakers. She could not help herself.

She walked over. She touched the top sweater, a soft blue, and found that it was cashmere. She touched a pile of cotton tees that were as high a quality and as finely woven as the sweaters. She saw a pile of running clothes—shorts, tights, pullovers. She glanced at the gleaming show boots—he had two pairs. His sneakers were well worn and muddy.

She gave his wardrobe one last glance, disturbed, and she quickly stripped off her trousers and twin set, and took off the red lipstick with a Kleenex.

Clad only in her own underwear—a pale pink cotton bra and pale pink cotton bikinis, she went to Lana's side of the closet, hoping to find something comfortable—and comforting—to put on. Lana had insisted in her letter that Kait only use Lana's clothes, makeup, and jewelry, which made sense. Of course, as no one was ever going to see her in her skivvies, Kait had used her own underwear. Her sister had actually left a tiny, lacy scrap of La Perla thong and a matching bra in the bag she had given her, but Kait drew the line at sharing underwear, and at the discomfort she felt certain the garments would provoke.

Kait rifled through designer wool suits; black, tan, and gray trousers; leather pants; Ralph Lauren blazers; expensive sweaters; and silk blouses. There was simply nothing to her liking. She eyed Lana's gym clothes—tights and a loose woven top would certainly do, except Lana would never be caught dead out of a gym clad like that and Kait knew it. There was not a single pair of jeans to be found. Lana had always been extremely well dressed, ever since they were children. Clearly, that had not changed.

Suddenly, Kait couldn't cope. Suddenly, the failure to find sweats and a tee brought tears to her eyes. Two days loomed ahead as if it were an eternity.

"Let's get this over with," Trev Coleman said.

Kait jumped three feet high and faced Lana's husband, clad only in her panties and bra. She felt her cheeks flame, and somehow did not run for cover. As she stood there, mostly naked, facing him, her heart going wild, she reminded herself that he thought they were married. But for a man bent on divorce, he was not very oblivious. In fact, damn him, he was staring.

"What are you doing?" he demanded, unsmiling.

Then she gave up. They were not married, she was not his wife, and while she thought she had decent thighs, he had just seen every inch of them. And his green eyes remained mesmerized by her cotton panties. "Would you mind? I'm getting dressed," she said through her teeth. And she heard them chatter.

His gaze jerked up, to her face, her mouth, her eyes. His color seemed to rise. "What happened to your underwear?" he said as tightly. His eyes jerked downward again.

She felt like throwing something at him. Instead, she grabbed a pair of pants off a hanger and hopped into them. "Nothing," she snapped. Damn it! She should have worn her sister's sexy designer underwear.

He now studied her carefully, from head to toe. Kait

didn't like the way he was looking at her, as if he was cal-culating the cotton underwear and her new haircut. He fi-nally said, his tone terribly neutral, "Are you on a diet or something?"

"I had the flu in New York. I didn't eat for a few days. I'm still feeling weak."

He finally lifted his gaze, and she saw that he was not un-affected by her; in fact, she saw a glitter in his eyes.

He turned abruptly and walked out of the dressing room. "We need to talk," he said from the bedroom. "Come down to my study when you're dressed." His tone was oddly polite.

Kait sagged against the wall, but there was no wall there, just two racks of clothes, which she fell into. She landed with a thump, grabbed a rack, and righted herself. She was quivering like a leaf and her cheeks remained on fire.

Was she attracted to this man?

She told herself that it was simply impossible.

He was good-looking and sexy, but that did not mean she found him desirable. He belonged to her sister. In fact, bar-ring instructions otherwise, Kait intended to do her best to help Lana salvage her marriage and her entire wonderful life.

Her spirits suddenly crashed and she sank down on the floor. "Damn it," she said, hugging her knees. How had she ever gotten herself into this?

She could come clean now, before it was too late. But then Trev Coleman would want to know why she was pre-tending to be Lana, and what would she say? He'd also want to know just where his wife was—and Kait couldn't betray Lana that way. Not without her permission. If she did, Kait knew it would be another ten years, if not more, before she ever saw her sister again.

No, she had promised to help her, and she had to keep that promise. More importantly, when this was over, they would be real friends and she would have a real family. In fact, when this was over, not only would Marni be her niece, but Trev Coleman would be her brother-in-law.

Kait cursed again, still hugging her knees. Now she felt sick to her stomach, sick enough to retch.

Resigned—and fearful of what Trev wanted to discuss—as if she didn't know!—she got up and pulled on a black V-neck sweater over the gray trousers. She had had enough of heels for one day and she went downstairs in her bare feet, trying to banish the expression she had just seen in Trev Coleman's eyes from her very treacherous mind.

He was attracted to her, too.

No, he was attracted to Lana, his wife.

In Kait's silly, plain cotton underwear.

His door was open; still, she knocked.

He was standing before the fire and when he turned to face her, she saw that he was a man very much in control of all of his feelings; a cool gaze swept over her. He saw her bare feet. "What's that?"

She tilted up her chin. "My feet hurt," she said.

He stared at her with the same calculating look he had given her before.

"I'm really tired," she said, and it was the truth. She had the urge to go upstairs and throw the covers over her head, just to escape him for a while.

Or was it to run from herself?

"Yeah." His smile was twisted. "Me, too."

She became alert. She did not like the sound of that, and she did not like the suddenly weary look in his eyes.

"This is a done deal, Lana," he said softly, his regard unwavering. "I have made up my mind."

Dread filled her. What should she say? What should she do? "You can't make a decision like this unilaterally."

"Unilaterally?" His brows drew together. "What the hell are you talking about?"

Uh-oh, Kait thought. "We can work this out," she said.

"Are you nuts? Have you changed your mind? We've been speaking about—no, arguing about—this for months."

Kait went into shock. Lana had known that this was coming—and she hadn't said a word. How could she have delib-

erately put her in such a position? And did his words mean
that Lana had agreed to the concept of a divorce?

"Why are you acting so dumbfounded?" He sat down,
moving some legal pads about as if looking for something.
Then he looked up, his green eyes skewering her. "This is
hardly a surprise. You knew this was coming."

Her mind was overactive now. How could Lana have
asked her to switch places when her marriage was on the
brink? And the answer was so easy—because she was in terrible trouble, and desperate enough to ask anything of her
twin sister. And it was only for two days. Kait began to
shake. Was her sister nuts? Surely she didn't think to throw
her marriage away!

Should she still attempt to salvage Lana's marriage for
her?

He was regarding her intently now, apparently having
given up his act of searching through the papers on his desk.
She said slowly, "Marriage is not something one throws
aside lightly."

He leaned back in the leather swivel chair. "Lightly?"
His expression hardened. "I am not the fool you took me
for when we first were married, Lana," he said, low and
dangerous.

She remained numb, but not numb enough to avoid
flinching. "I have no idea what you mean," she whispered
truthfully.

"No? Please! I suspected the truth a long time ago, but
didn't want to see it—I refused to see it. Because of Marni.
That, and because you are so damn beautiful and you had
your hooks in me." He grimaced. "Six months ago I finally
did what I should have done a long time ago—I sat down
and faced some cold, hard, ugly facts about our marriage,
about us." His expression was disgusted now.

Kait could only stare at him. What the hell was he talking
about? What facts had he faced? Why was she filled with
dread?

"I know now that I refused to see what was happening
right under my nose because of Marni," he said harshly.

"And I have spent the past six months coming to grips with the knowledge that Marni will be better off without you."

"Is that what you think?" She gasped. Kait stepped forward. This was a subject that she could not let slip by. "Every child needs a mother," she said hoarsely, aghast. "What do you mean—she'd be better off without me?"

"Only in functional circumstances with a functional mother," he said dryly. "I wouldn't exactly call you functional, my dear. Marni stays with me."

Kait cried out.

He leapt up. "What the hell is this? What the hell is this innocent act? You know you'd be hobbled by having her— you're too busy to be a mother. You've always been too busy to be a mother!"

An image of the beautiful child seared Kait's mind. If Trev thought he was taking Marni away from Lana, he was wrong! "She's her . . . my daughter," she managed, desperately wishing she could speak with Lana now. "You can't take her away from me!"

"She's *my* daughter," he retorted. "You want a good settlement from me, you'll give me full custody. And that is nonnegotiable." He bared his teeth, but not in a smile.

Kait managed to shake her head. "Absolutely not."

He was startled, incredulous. "I will have custody," he said, "and I will fight you tooth and nail to get it. If we go that route, do not expect me to be generous with you."

She had to get out. "I don't care about your money," she snapped. "This isn't about money! This is about a child!"

He burst into laughter. "Like hell! You don't care about money? Now that is a good one if I ever heard one!"

She stared, trying to comprehend his awful statement— did he really think that Lana cared more about money than their child?

"Baby, you set me in your sights because of my money, and we both know it," he said cruelly.

"No, that's not true!" She was horrified that he would think such a thing.

"No?" He stood. "Like you'd have looked at me twice if I

was some poor jerk making a couple hundred bucks a week. I should have listened to Rafe. He nailed you as a gold digger the moment he first laid eyes on you. But I refused to listen! Well, so be it. Now I am prepared to pay whatever price I have to, in order to get rid of you." He stared.

Kait was aghast. For one moment, their gazes locked, and cruelly—for there was such venom and loathing in his eyes. Kait could not stand being near him another moment—she could not bear his hatred. She turned and rushed from the room, so off-balance that she staggered. In the corridor, she hugged herself, gasping for air.

Lana did not pick up her daughter at school, but that did not mean she was a bad mother. That did not mean she should lose her daughter this way. Kait had not a doubt that Lana would fight tooth and nail for joint custody of her daughter.

And surely she loved Trev Coleman. Or surely, she had once, six years ago, fallen in love with him—and it hadn't had *anything* to do with his money.

She was blinded now. Blinded by hot tears.

Trev Coleman's expression blazed in her mind.

She slowly straightened. He didn't merely want a divorce, she thought, stunned. He hated his wife. She had seen it in his eyes.

But she had seen more than that. He didn't merely despise his wife; he hated her with a vengeance.

And he intended to have his vengeance, too.

THREE

Before she could truly comprehend the situation, before she could even begin to analyze it and consider its ramifications, the front door opened. Kait was standing near the window where she had left and lost her handbag. She glanced outside. The Land Rover was parked between her car and Trev Coleman's blue Dodge Ram.

Elizabeth was speaking in the foyer. "And I just baked them this afternoon."

A pause ensued. A soft, childish voice said, "Is Mommy home?"

There was something hesitant and tentative in Marni's tone; oddly, Kait's heart broke. She rushed into the foyer. "Marni!" she cried.

The little girl looked up, wide-eyed in surprise.

Kait cautioned herself not to be too emotional—she was Lana now, who missed her daughter, who had been away for a mere three days. She was not the aunt whom the child had never before seen, a thirty-two-year-old single woman who no longer enjoyed her career and was lacking love and a family. "Hello, darling," she said hoarsely, barely able to believe that the beautiful little girl standing by the door in her tiny navy blue blazer, pleated skirt, and knee socks was truly her niece.

"Mommy," Marni said, smiling a little, anxiously. Her

long, dark, curly hair was pulled back in a ponytail with a red ribbon.

"I have missed you," Kait breathed, kneeling and holding out her arms. "Come here, I need a hug."

For one moment Marni did not move; she resembled a surprised and confused doe caught in the headlights of an oncoming car. Then she smiled again and came forward. Kait swept her into her arms, far too hard, but the child did not protest. Instead, she clung.

Kait breathed in baby powder and baby shampoo, clean cotton and Ivory soap, and as she held Marni in her arms, she thought about what a treasure she was, and how lucky Lana was. And Kait believed that Trev Coleman had been exaggerating about everything he had accused Lana of. Perhaps his accusations that Lana was too busy to be a mother—that she was not functional as one—were the groundwork he was laying for his divorce case. Kait felt certain that she should not take Trev's opinion of her sister as gospel.

Lana surely treasured the beautiful child now in Kait's arms.

Kait pulled back a little and said, "I have a present for you." She had been at FAO Schwarz the moment they opened that morning in order to buy Marni a play stable that they could assemble together for all of her horse models.

Marni's eyes were wide and searching. "Really?" She smiled a little, her small mouth quivering.

"It's upstairs." Kait straightened and took her hand. "Do you want to help me unpack?" How right the child's small hand felt in her own!

Marni stiffened with surprise. Then she nodded eagerly.

"Marni needs a snack, Mrs. Coleman," Elizabeth said brusquely.

Kait glanced at her and saw disapproval and frostiness all over the older woman's face. She felt certain that her earlier instinct that Elizabeth was territorial where Marni was concerned was accurate. Kait intended to draw a new line in the sand. She smiled grimly at the housekeeper. "Would you mind sending up the milk and cookies?" She then grinned down at Marni. "We'll have a snack together while we unpack." Marni made everything—Trev's hostility, Max's coldness, Elizabeth's attitude—all worth it. Marni made the deception worth it.

Kait knew she would give up her own life to protect this child, much less switch places with her sister for a few days.

When Elizabeth did not respond, Kait looked over at her. The woman was staring at her as if she had grown two heads.

Kait's heart lurched. She really hoped that Lana wasn't as disinterested a mother as Trev claimed. But Elizabeth seemed to be regarding her with utter suspicion now. And Kait couldn't help recalling the sister she had known before they had gone off to different colleges. Lana had never been able to stay home, to be alone. She had always surrounded herself with friends—all of whom had been boys—and she had always been on horseback, on a bike, on a skateboard, on skis.

Kait had never assumed that she had become the baking brownies and making pot roast kind of wife, but many mothers had careers and hobbies and still were actively involved in their children's lives.

"I want to pack with Mommy," Marni said eagerly.

"What is going on?" Trev said.

Kait whirled and saw him standing with a strained expression directly behind her. "Marni is going to help me unpack. Besides, her gift is upstairs in my carry-on bag." She purposefully kept her tone light, as if he had not just declared he intended to take Marni away from her, which was tantamount to declaring war.

His jaw flexed. "Really?" His eyes were dangerous now.

Kait hesitated. Trev Coleman unnerved her as no man ever had, but that was because of the deception she was practicing on him. "Don't tell me I am not allowed to give Marni a present," Kait said as lightly, with a plastic smile.

"Marni needs to be at the stable in an hour," he said, clearly trying very hard to control his temper. He seemed explosive.

It took Kait a moment. "She is riding?"

He stared closely. "She rides every day after school at four o'clock. You know that."

A slip—but not a fatal one. "Of course she does!" Kait cried. Not about to release Marni's hand. "I just thought, after my having been away, we might change her schedule a bit."

"I want to stay with Mommy," Marni said.

Trev flinched as if struck. "But we are going hacking, darling, you and I. You love to hack with Daddy." He gave Kait a terribly cold glance. "You were gone for three days. It's never been a big deal before."

Kait knew she had been right—this man had somehow come to loathe his wife. Her urge to save her sister's marriage remained, but she also knew that she would be meddling now if she did. On the other hand, look at the position she was now in! A position Lana had chosen to put her in, making the decision without consulting anyone else—without talking it through with Kait. She took a huge breath. "Trev," she said, swallowing. She tried out a more genuine smile, hoping to soften him, but the mask that was his face did not change. "I've been doing a lot of thinking. We need to talk."

"Anytime," he said tightly.

Marni shook her head. Kait glanced down and saw a very stubborn look in her eyes. "I want to pack with Mommy." Her eyes held a warring light.

Kait stooped down. "I have a great idea!" she exclaimed. She did not want to antagonize Trev any further. "We have a whole hour to unpack, to play with your present, and have cookies and milk. Then I will bring you down to the barn and watch you ride."

Marni's eyes widened. "You want to watch me ride Prince Charming?" she exclaimed, clearly surprised.

"I most certainly do," Kait said, grinning. She tousled her hair, straightened, and looked up. Elizabeth and Trev were staring at her with consternation, disapproval, and even suspicion.

Kait stared back. She was afraid to understand that Lana never watched her own daughter ride. But that simply wasn't possible—was it?

Marni had to be the cutest short-stirrup rider in the world! Who wouldn't want to watch her ride her white pony?

"Why are you staring at me like that?" she managed quietly, with dread.

Trev looked as if he was about to grind down every single one of his lower teeth. He didn't answer—he simply strode out.

Elizabeth did reply. "Because you never bother to watch your daughter ride, Mrs. Coleman. Because you have come back from the city behaving as if you are somebody else."

Marni clung to her hand the entire way upstairs, and even once they had entered the master bedroom, she did not let go. Lana's garment bag and duffel sat in the middle of the room, where Max had apparently dumped them. And in spite of what had just transpired in Trev's study and the foyer, Kait's heart was singing. She would worry about Elizabeth's shrewd comment another time.

She smiled happily at Marni. "Close your eyes, sweetie," she said.

Marni obeyed, grinning.

Kait released her hand, knelt over the duffel, then froze. Slowly, she looked up.

At the foot of the bed was a beautifully upholstered bench. On the bench was her missing Gucci handbag.

"Mommy?" Marni whispered.

"One moment, darling!" Kait cried. She quickly opened the duffel and took out a gift-wrapped box. "Here you are," she said gaily.

Marni grinned eagerly when she saw the cheerfully wrapped big box. Kait sat down on the floor and patted it. Marni blinked in surprise, then, beaming at the gift, sat there beside her. Kait helped her unwrap the box, her pulse racing. Whoever had taken her bag, he or she had returned it. Why? Kait could only conclude that the matter had not been one of a simple theft. She was anxious to inspect it. But she still couldn't think of a single incriminating piece of evidence that had been in that bag.

Marni finished tearing off the wrapping paper. She saw the picture of the assembled barn on the outside of the box and she whooped. "Is it a stable for my horses?" she asked eagerly.

"It most certainly is. All you have to do is assemble it, and we can do that together." Pure love rippled over Kait. It was so hard to keep her hands off Marni, so she briefly stroked her hair.

Marni began to rip off the clear plastic paper and Kait helped her open the box. They spilled out its contents. "Look, a fence for a paddock," she cried delightedly. "And it's white, just like Daddy's!"

Kait patted her shoulder, just as there was a knock on the door, which remained widely open. She looked up at Elizabeth, who was carrying a tray. However, only one glass of milk was on it, and a small plate with two cookies. Kait got to her feet. "Thank you, Elizabeth," she said pleasantly. "I was hoping for milk and cookies too." She tried a smile out on the older woman.

Elizabeth's expression did not change as she set the tray down on a small round Chinese table, lacquered red. She glanced carefully at Marni and her gift. "Since when do you eat sweets?"

Kait stared. Her mind raced, because while she was a fairly healthy eater, she was a chocoholic. Here was an issue Lana had never addressed in her letter. But Kait could guess that Lana probably avoided chocolate and anything fattening at all costs. As a teen, she had been obsessed with her body image. She had started dieting then, even though there'd been no need.

Kait knew she could give up a lot of things, but chocolate wasn't one of them. She said quickly, "This is a special occasion, now, isn't it?" She smiled at Marni, who grinned happily. "If this isn't the time to splurge, when is?"

Elizabeth stared. Then she shrugged. "Fine. I'll be right back."

"Mommy? Come take one of my cookies," Marni cried. She got up and rushed to the table, reaching for a cookie. As she did, she knocked over the glass of milk.

Marni froze. Then she looked up with wide, stricken eyes—clearly expecting to be berated for the accident.

"It was just an accident," Kait said kindly, covering her small shoulder with her hand. "I'll clean it up in a flash. Elizabeth? Two more glasses of milk, please. *Whole* milk," she added on a whim, being perverse and relishing it. Lana probably only drank fat-free, or worse, soy.

Elizabeth seemed completely taken aback. She turned to leave and as she did, Kait realized Trev was standing in the doorway. And instantly she was angry—she did not want to share her precious time with Marni, not with him, not with anyone. She gave him a cool look, and went into the bathroom for some towels.

When she came out, Trev was on his knees, showing Marni how the barn should be assembled. Marni looked worriedly at Kait. "I'm sorry I spilled the milk."

"Who cares?" Kait smiled, wondering how to kick Trev out. This wasn't fair, especially when they only had an hour together—especially when she was only at Fox Hollow for two days. He rocked back on his haunches to study her. She gave him an angry glance and began to mop up the milk. "See? All gone, just like that."

"I want to talk to you," Trev said quietly, standing.

She faced him, trying to tamp down her anger. She decided to set boundaries. "I've been away for three days. I would appreciate some time alone with my daughter."

His eyes widened. "Since when?"

She put her hands on her hips, and then realized how that would look, and she dropped them. "This isn't fair," she said evenly. "Please let us spend some time together."

"I know what you're up to," he said flatly.

"I am not up to anything," she cried. Then she stiffened

and glanced at Marni. She forced a smile. "We're not fighting, sweetie," she said. "Really."

Marni bit her lip. "But you fight with Daddy all the time."

Kait stared, aghast.

Trev gave her an I-told-you-so look.

Kait breathed. "Look, we can talk later, at supper. Or whenever you want. But right now, Marni is going to help me unpack and we are going to start on her stable." She smiled as brightly as possible at him, no easy task, given the circumstances.

"Later," he said. He smiled at his daughter. "I'll see you at the barn." He walked out.

Marni looked after him, and then she looked at Kait with wide, worried eyes.

Kait sat down on the floor, pulling her into her lap. "There is nothing for you to worry about."

Marni's gaze was searching. "Daddy's mad at you. Really, really mad."

She flinched. "I know. But even mommies make mistakes."

Marni hesitated, thoughtful. "Daddy doesn't know you are a new mommy," she finally said.

Kait froze. Her ears thundered, her blood rushed. "What?"

"He doesn't know you are my new mommy," she said with a sweet smile. "It's my old mommy he doesn't like."

Kait could not move. *Marni knew.*

Somehow, the child knew the truth, that she wasn't Lana, not even close to it.

It was said that children were very perceptive and very astute. She'd even read that children could see things adults couldn't—like ghosts. Kait hardly believed that, but somehow, Marni knew that she was not Lana.

She was at a complete loss for words. She somehow smiled. "Even mommies change."

Marni grinned and laid her palm on Kait's cheek. "I *love* my new mommy," she said.

• • •

While Marni was taking her things from her garment bag and putting them in the walk-in closet, Kait rushed to her Gucci handbag, still reeling from the fact that, of all people, Marni had guessed the truth right away. She opened the purse, dumped everything out on the floor. The first thing she saw was her sister's cell phone and the second thing she saw was a folded scrap of paper.

She froze.

She had completely forgotten about that little scrap of paper. On it was the license plate number of Lana's Porsche, as well as the words "*level 3, row 2, space 4*," a note Kait had made for herself in order to find Lana's car when she arrived at Reagan National.

Kait tried to tell herself that the note wouldn't mean anything to anyone—she herself had often written down where she'd parked a car in a huge lot, after one day totally forgetting the spot in a discount outlet mall. But her attempt to smooth over the situation failed. Nobody wrote down their own license plate number as if they did not know their own car.

Numbly, she reached for her wallet, thinking that maybe the person who had taken and then returned her purse hadn't even seen the note. All of her credit cards—that is, all of Lana's credit cards—were there. So was Lana's driver's license. But the hundred dollars in cash that she had traveled with was gone.

She sat down on the bed, hard, eyes closing, flooded with relief.

It had been a simple robbery, nothing more.

It hadn't had anything to do with the switch.

She opened her eyes and felt like laughing out loud—so she did. God, her nerves were on end and she was simply paranoid and overreacting to every little thing. Then she sobered. That did not change the fact that she had been expecting an entirely different kind of welcome at Fox Hollow.

Very grim now, Kait hated facing a comprehension that

seemed inescapable. Lana had clearly alienated her husband, not to mention the housekeeper and that odd fellow, Max Zara. Nor did she seem to have a close or warm relationship with her own daughter. Kait was no fool. Marni had been anxious and worried when she had first been with her, and she had expected to be yelled at for her accident with the milk.

If only Lana had clued her in. But Lana had led her to believe that she had a wonderful and perfect family life.

Instantly, Kait realized that wasn't fair. Lana really hadn't said anything about her life at Fox Hollow. Kait had *assumed* that she lived a Disney kind of existence. She had *assumed* that her sister had everything a woman could possibly want—a perfect love, a perfect life.

Kait loved her sister. She had envied and admired her forever. Secretly, she had always wished that she were the popular one, the brave and fearless one, the sexy and flamboyant one. But she wasn't twelve anymore, or fifteen, or seventeen. She'd had her own share of life experiences, some good, some pretty bad. Life was never black-and-white and Kait had learned that as she matured. She found herself really thinking about her sister's nature then. Lana had always been an extrovert, but it was more than that. She was very passionate, and she had always been drawn to excitement and thrills. Which was why she was not comfortable staying at home. She had to be on a motorcycle racing around a dirt course, or a horse facing four- and five-foot fences that only the professionals attempted. She'd skydived, and Kait would bet her life that she'd bungee-jumped, too. Given her very nature, how could she not live life to its fullest? But in pursuit of her wild dreams, in pursuit of thrills and chills, she could also be insensitive and thoughtless at times.

She wasn't a bad person. In fact, Kait still admired her immensely. No one had her courage. But, like everyone, she had her flaws. She simply wasn't perfect. And clearly, she hadn't done the best job as a wife or mother.

Kait would never wish a situation like the current one on

her sister, but as it did exist, she hoped that Corelli's threats might make Lana appreciate all that she had a bit more.

And hadn't Lana done the most selfless thing in borrowing money from a man who had to be a loan shark in order to save Fox Hollow? Didn't that mean that she truly cared about Trev?

Marni came out of the bathroom, smiling proudly. "I put everything away," she said. "Come see, Mommy!"

Kait swallowed. *But there was no excuse for failing to watch Marni ride, for rarely picking her up at school, for having an anxious and emotionally needy child.* "Thank you." Kait smiled back, a rush of warmth overcoming her. She realized that she had fallen in love with her niece. But who wouldn't? "Let's see how you did," she said, jumping up and following the proud little girl into the walk-in closet.

She thought about Lana again. She would not be the first woman to be jilted by her husband, and perhaps Elizabeth's hostility was a result of her taking sides in a bitter divorce. If it were at all possible, tonight she and Lana would have a *huge* talk. Surely Lana would not agree to this divorce, surely she intended to fight for her marriage. If not, Kait intended to convince her to do so. She felt like pounding her sister on both ears, as if that might pound some sense into her so she might wake up. She had a beautiful home, a fabulous lifestyle, and the most adorable child in the world. Not to mention a to-die-for, sexy husband. How could she be so careless with such precious gifts?

"See? I hung up your suit and put the pajamas away, too." Marni cut into her thoughts.

"What a great job!" Kait cried, bending to hug her again.

Marni flushed with pleasure. "You smell so good."

Kait blinked at her. She had chosen not to wear any scent, because she favored soft, slightly sweet perfumes, and Lana had left Dolce & Gabbana in her purse, which was too heady and strong for Kait's taste. "I forgot my perfume; you must be smelling tea rose soap, sweetie," Kait said.

"I like it," Marni announced. "Can we do more packing?"

Kait smiled and pulled her close. "I think we're about finished," she said.

At precisely four o'clock, Kait and Marni were at the stables, Marni as cute as a button in her riding breeches and jodhpur boots. Kait had found a pair of paddock boots in Lana's closet, boots that had clearly never been worn. But she already guessed that her sister dressed to a T when she rode, unfortunately.

Kait wisely let Marni lead the way. The largest barn, she learned, had two dozen stalls and an indoor arena, and that was where she found herself. Trev stood in the aisle, in a navy blue polo shirt, tight tan breeches, and high field boots, the handsome snow-white pony already tacked and in the cross-ties. An older man was beside him. Kait recognized the pony from the photos on Trev's desk. A big, handsome bay gelding with four white socks and a star was also in the cross-ties; clearly, he was Trev's mount. Both men turned as they approached.

Kait was flooded with a tension she refused to identify. Trev's eyes were on her—she quickly looked away. But not before wondering why he wasn't an advertisement for Ralph Lauren.

"Hello, Lana," the older man said with a warm smile. He had a male rider's lean, wiry build. "How was your trip to the Big Apple?"

Kait was so surprised by this warm greeting that she could hardly speak. Then, "Fine."

"Been working Pride so he won't get too hot on you," the man continued. "He should be pretty steady when we work tomorrow."

It took Kait a quick second to realize that Pride was Lana's mount, and that she was expected to school with this man, who had to be the trainer. Lana had omitted all details of her equestrian life in her letter. Kait smiled, her lips feeling frozen. She knew she was not half the rider that her sister was. Lana had undoubtedly chosen not to mention her training, for fear of scaring Kait.

"Jim, I helped Mommy unpack," Marni announced proudly.

"Now did you?" The white-haired fellow grinned. "I hear your daddy's taking you for a bit of a cross-country ride today." He unsnapped the two leads and took off the pony's halter, slipping on his bridle.

"Daddy? Mommy wants to see me ride. Can't we school in the ring?" Marni pleaded.

Trev had untied his bay. He smiled at Marni, and did not look at Kait. "We'll warm up in the indoor," he said. "And your mother can watch you there."

A few moments later, Kait was hanging on the rail as Trev and Marni rode side by side at a walk. As she watched her niece, who had a beautiful seat even at the age of four, it struck her that there was no place she would rather be than exactly where she was, at Fox Hollow, hanging on to the gate of the indoor arena, surrounded by horses, their scent heavy and thick, while watching Marni ride with her father.

Her heart skipped again as her gaze settled on Trev Coleman. Trev, like most professionals, did not wear a helmet. That disturbed her, for she knew that even the most experienced rider could have a serious accident at any time, as even the most predictable horses could spook. Most men could not carry off breeches and high boots. They either didn't have the body for it, or were made effeminate in such attire. Not so with Coleman. Even astride, he reeked masculinity and male strength.

Kait forced her eyes to Marni. Her cheeks felt hot.

"Ready for a little trot?" she heard Trev ask.

Marni nodded.

Kait watched them both move into a rising trot, Trev keeping his mount at an unbearably slow pace to accommodate the pony's shorter stride. "Your reins are too long," he said. "Pick them up, sweetheart."

Marni did. Kait's heart swelled with pride. What four-year-old could post like that? She was working a bit hard, but then, a four-year-old child simply did not have the developed musculature of an older child. She murmured unthinkingly, "When did he start her?"

Jim turned. "I beg your pardon?"

"When did . . ." Kait stopped. She felt herself flush. Lana would know when Marni had first mounted a horse. "I can't remember when he first got her trotting so beautifully," she said lamely.

"She's been working at it really hard for the past few months. Her post just started coming together before you left," he said. "You all right? You seem different, Lana."

She faced him. "Actually, I was really sick in New York. I had the flu, and I dropped quite a few pounds very quickly. I'm still a bit shaky," she said. She was certainly going to have a relapse, as she couldn't possibly pretend to be Lana on a horse with her trainer—or Trev—watching.

His face fell. "Yes, well, I'm sorry to hear that. Take whatever time you need, Lana."

"I don't think I have a choice," she said.

He held her gaze, as if trying to read past her words, and he nodded.

Kait managed to bite back a huge sigh of relief. She was off the hook, for now.

Kait wandered across the lawns behind the house. Marni and Trev had taken off for their hack and she felt as if a weight had just been lifted off her shoulders. She realized that her temples throbbed from the stress of her arrival at Fox Hollow, and all that had followed. Kait stared up at the house, which remained a magnificent sight. This was a respite, she decided, that she had better enjoy.

And it was also the perfect time to call Lana. Maybe this time she'd pick up her cell phone—if she was even carrying it with her.

Kait glanced around. The barns were behind her and to her right, the house ahead and to the left, on the rise of the hill. Directly ahead the pastures swept away toward rolling hills and the horizon. Fall had overcome the countryside with spectacular vengeance, and every oak and elm was turning gloriously gold, red, and orange.

She was alone. No one was in sight, and no one could be watching. Kait dug her cell phone out of her front trouser pocket, quickly dialing. She was dismayed when she got her own voice mail.

Kait hesitated, then wondered if Lana might reprogram the code to retrieve messages. It was a long shot. "It's me," she said, looking around carefully. "You have to call me, ASAP. It's urgent! Leave a message with a time that you will reach me on my—your—cell and I will be waiting for your call." She hesitated, suddenly glancing up at the back of the house. But who would bother to lurk about in one of the windows, in order to spy upon her? She became uneasy. "Things are not going well here," she said tersely. "I *have* to talk to you." She hung up, staring at the house again, then quickly redialed the number, this time leaving a numeric message—her call-back number. Surely that would get her sister's attention.

She glanced at the house one more time, now slipping the phone back into her pocket. If someone was watching from the house, it was impossible for her to see. Kait decided she was being paranoid once again. She turned her back on the house and plopped down in the grass, not far from a huge old elm tree. The beauty of the autumn day and of Fox Hollow washed over her then. She would try to call Lana again, later. Kait wondered what Lana would have to say for herself when they finally spoke. The one thing Kait was sure of was that Lana would not give up Marni without a bitter fight.

Kait closed her eyes and instantly Trev Coleman's image assailed her. It stiffened her relaxed body immediately. In two days, he would be told the truth of who she was. She suddenly realized that, considering how he despised his wife now, he was going to despise her as well. After all, she was Lana's twin, and she had thrust this huge deception, this huge lie, upon him.

Kait sat up, more than disturbed, hugging her knees to

herself. She did not want Trev Coleman to hate her. Not now, and not ever.

Because he was Marni's father, because he was her brother-in-law, because they were also her family now, or they would be, after Lana returned and they told everyone the truth.

He was going to be very angry with both Lana and her. Kait simply knew it. And knowing that, she did not know what to do.

This entire scheme was a terrible idea. Why hadn't Lana gone to the police?

That in itself made no sense.

And the fact that someone was out there, in her past, who might help her pay off this loan shark also made little sense. Who could that person be?

Kait didn't want to analyze her sister's predicament now. It had sounded odd the moment she read the letter, but with Lana's life being in danger—and Marni's—there was no arguing with what Lana had decided to do.

Kait flopped back on her back. How to smooth things over with Trev Coleman—now and after they told him the truth? Her anxiety knew no bounds. She wanted to relax and enjoy the autumn afternoon, but how could she? The scent of horses was faint now, the scent of autumn strong. And it was heaven, being there. She sighed, then inhaled deeply, staring up at the sky. A flock of geese appeared, heading south. She watched them for a long time, until they disappeared from sight.

This was the kind of place no one in their right mind would ever want to leave.

Impulsively, she sat, unlaced her boots, and took off her socks and shoes. She lay back down, staring at the sky through the elm's leafy orange canopy, images of Trev and Marni dancing in her mind.

She closed her eyes and drifted off to sleep.

When she awoke it was dark.

Kait rushed to her feet, unable to believe she had fallen so soundly asleep—and for so long. She grabbed her boots, plunging her feet into them sockless. Socks in hand, she rushed up the hill. The back door on the veranda was not locked, and she slipped into the living room.

One light was on. There was also a pair of lit wall sconces in the entry on either side of the front door. But otherwise, the house was in shadow, and it was so quiet that Kait had the distinct feeling that she was alone. Where was everybody?

And why did the idea of being alone cause her to feel alarmed?

She hurried through a formal dining room with a trestle table and studded leather-backed chairs. The kitchen had one light on as well. She found and hit a wall switch. It became brilliantly illuminated.

A quick glance at the clock on the oven-microwave unit told her it was almost half past seven. Where was everyone? And why wasn't dinner on the stove—or in the oven?

Her stomach growled madly. The only thing she had eaten all day was two chocolate chip cookies and a glass of milk.

Kait left the lights on and hurried into the main portion of the house. As she did so, she glanced down the hall toward Trev's study, but the door was wide open, the room dark—he wasn't there. She paused by the stairs and strained to hear. She thought, but wasn't sure, she heard the sound of a television.

"Hello? Anyone home?" she called.

There was no answer. Kait started up the stairs carefully, which were unlit. The sound of a sitcom with canned laughter became clearer. She relaxed slightly. She hadn't met Trev's daughter from his first marriage, and undoubtedly Sam was in her room watching TV.

Kait followed the sound to the second door on the hall. The volume on the television was high. She knocked. There was no answer, so she tried again. Finally she opened the door a bit and poked her head in.

Sam sat at her desk, doing homework. She was a tall, thin girl with a cascade of iron-straight blond hair spilling down her back. She was wearing a black T-shirt and a short camouflage vest and a pair of jeans with a heavy studded belt. The television was on, but it faced her bed at the other end of the room. Sam clearly wasn't even listening to it—she had on a pair of headphones, and as she wrote in her notebook, her head was bopping to the music. "Sam?" Kait tried.

When Sam didn't even move, Kait crossed the room and turned the volume way down. Then she walked over to the teenager and tapped her on the shoulder.

Sam whirled, but did not stand. "What are you doing?!" she cried.

Kait smiled. She now noticed three hoops in one ear. "Hi! How are you?" she tried.

Sam blinked and did not smile back. Her expression was sullen as she removed the headphones. "What?" Then she looked at Kait's hair. "You cut your hair. It sucks."

Kait recoiled, shocked.

"I'm doing homework," she said sourly. She turned back to her notebook, giving Kait her back.

Kait remained stunned. So Lana had another enemy in the house. It simply didn't seem possible, but the evidence was right before her eyes. She tapped her on the shoulder again. "So I noticed. I just wanted to say hi."

"You're kidding, right?" Sam leaned back in her chair warily, facing her now.

"No, I am not kidding," Kait said firmly. And it flashed through her mind that this was too much—it had to end now. There were fences that needed mending. Four that she could count, if she wanted to include Max Zara.

"Well, you said hi, so, good-bye." She turned rudely, hunching over her open textbook.

Kait sighed. If she were very lucky, some of Sam's behavior might be attributed to adolescence and hormones. "Where is everyone?"

Not turning, not even moving one muscle, Sam said, quite clearly, "Dad went out. To dinner. In Middleburg. With Alicia."

Kait's heart seemed to stop. "What?"

Sam slowly faced her. She seemed amused. "You know.

Alicia. Your best friend. Alicia, who usually goes to New York with you—who actually spends more than you when you two go shopping."

Lana had mentioned a best friend named Alicia in her letter, but it had been two sentences—Alicia was a redhead who tended to drop by on whim and she was married to John Davison.

Kait was worried now. "But Alicia didn't come to New York with me this time," she said slowly.

"Nope." Sam grinned. "Guess she had stuff to do here—like have dinner with Dad."

Surely Sam was not implying what Kait thought she was. Surely Trev Coleman had too much decency to have an affair with his wife's best friend—and throw it in her face! "So they're really having dinner together?"

Sam sighed. "John is with them, hello!"

Kait was flooded with relief. "Oh."

"Dad doesn't cheat. Unlike *other* people." Sam gave her a hard look.

Kait didn't like what the girl was implying. She ignored the comment. "Have you eaten?"

She was incredulous now. "Have I eaten? I had pizza after school." She turned away.

"Where is Marni? Where's Elizabeth?"

"Marni is in bed. It's her bedtime." Sam gave her a look. "What planet did you come from? And how come you're not wearing lipstick? Where are your high heels?"

Kait stepped forward, but she was aware of flushing. This was not the first time Lana's family had remarked on the little details that differentiated Kait's style from her sister's. Kait knew she was really tired, and she resolved to be more stringent with herself tomorrow. "That's enough. Your rudeness is uncalled for. I may not be the best stepmother in the world, but maybe it's time to start over—maybe it's time I had another chance."

"Yeah, right." Sam turned away.

"I want a second chance, Sam."

Sam didn't answer.

Kait stared at her narrow shoulders, and then walked out, closing the door behind her. A moment later she heard the television blasting. She shuddered. Developing a relationship with Sam would be a difficult task, oh yes. But it was something she realized she wanted to do—that she had to do.

Fear pierced through her. She forced it away.

Farther down the hall, a bedroom door was open. Kait went to it, and saw Elizabeth seated at the foot of a small bed, Marni tucked up under the covers. They both saw Kait at once.

"Mommy! Where have you been?" Marni cried, tears streaking her face.

Kait rushed forward, horrified that her disappearance had caused Marni's distress. "Honey, I feel asleep outside in the grass," she said, taking her into her arms.

She heard Elizabeth snort, as if in disbelief.

"I thought you left, back to the city," Marni cried, near fresh tears.

"I would never leave without telling you," Kait soothed, stroking her long, curly hair.

Marni looked deeply into her eyes.

"I mean it. I love you, and I would never do such a thing."

Marni began to smile. "We had such a fun day," she whispered.

"I know. But we'll have lots more fun days, just like today," Kait said. And the moment the words were out, she froze.

This child thought she was her mother. Yet she also knew she wasn't Lana. What would happen when they tried to explain the truth to Marni? Just how on earth could they explain what they had done? And how would Marni react? And if Trev Coleman was furious with her, Kait, for this pretense, just how many more days did she have to spend with her niece?

The realization that when Lana came home there probably wouldn't be a fairy-tale ending to their deception was like a blow between the eyes.

Real nausea accompanied it.

Kait had finally found the family and home she had longed for ever since her mother had died when she was a child. She couldn't lose it all now. The concept was unbearable.

"Mommy?"

Kait forced a smile. She let her hand slide down to the child's nape. "Tomorrow will be a fun day," she said, and she was aghast, because her tone was as thick as her heart was sick.

Marni smiled and settled down in her bed. Kait tucked the covers around her. "I'll come and check on you later," she whispered, kissing her soft cheek.

Marni nodded, her eyes already closed.

Outside in the hall, Elizabeth confronted her. "I don't like this," she snapped.

Kait couldn't take much more—it had been an endless day.

"You're up to something, and whatever it is, it can't be good. But I won't stand by and watch you hurt that child," she continued. "Do you think he'll change his mind if you become a real mother now?" she demanded.

"Have you made supper?" Kait asked calmly.

Elizabeth started. "I assumed you'd eat the tuna you did not have for lunch. I am going to bed. Good night." She marched up the hall and went up the stairs.

Kait sagged against the wall. Is that what Elizabeth thought? That she was using Marni in order to change Trev's mind about the divorce? *Oh, God!* What if she were making a bad situation worse?

But Lana's life was in danger, and so was Marni's. Kait would move heaven and earth to protect them both.

And Lana would be home either late tomorrow or first thing the day after.

Kait tried to think. And then the world at Fox Hollow might very well blow up in all of their faces.

Kait fought for composure. Only one thing seemed clear.

She had a day or a day and a half at most to try to soften up Trev Coleman, to try to save her sister's marriage, and mend the many fences she had torn down.

But what was the point?

The point was that she desperately wanted to mend all of the fences Lana had broken, just as she couldn't bear the thought of Lana losing Fox Hollow, Trev Coleman, and her daughter.

Kait closed her eyes, trembling. But it wasn't her place to repair and heal Lana's relationships within her family. And in a day or two, she was going to have to leave, because Lana was going to return and all hell would break loose when Trev Coleman learned what the two sisters had been up to.

Why hadn't she thought of this sooner? Why hadn't her sister thought of this? Why had she, Kait, so blithely accepted her sister's promise that once she returned, they would finally be real sisters and real friends, and that Kait would become a part of her family?

Kate refused to think that Lana had been manipulating her with her promises.

But there was a bottom line. There was one fact that Kait knew for sure, beyond any doubt. *She didn't want to leave Fox Hollow.*

Not tomorrow, and not the day after that, not ever.

The realization was brutal.

She didn't want to leave. She loved Fox Hollow. She loved Marni. She wanted to be accepted, by Trev, by Sam, and even by grouchy old Elizabeth. She wanted to be a real part of this family.

But there was more. *She didn't want to leave because she wanted Lana's life to be hers.*

FOUR

It was impossible, Kait thought, stunned. She turned and made her way downstairs, not seeing where she was going. She hadn't even been at Fox Hollow for an entire day. Yet she wanted Lana's life?

Yes. She did. And it didn't matter that Trev hated her, because he didn't hate her, he hated Lana. And that was hardly the same thing.

Kait felt as if she'd been struck between the eyes. Had her own life become so miserable that she could step into her sister's shoes and want what she had so quickly, so badly?

She paused to reflect, because her life wasn't miserable. It was just . . . empty.

Her own life had been empty for years, and Fox Hollow was a magical place, and there was Marni, whom she adored as if she were her own daughter, and of course, there was Trev Coleman. . . .

But she mustn't allow her thoughts to go there. Trev Coleman belonged to Lana, and rightfully so.

And in that moment, she made a decision. In two days, Lana was coming home—to Fox Hollow, to Trev, to Marni. Amazingly, the concept somehow was painful. But it was a fact. Hard and cold. And when she did return, Kait would fight to her very last breath to mend every single rift Lana had created in the Coleman family. No matter how terrible the fallout from their deception, Kait would stand strong—

especially when it came to Trev Coleman. Somehow, she
would become a part of this family. As for the divorce, she
would do everything she could to convince Lana to fight for
her marriage. If she could—and she was determined as she
had never been determined before—she was going to try to
help Trev and Lana find the love they had once had. Surely
her sister still loved Trevor Coleman, no matter what they
were now going through. Kait knew Lana had not married
him for his money. In the end, she and Lana would be
friends as well as sisters, and Trev Coleman would be a
friend as well as her brother-in-law.

And she was not returning to New York.

She was staying in Three Falls.

She had savings; she would quit her job and buy a sweet
old house somewhere in Skerrit County, so she wouldn't be
too far from Marni. She had always wanted to work from
home, and it was time to seriously think about starting a
small home business. For the moment she could freelance as
an editor—she had so many connections in publishing from
her first job as an editorial assistant.

That decision made, she felt lighter, freer, than she had in
years. Kait walked into the kitchen, trembling but relieved.
And surely she could get her sister's marriage back on track.
Once they had been so happy; she had seen the photos, she
had seen the proof.

Had Lana returned her calls?

Kait hit the wall switch and dug her cell out of her pocket.
She turned it on and was dismayed to see that she had no
messages.

There was nothing Kait could do now except wait for a
return call or Lana's return home. She opened the refrigerator and was faced with a platter of rare tuna that looked,
well, raw. In Manhattan she enjoyed sushi, but now it was as
unappealing as diet Jell-O. She slammed the door shut.

Elizabeth had gone up to her room. Sam was holed up in
her bedroom and Marni was asleep. Trev was dining out
with the Davisons. Kait did not want to think about what
would happen when he came home, so she shoved him out

of her thoughts. She had seen a small shopping center on Highway 152 just before the turnoff to Northwoods Road, the country road where Fox Hollow was located. And there had been a pizzeria right there.

Nothing would be more comforting after this day than a pepperoni pizza and a few glasses of hearty red wine. Unfortunately, she would not be dining in her pajamas in her cozy living room, cross-legged on the floor, her back against her sofa with *Larry King Live* for company and the taxis outside blaring their horns. Unfortunately, she would be dining alone in Trev Coleman's huge house. Kait realized she was still shaken. She really needed an escape, but she wasn't going to get one. Not as long as she was posing as her sister.

She retrieved her purse, threw on one of Lana's beautiful leather jackets, and hurried outside and to the car. The grounds around the house were not lit, but there were front lights on the porch. It seemed stunningly dark, and except for the cacophony of crickets, so oddly quiet. New York never slept, but the darkness and quiet of the country night was splendid. Kait paused before climbing into the car, gazing up at a sky filled with brilliant stars. Who needed Larry King? Somehow she would make a cocoon for herself in the living room, and by morning, she would be fully up to the task at hand.

After all, she had been accepted as Lana; the worst was over.

A few minutes later she wanted to take back her thoughts. Driving at night in a city that was brilliantly illuminated, or on a city highway, was one thing, and trying to maneuver the Porsche down the hill in the blackness of the country night another. The first curve was sharper than Kait had recalled, and the Porsche went right off the road into a ditch.

Kait was so stunned for a moment she just sat there, panting. Then realized the little car had its two right wheels, front and back, in a deep rut, its two left wheels still on the drive. She had stalled out because of the abrupt stop, so she started the ignition. Carefully, she tried to drive back onto the driveway.

The Porsche groaned and rocked and did not move up and over the side of the road.

Kait stopped the attempt. She couldn't believe it. She turned on the interior lights and opened the dash—no flashlight. She looked in the side pockets of her door—as clean as a whistle. Ditto for the passenger door.

She got out, stumbling on the uneven ground, and instantly saw how precariously the car was angled between the drive and the ditch. The latter was two feet deep and muddy. She was a weekend driver at best—that is, she simply did not have the skill to get the sports car out of the ditch and back onto the road.

"Damn," she said. It was the perfect end to a perfect day. Then she stiffened. Walking up the driveway toward her was a man.

She glanced back at the house, but it was too far away for anyone there to be of any help—should she need it. She quickly moved to the trunk and threw open the lid. She tore off the compartment cover and withdrew a huge and heavy tire jack. It was about half past eight, so it wasn't that late, but who could be wandering about in the dark on Fox Hollow property?

The man didn't rush and he didn't slow. Kait stood by the trunk, unmoving, watching warily, as he came into the glare of the headlights. It was the workman, Max Zara.

Unfortunately, she was relieved.

"Gotta problem?" he said.

"I obviously do," she returned, throwing the jack into the trunk and slamming down the lid. "Do you think you can help me?" Anxiety filled her tone. She dearly hoped she had not damaged Lana's beautiful car.

He seemed to study her in the dark. "Nice night for a . . . drive."

She stared back. He seemed to find her situation amusing, and she did not like his innuendo. "I was on my way out to get something to eat," she said, trying to remain civil. "Is there a reason you don't like me, Max?"

He seemed taken aback. Then he laughed. "Like you damn well don't know," he said.

She didn't know. "Let's bury the hatchet."

"Like hell. If I get your car on the road, what are you going to do for me?"

She froze. Then, "I beg your pardon?"

He grinned. "You heard."

"I have to do something in return for your helping a woman in distress?" She was aghast; and what had she ever done to make him dislike her so?

He came closer. Kait stiffened. Tonight, he wore a flannel shirt hanging open over a men's white cotton undershirt. "I don't like teases, Mrs. Coleman. Never have, never will."

He was calling her a tease?

He was so close now that she could clearly see his expression, and she saw his sudden skepticism. "What's this? You seem surprised to have a spade called a spade. I'm real tired of you eyeballing me and sashaying around in those skinny pants of yours. I'm tired of you asking me to fix this and fix that just so you can do those funny yoga poses with an audience of one." He put two hands on his hips and from his expression, he was clearly getting worked up. "Now you just happen to drive off of the road," he said.

"You're nuts!" At least she now knew that Lana had not yet slept with Max. And the fact that she was so relieved told her she'd been worried to death about it. "Just forget it!" she snapped, and she turned, about to walk back to the house.

He seized her wrist and whirled her around so quickly that she fell against his chest. "Time to make good, Mrs. Coleman, on all you been offering up," he said softly, his breath, which was scented with beer, feathering her cheek.

"I'm not making good on anything—and I have no interest in you or anyone other than my husband!" Kait cried, for one moment aware of his superior brute strength. She yanked her arm back and he let her go. She stumbled, then quickly backed up. "How dare you!" She was shaken to the core.

"That was a test, Mrs. Coleman, and guess what? You passed," he snarled. "But what I'm damned if I can't figure out is why."

Kait was close to tears. "I'll walk," she said furiously. "And I'll call a tow truck!"

But before she could move, he said softly, "I can't wait to bring you down."

She froze. Had she heard him correctly?

He smiled, but it was an expression that told her that he was the hunter and she the prey.

Fear filled Kait. And what had he just meant? "I can have you fired for this."

He laughed. "I don't think so."

She wished, desperately, that she knew what was going on. Because clearly, something was going on—and she felt certain there was more to the conflict between them than Lana's flirtation.

He eyed her, then turned and slid into the car. Instantly, Kait leapt away from it, and a moment later he had the Porsche sitting pretty in the center of the driveway.

She was shaking as he stepped out of the car. "Don't let any bed bugs bite," he said, not nicely.

She ignored the innuendo. "Thank you for helping me with the car," she managed.

His gaze narrowed with suspicion.

She managed a smile and slid into the car, slamming the door closed. Inside, she hardly felt safe. She knew he was staring at her now. She kept her eyes on the road and drove away.

One quick glance in her rearview mirror showed her that he was still standing there in the center of the road, staring after her.

The road was deserted. It was eerie, but Kait knew that was only because of the unpleasant encounter with Zara. She did not want to think about him now, hurrying a bit as she drove, anticipating the lights of the highway. But avoiding a distinctly bitter memory of their recent exchange was impossible. She remained unnerved, even frightened.

She'd automatically left her cell phone on the dashboard by the stick shift; she reached for it and saw that she still had no messages. Despairing, Kait put the phone back down. She felt as if she were in quicksand, and a call from Lana might put her back on solid ground.

But maybe she was in quicksand. There were so many hostile currents around her, and Max could no longer be discounted as insignificant. Even if he were only a redneck with an ax to grind, he seemed dangerous, and he was after her.

He had made himself clear.

She should ask Trev to fire him. It would be not only in her own best interest, but in Lana's.

A moment later, the glare of headlights behind her winked once. She was no longer alone on the road, she thought, taking the corner. She glanced in her rearview mirror again as the road straightened out, and saw that she had not been mistaken; a car was a half a dozen lengths behind her, cruising steadily at her pace.

The highway was ahead. It was a country highway, with only two lanes, and Kait was surprised to see that it wasn't well lit, and there was hardly any traffic. One car passed, heading in the opposite direction. Kait paused at the stop sign by a diner boasting several parked cars and she turned right. A moment later she saw the car that had been behind her on Northwoods Road was also turning right.

It crossed her mind that she was being followed, but that was simply absurd. No one had any reason to follow her.

But just to be sure, Kait decided to take a left at the next deserted four-way intersection.

The car also turned left.

She became stiff with tension. Was she being followed? She couldn't help noticing that the other car was staying the same distance behind her, no matter what she did. She accelerated, was briefly relieved when the other car did not, and then her heart sank. For after a minute, it accelerated, too.

She was being followed.

But why?

The answer was obvious. She was Lana now, and Lana owed a man named Paul Corelli a large sum of money. What if Corelli had sent someone out to chase her, frighten her, or even hurt her? What if Corelli meant to terrorize her until she paid up? Her heart racing wildly, Kait hung a U-turn, hit the gas, and sped back down the highway. She glanced back—the other car had stopped, pulling over on the side of the road, but he or she was not making the same U-turn. He or she had decided to call it quits.

Kait began to shake uncontrollably.

It had to have been someone sent by Corelli following her; there was simply no other explanation. Even though Lana had been given an entire week to pay off her debt, Kait had seen enough movies which she felt were based on fact to feel that some extra arm-twisting might be on the agenda. She had no desire to have her own arm twisted, or worse.

She had an awful feeling that she was in over her head.

Why was Lana doing this? Why hadn't she confided in Trev? Even if he truly hated her, she knew, without a doubt, that he would help her out of her predicament. Why hadn't she gone to the police? It still wasn't too late to do so.

Kait pulled into a gas station and collapsed over the wheel. Her body continued to shake, but not as badly as a moment ago. Then she reached for her cell phone. She dialed her sister again, and this time, when her voice mail came on, she hung up in fury and frustration.

And after she hung up, a terrible thought occurred to her.

Lana had never said anything about Kait being in danger once they switched places. But now that she had taken her sister's place, was she in danger? And if so, what kind?

Kait told herself not to panic. Corelli wanted his money,

so he might frighten Lana, but he would not kill her, because a dead woman couldn't pay up.

But he could hurt her, and badly, to encourage Lana to find the money.

Fear sickened Kait.

Still frightened and now angry at her sister, Kait pulled on a pair of indigo gym tights, a loose but short-waisted waffle-weave top in a lighter blue, and a pair of Trev Coleman's thick wool winter socks. She uncorked the red wine she'd found in a wine rack in the dining room, located CNN, and leapt into bed with the carton of pizza. In the end, the living room hadn't seemed like the sanctuary she needed, especially as it lacked a TV. There was a television in Trev's study, but she didn't dare dine there. She had also placed her cell phone by her thigh. She hadn't planned to keep it on while in the house, not when she didn't have any idea of when Trev would return home, but she was desperate to talk to Lana now and she would take her chances.

And that brought her right back to another subject. The one of cohabitation. The one of this particular master bed.

He had asked Lana for a divorce. Well, actually, he had told her that they were getting one. Surely he was not intending to share a bed now with his wife. Or was he?

In spite of the pizza and wine, Kait found it really hard to concentrate on anything other than Trev's returning home and what might happen when he did.

Larry King was on; he was interviewing Mel Gibson. Kait could not focus on the interview, but after a half a bottle of wine—and having eaten two-thirds of the pizza—she was finally becoming relaxed. In fact, her lids were closing when Trev Coleman casually walked into the room.

She sat up like a shot, fully awake.

He blinked at her.

"What . . . what are you doing?" she managed, then realized that was a very stupid question. She clearly had her answer now.

"What am I doing? I forgot my toothbrush," he said. His green eyes moved over every inch of her body, carefully and slowly. He was wearing a suit. He had dressed up for his dinner date with Alicia and her husband. Unfortunately, he looked like an ad for *GQ*, a very sexy ad. And there was an expression in his bedroom eyes that made Kait certain he'd had a few stiff drinks.

She swallowed. "Does this mean . . . you're not sleeping here?" She intended to sound elated.

"It means I moved out the essentials, but forgot my toothbrush. I'm sleeping in the guest room downstairs. What are you doing?" His eyes had landed on her socks. No, on his socks.

"Eating, watching TV. Getting ready for bed."

He folded his arms across his chest. "This is interesting."

"It is?"

"Since when do you eat pizza? Since when do you eat in bed? Since when do you sleep in gym clothes? And my socks?"

Kait couldn't manage sitting in the middle of his bed a moment longer, with him standing at its foot. She slid to her feet, crossed her arms. "I think I'm having a relapse. I don't feel well; I think I have a low fever," she lied.

"Really?" His brows were a few shades darker than his hair. They arced upward. "So you're drinking red wine, which is dehydrating?"

"It's been a hard day," she cried.

"Yeah, I'll bet." His stare left her and moved to the bed. "Expecting a call?"

Her heart did stop, missing a series of beats. She followed his regard and it landed on her cell phone, lying there by the folded back quilt. "Uhh . . ."

His gaze slammed to her face. He seemed to flush then. "I don't care," he snapped, and he strode into the walk-in closet, tearing off his suit jacket.

Kait snatched up the phone and thought, He does care. He's angry—he's very, very angry with Lana.

He returned instantly, pulling off his tie. "I know what you're up to," he said harshly.

She was alarmed. "You do?"

"Yes, I do! You've decided on a new act, because you think that wide, innocent baby blues and a lousy fashion sense and a sudden doting interest in my daughter will make me change my mind! Either that, or you're trying to keep me off balance," he ground out.

She shivered. "I'm not trying to do any of those things," she whispered. "I'm cold. You have nice socks."

"Cut it out!" he shouted.

She was so taken aback by his yelling at her, that she was briefly at a loss for words. And he seemed as surprised by his own temper. They stared at each other, and Kait felt that her own eyes were as wide as his.

The cell phone rang.

Kait realized she held it and she was aghast. Stupidly, she looked at it. It continued to ring.

"You have a call," Trev said softly, dangerously. "Aren't you going to answer it?"

She failed to breathe. "It's not important," she began.

"Answer it," he snapped.

Kait obeyed, stiff with fear—it was the worst possible timing for Lana to call. "Hello?" she said carefully.

"Lana, it's John. We missed you at dinner so I thought I'd call and see if you are okay."

For one moment, she couldn't understand who was on the other end of the line. She met Trev's cold, relentless gaze. As she did so, the comprehension clicked—it was John Davison, Alicia's husband.

"I don't accept solicitations at this number," Kait said. She hung up—and powered off.

Trev stared, his face so hard it was in danger of cracking. Kait stared back, not daring to even breathe. She reminded herself that he couldn't know that she had been desperately awaiting a call from his real wife, and that she, Kait, was an impostor.

"You are one bad trip," he said. "And the sooner this is over, the better." He turned.

Kait thought about her sister and her niece. She ran after him and gripped his arm. It was like grasping steel. "Please give me another chance," she cried. "Please don't do this, not to us, and not to Marni!"

"There is no us," he said. And his gaze slid over her in a frankly sexual and appraising way. "But you could try to persuade me to change my mind with that hot little body of yours."

She leapt away from him as if burned, but his sensual tone and what he clearly wanted from her tightened her body in a way she had forgotten about. "No," she whispered, licking her lips. "Because marriage is a sacred union—"

He actually laughed. "You don't give a shit about marriage and you never have. But we both know you love sex." His eyes gleamed.

She could imagine him coming down on top of her on the bed, his mouth moving over hers. She had to think straight! "Because . . . because I'm the mother of our child and because I love her," she said hoarsely, refusing to back down, refusing to be derailed. "I know I've been lacking as a mother, but no more. I'm turning over a new leaf. Trevor, I swear. And I intend to prove it."

His eyes widened, and they were hard. "Damn it. You never call me Trevor. What the *hell* is going on?"

She flinched. She had better not make any more mistakes, or he was going to know that she was not Lana. She wet her lips again. His eyes followed the motion of her tongue. She backed up. "And maybe we can still find the love we once had."

"The love we once had?" He was incredulous. "We never had love. Or rather, you never did. What we had was something completely different, and you know it." He was furious now. His eyes moved to her breasts, which were bare beneath the waffle weave and perfectly molded by the soft, giving fabric.

She couldn't breathe. She wanted to protest, but without enough oxygen, she didn't try.

He finally lifted his glittering eyes. "I am not going to change my mind," he said flatly.

It was very hard to think. How could a man's mere but charismatic presence, his heated eyes, arouse her body so much? When he did not belong to her, when they were in the midst of a battle? But he was staring at her mouth. "Never," she whispered, "say never."

His jaw flexed. "You know," he said slowly, taking a step forward, "that getup is a helluva lot sexier than those expensive teddies and nightgowns you wear."

He was still moving forward. She was frozen—because comprehension was crashing over her like a waterfall—and so was disbelief. "It . . . is?"

He paused before her. "Yeah. It is." He lifted his hand and through the waffle weave, he touched her very erect nipple with his thumb.

Kait cried out.

Trev seized her, crushing her body against his, his mouth going to her neck, where he used his lips, his tongue and his teeth. His body was all muscle, and he was very aroused. Kait's entire body turned into mush, while her brain became frantic. *This could not be happening. . . .*

Suddenly he pushed up her top and latched on to her nipple, sucking it hard.

Oh, my God. It was happening. . . . Her brain started to shut down. Electric desire coursed over her, through her, pooling in her loins.

He palmed her crotch. She wasn't wearing anything beneath the tights, and she could practically feel his skin. His hand was large, hard, warm, and very, very possessive. He began to rub her rhythmically and she arched forward, for more, more, more, throbbing desperately, frantically, beneath his searching fingertips.

His mouth and tongue stopped their dangerous, wonderful torture. "You're already ready for me?" he gasped.

Kait met his eyes and saw surprise. And in that single moment, sanity returned. She thought, *He is Lana's husband!*

And at that precise moment, his gaze darkened and he cursed. He pushed her away just as she leapt back from him. Grimly, his face still strained with lust, he stared at her as if she were the devil.

It took another moment for her brain to work the way that it should. "You had better go." She was trembling, and foolishly, she wanted to cry.

His eyes narrowed with suspicion and hostility. "You've got me going good with your little act—the big eyes, the cute haircut, the mommy routine. Guess you win this round."

"No," Kait whispered in anguish. "I'm not playing a game. . . ." But she was, and it was a terrible game, a game of lies and the betrayal of all trust.

He suddenly seized her arm and shook her. "Like hell you're not!" He was furious now, but whether with her and her "act" or himself, she did not know. "You know what? Bottom line is I'm a man. And we're still married. It's been a long time since we slept together, baby. And right now, I can't think of a better good-bye."

It had been a long time since he'd slept with Lana. "How long?" she demanded breathlessly, having to know.

"What?" He was incredulous.

She had to know. "Refresh my memory, please!"

"The night of the May Day Ball," he said. "You don't remember the way we fucked each other's brains out in Sara Lee's bed?"

She folded her arms tightly across her aching breasts. "I remember. I wanted to see if you remembered." It had been almost six months since he had slept with Lana.

Disgust covered his face. "Bullshit. You didn't remember because there have been a dozen guys since." He shook his head, appearing explosive. "You're right. This was one bad idea." He turned abruptly.

"Wait!"

He halted, not facing her, his shoulders stiff.

Her cry had been an impulsive one. What was she doing?

She had to let him leave. Otherwise, they'd be making love on the floor. She closed her eyes, still consumed with wanting him, but now, completely sane and knowing that she shouldn't and that she couldn't allow anything else to happen. "I'm sorry," she finally said.

He walked out.

Her night had been a sleepless one. Mostly because of Trev Coleman, but also because someone had followed her to the pizzeria last night, and all night Kait had tossed and turned, worrying over what might happen next—with Corelli, with Lana, with Trev Coleman. But she was up at half past six, sipping black coffee, and rousing Marni at seven. Marni smiled sleepily at her, then sat up like a shot. "Mommy!" she cried.

"Time to get up, sleepyhead," Kait said, tousling the child's dark, curly hair. She had gleaned the fact that Marni had a schedule and Elizabeth kept her to it. She was up at seven and being driven off to school at eight.

Marni was wide-eyed and beaming. "But what are you doing here, Mommy?"

"Helping you get ready for school," she said, giving her an impulsive hug.

There was a harrumph from the door. Kait knew the sound had been emitted by a disapproving Elizabeth, so she smiled very brightly and faced her. "Good morning." Her tone was as radiant.

Elizabeth stared, her expression rather unpleasant. "Am I to understand that you will bathe and dress her today?"

Still smiling, but aware now that the older woman had dropped any façade of liking Lana at all, she said, "Yes," with an elevated set to her chin.

Elizabeth turned and walked out.

"Let's go," Kait said cheerfully.

Marni leapt from the bed, babbling a mile a minute.

Kait and Marni were devouring plates of pancakes. Or rather, Kait was devouring hers, as if she had not eaten most of a pizza the night before. Marni was talking about her best friend, Susie, Susie's dogs, and the fact that apparently she had been promised a corgi puppy by Trev. Jim's dog was about to become a father.

A back door slammed. Kait didn't have to be told who was coming into the house, she simply knew. Pancakes turned to balls of glue in her throat. She froze over her plate.

A hot memory of the night before rushed over her. Trev Coleman strode into the kitchen and she simply had to look up. He was in his faded jeans, a beige wool sweater, and a royal blue zip-up shell. He was in his paddock boots, so he had clearly come from the stables, and he was sexier than any man had any right to be.

She tried not to choke as his gaze slammed into her, even as she felt herself flush brilliantly.

His eyes as they met hers were cold. Then he smiled and bent over Marni, his expression changing, becoming impossibly soft and warm and tender. Kait's heart leapt as she watched him brush his mouth just barely over her niece's hair. "How's my best girl in the world?" he asked.

"Mommy woke me up this morning! She helped me with my bath!" Marni exclaimed excitedly. "Look! She picked out the pink ribbon in my hair!"

"Aren't you the lucky one?" Trev murmured.

Elizabeth slammed a pot down on the stove.

Kait finally swallowed the lump of now-tasteless dough. It hurt so, his hating her, especially when she considered herself a kind and considerate person—especially as he didn't even know her.

Then Trev glanced up at her.

Kait flinched but held his stare.

A small smile twisted his mouth. "I'm taking her to school."

Kait gasped—and so did Marni. "No, Daddy! Mommy's taking me! You never take me—you school the horses in the morning with Jim!" she wailed.

"Honey, today I am taking you to school." From his tone, there would clearly be no argument, no debate. Or at least, not from Kait. She got up silently and carried her plate to the sink, where she slid several untouched pancakes into the disposal. Her appetite was gone.

"I want Mommy to take me to school," Marni said firmly.

Kait turned. Marni had an expression of sheer determination written all over her face, and she could see that a huge clash of wills was imminent, because her father had the exact same expression.

Before Trev could speak, Kait hurried between them. "Listen, sweetie. I'll pick you up! Being as your father wants to take you," she added. She didn't turn but she could feel Trev's astonishment.

Marni blinked. "Really?"

Kait nodded.

"Okay." Marni attacked her pancakes with gusto.

Trev turned.

Kait tried to smile, lost her nerve, and said, "Gotta use the bathroom." She fled.

The house felt empty with Marni and Trev gone. Kait hurried outside, aware that Elizabeth remained in the kitchen, tidying up after breakfast. She inhaled, still shaken by the brief but completely hostile encounter with Trev, and then had no choice but to fully appreciate the beautiful fall day. There was a soft breeze whispering through the gold and red leaves of the trees overhead, big fluffy clouds were drifting lazily through the sky, and a horse was whickering from one of the paddocks.

If Trev Coleman hated her now, how would he feel after Lana returned and they told him the truth?

Kait shuddered. Her confidence was low now. And her determination to fight for the family's future—for Lana and Trev's future—for her own future—remained. But she was afraid the outcome might not be the one she planned on.

She dug her cell phone out of the pocket of the leather jacket she was wearing and turned it on. There was no voice mail icon on the screen. Lana had not called her back.

She was not really surprised. In fact, she now believed

that Lana did not even have her cell phone with her. And if she had made it through yesterday—and last night—she could make it through one more day. Kait refused to recall his touch and the feeling of his hard aroused body against hers.

Lana would come home late tonight or tomorrow morning.

Her heart lurched, as if with dread. Suddenly she wished to delay her sister's return, in spite of being followed last night. She put the cell back in her pocket and walked slowly down to the first barn, where she had been yesterday. She told herself that the sooner Lana returned, the better—for the sooner they ended this charade, the better their chances of finding a reconciliation with Trev. And as intimidating as Trev Coleman could be, she would not turn tail and run. She had made the promise to herself and she would keep it. In fact, she would dwell on a rosy future, a future where everyone was happy and she was living a few miles away and just down the road. A future where she often came over to visit and see Marni.

Doubt warred with hope.

Kait walked over to the nearest stall, where a handsome, brilliantly chestnut horse was staring through the bars. He had no markings, and his coat gleamed like satin. "Hey, boy," she murmured, frowning now. Who was she fooling, exactly?

Not only didn't she think the odds very good of Coleman ever liking her, Kait London, not after the switch; last night she had been insanely attracted to him. Would she ever forget what it had been like to be even briefly in his arms?

Did she really want to see him back with her sister?

The question was a terrible one. Kait didn't dare consider it. She had her—and Lana's—future mapped out. It did not include any sexual attraction or any other feelings whatsoever on her part for Trev Coleman—other than purely platonic ones. She realized she had a huge headache, undoubtedly her just deserts.

"Ain't he grand?" Jim's voice startled her, referring to the chestnut.

"Sure is," Kait said.

"He's coming along, since you left. Should have a good season in Ocala."

Kait nodded, and as she glanced around, she saw a handsome blood bay with a star. He snorted gently at her. The nameplate below read PRIDE OF RHODOS, LANA COLEMAN. Her heart lurched.

"You look better today. Not so tense," Jim remarked.

She inhaled, walking over to the bay as if a somnambulist. He blew softly at her; she stroked his velvet muzzle. "I'm still weak," she murmured. What she wouldn't give to ride this horse. And what if she did?

Jim knew she was ill. Better yet, they didn't have to school. She could just go out for a simple little hack. She whirled. "Jim? I think I'll hack him a bit. I've been out of the saddle too long."

Jim grinned. "That's my girl. I been longeing him while you were gone, so he's not too full of himself."

"Great!" Kait cried, somehow hugging him impulsively. Excitement was thundering in her veins, but she did manage to catch his surprise. "Be right back," she declared, and she dashed from the barn at a run.

He laughed. "Slow down! Pride ain't leavin' without you!"

As she hurriedly pulled on breeches, a turtleneck, and microfiber vest, anticipation of riding the gorgeous horse chased away some of her doubt and fear. Besides, dwelling on her worries wouldn't help anything; she did have work to do and not a lot of time to do it—surely she could defuse Trev's utter hostility, not to mention that of Elizabeth, Sam, and Zara. And then there was Marni, whom she would pick up at one-thirty. Maybe they'd go to a movie, or to a toy store. But first she would ride across the beautiful countryside on one of the most handsome horses she had seen in years.

Kait tossed Lana's cell phone in the garbage.

Twenty minutes later she was back in the stable, somewhat stunned to find Pride completely groomed and tacked and ready to go. "I would have tacked him up," she muttered, instantly going to his head, taking the reins and stroking his strong neck, her helmet in her other hand.

Jim gave her a look, but he was whistling. "You never bother," he said.

She should have known. Unable to wait, Kait led him outside and to the mounting block. The moment she settled in the saddle, she felt as if everything would turn out just fine.

And the saddle fit her perfectly, being as she and Lana were the exact same height and close to the same size. "See ya, Jim." She grinned.

"Enjoy yourself," he called, turning away.

Kait left the barns at a walk, heading out into the open fields, quickly fusing with the horse's rhythm. She chatted with him as birds winged overhead, just to soothe him and herself. But he was quiet, although eager to take off. Finally she patted his neck. "Let's try a trot, fella."

He obeyed, and she worked a little to hold him back and keep him collected. His stride was huge but fluid, and she felt herself grinning with pleasure. Ahead, she saw a small log lying across the trail.

She shouldn't, but why not?

She nudged him into a canter and a moment later they soared effortlessly over the log.

Kait laughed out loud, slowing back to a trot, patting his neck with encouragement.

Then she saw a split rail up ahead. Clearly fences were scattered about for cross-country riders like herself.

She hesitated, because it was about three feet tall, and she was out of shape. Then she urged him forward. Ears pricked, he cantered to the jump and over it as effortlessly as if it were a tiny pole an inch or two off the ground.

"My, you are something!" Kait settled down to ride now, and at a canter they took half a dozen fences. Kait was pleased. Her balance was good, and for someone who did not know her mount, she was pretty much in sync with him. On the other hand, Pride was clearly a great athlete, and he was easy to ride.

A big chicken coop was ahead, painted red. It was triangular in shape, and about half a foot higher than the previous fences. Kait gathered Pride under her as they approached, silently counting off the distance.

Four.

Three.

Two.

She was about to breathe "one" when a shot rang out.

Pride bolted sharply left, around the fence, and Kait heard something—a bullet?—whistling past her ear. Kait lost her balance, and a moment later she was flying through the air, over the horse's head and the edge of the fence.

She landed hard on her back, her head snapped back, and for an instant, there was haze and shadow. Then she blinked, breathing hard, realizing she had taken a spill and she had hit her head.

Then the world stopped.

There had been a gunshot.

Someone had fired a gun.

It was hard to breathe. *Someone had tried to shoot her.* Terror overcame her. It was almost impossible to think. But disconnected words like "Lana" and "Corelli" and "the killing kind" echoed in her mind. Slowly, beginning to pant, she rolled onto her side and crept over to the bottom of the coop. From the corner of her eye she saw Pride, a few yards away, gazing at her.

She didn't move. Someone had just fired a gun. *She had heard the bullet whiz by her cheek.*

Which meant one thing.

Someone had taken a shot at her.

Someone wanted Lana dead.

Sweat trickled into her eyes, blinding her.

FIVE

Kait scrambled the few inches between her and the very bottom of the wedge-shaped jump. She pressed her face into her arms, still on her belly, her heart pounding so hard now that her body was shaking.

Someone had lied to Lana. They hadn't given her a week to pay off her debt—they were collecting now—with her life.

She didn't know what to do. She was afraid to get up. She was afraid that if she stood up someone would shoot her, and this time fail to miss.

She choked once on a sob.

Kait told herself that unraveling now would not help. She *had* to think.

Lana had never mentioned that Kait would be in danger if she took her place. Kait assumed that Lana had believed that any danger lay in the future, if she did not deliver the cash. Could a hunter possibly have been so careless as to shoot at her and her horse?

Kait wanted to believe that. She also knew that the people after Lana would rather have their money than her corpse. She couldn't relax.

How the hell was she going to get out of there?

Kait quickly shifted up into a sitting position, her back against the jump, hugging her knees to her chest. Would Pride come if she whistled? Should she attempt to mount the seventeen-hand gelding from the ground and then gallop away?

Who was she fooling! She could never get on the horse without a leg up or a mounting block. And now, her sweat was interfering with her vision as it trickled down from her forehead and temples into her eyes.

Pride snorted.

Kait stiffened, as the sound had been uneasy. She froze, straining to hear.

A twig snapped.

Not near the gelding, but to her right, in the direction of the woods—where the shot had come from.

She heard brush rustling.

Kait was on her knees; she crawled through the dirt and grass to the other edge of the coop. She dared to peer around it.

She saw nothing except an expanse of silvery birch with an occasional oak tree, the sun streaming through the golden glade. But her vision was limited now.

Pride snorted again. She heard him paw the ground.

"Easy, easy," she said, low and rough. On her belly, she shimmied forward a foot and paused. The woods shimmered and danced before her in the sunlight, orange and red and gold. Kait's gaze swept through the glade. And then it paused, her entire body stiffening. She reversed the sweep of her eyes, going back the way she had come. A shadow. She paused. She stared, straining to distinguish the shapes in the woods. The shadow was darker, greenish, unmoving. It was attached to a heavy oak tree.

Comprehension seared her then.

It was the silhouette of a man.

Someone as motionless as she.

Someone camouflaged.

Standing there, waiting for her to get up.

Kait wiggled rapidly back behind the jump. A branch snapped loudly from the woods, so loud that at first Kait was certain it was another gunshot. Pride snorted and took off.

But it *hadn't* been that man firing a gun. It had been a

branch breaking off. Still on her belly, Kait scrambled to the opposite side of the coop, to see Pride disappearing at a gallop in the direction of home. Despair seized her.

Another twig snapped, but softly, and it sounded damn close.

Kait crouched. She dared to peek over the top of the jump this time. As her vision tore back and forth across the woods, she could not find the silhouette of the man she had seen a moment ago.

He was gone.

That is, he had *moved*.

Kait leapt up and began to run, waiting for the sound of a gun to ring out. But no gunshot sounded as she raced desperately across the short distance between the coop and the next fence, a split rail. There, she slammed into a post, breathing hard. And still no one shot at her; a bullet did not slam into her back as she had expected.

Was it possible?

Had he gone?

But if so, why?

Had the shot been a warning?

What if it had been a threat? Just the way that being followed the night before may have been a threat? Kait relaxed very slightly, and using her hand to shade her eyes, she scanned the countryside. Her run had taken her into the center of the open pastures, farther from the woods. It felt like a miracle, but as far as she could see, she was alone.

She slumped against the split-rail fence and removed her riding helmet. She was aware now of a throbbing pain in her head. Automatically, she touched her scalp, wincing. A lump had formed there.

She turned to look all around again. She was definitely alone.

What was going on? Determination suddenly filled her. It was time for answers, it was time to go to the police. If only she could reach Lana. But Kait had given up on that. The question was, could she hang on for a few more hours or until the following morning, depending on when Lana returned?

Was Lana's life in danger? Was Kait's?

Kait didn't want to suddenly think about a fact of her life while she was growing up. But she, Kait, had always been the sincere and honest one. She had never been able to dissemble or lie.

Lana had always been able to exaggerate the truth, or omit it, to suit her needs. She had, once or twice, been caught in an outright lie. On those occasions, Lana had always been in a jam. Her ability to dissemble had extricated her from some serious trouble, even once when she had been caught shoplifting with a boy. But that had been years ago.

Kait stiffened. What if Corelli hadn't lied to her sister about giving her a week to pay off her debt? What if Lana had lied to Kait?

It was simply impossible that her sister would knowingly put her in danger. Wasn't it?

Kait didn't know what to believe. She still couldn't understand why Lana hadn't gone to the police. And she still couldn't imagine who might be in Lana's past who would now come forward and hand over a large sum of money to pay off her debt. Something was wrong with the entire situation.

Kait tucked her helmet under her arm and began the long walk home.

Five minutes later a horse and rider appeared on the far side of the rolling fields. Kait paused, somehow knowing who it was. The rider had pulled his mount up too, and even though he was a good distance away, Kait knew the moment he had spotted her. An instant later he was moving his mount into a hand gallop, and then horse and rider were flying over a four-foot stone wall. A moment later Trev Coleman was pulling up his big bay gelding right in front of her. He was a superb equestrian.

His eyes locked with hers. "Are you all right?"

By now, her head was really hurting. She started to nod, and to her horror, felt like bursting into tears. She fought the unwelcome urge. "Yeah."

He leapt down from the bay, his eyes never leaving her. "Pride appeared back at the barn. You took a fall?" He was very calm and matter-of-fact. His gaze had swept over every inch of her, and as she was covered with grass and dirt, not to mention horseless, the answer had to be obvious.

She felt like rushing into his arms. She wanted to tell him everything. Instead, she swallowed and clutched her helmet as if it were a life vest and she was in the deepest of seas. How much of the truth could she reveal? Lana was in trouble—and Trev should know about it. "Any hunters around here?"

His eyes widened. "This is private property."

That almost answered that. She hesitated.

"What the hell happened? How the hell did you fall off your horse?" Trev demanded.

She had to tell him. "Someone shot at me. We were about to take the coop. Pride went one way—I went another."

For one moment, he seemed simply astonished. Then, "No one shot at you."

"Trev!" She began to shake all over again, when she had thought she had recovered her composure. "It was a gunshot. And I felt the bullet whiz past my cheek!" And she looked him right in the eye.

He was very still. His expression was impossible to read. Then, "Are you certain it was a gunshot—and not something else?" he asked so quietly that she felt like kicking him.

"Yes!" Tears filled her eyes.

He touched her shoulder, clasping it. "Take it easy. You're okay."

She looked up at him, almost swooning with gratitude. "I'm scared." And she wanted to blurt out to him that it was undoubtedly some loan shark named Corelli. But she couldn't—she had made her sister a promise, and she had only a few more hours to hold to it.

"Lana, I don't believe someone shot at you. Why would anyone do that?"

Kait pressed her lips firmly together, instead of answering him.

"You may not be Miss Popularity in this county, but no one wants you dead." He wasn't smiling, though. He was grim. "Or at least not badly enough to do something like really shoot at you."

"That was unkind," she said tersely.

He gave her a thoughtful look. "You have more enemies than a bus full of cops. You make enemies the way bees make honey."

Kait was taken aback. "That's not true!"

He shook his head, exasperated. "If you want to deny the fact that every woman and half the men in this county hate you, so be it. Have you ever heard a gun being fired?"

Why would all the women in the county hate her? And half the men? Kait was afraid to know what he meant. "On TV. In the movies."

"See? It wasn't a gunshot, Lana."

She grabbed his arm. "It was a gunshot!" A wave of dizziness swept her, but she ignored it. "Someone fired a gun. And I saw a man lurking in the woods afterwards! Then he was gone."

His jaw flexed. "Hunting season starts in two weeks. I'm calling the police when we get back."

She met his green gaze. "Is that what you think? That someone decided to look for game on your property—and somehow fired at me?"

"If a shot was fired, there is no doubt in my mind that is what happened," he said firmly. Suddenly he handed her the reins. "Put on your helmet, Lana," he said very softly.

She stiffened.

"And get on Scandal."

She didn't move, because she couldn't. All she could think about was being astride Pride as they moved closer and closer to the jump—and the bullet screaming past her face.

He didn't move either. His eyes were steel.

There was an old saying every rider knew—if you fall off, you get right back on, otherwise, you might never get on again. It was even more important if the fall had occurred while jumping.

"You're a damn good rider. That fence is nothing for you, and less than that for Scandal."

She nodded, trying to compose herself and failing miserably. Worse, she was really feeling shaky now. She put on her helmet, wincing as she did so, and as she fastened the strap, she looked at him. He nodded, his smile slight and meant to be encouraging.

It crossed her numb mind that he didn't hate Lana after all.

Even more dispirited, Kait looped the reins over the bay's head, while her pulse pounded with increasing anxiety. She knew she had to find calm, because one could not ride a fence while consumed with stress and fear. Trev moved behind her, undoubtedly to give her a leg up.

Instantly, she became aware of him as a man, a husband, a lover, and a friend.

She closed her eyes, gripping the pommel. Is that how she saw him? As a complete partner? But he wasn't her partner, and he never would be. He still cared for his wife. Why else would he have raced from Fox Hollow to find her when Pride had returned without his rider? Why else would he be making her jump again? If he didn't care, he wouldn't care if she ever got on a horse another time.

Still, he was standing an inch or two behind her. It would be so easy to turn and melt into his arms. Not for sex, but for comfort, safety, love.

How could this be happening?

She opened her eyes and not turning even once, lifted her leg as he boosted her up.

"Take some deep breaths," he said as she dared to look down at him. "Long and slow." He shortened her stirrup for her, all business now.

Kait obeyed, while he moved to the other side to shorten

her other stirrup and then check the girth. Finishing with the girth he glanced up, their eyes meeting.

Her worry must have showed. He clasped her knee. "You've jumped this fence a hundred times. You can do it with your eyes closed, and so can Scandal."

Kait nodded, thinking he'd die if he knew she'd only jumped it once—not even, considering she had fallen off. It crossed her dazed mind that this was the perfect time to come clean.

He said, "Canter a small circle, keep him collected, and let him pick the distance. All you have to do is sit there and look pretty. Okay?" He slapped her thigh. "Sit tight and deep," he added, a warning. "Stay behind the movement. You know what to do." He nodded at her, stepping away.

"Piece of cake," she rasped. His gaze shot to hers, reflecting worry, and she looked away. She gathered up the reins, filled with tension. The horse beneath her shook his head, clearly anticipating action. Or was he aware of the fact that she was frightened and worried and an unfamiliar rider? Breathe, she told herself. They circled easily, slowly, the bay's ears pricked and forward. Kait tried to relax, but it was impossible, even with the graceful horse beneath her. The jump loomed ahead as they approached.

She tensed.

And Trev must have seen. "Relax. Deepen your seat. Sit *up*," he snapped.

They were four strides away. Kait obeyed. The horse beneath her was a beautiful mover—as comfortable as a rocking chair. Thank God for that. She could do this. She had to. Trev Coleman was watching.

They were two strides away.

The bullet had whizzed past her cheek.

Kait forced the thought away.

"Grab his mane," Trev said harshly.

Scandal was soaring into the air. Kait had a hunk of mane. They landed and Kait was thrown a bit forward and knew she'd botched it, but at least she hadn't chickened out, and at least they had gone over—not around—the damned coop.

She pulled the bay into a trot, turning him, and with a flush she halted before Trev.

He was staring in a way she now recognized—his eyes said, What the hell is going on? But he quickly smiled. "Good girl. You got the job done. That's what counts."

"I landed in a heap on his neck," she said with regret, patting the bay for being so steady and good. She avoided Trev's green eyes now. He knew something odd was going on. Lana would never be tense like that, not even after a fall. She would never collapse after a jump. "I'm sorry."

"You were frightened," he said. "You were scared of the fence."

Kait couldn't move. She felt his confusion, uncertainty, his doubt. She simply knew that he was trying to comprehend how Lana, who was not afraid of anything, had been afraid of that little chicken coop. She said, "I was expecting a bullet to hit me in the back."

He didn't look away. "I guess that explains it."

Kait nodded shakily but refused to hold his gaze—it was too penetrating—because if she did, he might be able to tell that she was lying and that she was not her sister.

But he was going to find that fact out pretty soon anyway. She inhaled. "Trev?" The truth was on the tip of her tongue.

"You stay on Scandal. I'll walk," he said, his tone very grim and his head down. If he had heard the tentative question in her tone, he was ignoring it.

They started back across the field in the direction of Fox Hollow, with Trev pacing by her leg and the bay's side. Kait's heart raced. Why was her courage suddenly, completely, failing her now? This was the time to tell him, and to hell with the promise she had made. Kait glanced at him, catching his devastating profile. The words stuck in her throat. She'd realized a moment ago that he couldn't possibly hate Lana after all, and Kait knew she was supposed to be thrilled with her comprehension, but she wasn't. She was, in fact, dismayed. And simply put, that was very wrong.

Because Trev Coleman and her sister deserved a second

chance. Because she intended for them to have a second chance.

She closed her eyes, fought to take the high road, then opened them, deciding to wait until Lana returned and let her handle the deception, which was her idea. And the marriage—which was her marriage—her way. . . . But now was a good time to start mending Lana's broken fences. And there was an upside—Trev Coleman could be kind and pleasant when he wasn't pushing Lana away. "Trev?" Trepidation filled her tone yet again.

He glanced at her.

"Thanks." She smiled a bit at him, her eyes searching his.

His expression hardened. "This doesn't change anything." But he didn't look away.

"Why not? It's clear now that you still care . . . about me." God, her own words hurt!

"I'm a human being, Lana. A compassionate one, as you should damn well know."

She hesitated, felt the beginnings of a flush. She could not help her unruly self. "There was more than compassion on your mind last night."

He stumbled. His regard whipped to hers, glimmering with anger. "Do you expect me to deny it? I'm not a hypocrite. Compassion was the last thing on my mind last night."

"Then why? Why go through with a divorce when there is hope?"

"Did I say there was hope? Going to bed with you has nothing to do with hope." He seemed very angry now.

"Why are you so mad? What have I done now?" she whispered. "For God's sake, someone just shot at me!"

He faced her, halting the horse. "That's just it!" he exclaimed. "Those baby blues, all wide-eyed and startled, and . . . hurt! I'm the one who's been hurt, not you, so just cut out the nice-nice act!" He released her reins and strode ahead of her, then tossed back, "And no one shot at you, damn it!"

"It's not an act," she tried to say to his set shoulders and rigid back.

He kept going.

Eventually, she gathered up the reins and followed.

Kait locked the bathroom door, took two—not one—Motrin and a hot, hot shower. She was toweling off and regarding her ultra-pale reflection in the mirror when there was a knock on the bathroom door. She tensed.

Only one person could be standing there. "I'm not dressed," she said quickly, reflexively. She held the towel up over her breasts as if Trev Coleman could see through the door she faced.

He said, his tone wry, "Doc Mitchell will be here in five."

She inhaled, and caught a glimpse of her startled expression in the mirrored wall behind the pedestal sinks. Another player had just entered their drama and she wasn't up to continuing her Lana charade. What she needed was rest. "I don't need to see a doctor."

There was a pause. "Are you all right?"

"Yes, that's just it, I'm fine!"

A few seconds ticked by. "I think he'd better look at you anyway." Then his footsteps sounded as he walked away.

Kait stared at herself in the mirror, resigned. If she had fooled Trev Coleman, she could surely fool Mitchell. Besides, her head hurt, and maybe it should be looked at.

She slid on a clean pair of gym tights and one of Trev's sweaters. She unlocked the door and stepped out of the bathroom. The bedroom door was open, and a heavyset man with a kind smile stood there. Trev was with him, still in his riding clothes. "Hello, Lana," the portly doctor said.

Kait forced a smile. "Doc."

He seemed startled by her having called him Doc.

"Mitchell," she added quickly.

The doctor looked at Trev and they exchanged a glance. "She may have landed hard," he said. "I can tell her head is hurting her."

How did he know that? she wondered.

Dr. Mitchell smiled at her. "So let's have a little look, why don't we?" He started toward the bed.

Kait didn't move. "Would you mind?" she asked Trev.

He shrugged and walked out.

Kait went to the door and closed it behind him. When she turned, the doctor was staring at her in surprise. She managed a tight smile and walked over to the bed, sitting down.

"What are you doing?" he asked mildly.

His eyes were so gentle that she told him the truth. "I have no idea."

He patted her back. "You are cute as a button in that haircut, Lana. Makes you look like a college girl."

She met his gaze. "Thanks."

"Trev like it?"

She tensed. "I don't think so. But then, he doesn't like me much, now, does he?" This man had a demeanor that encouraged her to confide in him.

Mitchell sighed. "Relax while I feel around," he said, his gentle hands going to her scalp. "It's never too late to patch things up, or at least, that's my motto."

She winced. "Do you think we can?" She was beginning to realize that Mitchell was more than a doctor, he seemed like Trev's friend.

"Well, it depends. A lot depends on you." He smiled at her. "Got a bit of an egg here, now, don't we?"

"It hurts," she admitted. "What should I do? If I want him back?"

He had finished examining her head and he sat down beside her, studying her, perhaps to see if she was sincere. "Why do you want him back . . . now?"

She swallowed. "Marriage is a lifelong commitment. And then there's Marni."

He stared at her without saying a word.

She shifted nervously.

"Odd words from you," he said, but not with censure. He seemed puzzled. "How are you feeling?"

"I have a raging headache. And sometimes when I stand

up I'm a bit dizzy. I'm a tad nauseous, too," she said truthfully.

"You may have a small concussion. You haven't said anything about love."

"I love him," Kait said. And she felt her cheeks turn red, but she refused to consider why.

He stared into her eyes, shook his head as if to shake some sense into himself, and stood. "I believe you," he said. "I see nothing but sincerity in your eyes." He shook his head again. "I know we've had our differences, although I've never tried to judge you, and I admit, I had my doubts from the moment you two announced your engagement." He smiled then. "I'm happy to see that you've done some soul searching. Marriage is a big commitment."

Kait certainly agreed with that. And she sensed that she had an ally here—at long last.

"Shall we get back to business?" Mitchell asked with a smile. Kait nodded. "Have you thrown up?"

"No. Not even close, just the upset stomach."

"That's good. Tell me about the fall," he said, sitting down beside her again.

Kait told him, omitting any reference to a gunshot. When she was through, he patted her hand. "You have a small concussion, I am certain of it. But I want to take X rays, and we can do that this afternoon or early tomorrow. Meanwhile, no activity! I want you to stay in bed and rest."

"For how long?" she asked, suddenly curious. Maybe she would be invited to stay at Fox Hollow once Lana returned, until she had fully recovered from the fall.

"Let me look at those X rays before we decide," he said with a pleasant smile, standing and gathering up his medical bag. "I'm giving Trev a prescription for the pain. Tylenol with codeine. I'm sure you won't need it after tomorrow."

Kait nodded and hesitated, biting her lip. "Dr. Mitchell? Do I have a chance? Or does Trev really hate me?"

He stared for a moment, and she knew that she never called him Dr. Mitchell. "I don't really know," he said after a pause. "If I hadn't just had this talk with you, I would have said no. But I think you have been doing some real home-work on yourself. I think, once Trev realizes you are sincere, you might be able to win him back."

Kait managed a smile. Why wasn't she happier with his assessment of Lana's chances of winning Trev back?

There was a knock on the door.

Mitchell, bless his kind soul, turned to her. "Do we let him in? You look as if you are expecting the executioner."

Kait managed a rueful smile. "I'm too tired to fight with him, and he seems to relish the combat." Then, "How awful do I look?"

He was amused. "You're a beautiful woman, concussion or not." He winked and told Trev to come on in.

Trev walked in and his gaze met Kait's. "What's the diagnosis, Mitch?" He was abrupt.

"No combat," Mitchell said, with a smile at Kait. "Doctor's orders."

"What?" Trev looked from Kait to Mitchell and back again.

Mitchell touched his sleeve. "She has a concussion. She needs rest. We'll talk about it on my way out."

Trev's expression changed. "I'm not surprised." His jaw seemed to flex.

"Hey, doesn't she look like the cutest college student in that haircut?" Mitchell sent Kait a wink.

She knew what he was doing. He was trying to get Trev to begin to come around toward her. Silently, she blessed his good-hearted soul.

Trev glanced at Mitchell. "It's okay," he said, clearly refusing to give an inch. Then he faced her. His gaze swept over her face, finally lingering on her mouth. "We'll talk later," he said firmly. And he followed Mitchell out.

Kait hugged a pillow to her breasts. Mitchell was a real ally, but would he be Lana's friend when the truth came out? And was Trev concerned about her? It certainly seemed so.

She reminded herself that he was concerned about Lana, his wife, not about her, Kait London.

If only her head wasn't killing her.

Kait lay down carefully and closed her eyes, tension draining away like an ebbing floodtide. Exhaustion claimed her. A moment later someone was shaking her and calling Lana's name.

"Lana? Lana! Wake up!"

Why was she being called Lana? That wasn't her name. Kait opened her eyes and looked into the most devastating pair of sooty-lashed green eyes she had ever seen. Instantly, she recalled her switch with Lana and the jumping accident, as instantly, she recalled that someone wanted Lana—meaning her—dead. She sat up with Trev Coleman's help. Relief flooded his features.

He sat down by her hip. "I hate to do this to you, but you can't sleep right now," he said.

"What?"

"For the next twelve hours, Mitch wants me to keep a close eye on you. You'll have to be woken up every half hour," he said.

She just stared. She already knew the reason why—if she had a serious head injury, she might fall asleep and wind up in a coma. "Mitch said it wasn't serious," she said, suddenly afraid. She had landed hard. Fortunately, if memory served her correctly—and she was not sure it did—she had landed on her rear and then her head.

"He's making an appointment for us at the hospital. I just sent Max out to get you that prescription for painkillers," he added, finally attempting a smile.

Something very much like love flooded her chest in the vicinity of her heart. "Thanks," she whispered, reaching for his hand without thinking.

He looked from her face down to her palm as it clasped his. Then he pulled away, standing. "I need to go get Marni," he said tersely.

Marni was expecting Kait to pick her up at school. Kait struggled to stand up. "Oh, God! She's expecting me! I have to go!" she cried. Marni was coming to love and trust her and she could not disappoint her now.

"Like hell." He was staring at her as if she were an alien from Mars. "I'll explain what happened."

Tears came to her eyes. "But that isn't good enough! I can't let her down," she said, shoving off the covers and leaping from the bed.

The moment she did a huge wave of dizziness engulfed her. Trev caught her and held her upright, his arms hard and strong around her. "What the hell do you think you're doing?" he asked harshly.

She didn't move away. Her breasts were flattened by his chest. "I want to come too," she said. "Please."

"You're so dizzy you can't even stand up! Besides, Mitch gave orders, and we're following them." He somehow maneuvered her over to the edge of bed, where she simply had to sit down.

"I'll go get her now, and Elizabeth can watch over you," he said grimly.

Kait nodded, tremendously upset. Marni was only four. She wasn't going to understand and Kait didn't need to be a child psychologist to know that.

Trev walked to the door. Kait said, "Don't scare her. Tell her it was a little fall and I will be up and about in no time."

He turned abruptly and looked at her. Confusion, doubt, and suspicion were clearly reflected on his face. He said, "I wish to hell I knew what was really going on."

Kait didn't move.

Neither did he.

"What does that mean?" she asked unsteadily.

He stared, a familiar coolness now in his eyes. "It means I know you damn well. And this is *not* you. My wife wouldn't care about picking Marni up at school, not after the accident you had today. This has gone too far, Lana. This act of yours has to stop." He was angry.

Her heart stopped. She failed to breathe. Tears wanted to come to her eyes. "Trev, please. It's not an act. Not anymore. Please try to believe me!"

"You've even got Mitch on your side! How the hell did you manage that?" He was even angrier now.

"I told him the truth," Kait whispered. "I told him how I feel."

He stared.

Kait inhaled. "Trev? I need to ask you something. It has to do with who may have taken a shot at me."

He started. "What?"

"Have you ever heard of someone named Paul Corelli?" she said, her cheeks heating, her mind spinning, almost unable to believe what she was about to say, about to do.

"No." He was abrupt, mocking. "Let me guess. Another jilted lover?"

Kait gasped.

He folded his arms across his chest and waited.

She swallowed, praying he was wrong about her sister. "Remember when we were in trouble with the banks? Remember when they were going to foreclose on Fox Hollow?"

His eyes widened. It was a moment before he spoke. "What the hell are you talking about?"

An inkling began, a horrible one. "I'm talking about the time when we were about to lose Fox Hollow."

He stared. "What game is this? I was never on the brink of losing Fox Hollow. I own Fox Hollow free and clear and I always have," he said.

SIX

The pain had returned. Her head throbbing, Kait stared as Trev walked out of the room, almost slamming her door behind him.

Lana had lied.

Fox Hollow had never been in danger of foreclosure. Trev owned it free and clear. Why would Lana tell Kait such a story?

Why would she ask Kait to switch places with her?

Did this mean that she did not owe money to someone named Paul Corelli? And if that was the case, why was Kait at Fox Hollow, pretending to be her sister? If that was the case, why had someone followed her last night, and tried to shoot her this morning? *What the hell was going on!*

Kait's instinct was to run after Trev and explain everything and beg him for his help.

But instead, she gripped her head as she sat on the bed, trying desperately to think. Lana was not malicious; her lies were always meant to avert trouble. Clearly she was in trouble now. There was no other possible explanation for her to lie this way to Kait, and ask Kait to switch places with her.

Kait was terrified. She felt like a blind person trapped in a huge dark maze, with pitfalls awaiting her every turn. What should she do?

She told herself to calm down, to breathe. And as she tried to inhale slowly, deeply, and exhale the same way, she began to think coherently. Lana would return. Kait chose to believe she would return as she had promised, in two days—which meant in a few more hours or the following morning. Could she, Kait, hang on until then—until she knew what the stakes really were?

Kait swallowed, thinking the worst. Lana had to be in danger. Her life had to be at stake. Only such jeopardy would justify such a monstrous lie and their deception on her family. If Kait came forward now, might she inadvertently put her sister in even more danger?

It was hard to say. Being as Kait had not a clue as to what was really happening, sitting tight seemed to be the only possible solution now. And the more she pondered, the more staying put seemed like the least of all evils because the only conclusion that seemed likely was that Lana's life was in real danger, and she had left Fox Hollow to do something about it.

Kait shivered. *Did that mean that she was in danger, too?*

Kait already knew the answer to that. Her riding accident was proof that her own life was on the line as well.

But why? If Corelli did not exist, who was after Lana?

Trev Coleman had said she had many enemies.

Kait shivered again, panic trying to claim her once more. He had also said no one hated her enough to want her dead. Very uneasy now and quite simply overwhelmed, recalling Max Zara's hostility, and then Elizabeth's, she walked quickly into the bathroom to retrieve Lana's cell phone from the trash, hoping against hope that Lana might try to call her. But to her dismay, the phone was gone.

Lana would never call her at the house. Kait sat down on the edge of the tub with tears filling her eyes, overcome with dismay. How would Lana ever reach her now? If only she dared go to Trev! In fact, she wanted to huddle in his arms. But being as Lana hadn't done so, Kait knew now that she had better not, either. She was terrified that anything she might do would make her sister's dilemma even worse.

But damn it, Lana should have told her the truth!

Grabbing a tissue, Kait wiped her eyes and returned to the walk-in closet. Surely there must be some clue somewhere. Grimly she went to Lana's side of the closet and began a thorough search of every shelf and every drawer, but other than finding clothing and accessories, she only found a few receipts. Her pulse accelerating, she began searching through Trev's things. She shoved aside jeans and slacks, socks and underwear. She was on her hands and knees, rummaging on the floor behind his shoes, when she realized that she was not alone.

The closet door had been open, and slowly, she turned. Elizabeth Dorentz stood in the bedroom, watching her.

Kait stared defensively back, but her heart lurched with more dismay. This woman disliked her. She did not know why, but her feelings were all too clear. Was she one of the women in the county who hated her? And, if so, why? "Are you spying on me?" she asked tersely, slowly getting to her feet. Too late, she realized she had left the closet looking as if a burglar had ransacked it.

"Spying? Hardly." Elizabeth was holding a tray. Her face was an expressionless mask. "Your painkillers. Max brought them."

She stared. *But nobody hates you enough to want you dead.* Trev's words echoed in her mind, loud and clear. Someone hated Lana enough to want her dead, Kait felt certain.

"You're staring," Elizabeth said calmly. "Have I grown horns?"

But it was absurd to think that Elizabeth had taken a potshot at her. Or was it? "I don't know. Have you?" Kait stepped into the bedroom, her shoulders defensively high.

"What does that mean?" Elizabeth asked sharply.

Kait stared back. "What have I ever done to you?" she finally asked softly, "to make you dislike me so?"

Elizabeth's eyes widened. Then she set the tray down, shook her head, and began to leave the room.

"Wait!" Kait cried. "I mean it. I am serious."

Elizabeth turned around. "I doubt that. Trev might believe you somehow fell from your horse and now are injured, but then, you have played him for a fool from the moment he first laid eyes on you, haven't you?"

"I did fall from my horse," Kait said. "Someone shot at me, Elizabeth."

Elizabeth made a disbelieving sound.

"You still haven't answered my question," Kait said. "You can't hate me because we fell in love!"

Elizabeth folded her arms. "You don't love Trev. You never have."

Kait stiffened. "That's not fair." Trev's accusation that Lana had only married him for his money came to mind. It was too terrible and ugly to contemplate, and she shoved his words aside. Still, the kernel of their meaning simply would not budge; it had been implanted in her mind.

Elizabeth's face darkened. "You never have loved him! I have known him since he was a small boy. I consider him the son I never had. I bandaged his scrapes and cuts, I encouraged him before every show, I picked up his tuxedo on prom night! I sat with him as his wife wasted away, day after day, dying. I love him just as I loved his father, deeply and selflessly. That is why I am still here, at Fox Hollow, holding it all together! And that is why I am intolerant of your shenanigans."

Kait recoiled at the look of anger on her face, even as she tried to absorb this. Why hadn't Lana mentioned this to her? "You were involved with his father?"

"Oh, please! As if you don't know. Edward's wife also died, but in a tragic riding accident. Trev was a small boy; he needed me—just as Edward did." She stared closely at her. "I am wondering what you hope to gain by this charade of yours."

Kait shivered. Did Elizabeth suspect that she was Lana's twin, or did she think her to be Lana, and playing a dangerous game? In either case, Kait realized that she was walking on eggshells here. And then she realized that she was determined to continue to cover for her sister until her sister returned, until Lana could explain precisely what was going on and who wanted to kill her—and why.

"Someone shot at me today," Kait said tightly. "That's why I had a riding accident. Someone tried to shoot me. I think that person wants me dead."

Elizabeth stared. It was impossible to gauge her reaction to Kait's words. The woman had an iron will, the most superb self-control.

"Do you have any idea who might hate me enough to try to shoot me?" Kait asked harshly.

Elizabeth blinked. "No."

Kait had hardly expected her to confess. However, her next words truly surprised Kait.

"I do not know who might hate you enough to want to murder you, Lana," she said with a poisonous smile. "But I do know that you don't have a single friend in the entire county. What I do know is that you have many, many enemies."

Kait stared, unnerved. Was Elizabeth implying that she was hardly surprised that someone wanted her dead?

"Just for fun, why don't you tell me who I'm up against?" Kait asked without thinking.

Elizabeth blinked. "I have no idea," she said, turning to leave.

Kait raced after her and grabbed her arm. "Let's say the intent was not murder. Let's say someone only wished to hurt me, or even frighten me."

Elizabeth shook free. "To hurt you as you have hurt them? Oh, I don't know. But I would count backwards if I were you." Her blue eyes blazed.

"Count backwards? And just what am I counting?" Kait asked with dread.

"Your lovers and their very angry wives," Elizabeth said.

When Kait awoke, she was completely disoriented. The sun was shining brightly into her room, as if it were midmorning, but she knew it was the late afternoon. In fact, distorted images flitted through her groggy mind: Pride standing riderless in the field. Trev cantering over to her, his face a mask of concern; then his face near hers as he shook her, asking her to wake up. Another image of Dr. Mitchell followed, and suddenly Kait was completely awake. Dear God. Someone had tried to kill her, and Lana had lied to her about the reason for the switch.

She blinked and the amount of sunlight streaming into the bedroom did not change. Kait struggled to sit up, stunned and then horrified—how could it be the morning? She had lain down right after the tense and hostile exchange with Elizabeth Dorentz, after swallowing the prescribed painkiller. She blinked at the grinning clock on the bedside table, and realized it was eight the following morning.

Though she dimly recalled someone checking on her several times, it seemed she had mostly slept through the entire night, which meant that Lana had not yet returned.

Or had she?

What if she had returned last night, and Trev Coleman now knew everything? Kait threw off the covers, a knot of tension inside her chest, aching terribly, like heartburn. And she had missed Marni.

Kait got up, more than dismayed. By now Marni had left for school, and as upset as she was to have disappointed her niece, she was terrified of the reception she might find downstairs. She reminded herself that the upside of the equation was that she would finally have answers from Lana if she was back—she would finally have the truth.

She quickly brushed her teeth and showered, then dressed in a pair of beige slacks and a turtleneck sweater. It was nine o'clock; downstairs, Sam was in the kitchen, slathering something goopy and beige onto toast. The tall blonde turned, saw her, and turned away. Today she wore all black—a black V-neck pullover, a black leather vest, black jeans, and a big black belt with silver grommets. Her shoes were black Keds.

Kait felt a flash of relief. Sam was acting as if Kait were Lana, not an unknown twin sister of her stepmother. Kait cleared her throat. "Did I miss everyone?" she asked nervously.

Sam didn't answer. She carried the plate of toast over to the breakfast nook with a huge glass of green juice that looked healthy but unappetizing. She sat down, drank, and ate.

"Good morning," Kait tried. But she was certain now that Lana had not come back. Sam would be acting far differently if she had, and the firing squad would be waiting for her.

Sam didn't look up. She pulled a newspaper forward and seemed to read the front page.

Kait hesitated, went to the coffeemaker, and poured herself a coffee. Today she needed sugar, and she found a jar in the cupboard. She added milk and went and sat down across from Sam. The teenager looked up.

"You may be sixteen, but that is no excuse for bad manners," Kait remarked, her gaze moving over Sam again. She realized that Sam's sweater was extremely expensive—it was cashmere and of the highest quality, Kait felt certain of it. But perhaps she was allowed unlimited spending. Yet Trev didn't seem like that kind of father.

Sam finally looked at her. "You're not wearing any makeup."

Kait smiled. "It's too early for makeup."

Sam stared. Mostly at her face and hair. Then she stood up. "You look weird naked like that," she said abruptly. "You look like a geek!" She thrust her slim body away from the table, and then snatched up her juice.

Kait also shot up. She had had enough, and to hell with the consequences. She grabbed Sam's thin arm. "What have I ever done to you?" she asked.

Sam shrugged free. "Are you kidding?"

"No, I'm not. I had a riding accident yesterday, or didn't anyone tell you?"

Sam folded her arms across her chest. "I heard," she mumbled.

"I have a concussion. My head happens to hurt. But more importantly, your rudeness is intolerable."

Sam snickered. "Did you suffer memory loss, as well? That might be why you forgot to put on your face—and why you're drinking coffee with *cream?*"

Kait suspected that Lana drank her coffee black. "I didn't even think about it. I'm hungry." That was the truth.

"Right." Sam turned to go.

"Wait." Kait moved in front of her, blocking her way. "Why don't you like me? Is it because of your mother?"

"My mother?" Sam seemed startled. "My mother died

when I was nine. Sometimes I can't even remember what she was like." She seemed upset and she stomped away, finishing her juice and putting the glass in the big state-of-the-art stainless-steel sink. Then she turned. "But she was a lot more beautiful than you!"

Kait stared at her back. If Sam's mother had died seven years ago, there had been a year or less between her death and Trev and Lana's marriage. She would imagine that Sam had had an extremely difficult time with the marriage, and that might explain her hostility to Lana. It suddenly occurred to her that Trev as well may have been in the throes of grief when he had met her sister.

She didn't like the implications of her thoughts. But there was no way for her to avoid them now—he hadn't been ready to settle down with another woman, not on the heels of his wife's death.

Suddenly Kait felt as if a huge curtain were going up, laying bare the weakness of all the excuses she had been making for her sister. Suddenly she felt as if she were on center stage, drowning in bright stage lights. Lana loved beautiful things. She loved clothing and jewelry, and now, apparently, expensive horses and sports cars. Trev had been newly widowed when they had met. Had she been attracted to him because of his wealth?

He owned Fox Hollow outright. That made him a fairly wealthy man.

Dismayed, Kait had to sit down.

"You gonna faint?" Sam asked.

"I hope not." Kait gripped the edge of the kitchen table grimly. "So then what is it, if not your mother?" she asked.

Sam turned, leaning against the sink. Her smirk was not pleasant. "What is it? It's because you are a total bitch."

Kait gasped.

Sam didn't blink. She said, "If you think, just because you fell off your horse—if you really did—that I am going to forget all the times you have walked into a room and not even seen me there, forget it! If you think I am gonna forget how you have fucked my dad over, forget it! A riding accident doesn't change *anything!*" With that, she went to the center island, hefted up a maroon backpack, and hurried from the room.

Kait was reeling.

Then footsteps sounded and she turned with dread. As no door had slammed closed, whoever was in the hallway had already been inside the house, apparently lurking about. And the footsteps were heavy and male.

Max Zara appeared in the doorway. Their gazes locked.

He hadn't shaved, his short hair was disheveled; he looked as if he'd just gotten out of bed. And his blue eyes were hard as he regarded her. How much had he overhead? Enough, apparently, Kait thought. Had he enjoyed her exchange with Sam?

He smiled at her, but not pleasantly. "Not about to win any popularity contests around here, eh?"

She stared at him and simply knew he had been the one to go into her room and take her phone. It hadn't been a maid. And he had also been the one to take her Gucci bag.

It was sheer gut instinct, but so powerful, Kait did not have a doubt.

Had he taken a shot at her, too?

Suddenly it crossed Kait's mind that he was hardly stable boy material. She didn't know much about him, but she'd bet he'd had more than a high school education—not only that, he was definitely from Brooklyn or Queens. So what was he doing down in Virginia, working on a horse farm?

It was hard to breathe properly. *This man was not what he seemed.*

"And you?" she said hoarsely. "What do you want?"

His next words stunned her. "What do I want?" He laughed as he poured himself a cup of coffee, as nonchalant as if he owned the house, no, the world. He didn't look up. "What I want, Mrs. Coleman, is to bring you down."

Kait's headache was minor enough to forgo a painkiller and take straight Motrin. When she had seen Max drive off from the house in a beat-up Toyota pickup, heading toward the far barns or even the road leading to the highway and town, she took off on foot toward the stables. Determination filled her now. Zara's parting words told her that she was right—there was more to the man than met the eye, and damn it, she was going to find out if he was the one after her and Lana.

She had gleaned that there were several apartments over the first stable as well as an office in the back, which Jim used. She had learned that Max lived in one of those apartments. She was going to search it in the hope of finding her phone and learning who he really was—and what he had meant by his statement that he intended to bring her down.

She was ill. That statement had been a very personal one. Had he meant that he intended to kill her? Did this man want vengeance, and, if so, why?

It crossed her mind that her sister might have disappeared because she couldn't take living at Fox Hollow anymore.

But Kait dismissed that thought, because it implied that she wasn't coming back.

No one was about as she entered the barn where Pride and Scandal were stabled. All of the horses had already been turned out, and Kait only saw a solitary groom, a young red-headed man who was mucking out a stall. He looked like a high-school student, and Kait suspected he was a local kid in need of a part-time job and some cash.

She knew she had to work fast. She had no intention of being in Zara's apartment when he returned. She found the apartments at the back of the barn, above the ground floor. The first apartment was clearly unused, but the second one had plates in the sink of the kitchenette, and the bed had barely been made, the covers tossed up. A blue chambray shirt hung on the back of one of the two kitchen chairs at the small, square table there, and she knew she was in the right apartment.

Bingo, she thought with satisfaction.

Her heart had picked up an accelerated beat. Kait remained on the threshold, glancing behind her just once, to reassure herself that he wasn't standing there. Then she faced the studio carefully, taking one quick glance at her watch. It was half past nine. She intended to be out of there in fifteen minutes flat.

She quickly took in the apartment. The window in the kitchen area looked out over the far pastures and in the direction of the country road. The window over the bed looked out over the fields where she had been riding yesterday. The studio was basically furnished, and other than the bed and kitchen table and two kitchen chairs, there was a big tweed easy chair, a small-screen TV, a beige sofa, an oak coffee table.

She closed the door behind her and went swiftly to the kitchen area. She opened the closest drawer, and found it to be a catch-all. She smiled grimly, pulling out a handful of receipts, paper clips and pens, a notepad that was blank, Scotch tape, and scissors. His name, she read on the receipts, was Max Zara. So he was not lying about that.

He had shopped at Wal-Mart, Ace Hardware, Kroger. And he had rented some videos.

There was also a package of condoms in the drawer. She didn't want to even think about whom he was seeing.

Kait shoved everything back in and then went through the rest of the kitchen. She found pots and pans, cooking utensils, dishes, silverware and glasses, everything she would expect. She turned to the closet, as there was no bureau to go through. It was nine-forty.

She moved more quickly now. His jeans were folded on one shelf, a half a dozen button-down shirts, chambray and flannel, hung on the hangers. She ignored a pile of black bikini underwear and equally black socks.

There were no drawers in the closet. She hesitated, and began going through his shirt pockets. She found a small scrap of white paper, realized it was another receipt. She sighed, then started and looked at it again.

It was dated two days ago. Exactly.

And it was for a taxi.

In fact, Kait was one of those rare people who kept her taxicab receipts. She now recognized the stub in her hand. It was for a New York City Yellow Cab.

Two days ago—exactly—she had left Manhattan, taken a cab to La Guardia, landed at Reagan National, found Lana's car, and driven to Fox Hollow.

Two days ago she had been woken up at one in the morning by Lana's telephone call.

Two days ago—exactly—Max Zara had been in a taxi in Manhattan.

Coincidence?

She was far more ill than before.

Did he know?

Did he know that she wasn't Lana?

Kait had to sit down, and hard. This man might have followed Lana to the city, and he might have seen them together. Kait didn't think it was a terrible leap of faith to make. And if so, what kind of game was he playing? Why hadn't he confronted her, or told Trev? *What did he want?*

Who the hell was he?

She looked at her watch again, and became filled with panic. It was nine-fifty. She had promised herself that she would spend no more than fifteen minutes searching his apartment, because she was terrified of being caught. Those fifteen minutes were gone.

How much did he know?

He was the enemy, she thought unsteadily, and she needed five more minutes, desperately.

She rushed to the kitchen window and looked out. She froze, because a truck was coming up the driveway, but from this distance she couldn't tell if it was Trev's brand-new Dodge Ram or Zara's beat-up Toyota. Both were blue, although Trev's paint job was cobalt, metallic, and brighter.

She ran to the bed and quickly checked out the two drawers in the cube that served as a bedside table and knew her time was up. Still, breathing hard, she flipped the pillow aside, but nothing lay beneath it. Shit. She ducked under the bed. A suitcase lay there.

Kait hesitated, imagining Max Zara parking outside. She pulled out the suitcase, went to open it—and found it locked.

A car door slammed, not terribly distant.

She froze.

Then she lifted the suitcase and grunted. It was heavy—something was inside.

It was too big to shake, but she tilted it, and heard and felt objects falling to the lowered end. Kait shoved it back under the bed, leapt up, and ran to the door. She pressed her ear to it, while sweat trickled down her collarbone and between her breasts.

Silence greeted her.

She cracked open the door and peered through. The short, dark hallway was empty. Kait slipped out, carefully closing the door behind her, not making a sound. Then she moved as quietly as possible to the top of the stairs.

A voice drifted up to her, faint, the words not distinguishable, the voice unfamiliar. It sounded young—and she guessed it belonged to the groom.

Then a too-familiar rumble answered. Max Zara said something about going outside. Kait clung to the narrow railing on the stairs.

There was only silence now.

She inched down the stairs, one at a time, pausing when a floorboard creaked loudly enough to wake the dead. She stared at the ground floor, expecting to see Zara rush in, demanding to know what she was doing on the stairs that led to his apartment. He did not appear.

She took a gamble and ran down the rest of the steps, turned the corner, and entered the corridor between the twenty-odd stalls. It was, thank God, empty.

She slowed her stride, reminding herself that she had every right to be in this part of the barn. As she reached the other end, where the barn door had been raised and was open, she recognized Max's beat-up pickup truck parked just outside.

She paused before stepping into the sunlight. Max and the redheaded groom were standing by a tractor, which was hauling a cart of baled hay. He saw her instantly, his head whipping toward her, and he stared.

And as their gazes locked, she suddenly recalled that she had closed the door to his apartment—but it had been open when she found it.

SEVEN

"**D**o you always make house calls?" Kait asked.

Mitch smiled at her, having just examined her. "Yes, I do. I am a bit old-fashioned when it comes to my practice," he said good-naturedly. "That lump is half the size. Very nice, indeed."

Kait glanced across the bedroom. Just after Sam had left, Trev and Mitch had walked into the kitchen. It remained early morning, and Kait was on pins and needles, waiting for a call from Lana, a call that would tell her she was on her way back to Fox Hollow. Now, Trev stood with his shoulder against the doorjamb in his faded jeans, paddock boots, and a canary yellow sweater that did amazing things to his coloring and eyes. His expression was inscrutable.

If he remained worried about her, he did not show it.

"Any dizziness or nausea?" Mitch asked.

Kait hesitated, her gaze on Trev—their eyes briefly locked. She tore her glance away. "I think I'm pretty much okay," she said, with another glance at Trev. "No dizziness, no nausea. I slept like a rock last night."

His eyes narrowed.

"Well, I am happy to hear that." Mitch stood. "Stay away from the horses for a week or so, and no exercise, other than a pleasant stroll. Other than that, do what you feel up to. We can forgo X rays, since you are well on the mend, my dear."

Trev came forward. "That was a quick recovery," he remarked.

Mitch glanced at him. "The lump on the back of her head is half the size it was yesterday, Trev. Which is very good news."

Trev eyed her. Kait realized that now that her riding accident was safely past, he was back to being hostile and suspicious of her. It simply wasn't fair. She also appreciated Mitch defending her. She had the feeling this was not the first time that he had done so.

"I'll walk you out," Trev said to his friend.

When they left, Kait followed them, keeping a good distance behind. She watched them going downstairs, and heard Mitch say, "You really should give her a break. She didn't fake that lump on her head."

"That's about the only thing she hasn't faked in our marriage, and you know it," Trev said harshly.

Kait was grim. She didn't want to hear any more. But she moved to the top of the stairs anyway.

"You were pretty upset yesterday. Did you call the police?" Mitch asked.

"I spoke with Rafe. He agrees with me that if someone did take a shot, it was merely a hunter trespassing on Fox Hollow property and violating the game laws," Trev said firmly. "I think he intends to speak with Lana sometime today."

"Well, I do agree with that hypothesis. Lana couldn't possibly have angered someone enough to make that person take a shot at her, for goodness' sake," Mitch said.

Trev laughed derisively. "You are the most benevolent person I know. I hate to tell you, Mitch, but you are completely wrong. I can think of a couple of women—and men—who'd love to attend her funeral."

Mitch paused. "Look, Trev, I know she's disappointed you. I—"

"Disappointed me?" He was incredulous. "She's fucked everybody I know, right beneath my nose! She neglects Marni, and as for Sam, she never tried, not from day one, to be a mother to her. She is selfish and grasping, and I, for one, am sick of it. Besides, I happen to know for a fact now that she targeted me way before she met me."

"What does that mean?" Mitch asked.

"She was looking for a rich sugar daddy. I fit the bill. Especially because Mariah had just died and I was vulnerable. I was a mark, Mitch, and it took me a long time to figure it out."

For a moment, Mitch stared. "I hope you're wrong," he finally said. "Give her a break anyway, will you? In case you haven't noticed, she seems to have changed. People do change, Trev. There's something different about her."

"Yeah, she cut off all of that gorgeous hair."

Mitch laughed. "You know that's not what I meant."

Kait hung over the rail as the two men disappeared from her view. She was reeling. Was that how Trev viewed Lana? And surely, surely, he was wrong!

She managed to straighten, so stunned she had but one thought—there was never going to be a reconciliation between him and his wife. She closed her eyes, hanging on to the railing. And she realized that a part of her was terribly relieved.

Kait knew she shouldn't be relieved. She tried to think. Lana could not possibly have been so calculating as to single out a rich widower just to marry his money. And as for Trev's comment about Lana sleeping with everyone he knew, that was surely a gross exaggeration.

But Elizabeth had made a similar comment, and so had Sam.

Lana had always been extremely popular. She'd always been able to get any boy she wanted. She hadn't been good at going steady, either—she'd changed boyfriends the way Kait read books. There had been quite a few broken hearts at Darien High School, and not just male ones. Too many pretty girls had lost their boyfriends. In fact, upon graduation, Lana hadn't been all that popular anymore, Kait realized with a jolt. There had been a lot of enmity against her seething just beneath the surface.

. Just the way there was now.

Kait had always looked the other way, partly because she didn't want to see Lana flaunting the football team captain on her arm when his girlfriend was so hurt, and partly because she had her nose buried in her books and it was easier to make excuses for her sister than to condemn her for her ability to entice any boy she wanted her way. Kait was afraid.

She was afraid the time had come to stop making excuses for her sister.

But she hadn't heard Lana's side of the story yet. And Trev Coleman wanted a divorce. No situation caused a couple to become more hateful, or to twist the truth more. And Sam, Elizabeth, and even Max Zara were all clearly on Trev's side.

Lana was her twin. And she was in terrible trouble. Kait intended to continue to give her the benefit of the doubt until she heard what she had to say for herself.

Besides, she wasn't a bad person. She was wild, restless—an adventuress in every sense of the word. She had unquenchable energy, and a love of excitement. She never set out to hurt anyone, not deliberately. Kait was certain of that. Kait still admired her immensely, and she still wanted the relationship with her that she had never really had.

Kait glanced at the bedside clock. It was half past ten. Lana should be calling at any moment—except that Kait no longer had her cell phone. Would she contact Kait at the house?

Or would she simply walk through Fox Hollow's front door?

Kait walked into the kitchen, where Elizabeth had all kinds of vegetables on the counter and lettuce in a colander. It was noon, but Kait didn't care about the time except for the fact that she was expecting to hear from or see her sister at any moment. In spite of her extreme state of anxiety, her stomach was growling wildly, no doubt due to the fact that she hadn't eaten well in two days and nothing yesterday. She opened up one of two stainless-steel refrigerators and found it stocked with bottled water, both sparkling and flat, cans of soda, cartons of juice, milk, and soy milk. She closed the door and opened the adjacent one.

Where was Lana now? Was she in a taxi and on her way to Fox Hollow, having already landed at Reagan National? Her heart lurching, Kait pulled out a loaf of whole-grain bread, then a jar of mayo, a wedge of cheese, and a package of sliced turkey. As she turned, she realized that eyes were drilling holes into her back.

She glanced over her shoulder. Elizabeth said, "What do you think you're doing?"

"I'm ravenous. I'm making a sandwich and then I'm going to get Marni." A thought occurred to her and she leaned against the counter. "Did a maid find my cell phone? I seem to have misplaced it."

Elizabeth blinked at her, then walked to a drawer at the far end of the counter and opened it. From where she stood, Kait saw that the drawer was a neatly organized catchall. From amidst the many sections holding pens, paper clips, receipts, and other miscellaneous items, Elizabeth withdrew a cell phone.

Kait almost fainted. Then she almost leapt at Elizabeth to grab it from her. Somehow, miraculously, she did not move.

"Theresa found this in the trash."

"That's mine," Kait managed breathlessly. She forced a smile as she sauntered over, her heart pounding in excitement. She knew there was a message there for her. She took the phone quite calmly, silently applauding herself for her theatrical skills, and glanced at the LCD screen. Her heart sank like a rock.

No message icon was there.

"You seem to have been expecting an important call, Lana," Elizabeth said.

Her hands began to shake. Quickly, Kait turned away from Elizabeth, in real disbelief. This was not fair! Why the hell hadn't Lana called? She was supposed to be back at Fox

Hollow now, or at any moment! Where was she? What was going on?

Kait told herself that Lana was running late. People ran late all the time.

Still, Kait had been desperate to learn what was really going on, ever since she had realized how hugely Lana had lied to her about the reason for their switch. She forced herself to think. Surely she would hear from her sister at any moment.

Then she realized that Elizabeth was staring at her back again.

Kait turned. "I can feel your disapproval. What crime am I committing now?" Her tone was sharp, but she could not moderate it.

"I just do not understand. You don't eat sandwiches and you don't eat at noon; you cut your hair which you were extremely vain about, you never seem to wear makeup and you used to sleep in it, and now you're going to pick Marni up at school? I do not like this one bit."

Kait didn't know what to say. But she would remain in her role as Lana until Lana gave her the go-ahead to come clean. "I'm still shaken from the fall yesterday," she said slowly. "And I did a lot of soul searching these past few weeks, especially in New York, when I was cooped up with the flu. I got tired of all that hair, of that boring matronly look. Is that so odd? And I had a makeover at the salon. I was strongly told that less is more at my age. What is so unusual? A grown woman can't decide to change a bit? And I am starving, Elizabeth. I hardly ate yesterday!"

"No." Elizabeth stepped forward, her square face rigid with tension. "You think to con Trev yet again, don't you? The sexy seductress failed—he got tired of *her*—so now you are playing the devoted mother, the innocent ingénue, the sweet girl next door."

"I've *always* loved my daughter," Kait said, turning back to the counter, where she began slapping together a sandwich. She did not want to become angry now. And especially not with Elizabeth—but it was hard not to be angry—and she was becoming angry with her sister, too. But why couldn't Elizabeth mind her own business? The answer was simple—because she genuinely loved Trev and Marni.

"He won't fall for it. He's too smart now," Elizabeth said. "Even if that haircut was very clever, indeed, the most clever thing you have ever done, really, other than to pick him up the way that you did when the two of you met."

Kait stiffened. She faced her adversary now. She certainly understood what she meant about her hair, because when she had cut her own hair several years ago, everyone had told her how it played up her eyes and made her look a decade younger. But what did that comment about picking Trev up mean? "I don't know what you're talking about," she said harshly.

"Really? He was grieving for his wife, Lana. His heart was broken! He had a Friday business meeting and you showed up, took one look at his Rolex, his custom-made suit, his Italian shoes, and you knew a good thing when you saw it. The next thing I know he is calling me from New York and telling me he is staying for the weekend. And on Monday he returns—with you. Now that was fast work, indeed."

Kait had to look away, gripping the kitchen counter. So that was how they had met—at a restaurant or bar, and it had been a whirlwind love affair.

Were Elizabeth's accusations inherently possible?

Who met someone on a Friday afternoon, spent an entire weekend, then brought that person home?

Someone being conned . . .

Kait hadn't heard her sister's side of the story yet. She managed to smile grimly at Elizabeth. "Did it ever occur to you that we fell in love, madly?" But even as she defended Lana, that notion dismayed her, too.

"No, it did not, as Trev is a rational and deliberate man. But he was very vulnerable then. And you took complete advantage of him." She turned away, grabbing a a paper towel and disinfectant and wiping down the counters angrily.

Kait went to the center island and sat on a stool. She

sighed. She did not want to fight with anyone, not even Elizabeth, and just then she had a terrible sinking sensation—like she was in over her head. Too many people believed that her sister was malicious. Kait refused to accept their point of view. *But where was she?*

She was coming back to Fox Hollow, wasn't she?

Kait knew that she was. She didn't know why she had even had a moment's confusion or doubt. She cradled her temple in her hands, composed herself, and looked up. "What would it take for you to give me a second chance?" she asked, meaning it.

Elizabeth did not turn around, now disinfecting the sink. She snorted.

"People change." As Kait spoke, she thought about Mitch. He was a sweetheart. "Things happen. People realize their mistakes and reverse their entire lives."

Elizabeth said, "I was making you a salad for lunch. I'll set it aside for supper, instead."

Kait got up, suddenly weary, and placed her sandwich on a plate, and said, "Thank you." Then she walked out, wondering what it would take to win Elizabeth over.

For even though Lana was returning in a matter of minutes or hours, even if she and Trev did not work things out—and Kait wasn't as optimistic on that point now—Kait intended to remain an aunt to Marni, her plans to stay in Three Falls hadn't changed. She would be the aunt next door, so to speak. She was going to win Elizabeth, Sam, and Trev over—even if Lana and Trev did divorce, even if they remained hostile to one another. Elizabeth's animosity did matter. It mattered greatly, because in every way she was a member of the Coleman family.

Why had her sister run roughshod over everyone at Fox Hollow?

Her head hurt her now. Kait returned to the kitchen for a Motrin, then plopped down in the living room in the chair she had eyed her first day at Fox Hollow. It was as comfortable as it looked. She put her feet up on an ottoman and looked out the huge windows facing her. The view of the rolling fields and distant hills was spectacular. It was also vastly comforting. God seemed to be everywhere at Fox Hollow, so close she could almost feel Him. Hadn't Lana felt any of this?

"I heard you took a spill! Are you all right?" a woman said, approaching from behind.

Kait's feet came down and she turned and saw a very pretty, slightly plump redhead in tan slacks, a pin-striped shirt, and a red cardigan. Her diamond ring was large. A gold Cartier watch glinted on one wrist. A diamond hung on a gold thread in the vee of her crisp shirt. She was smiling, but anxiously, as she hurried into the room. Of course this was Alicia—Lana's best friend. Trev had had dinner with her and her husband the first night Kait had been at Fox Hollow. "Hi." Kait managed a smile, unsure of what to expect.

Alicia stopped, staring at Kait's hair, her eyes wide with surprise. Kait smiled. "I got a chop job."

Seeming stunned, the redhead now took in Kait's paddock boots, which, while gleaming with polish, were, nevertheless, a distinct stable statement. Then she looked at the sandwich on the plate. "Are you all right?" she managed, her coral-stained lips barely moving. "I heard you *fell* off your horse over a fence, Lana."

"I'm fine." Kait smiled again. "I mean, we did have a bit of an accident, and I did hit my head, but I'm fine."

Alicia sat down on the ottoman beside Kait's chair, reaching for her hands. "No one told me until this morning! Why didn't you call me yesterday when it happened? I would have come right over," she cried.

Kait looked into her hazel eyes and thought that Lana seemed to have a friend here. "I'm fine. It was scary. . . ." She stopped. Alicia was Lana's best friend. Maybe she knew what the hell was going on.

Alicia still held her hands. "You're a superb rider. I can't imagine you having a fall! And whatever possessed you to cut your hair? I mean, it's cute and all, but . . . it's so not you!" She finally released Kait's hands, seeming bewildered.

It wasn't Lana at all. Temptresses did not have short,

wispy hair. Temptresses had long sultry locks. "I was temporarily insane." Kait was wry. Did she dare pump Alicia for information?

Alicia blinked, then smiled. "Well, I like it." She grinned. "I like it a lot! But you didn't clue me in!"

"It was spur of the moment," Kait murmured.

Alicia touched her own, heavy, shoulder-length mane. "Should I cut mine?"

Kait started, regarding the redhead's pretty face. Being as she was a bit overweight, and she had round, plump cheeks, she knew that her own hairstyle would never suit Alicia. Besides, the blunt cut was extremely conservative—Alicia, while probably thirty or so, was a bit matronly for her age. "Honey, you have gorgeous hair. Do not cut it."

"I really don't want to," Alicia said, with relief. "But it looks so cute on you!" She hesitated. "Does Trev like it?"

Kait also hesitated. "I have no idea."

Alicia reached for her hand. "Is everything okay?"

Here, at last, was a friend and confidante. "He's handed me my walking papers," Kait said.

"What?"

"He gave me divorce papers about one second after I walked through the door," Kait explained.

Alicia stared, dismayed. She stood and paced, then said, "How can I help?"

"Can I win him back?" Kait asked.

She was startled. "I thought you wanted out! You said you were sick and tired of marriage. That you needed to move on."

So that was how Lana felt.

Alicia lowered her voice. "I even got the feeling that you might not bother to come back from New York."

Kait shot to her feet. "You did?"

"Well, it was just an idea. I mean, you never suggested anything. But I know how much the two of you have been fighting. I know how mad Trev is at you. I know you hate it when people are mad at you." She shrugged. "It's been awful in this house. I couldn't blame you if you moved out."

Kait stared at Lana's friend. Lana was going to return at any moment. Of course she was. Alicia was a bit of a bimbo, Kait thought. She shouldn't really trust her judgment. On the other hand, out of the mouths of babes often came the wisdom of the gods. . . .

"I'm not sure what to do," Kait finally said softly. And why was she somewhat relieved that Lana was finished with her marriage? Kait knew she had to get a grip on her attraction for Trev Coleman. Otherwise, how could she help Lana salvage a life that she should never give up?

Alicia put her arm around her. "You're so beautiful. In the end, it will all work out. And there's always Farrell."

"Farrell?" Kait echoed, with unease and before she could stop herself.

Alicia gave her a knowing look. "He'll love you forever," she said.

God, who was Farrell? Kait shuddered inwardly, because she wasn't ready for another player, oh no. And especially one who might be in love with her sister. She tried to decide what tack to take with Alicia. "Why does Trev hate me? Does he hate me?"

Alicia started—and then she flushed. "Why are you asking me that?"

"Because you're my friend—because if anyone will tell me what I don't want to hear, it's you."

Alicia blinked. "You're acting oddly. It's frightening me."

Kait smiled quickly. "I'm under a lot of stress." That was a terrible understatement!

"I mean, it's not just your hair. Where's your *lipstick?*"

"I switched to gloss," Kait said patiently. "I also had a makeover at the salon."

Alicia came over to her and put her arm around her. "At our age, we need a bit of help with what Mother Nature gave us."

Kait looked at her heavily made-up eyes. "I guess you're right. So? Does Trev hate me?"

Alicia let her arm fall away from Kait's waist. She hesitated.

"You can tell me the truth."

"I don't know. No one can run him around like you. Oh! I didn't mean that the way it sounded!" she cried.

"That's all right," Kait said solemnly, dismayed. When Lana returned, would she be able to turn Trev around, seduce him into falling for her all over again?

It was what Kait wanted. But now, suddenly, the whole concept felt horrible, unbearable.

"What I meant was, he's no different from any other man, and you are so beautiful and they all flock to you without your hardly doing anything! I mean, all you have to do is smile to make a man fall in love with you," Alicia said earnestly.

"That's hardly true," Kait said stiffly. She had a burning question, but how to ask, and did she dare? "Does he know about . . . my love affairs?"

"Uh . . . well, you sort of threw every one in his face," Alicia muttered. "Why are you asking me these questions?"

Kait couldn't answer. She just stood there, horrified.

Alicia smiled quickly. "Will you be going to Parker's gala on Saturday?"

Kait knew that the answer was no—by Saturday, she would be Kait London again, and the entire family would be in a terrible showdown. "I'll ask Trev what he wants to do," she finally said.

"Ask Trev? He always goes to Parker's gala. He told me he's going. He told me the other night when we had dinner." She hesitated. "John was disappointed that you didn't join us. So was I."

Kait couldn't really tell her that she hadn't been invited. "It didn't seem right, not after he handed me those divorce papers."

"What are you going to do?"

Kait froze. "Do?"

Alicia sat down and crossed her legs. "Well, you said you wanted a divorce. Now you sound like you've changed your mind."

Kait responded in the only possible way, truthfully. "I

have no idea what I'm going to do or what is going to happen next."

Alicia stared. Then she said, "Please don't jerk Trev around. You two were happy once, but . . . so much has happened since then. He's a good man. He deserves some happiness, Lana."

Kait stared. "How long have you known him?"

"What?!"

Kait wished she had thought before speaking. She stared at Alicia, aghast, not knowing how to get out of her terrible slip.

"We grew up together," Alicia said. "But you know that. Trev is the brother I never had."

"I know," Kait said in a rush. "I meant, how long have you known he wants a divorce?"

"Oh." Alicia's expression lost its puzzled look. "A few months, I guess. The same as you."

Kait went to the sofa and sat down beside her. "There's something I haven't told you," she said.

"What's that?"

"I had that fall yesterday because someone shot at me."

Alicia turned white. "I beg your pardon?"

"Someone shot at me. Alicia, I think someone is trying to kill me," Kait said.

EIGHT

Alicia covered her heart with her hand and sat down, wide-eyed. Then she said, "Maybe you should have been more discreet, all of these years."

Now we're getting somewhere, Kait thought. "More discreet? How?"

Alicia regarded her closely. "You have been so open about your affairs. I don't know, maybe one of your lovers or one of their wives has decided to pay you back."

Kait had somehow sensed that it was coming to this. Her sister, clearly, had been terribly unfaithful to Trev Coleman, and hadn't bothered to even try to hide her affairs. How could Lana have behaved in such a miserable and hurtful way?

Kait turned away from Alicia so she could not see her face. She was more than upset; she was angry. Now she understood why Trev was angry, and why, perhaps, he even hated his own wife.

Why would anyone cheat on Trev Coleman?

Kait believed in fidelity and commitment. Still, she knew that life could take unusual twists and turns, and while she wanted to blame Lana now for being an adulteress and disloyal, she did not yet know her side of the story. She had to have one.

"Are you all right?" Alicia asked softly. "I'm not trying to pass judgment, Lana. You know I'd never do that. You know I'd hoped you and Trev would work things out, until you told me it wasn't ever going to happen. Now I just want you both to be happy. I hate seeing you hurt each other this way."

Kait turned. "Who do you think shot at me?"

Alicia was taken aback. "I don't know. I really don't have any idea who would be so crazy to do something like that."

"Mrs. Coleman! Isn't this a surprise!"

Kait smiled at a pretty, young woman with pulled-back blond hair, but she was looking past her at the kids crowding the lobby of the school. Some very young children were present, and clearly the school had programs for twos and threes as well as fours. Then she saw Marni, who saw her at the exact same time.

"Mommy!" she cried, her smile brilliant with surprise and happiness.

Kait smiled at the teacher, whose name she had not bothered to discover and hurried past her. She knelt and hugged her niece. "Hi, sweetie. How was school today?"

Marni beamed at her. "It was great," she said, "I made a Halloween picture for you."

"That's wonderful," Kait cried. "When can I see it?"

"It's not finished."

Kait stood, stroking Marni's hair, which was pulled back into one big fat neat braid. "I'm sorry about yesterday, honey. I fell off my horse and hit my head. The medicine Dr. Mitch gave me put me right to sleep."

"I know." Marni smiled up at her, taking her hand. "Daddy told me."

"Were you angry with me for not picking you up yesterday?"

"A little. But Daddy let me sleep with you for a while. I saw you were really sick," Marni said very seriously.

As they started out of the lobby, Kait smiled at the blond teacher, who said, "I am so pleased to see you, Mrs. Coleman. I take it you have recovered from your riding accident?"

Kait started and paused. Was Three Falls such a small

town that even Marni's pre-K teacher knew about her fall? Then she realized what had happened. "Oh, I'm fine. I guess Marni told you about it?"

"No, actually, I heard about it at the deli this morning when I was picking up a coffee and a bagel." The woman had hazel eyes and they settled on her. Her smile suddenly seemed fixed, her gaze quite curious.

Suddenly Kait realized just how small Three Falls was. She didn't know the actual population, but she bet it was a mere few thousand. And that meant that everyone knew everyone else's business. Kait managed a smile, and with a wave, she and Marni left. "You have a very nice teacher," she said.

"Ms. Harding is very nice," Marni agreed. "She asks about Daddy a lot. She smiles at him a lot too, when he comes to school. I think she loves him." Marni smiled at her.

Kait would bet heavily that Ms. Harding had a crush on Trev Coleman. Was she waiting in the wings for Lana's divorce so she could take her best shot at him?

Kait halted in midstep. Trev Coleman was handsome and wealthy; he was a catch. Undoubtedly the entire town—no, the entire county—knew he had a cheating wife and that a divorce was imminent. How many women were out there, eagerly awaiting the event, and hoping to eventually ensnare Trev for themselves?

It was a dismal thought.

Kait hoped one of them wasn't insane enough to try to kill Lana to expedite matters. And how was she ever going to discover just who Lana's old lovers were? Although Lana would be back at any moment, Kait was trying to put together a list of suspects. So far it was short and weak. Max Zara was on it, as was Elizabeth Dorentz. But, in truth, Kait didn't think either person crazy enough to try to murder her sister—or herself. She didn't think either of them had enough motivation.

No, it had to be a jilted lover, or a very angry wife.

"Mommy?"

"Sorry!" Kait cried, realizing she was standing in the middle of the sidewalk, while other mothers and nannies were on the curb with their children, chatting before getting into their SUVs and station wagons. She smiled at Marni, but now the biggest question of all loomed. *Where the hell was her sister?*

She reminded herself that it was only one-thirty in the afternoon. Yes, Lana had said in her letter that she would be back in two days, and that was now. In fact, Kait had arrived at Fox Hollow exactly forty-eight hours ago. Lana was obviously running late, Kate decided.

Marni cut into her thoughts. "Mommy, are you and Daddy getting a divorce?"

Kait looked into Marni's worried eyes and was horrified. "What do you mean, Marni?" Kait asked very quietly, but inside she was not calm at all. Inside, she was stunned and furious.

Marni was downcast. "Daddy told me. He said it was time for you and him to just be friends and to live in different houses. He said you would still love me. Mommy, I don't want a divorce! I don't want you to go away!"

Kait swept her up into her arms, hugging her hard. Tears filled her eyes. "Neither do I," she said impulsively, and then she was aghast. Kait could not release Marni. She held her and thought about the fact that she didn't want to give up her new life at Fox Hollow.

Kait was horrified with herself.

It wasn't *her* new life. It was Lana's life and Kait must never forget that—even if it was one she hadn't seemed to care very much about.

But that wasn't fair. Kait still didn't know her sister's side of the story, and Lana was in terrible trouble, and someone had taken a shot at Kait to prove it.

Kait closed her eyes, still embracing the child who felt like her own daughter.

Three hours later, Kait and Marni drove up to the house. Marni saw the black-and-white police car at the same time as Kait. Marni cried out in childish excitement, while Kait gasped, wondering why the Chevy Blazer was parked in front of their door. And then she knew.

Lana had returned and they were both going to jail for fraud.

"Mommy! Do you think bad people came to the house?" Marni cried, wide-eyed.

Kait parked the Porsche and turned off the ignition. She tried to calm down. It was simply impossible. It had never before occurred to her that what she was doing might be illegal as well as wrong.

What if it were worse than that? What if something had happened to Lana, what if whoever was after her had somehow gotten to her?

"I'm sure that nothing is wrong," Kait managed as reassuringly as possible. But she did not believe her own words. Why else would the police be at the house? The windows in the SUV were rolled down, and she could hear the police radio crackling, with occasional outbursts of operator and officer dialogue. This had to have something to do with her sister and the danger she was in.

Kait tried not to panic. It was no longer early afternoon. It was after five P.M. Lana should have been back hours ago, and if she was running this late, she should have called. What had happened?

And something had happened.

Kait was afraid.

Marni was already pushing open her car door. "Uncle Rafe! Uncle Rafe!" She shouted happily.

Kait tensed as Marni bolted from the car. Lana had mentioned that Trev had a younger brother, Rafe Coleman, but hadn't given any details. Why had he shown up now, of all times? Kait couldn't handle another family member, another potential confrontation. Because clearly Trev's brother would be on Trev's side.

Marni was already racing up the front steps to the veranda. Kait stepped out of the Porsche, almost twisting her ankle on the uneven ground. She had stopped wearing Lana's high heels the moment she had arrived at Fox Hollow, but today she had decided to remain completely in character. She was wearing one of Lana's elegant pantsuits with a pair of ankle boots. In real frustration, she cursed.

She was perspiring now.

She prayed her sister was all right, and that her being hurt wasn't the reason the police were there.

The moment she entered the house, Trev came blasting out of the living room, tightly clutching his daughter's hand. "Where the hell have you been?" he shouted wildly at her.

And she saw his fear. "What?"

He gave her a look filled with rage—a look of murderous fury—and swept Marni up into his arms. Kait recoiled, although, in that moment, she understood. This had nothing to do with Lana at all. "Where have you been all afternoon?" he ground out, kissing Marni's cheek.

An officer in a black standard-issue jacket, a big gun in his holster, a Western-style hat on his head, stepped out behind Trev, as did Elizabeth and Max. Elizabeth was as white as a new sheet, and Max Zara was, well, speculative.

"We went to the movies," Kait said quickly. *Trev was enraged. He was enraged with her.* "I'm sorry. I didn't mean to—"

"You went to the movies?!" Trev choked, still furious.

"Daddy, we saw *Beauty and the Beast.* It was so much fun! And we had ice cream," Marni cried. She looked extremely anxious now.

Instantly, Trev kissed her again. "I didn't know," he managed harshly. "Thank God you are all right."

The officer wore a badge on his bomber-style jacket with SHERIFF engraved on it. He was dark-haired and far too handsome for an officer of the law. He was staring at Kait. The moment she realized it, their eyes met, and Kait saw Irish green eyes framed by thick sooty lashes and she knew who this man was.

Trev's brother was the county sheriff.

Rafe Coleman did not smile at her. He turned to his brother and slapped Trev's shoulder. "Well, they are back

safe and sound, and I'm taking off. We have a bit of an alter-
cation on the other side of town."

Trev set Marni down but gripped her hand. "I'm sorry,
Rafe. I'm sorry for the false alarm."

Rafe was hard to read. His expression was implacable.
He shrugged. "False alarms happen all the time." He glanced
at Kait with a narrowed gaze. "She never took Marni for an
afternoon before. You did the right thing, calling me. How
would you know she was taking Marni to the movies?" His
gaze remained on Kait. It slid over her features, slowly,
coolly, one by one, lingering on her hair and eyes. Then he
looked her up and down.

The look was *not* a sexual one.

And Kait knew a dangerous adversary when she saw one.
She stepped back breathlessly, as if that might put a real barrier between them.

"Lana, I'd like to speak with you about that gunshot you
think was fired. You care to come down to the office and
make a statement?"

"I . . . of course." Kait looked from the swarthy, dark-
haired sheriff to Trev. "I'm sorry," she said, certain she was
ashen. "I had no idea I would frighten anyone this way." She
stared at Trev, wanting to beg him not to be this way. He
hated her. This was the second time she had seen it and she
had not a doubt as to his feelings now.

Then she regrouped. He did not hate her. He hated Lana,
his wife.

"A deputy will take your statement if I'm not there," Rafe
said.

Kait started, suddenly realizing that Rafe Coleman—the
county sheriff—didn't find her having been shot at significant at all, or at least, not significant enough for him to in-
volve himself. Their gazes met again and she recoiled. She
was afraid of this man.

Then Rafe nodded, tipping his hat at Elizabeth and
chucking Marni under the chin. "Later, sweetheart," he said
to the little girl. He glanced at Trev. "Walk me out."

Trev nodded and the two brothers strode out. Kait stared after them, dismayed. She had no doubt they were discussing her. But what, exactly, were they saying?

She followed them into the foyer, and as they stepped outside onto the veranda, she went to the window, watching them. They were two handsome, masculine men, one dark, one tawny-haired, both obviously brothers. She could not hear a word they were saying, but Rafe was speaking, with controlled urgency. She did not like it at all.

Her head began to ache. She clutched her temples, no longer able to avoid the most worrisome thought of all.

Did Trev Coleman hate Lana enough to want her dead?

A few minutes later, Trev returned to the house. Kait had somehow known he would want to talk to her, and she was seated in the living room, her hands in her lap, grasping a brief moment's respite. As he entered, she looked up and their eyes met. He was grim.

"We need to talk," he said flatly.

"I said I'm sorry," she began sincerely.

"Since when do you take my daughter to the movies?" he demanded. "Much less pick her up at school? *Since when, Lana?*"

Kait stared, her mind racing, more worried now about her sister than about the confrontation with Trev. Then she saw Marni peering around the corner into the room, a Breyer's horse model in her hand. "Let's go into the other room," she said quietly.

Marni hurried forward. "Daddy?"

Instantly, he stooped to her height. "What, honey?" he asked gently.

Somehow, watching him like that, seeing how much he loved his daughter, hurt too terribly for words.

This man was capable of kindness and compassion and deep, abiding love.

"Mommy's not bad anymore," Marni said plaintively.

Kait froze.

Trev stared, then scooped her up into his arms. "Of

course your mommy isn't bad," he said gently. "Your mommy has never been bad. Mommies aren't bad, honey."

"No," Marni protested with a serious shake of her head.

Kait's mind came to life. She knew she had to stop her now. But when she opened her mouth to speak, no words came out. She now knew how it felt to have one's neck on an executioner's block.

"Mommy is a new, nice mommy now," Marni said very plainly.

Kait thought she might faint.

Trev stared at his daughter.

Kait stared at Trev, speechless, sweating.

"Yes, she is a new, nice mommy," Trev said. He stood. "Elizabeth?" he called. "Why don't you give Marni some supper?" He smiled down at his daughter. "I need to talk to Mommy. Go into the kitchen, honey."

Marni shot Kait a grin, as if to say, See? It's all right now; I told him you're new and nice.

Kait somehow smiled back, and then she and Trev Coleman were alone.

"I can't take it anymore," Kait whispered earnestly. "It was only a movie. I stupidly didn't let anyone know what we are doing, and it will never happen again. I'm sorry!"

He strode to her, and she flinched as he loomed over her. *"Stay away from my daughter."*

Kait gasped.

He was trembling. "Did you hear me? I know what you're doing—I've known it the moment you got back from New York with your new sainted mother act! I won't have it," he said tightly.

It was hard to stand straight and tall before him, because he was frightening. She had never seen anyone so angry and even desperate, and she wondered if he even had control of his temper now.

"It's not an act. I'm not . . . I'm not who you think I am. I love . . . our . . . I love Marni. With all of my heart. I really do."

"Not an act? You love Marni?" He was incredulous. "You're using Marni for your own selfish ends, that's what you're doing."

"No," she tried.

"I'm divorcing you," he continued harshly, his green gaze on hers. "And it will be good riddance! Marni stays with me. Full custody. I will pay you off and you know it! But if you keep this up, it will be war, Lana, and I promise, I will win— or die trying."

Kait stared into his furious eyes, reeling. "Calm down," she finally said. "Your anger won't solve anything."

"Calm down?" He was incredulous. "My anger won't solve anything? Have you just come down from the moon? You are trying to make her love you at the eleventh hour— and it's working! Then we'll split, and her heart will be broken—and you expect me to calm down?" He began shaking again. "Or do you expect a judge to let her choose who she lives with! Are you hoping she'll choose *you?* You haven't done enough? Is this your way of hurting me one last time? What about how Marni feels? You're going to hurt her too!"

Kait met his eyes. She agreed with everything he was saying, except she wasn't Lana. She had an overwhelming urge to rush forward and hold him and soothe him and somehow heal his wounds. Of course, that was not to be. How could Lana have used and hurt this man so? How? And where was she? Now was the perfect time for her to walk through the door so Trev could learn the truth—a truth he was entitled to!

Kait even looked at the doorway, but her sister wasn't standing there.

She closed her eyes. How much more of this deception could she take? Could the police protect Marni from an enemy that no one except Lana even knew the identity of? Should she tell him everything now?

Lana, where are you?!

"Well?" Trev was shouting now. "Answer me, damn it!"

She looked into his eyes and could not speak. She loved Marni with her every breath and more, and until she knew who she was up against, she was not going to take the chance that coming forward might jeopardize the little girl. Her decision had been made.

If Lana did not return, if she did not contact her, Kait was going to begin her own investigation. She would find her sister, find out what was happening, and then do whatever had to be done to protect Marni, Lana, and even herself. But Marni came first.

Kait shuddered with relief. Making a solid decision for the first time in days felt right and it felt good.

"Jesus Christ! You never quit!" Trev shouted at her.

Kait realized a tear had trickled down her cheek. She wiped it away, looked up and met his hostile gaze. "I'm sorry. I said it before and I meant it."

"That's it?" Trev asked in disbelief.

"I'm sorry for everything," she said firmly. Her strength seemed to be returning now. "I regret everything I have ever done to hurt you and Marni. I'd like for us to have a truce."

He snorted. "Have your lawyer call mine, and soon, Lana. I want this farce over with yesterday! And stay the hell away from my daughter," he added warningly.

She stood. "That isn't fair and you know it."

"I don't think life is fair, do you?"

"Marni had a good time today."

"And what about tomorrow—when you're gone—or when you have returned to your usual cold and uncaring self?"

"Talking to you is like talking to a wall," Kait snapped. Because he was undoubtedly right. She had to assume her sister was alive, and when she did return, Marni would have her real mother back in her life again. But she would also have her aunt, no matter what Trev had to say about that. "And what about *your* selfish behavior?"

His eyes widened. "My selfish behavior?"

"Yes! You told her that we are divorcing. That was uncalled for!" Her hands found her hips.

He stared. "My, my. Have we become the epitome of moral indignation? Please!"

"You had no right," Kait flared, meaning it.

"I gently explained it to her, in terms a child can understand."

"Really? And what terms are those?" Kait demanded, trying to get a grip on her rising temper.

"We're going to live in different houses," Trev said vehemently. "That sometimes people grow up just like children, and when they do, they change. And when they change, they need to move away from each other. That is what I said."

"I'm sure she understood that," Kait said sarcastically.

"She is upset. She'll get over it. She'll get over it a lot faster if you move out of the house and stay away from her."

Kait stared at him with dread prickling along her nape. There was also a surge of panic. "You want me to move out?"

"I think it would be best. Don't you?"

She was not moving out. The thought of leaving Fox Hollow was more than painful. God, it was a thought she could not bear! "We should reconcile, for Marni's sake," she said slowly. Could he force her out? "You can't make me leave."

His eyes widened and then he laughed. "Like hell I can't!" He started toward the closed door.

His words terrified her. Vaguely, Kait saw Sam standing there, a look of savage satisfaction on her face, and as vaguely, she saw Trev pause and exchange words with his teenaged daughter. *Oh, dear God.*

Her reaction to the mere idea of leaving Fox Hollow told her what she did not want to know, what she had avoided admitting, even to herself.

Something had changed terribly, somehow.

Kait did not want to leave Fox Hollow, not ever—and she was afraid it wasn't just because of Marni.

Kait watched Sam and her father walking away from the study, refusing to analyze her wayward emotions now. Instead, she thought about Sam. Had she been eavesdropping? Kait thought so. Unfortunately, there had been no mistaking the look of ugly pleasure on her face just a moment ago. She knew about the impending divorce and she had heard that Trev wished to boot Lana out of the house. She seemed to want Lana to suffer.

Then Sam turned and glanced over her shoulder at her. Her face was expressionless now.

Kait did a double take. Sam was wearing a beautiful lipstick-red cashmere sweater, one with wide deep ribs, a very high turtleneck, and cuffed sleeves. Hadn't she almost worn that sweater last night? Hadn't that sweater been in Lana's closet?

Kait was certain that Sam was wearing one of her step-mother's sweaters. And she hadn't asked permission, either.

An image of Sam in the kitchen that morning came to mind. She had been wearing a very nice black V-neck beneath a leather vest, one that had looked far too expensive for a young girl.

Was Sam stealing from the stepmother she despised?

Kait wished the notion had never occurred to her, but unfortunately it had. Almost reluctantly—but resolved now not to leave a single stone unturned in her sister's life—she went up the stairs as Sam and Trev disappeared into the kitchen. It crossed her determined mind that she should ask Sam about the sweater; she pushed open her bedroom door instead.

Sam's room was a mess. Her desk was covered with books and CDs, two empty cans of Diet Coke, a bag of pretzels, and, of course, her PC. She had a set of shelves containing horse models on the adjacent wall, which gave Kait pause. At some point, Sam had been following in Trev's footsteps. A few framed photos were on the lowest shelf, including one of a handsome boy about Sam's age, with black hair and an infectious grin. A guitar and scattered music sheets lay in the corner between the desk and wall. Her backpack lay on the floor, alongside a fringed suede handbag. The backpack was open, and half of its contents—makeup and schoolwork—were on the floor. Magazines, an old and tattered stuffed animal, and an empty Fritos bag covered the unmade bed.

Kait went to the antique pine bureau in the corner of the

otherwise pleasant blue-and-white room and opened the top drawer. She started at the sight of red and black lace bras and thongs. A tag screamed VICTORIA'S SECRET at her.

Was this appropriate for a sixteen-year-old girl? Kait didn't have a clue. She started to shut the drawer, when the set of sexy ivory underwear caught her attention. It was not the inexpensive cookie-cutter version bought from a catalogue. She lifted it out. It was La Perla, and she recognized it immediately—it was Lana's.

Sam was stealing from her stepmother. Dismay filled her.

Surely it was not serious. Kait hoped it was Sam's way of acting out her confusion and anger. She tucked the ivory lace ensemble back in the drawer when her fingers brushed something cold and hard, something metallic. Kait's grasp closed over something that felt like steel, with an odd little spike jamming her finger. What was this?

She lifted up the object.

It was a gun.

NINE

Kait left Sam's room filled with trepidation. Her first instinct was to rush downstairs and tell Trev what she had found. However, he was furious with her. This might not be the best time to point out that his daughter was stealing from her, or that she had a gun.

Kait hung on to the railing, looking down from the second-floor landing into the foyer and an edge of the living room. Her heart lurched with dread. One question simply could not be avoided: Did Sam hate her enough to want her dead?

Had Sam been the one to shoot at her?

Sam was tall—Kait thought her to be five foot nine or ten. The shadow she had seen in the woods had been an adult—or someone as tall as an adult. She had merely assumed the shooter to be a man.

She was ill.

Was Sam the one?

How could she ever voice her fears and suspicions to Trev?

She heard his footsteps below her before she saw him, and she tensed. He came into her line of vision and she watched him with anguish. She didn't want to fight with him—she wasn't Lana, damn it, and she did not want him hurt now, any more than he already was. What should she do?

He swung around the edge of the banister and began hurrying up the stairs. The moment he saw her, his naturally exuberant stride slowed. Their gazes collided.

She didn't move.

He reached the landing where she stood. "What are you doing?"

She wet her lips. "Nothing."

One brow lifted and he went past her. She hesitated, and followed. This might be a good time for a private and difficult discussion after all—he seemed much calmer than he had been when he had been shouting at her about the divorce.

She realized he was going into the master bedroom, which had become her bedroom, as he was sleeping elsewhere. Suddenly an inkling began, one that caused real dismay. "What are *you* doing?" she asked, following him into the room.

"Changing my clothes," he said, disappearing into the walk-in closet.

She glanced at her watch—at Lana's beautiful Chopard—and flinched. It was close to six. Was he going out for the evening again? And if so, with whom?

He had his back to her, but he had nothing on but tight white jockeys. He reached for a pair of dark gray trousers. "What is it?" he asked, turning.

She stared at his beautifully sculpted chest, dusted with a touch of dark hair, and then at his flat, rock hard abs, and finally at the way his briefs molded his groin. *Oh, my.* And his legs were long, hard, and muscular; his thighs and calves belonged on a soccer player, not an equestrian.

She swallowed, mesmerized.

"What the hell are you doing?" he demanded.

Her gaze flew up and clashed with his. He seemed angry now, while her mouth was so dry that she could not speak.

An endless moment ensued. The silence was thick, but Kait could hear her pulse drumming. This man was so beautiful. Had Lana been insane?

"If you keep staring, maybe I'll change my plans and get that good-bye I'm owed," he said harshly.

She blinked. He wanted to make love. In fact, it had become rather obvious. She felt her cheeks heating.

"Like you've never seen a man aroused before?" His laughter had a rough edge now. He dropped his trousers right on the floor. "Take off your clothes, Lana," he said.

She was so dazed that her first response was a wild, internal longing! And he knew it, because he smiled and started for her.

But there was a reason why she could not do this, even if she was shaking with urgency, even if her blood was running hot and primitive inside her. And that reason was simple—her sister.

He belonged to Lana.

While, she, Kaitlin London, was a temporary substitute and a complete fraud.

He was smiling, seeming amused. His hands closed on her shoulders. "You know what?" he said in a rough whisper. "I like this act. I like the virginal thing, the cute wispy hair, the big astonished eyes. I like it a lot. It's a helluva switch."

A switch. Oh, yeah, this was a helluva switch. She had to get a grip. It was almost impossible, considering his hands were making her pulse race more rapidly as he was drawing her forward. Her sweater brushed his chest, making her nipples harden. "You're going out," she managed.

"I'm meeting Mitch and Sara. We have time. No, I'll cancel," he said, his mouth close to hers. "So we can enjoy," he added in a very sexy murmur.

Lana's cell phone began to ring.

It was in her back pocket, and she was so startled that she flinched. In doing so, her body brushed against his erection.

"Ignore it," he muttered, sliding his hands up beneath her sweater, his palms hard and callused on her bare, tingling back.

Kait leapt away, reaching for the phone. She didn't have to look at the LCD to know that the caller was Lana, finally. Kait ran for the door, glancing back at Trev Coleman as she did so.

He looked shocked.

"I'm sorry," she whispered, and then she dashed through the bedroom and into the hall. She pressed TALK. "Don't hang up," she cried.

Once safely outside, where the sky was now turning to dusk, Kait said, "Thank God you're all right! I've been so afraid!"

"Are *you* all right?" Lana asked. Her tone seemed wry.

Kait began walking away from the house. She felt eyes on her back, but did not care. Not now. "Where are you! When are you coming back? Someone shot at me, Lana! And Trev has handed me divorce papers!"

"Slow down," Lana said calmly. "I didn't think it was a good idea to tell you that a divorce was imminent. You had enough on your plate already."

"You knew? Just how the hell did you think I could manage this—him—when he hates you so?" Kait demanded furiously.

"How could I not know that my marriage is over?" Lana asked dryly.

Kait envisioned her sister then. She would be composed, even amused, as that was her outlook on life. "I don't think this is funny. You have a wonderful husband and a gorgeous daughter and you're not upset!" She almost added that Trev Coleman wanted full custody, and that she thought he intended to slowly but surely cut Lana out of her daughter's life. But that was not a subject to go into now.

"I think you're the one who is upset. But, then, you were always the truly romantic one." There was a nostalgic smile now in Lana's tone. "Remember when I caught you reading that trash, what was it, something like *Sweet Eternal Love*?" Lana actually laughed. And then she said, "Have you fallen for Trev, Kait?"

"What?" she whispered.

"I knew you'd like him," Lana said, seriously now. "It's why I never wanted you to meet him before. I knew he'd like you, too. In fact, he married the wrong twin, now, didn't he?

If you've been wondering why I never told you about my marriage, well, there's your answer."

Kait was so stunned she could hardly think.

"But it's over now. It was a mistake. You can even have the husband, if you like," Lana said with a laugh. "As for Marni, well . . ." She trailed off.

Kait had halted. She stood fairly close to Trev's spanking-new Dodge Ram. She felt perspiration gathering on her brow. "What?"

Lana sighed. "It's over with Trev, Kait. It's been over for a long time. I'm sick and tired of him and his morality—I am tired of always being judged. I was expecting the divorce papers, and as soon as I get back, I am taking them to the best lawyer I can find," Lana said harshly.

Kait began to tremble. "He loved you. I think, maybe, he still does."

Lana did laugh. "He hates me now, but he does like sex."

She flinched. Somehow, she had already gotten that very impression.

"Are you still there?" Lana asked after a pause.

Kait felt as if the ground beneath her feet were tilting wildly. She must not think about what had almost happened a few minutes ago. "Yes. Are you on your way back? And what is going on?! I know you lied to me about the foreclosure, Lana. Trev owns Fox Hollow free and clear."

"He inherited it from his father. Actually, he's partners with his brother, but Rafe has a hands-off policy."

"You lied to me. But someone shot at me—thinking I'm you. What is going on?" Kait demanded tersely.

"I was afraid to tell you the truth. I still need a few more days," Lana said. "Please, Kait, on this one, you have to trust me."

"A few more days?" Kait gasped. "No! No way! Trev needs to know the truth, and I suspect we need to go to the police." And she wasn't going to trust her sister without an explanation.

"I didn't lie when I said I was in terrible trouble. Someone is after me! But I have no idea who shot at you at Fox Hollow. That can't have anything to do with my situation. I do owe someone a lot of money, Kait, but I can't say why, and he won't hurt me yet, because he wants to get paid back. Nobody shot at you. I mean, I do have a lot of enemies in the county, but I don't think any of them would have the guts to attempt murder. Not even someone's angry wife." She was amused.

Kait gripped the phone. "So it's true? You've had . . . affairs?"

"I told you, I don't love Trev. Of course I've had affairs. And it's not like there are any single guys around in Skerrit County, not our age, so do not go judging me, either."

"Lana—you're putting me in danger," Kait said slowly.

"I would never do that!" Lana cried. "Nobody shot at you! And if someone did, why, it was an amateur. Just hang in through the weekend, Kait, and then I'll return and we'll tell Trev everything. By then, we won't have to go to the police. I am sure of it."

"Trev already hates you. He will hate me, too, when he knows what I've done."

"He'll forgive you . . . in time. When he realizes the kind of person you are—when he realizes you are nothing like me. Kait, I am desperate." She was pleading now.

"I realize that. But you have to tell me exactly why you are desperate! Otherwise I am telling Trev everything—not to mention the police!"

"Rafe Coleman hates me. If you go the police, they will throw the book at you. You can do time for this little switch of ours, Kait. I wouldn't want to see that happen."

Kait stared into the night.

"Are you still there?"

Kait nodded.

"It's only for a few more days," Lana said urgently. "And you don't have a choice, Kait, because the one thing I know you would never do is put my daughter—your niece—in danger."

Her words were a terrible blow. "So you didn't lie when you said she'd been threatened, too?"

"I'd never use Marni that way. Why do you think I'm doing this? I may not be the best mother in the world, but I would do anything, *anything,* to protect her from harm. I cannot let her pay for my stupid mistake. They know she's my Achilles' heel. God, what if they kidnap her? What if I never see her again?" Lana cried.

Kait leaned heavily on the side of the truck. "All right! I'm staying put! But I don't understand any of this!"

"The only thing you have to understand," Lana said softly, "is that I am a fool, and now I am paying a terrible price for my past—and my daughter very well could, too."

"No," Kait said through numb lips. "I'd give up my life for her. We can't let anything happen to her." Tears were betraying her now.

"I know. She's the best thing that ever happened to me," Lana said softly, with a smile Kait could feel.

Kait pulled herself together. "How should I handle Trev?"

"Calmly, kindly—be yourself," Lana said.

An image of him standing facing her in his underwear assailed her. "And if he becomes amorous?" she asked tersely.

There was a pause. "Has he hit on you, Kait?"

"He thinks I'm you!" Kait cried grimly.

Lana was amused. "I think you can handle it. Do what you think is right. But, then, that is always what you do—isn't it?"

"This is not the time to be cryptic!" Kait nearly shouted. She remained stunned, but the fact that they were continuing the deception was truly starting to sink in. And she still did not know anything other than that two lives were in danger, her sister's and Marni's.

Kait felt more moisture gathering in her eyes. She sat down. There was nothing to sit on except the ground, so that is where she sat. If she had to pretend to be Lana for the next month—the next year, she'd do it, if it meant protecting Marni.

"Kait, I am counting on you."

Kait nodded, her hands clammy now, then realized her sister couldn't see her. "You can count on me," she whispered hoarsely. "You know that."

"Yes, I do. Because we're twins, and if I can't count on you, who can I count on when the chips are down? And you can trust me, Kait."

Kait knew their call was coming to an end. Her heart seemed to have been misplaced—it seemed to be in her throat, choking her. "When will we speak again?"

"I'll call you as we decided, when I'm coming back, right after the weekend."

Kait was breathing hard. "Lana—I'm scared. This is so hard. It's hard lying to Trev and . . ."

"And what?"

"And loving Marni so much," Kait whispered finally.

"I know. I can't thank you enough. Kait, when this is over, everything will be the way it should be. I swear. We'll be a family again, even after the divorce. That's a promise."

Kait couldn't speak, so she nodded.

Lana understood, because the phone line went dead.

Kait sat very still. *We'll be a family again after the divorce.* Her breathing was tight. There was nothing, she realized, she wanted more than for this horrid deception to be over, for everyone to be safe, and for her to be a part of Fox Hollow. She knew she must not think about Marni's life being in danger now. She didn't dare. She might unravel. Kait closed her eyes and prayed for everyone's safety, even her own.

Now, she wished she'd had a chance to ask Lana about who might have shot at her. Lana hadn't taken it very seriously, just as Rafe Coleman hadn't. Maybe they were right, Kait thought, and she was wrong.

Her head ached now. It was time for bed.

Then she thought about who was upstairs in the master bedroom and her heart lurched, but not with dread. *I don't love Trev . . . I haven't in a long time.* Her sister had every intention of getting a divorce, and Kait no longer intended to meddle. Besides, it had become pretty clear that Trev Coleman deserved better than Lana.

"What are you doing?" Max Zara's voice drifted over her.

Kait opened her eyes and looked up. She had remained seated on the ground by the Dodge's back tire, and he stood by the tailgate, one arm propped on it, staring down at her. Surely he had not been listening to their conversation—because she had used Lana's name, hadn't she?

"I felt faint," Kait said quickly, her mind spinning. She moved to get up, wishing she'd had the chance to ask Lana about Max.

He reached down and hauled her to her feet, his grip warm and strong. Their eyes met and held.

Kait didn't like the directness of his regard. She didn't like the grim expression on his face. She didn't like the way his eyes searched hers, as if seeking out her secrets and her lies. She looked away.

"Maybe you had better go back inside," he said quietly.

She had to look back into a pair of brilliant baby blue eyes. She wanted, desperately, to ask him what his role in all of this was, and why he was so hostile to her sister—what was going on between them. But Kait could guess. "How long have you been working here at Fox Hollow, Max?" she asked slowly.

His eyes narrowed. "What an odd question."

Kait knew why it was odd. It was odd because Lana would have been there when he first was hired. "I can't seem to remember when you first started working here," she said. "Must be that little bump on my head."

"Yeah, must be from that little bump—which you got from that odd little riding accident," he said.

Their gazes locked.

Kait couldn't look away from him, and she knew he knew that she was not her sister.

He shrugged then. "Almost two months. Can't say I blame you, though, for not knowing precisely when I started here. You didn't look at me the first week. I might have been a doorknob or some such thing."

"I was preoccupied," she said, her mouth dry, her temples throbbing. "And I am sorry if I have been rude in the past," she said.

He didn't comment. Kait gave him an uncertain but somewhat grateful smile. He did not seem at all smug or hostile now.

He did not smile back. Instead, his gaze wandered past her, behind her.

Kait suddenly sensed who was there and she turned abruptly.

Trev stood on the porch, now clad in his dark gray trousers and an elegant sports jacket, watching them. Kait felt herself begin to flush. Surely he would not think that she was carrying on with Max, would he?

So it's true? You've had . . . affairs?

I don't love Trev. Of course I've had affairs.

You can have the husband. . . .

This was not the time to recall Lana's words. Trev started down the steps. Kait felt frozen in time and place. Of course he would think the worst of her, because Lana had no morals, not when it came to her husband and her marriage. When he was at the Ram's door, she could finally see his face. His expression was completely closed. And he did not look at her—it was as if she were not standing mere inches away.

He opened the door to the cab and slid in.

Max turned and walked around the tailgate, apparently toward the back of the house.

Kait did not move.

How should I handle Trev?

Be yourself.

He married the wrong twin.

He turned on the ignition.

Kait walked up to his door, trembling. Lana was crazy! "It's not what you seem to be thinking," she said slowly.

He glanced at her. "I'm not thinking anything," he said. "Do you mind?"

His cold words stabbed through her with chilling force. She inhaled and stepped away from the truck.

He reversed, turned, and drove away.

Kait stared after him for a long time, wishing she could tell him the truth; somehow knowing, with her foolish heart, that he would be able to help them if she did. But she had promised her sister differently, and this was now about Marni more than anyone else.

Kait had taken Marni to school, ignoring Elizabeth's disapproval and a very cold shoulder from Trev Coleman. Now she got out of the Porsche in front of the main barn. Instantly, she saw Zara standing in the corridor, as the wide door had been raised to accommodate his truck. Kait paused. The sight of him standing there made her recall that moment the night before when she had felt certain he knew she wasn't Lana. But if he knew that, surely he would confront her or go to Trev with his accusations.

Last night, his hostility had disappeared. Why?

And why did he keep a locked suitcase in his apartment?

Zara had seen her. Kait saw that he was unloading bags of feed. He paused to watch her approach.

He had only been at Fox Hollow for two months. He was hardly stable boy material. So just who, and what, was he?

Now that Kait had another few days to get through, she did not intend to leave her back unguarded, not even for a moment. Maybe Lana was right. Maybe no one had taken a shot at her, or maybe, as Trev had said, it had been a careless hunter who was trespassing. Kait hoped that was the case. Still, Sam had a gun and Lana had too many enemies to even count. She would stay in a state of alert.

Kait went forward. "Hey," she said, managing a tight smile. "Is Trev around?"

Max nodded in the direction of the indoor arena.

Kait nodded in thanks and moved past him, crossing the long corridor, aware of his regard to her back. Only one horse was in a stall; the others had been turned out.

She stepped into the indoor arena. Trev and Jim stood in its center with a magnificent chestnut with four white socks and a blaze on a longe line. She hung on to the gate, watching as Trev worked the animal at an extended trot. If he had seen her, he gave no sign. And it was simply impossible that he hadn't seen her.

I don't love him . . . He married the wrong twin.

Her heart accelerated. What was wrong with her sister? Why would she say something like that? Never mind that she was foolishly and maybe hopelessly physically attracted to him. Of course he hadn't married the wrong twin.

But she knew that if she were his wife, she'd never ever betray him, and she would treasure her every moment at Fox Hollow and enjoy raising as many children as they dared have.

Her thoughts were frightening her. Kait switched them off, focusing hard on Trev and the chestnut horse.

"Walk," Trev said firmly. "Waaalk."

The chestnut obeyed with an impatient shake of his head.

"Whoa," Trev said, in the same tone. "Whoooa. Good boy, son. Good boy."

She watched him walk up to the gleaming chestnut, stroking his neck and praising him. His hands were large and so was his stroke. The horse visibly relaxed under his touch, clearly enjoying the caresses and strokes. Her heart tightened. She tried not to think about what had almost happened last night before he had gone out. But she'd never erase the image of him standing there in his tight white jockeys with an utterly sexy gleam in his eyes—and an intention he had no right to.

Trev led the chestnut toward the gate where Kait was standing. He continued to act as if she were not present. Kait knew why. He thought that Lana was flirting with Zara, or even sleeping with him.

Jim was at his side. Kait had learned that he had been a rider for the Canadian Olympic team in his day, and that until recently he had lived in Toronto. He smiled at her. "How are you today, Lana?"

"Much better." She returned his smile, and then felt her expression tighten as she looked at Trev.

He was finally looking at her, his hand on the gate. "Excuse me," he said.

She realized that she was in the way. She leapt aside as he swung open the gate and led the chestnut out. She trailed after him, Jim, and the horse. She was more than dismayed by his behavior toward her. Finally Trev handed the horse over to the trainer and started down the corridor.

Kait hurried after him. "Trev, wait!"

His long, athletic stride slowed—briefly. "I'm busy," he said, not looking back.

She ran and caught up with him as they stepped outside. "I'd like to talk to you," she said, filled with dread. He was punishing her, but why? Because he thought she had been in Max's arms last night? Or because she had rejected his advances again? In either case, he was not in the best mood and she had to discuss the fact that Sam had a gun in her room.

He slowed but did not stop. "Can't it wait?"

She gripped his arm. "No, Trev, it cannot wait."

He looked at her, really looked at her, for the first time since the night before. Then his eyes dipped to her mouth, which had nothing but a dab of clear gloss on it. He looked away. "What is it?"

She hesitated. She had rehearsed how she intended to proceed, and she had decided not to tell him that Sam was taking Lana's sweaters without permission—and God knew what else. That discussion could come at another time and, hopefully, Lana would be the one to participate in it.

"What is it?" he asked again, this time with impatience.

"There's no easy way to say this." Kait took a breath. "I found a gun in Sam's room."

He blinked. "I beg your pardon?"

"Trev, I found a gun in her room. Are you aware of the fact that she has a gun?"

"No, I am not. This must be a mistake," he said grimly. "Christ, it has to be a toy."

"It's not a toy. I'm sorry."

"Where is it?"

"In her underwear drawer. I'll show you, if you like." She could see now that he finally comprehended what she had said, because he was becoming increasingly upset.

He nodded and they took off up the hill toward the house. "I'm sure it's a toy. These days they make incredibly realistic toy guns."

"Ever since a cop shot a kid with a toy gun, manufacturers have stopped making those kinds of replicas, and stores don't sell them," Kait pointed out.

"Are you trying to soothe me?" he said, his face impossibly tight now. "Because you're not doing a damn good job!"

She touched his elbow as they trotted up the stairs to the veranda. "I'm sorry. I never expected to find a gun in her room."

He suddenly paused, one hand on the front door. "What did you expect to find?"

She hesitated. But she was prepared for his question. "I thought, maybe, she had borrowed my cell phone."

He stared, his green eyes too piercing for comfort. "Now why would you think that?"

"Because I misplaced it and couldn't find it."

His look told her he didn't buy her excuse for a moment, and he shoved through the front door, not even waiting for her to follow. But follow she did.

He didn't knock, apparently because Sam had left for school sometime after Kait had driven off with Marni. He glanced around, seeming startled. "What a pigsty," he mumbled.

"Most teenagers are sloppy," Kait said quietly. "I don't know why, but I'll bet it's a developmental issue."

He gave her a grim look and nodded at the room's single bureau. "There?"

Kait nodded, walking past him. She suddenly wondered what she would do if the gun was gone. She shuddered at that thought as she opened the drawer. But right there, peeking out from all the scanty Victoria's Secret bras and thongs, was the gleaming steel muzzle.

Trev came to stand behind her, gazing over her shoulder. "What the hell?"

Kait knew he was looking at his daughter's too-sexy underwear. She glanced at him. He was flushing. "Is this appropriate?" he stopped. He touched the ivory La Perla bra. Kait knew he recognized it. Now, he did not speak.

The gun's nozzle poked through the bra's straps.

Kait stepped away. She felt terrible for him.

He took out the gun. "It's real."

She touched his shoulder. "I know. I'm so sorry."

His back was as rigid as a board. "This isn't hers. It's that damn Jenkins kid. He's always in trouble—he's bad news. I *know* this isn't hers."

She said, very cautiously, "Does Sam know how to shoot?"

"Yeah. She wanted to learn when she was about thirteen, and Rafe gave her some lessons. We both felt that around here, it's a good idea to understand and respect guns. It's a solid Republican county. She's actually a pretty good—" He stopped.

She was chilled. So Sam knew how to shoot—and she was a good shot.

Their eyes met. His eyes were wide, agonized.

She touched his elbow to steady him. Was he thinking what she was thinking? That Sam hated her, and that in the throes of a difficult adolescence, she had made a terrible mistake?

"I'm going to get to the bottom of this," Trev ground out. He was more than upset now, he was angry.

"You should have a long talk with her. What time will she be home?"

"Who knows? I'm not waiting for the end of school." He was checking the gun and he cursed.

"It's loaded?" Kait gasped.

Cartridges fell into his hand. "Yes." Fury was in his eyes. He pocketed the cartridges and jammed the gun into the waistband of his jeans.

Kait grabbed his arm before he could stalk out of his

daughter's room. "Stop. You're upset. You need to calm down, and I don't think dragging her out of class is the right thing to do right now."

"I'm dragging her out of class by her goddamn hair, that's what I'm doing," Trev said, turning livid green eyes on her. "And I think I'll grab Gabe Jenkins while I'm at it! I forbade her ever seeing him again!" he cried.

"Please, stop and think." She didn't release him. "You're so angry I doubt you can see straight. If you approach her this way, you'll put her on the defensive and make it worse!"

"Worse? How can it get worse?" He was disbelieving. "We find a loaded gun—a frigging loaded gun—in her room—not to mention that she's stealing your underwear!"

Kait let go of his arm. She winced.

"Why would you protect her? You don't like her—you never did. How long has this been going on? That was your red sweater she had on last night, wasn't it? Damn! I thought I recognized it," he cried, not waiting for her answer.

She slipped her hand in his. "C'mon. Let's sit down. Just for a minute."

His eyes met hers, skipped away, then came back. She saw desperation there. "How long has she been stealing from you?" he asked roughly.

Her heart broke. She wanted to touch, no, stroke, his brow. "It's not stealing. It's borrowing," she said as roughly.

"Why are you protecting her? I have no doubt she didn't ask permission."

Kait hesitated. Maybe it was best that he knew the entire truth about his daughter. "No, she didn't."

"That's stealing in my book," he said grimly. Then, "It's illegal for a minor to possess a handgun without parental consent!"

Kait pulled him over to Sam's bed. "Sit down, please."

He looked right into her eyes—and maybe her heart, too—with all of his defenses down. And as Kait looked back into his green eyes, as she saw how much he loved Sam and how scared he was, her heart went out to him. She wanted to see this man happy. And God, she knew now that meant his divorcing her sister so he could have the peace and serenity he and his children deserved.

He sat down, cradling his face in his hands. Kait touched his solid shoulder, and he looked up. Their gazes locked.

And the look he gave her knocked the breath out of her lungs, it tightened her body, it made her want to take him in his arms, touch him all over, take him inside her, taming the lion and freeing the man.

She smiled a little and sat down carefully beside him. But she was terribly shaken. "We should look at this one piece at a time. We don't know why Sam has been borrowing my things. She's at a very tough age, and she wouldn't be the first adolescent to engage in this kind of behavior. My first thought isn't that she hates me—which is all my fault, I might add—but that she wants either your or my attention— or maybe both of our attention."

He stared, his stare unwavering. She saw his eyes soften. "Since when did you become so kind?"

"I don't know. Let's not talk about me right now, okay? I think we should leave the issue of Sam taking my things alone for now. It's a good issue for a psychologist, Trev."

He continued to stare at her, appearing absolutely bewildered. "You're right." He glanced up at the ceiling and shook his head. "I never, ever thought I'd see the day where I'd be telling you that you're right." He smiled a little at her.

Her heart burst into song. *What she wouldn't do for a lifetime of those smiles.* Then she realized the direction of her own thoughts, and she was completely stricken again. Kait managed to smile back, no easy task now. "So we should focus on the gun," she said firmly.

His expression hardened. "It *has* to be Jenkins's."

"I hope you're right."

He faced her more fully. "I can't wait until tonight to speak to her. I just can't, Lana."

She understood. "But you're calmer now. If you go get her at school, you have to stay calm like this. Shouting at her won't help. In fact, I'll bet she won't tell you a thing if you do scream at her."

He was staring again, the way he had before. He stood and gazed down at her. "Maybe it was that knock on the head you took when you fell. Because I would almost swear that you are a different person since then."

Her heart raced with alarm. She also stood. "Nope. Sorry, it's the same old me. But, hopefully, a bit more introspective, a bit new and improved." She hesitated. "I have so many regrets, Trev."

"I just don't get it," he said with a shake of his head.

She shrugged, attempting a light, who-knows kind of expression.

He hesitated. "Thanks," he said. "Thanks a lot."

She melted from her head to her toes, and it was frightening, how one heartfelt word could have such an effect upon her. "You're welcome," she said.

She paced downstairs after Trev left, wishing she had been invited to go with him, but knowing that wouldn't have been right and she would have ended up staying at Fox Hollow anyway. Worry filled her. Sam was at a tough age, and Trev was extremely upset. But now, she could only hope for the best when she feared an escalation of emotions and conflict.

Elizabeth came out of the kitchen to stand with her hands on her hips, staring at her. She didn't say a word, but her expression clearly indicated that she wanted to know what was happening. Kait was tired of Elizabeth's disapproval and hostility, both silent and acknowledged. She slipped past her, into the kitchen.

She might as well wander over to the barn and see if Max was around. Snooping in his suitcase would keep her mind off Trev and his daughter and might solve the mystery of who and what he really was. She took a small paring knife from the knife drawer and slipped it into the back pocket of the black trousers she wore. It was hard to believe that she was really going to break into someone's personal possessions. Kait was nervous.

"What are you doing?"

Kait smiled at Elizabeth without animosity. "What I am not doing is stabbing someone in the back," she said, and she went out.

It was a gray, wintry day, as if, all of a sudden, winter had decided to descend upon Skerrit County with a vengeance. Kait was only wearing a white button-down shirt with slacks, and she shivered. Tomorrow she was going shopping for some casual clothes—and Trev could write it off as more of the odd behavior he could not understand or explain.

Max's Toyota was gone. Her anxiety had increased, but at least he was not around. A moment later, as she stepped inside, she saw that the redheaded boy was in the feed room, but no one else was about. The coast seemed free and clear.

Now Kait could use a bit of her sister's nerve. She paused in the open doorway. "Hi. Max around?"

"He's down at the broodmare barn."

This was the perfect opportunity, then. Kait thanked him and hurried out. A moment later she was racing up the narrow, dark stairs to the two apartments above the barn.

This time, Max's door was closed. She reached for the knob and realized it was locked. Dismay flooded her.

He had not kept his door locked before. What did this mean?

She juggled the knob, but without success. She paused and stared at the closed door. Last time, his door had been wide open. Had he known he'd had an intruder the other day? She was sorry she had automatically closed the door when she had been through going over his studio, but was that necessarily a giveaway?

She knew Max Zara was not all that he claimed to be. He was intelligent and he was astute, and she'd bet he'd had a college education—at least. The door was now locked for a good reason. Kait was more than nervous now, for this was really breaking and entering. But she just felt that Max Zara was the key to many secrets at Fox Hollow.

Kait pulled out the paring knife, but the point would not fit in the simple lock, which was a small slit in the center of the knob. She frowned. This was a simple lock—one had only to twist a raised button on the knob's other side to lock it. She hesitated, and slid the knife between the door and jamb.

She hadn't ever done this before, but she'd seen movies where a lock was jimmied with a credit card. She slid the knife upward and—Voilà. The lock clicked free.

Kait inhaled for courage and pushed the door open—but it did not budge. *He'd added another lock on the inside.*

He was on to her.

Or he knew someone had been in his apartment the other day.

Suddenly determined, Kait walked breathlessly to the adjacent apartment and found that door open. She walked into the dusty, unused flat, which was similar to Max's. Then she saw the window. It was on the same wall as the window in Max's flat, and if she did not miss her guess, no more than ten feet separated them.

She hurried over, shoved it open as far as it would go, and looked down. She was on the second story, and if she fell she would probably break an ankle, if not her neck. She leaned out and found that she had overestimated the distance between the windows. Maybe six feet separated them—and Max's window was wide open.

And a gutter ran along the roof of the barn, with a small ledge a few feet below the windows. It was only a few inches wide, but she had small feet. And heights had never scared her, not until now.

She had come this far. She had three more days to survive before Lana returned. She couldn't turn back now.

Kait closed her eyes, took a deep breath, then opened them and stepped carefully through the window, standing on the narrow ledge by holding on to the gutter. With the front of her body pressed flat against the building, she inched over to Max's window. It was hard to breathe. She tried not to think about falling. Instead, she told herself again and again that the answer to who Max Zara really was, was inside that locked suitcase.

A moment later Kait was heaving herself through his window and onto his apartment floor.

She landed on her hands and knees, and she began to laugh.

Her laughter was a bit hysterical, but, by God, she had done it. Not only had she gotten past his doubly locked door, she'd climbed a window ledge to do it. Ridiculously, she felt proud of herself.

If only Lana could see her now.

Kait stood, dusted herself off, wiped sweat from her cheeks, and hurried over to the bed. She knelt and pulled out the locked suitcase. She tried the point of the knife in the small padlock, with no results.

Kait sat back on her haunches. If a baggage handler could break into just about any kind of locked bag, then so could she. She tried to jimmy the lock again. It did not click open.

What the hell, she thought. Inhaling, she seized the bag and dug the knife into the vinyl. It was amazingly strong. Kait forced the knife through the fabric, widening the tear until it was big enough for one of her hands. She reached in, and for the second time in twenty-four hours, gripped cold, lethal steel.

He had a gun in his bag.

For one moment, she did not move, absolutely stunned, and then she pulled it out.

She inhaled harshly. This gun did not look at all like the rather generic one she had found in Sam's room. This gun was big and very dangerous in appearance, it looked like the kind of gun Clint Eastwood had wielded in too many movies to count. That is, it looked like the kind of gun meant to kill.

"Damn," she said, barely able to get the single word out.

She laid the gun aside, hesitated, and stuck her hand slowly back in the suitcase, with the kind of dread one has when one expects to get bit. This time, her hand closed on leather.

But it was long and narrow and she somehow knew without pulling it out that it was a sheath, and in it was a knife.

She extracted the object and found that she had been right. Worse, the knife wasn't a simple knife—it was a long, slim dagger, the kind that was meant for very bad purposes indeed.

Who the hell was Max Zara?

And why was he at Fox Hollow?

Kait knew beyond a doubt that he was at Fox Hollow because of Lana—or because of the trouble she was in. For there was no other possible explanation. But she had been right about one thing—he was hardly a stable boy.

But whose side was he on?

Kait had a bad feeling. She hoped he was a cop. But cops didn't carry stilettos. And he hated her sister.

And maybe she had better get right out of his apartment, before he found her there.

Kait stuck the knife back in his suitcase, and was about to do so with the gun when she heard the sound of a lock snapping open.

Then she heard the door.

This could not be happening. . . .

Panic flooded her.

"What the hell are you doing?" Max Zara asked oh-so-calmly.

Slowly, still on her haunches, Kait turned.

TEN

It was so hard to breathe.

Max closed the door behind him, his movements casual and somehow infinitely threatening. "What are you doing?" he asked again, his eyes moving briefly to the gun.

She was still holding it. She dropped the gun and leapt to her feet. What was she doing? Why, she was checking him out, and, in fact, she had just broken and entered his apartment illegally. What excuse could she possibly come up with?

What if he was the one after Lana? What if he was the one who had taken a shot at her?

Kait quickly told herself that if he wanted her dead, he'd had ample opportunity. No, he didn't want her dead—not yet.

She was not relieved.

He folded his arms across his barrel-like chest. "I think I should be the one asking questions," she said, her tone a rasp.

This seemed to amuse him. "Really? I'm thinking about calling the cops." But his tone was mild.

Kait swallowed and accepted what had to be a bluff. "Go ahead. Because you have a gun and a knife, and I don't think you have a permit for the gun, and as for the knife, well, isn't a weapon like that illegal?" Who the hell carried a stiletto around?

Someone very, very dangerous. Someone with lethal intent. Someone outside the law.

He hadn't moved. He had a slight smile on his face. "Actually, the knife isn't illegal, and I do have a permit for the gun."

She tried to shake the cobwebs from her brain. "Can I see the permit?"

He seemed to laugh. He dug a wallet out of his jeans and opened it, revealing a gun permit that looked authentic. It even had his photograph on it. "Happy?"

"No."

She had to get out of there, as soon as possible.

"Why? Because I've found you in my apartment, where you have no right to be? What were you looking for, Mrs. Coleman?" His eyes narrowed. "I mean, unless I miss my guess, this is not a social call."

"I'm sorry. I had no business snooping." Kait forced a smile and tried to move past him.

His hand clamped down hard on her wrist. "Why the rush, Mrs. Coleman?" He breathed, turning her back around. He wasn't smiling now. "You seem frightened."

"I'm not frightened," Kait lied.

"Really." He released her. Kait couldn't move. "You haven't answered my question, Mrs. Coleman. What are you doing up here?"

She looked into his cool blue eyes and did not see any heat. She did not see any anger, any desire. New fear added to her tension. She somehow felt that this was a game, that he was toying with her. And she desperately needed an excuse for going through his things. "I don't think you are who you say you are."

He dared to laugh. "No? I hate to tell you this, but I'm a fairly ordinary guy whose wife dumped him, who lost his job, who works in a stable because it pays the bills and puts a roof over my head."

Kait didn't believe him.

"And I'm NRA through and through, which is why I have a gun."

Kait still didn't believe him. She didn't think he was an ordinary guy, not for a moment. He had the sharpest, most probing gaze she had ever seen, and she hadn't imagined either his loathing or the sexual tension in him when they had first met.

But both were gone now.

What if he knew everything? What if he had heard her entire phone conversation last night with her sister? What if he knew she wasn't Lana, and that was why he wasn't attracted to her now, that was why he was no longer hostile to her?

"Most people ask questions when they have doubts about someone. You went to a lot of trouble to get in here," he said softly, cutting into her thoughts.

She wet her lips. "Someone took a shot at me the day before yesterday, or have you forgotten?"

"I haven't forgotten. But you've aroused a lot of emotions in this town since you first came here, now, haven't you . . . Lana?"

He'd never called her by her sister's first name before. The way he murmured it sent a shiver of fear down her spine. "I have many regrets. My behavior recently is certainly one of them."

"Really?" Now both brows lifted. "Undergoing a change of heart?"

"Yes." She tilted up her chin aggressively. "I really am sorry for the past. I'm sorry if I ever led you on. Now I have to go. Trev will be looking for me at any moment."

"Trev went to town," he said calmly.

Kait turned grimly, and to her relief he did not seize her arm from behind. But her relief was short-lived when he spoke.

"A word of advice."

She halted and didn't dare turn around.

"Keep to yourself," he said. "You may have had a change of heart, but this is a small town with a big memory. I'd hate to think of what might happen to a pretty girl like you if you don't."

She whirled to face him. "What do you know?" she cried. "Do you know who shot at me, and, if so, why?"

His smile was fixed. "I know as much as you, and if I were you, I'd lie real low."

Kait stared into his eyes. They were hard now, hard and cold but not malicious. Had she been mistaken? Was this man on her side?

"Oh—and next time you feel like going through my things? I might not be so mellow about it." He smiled without humor.

Kait had just entered the house, still stunned by her encounter with Zara, and worse, thoroughly confused, when she heard a car's engine outside. She whirled and ran to the window beside the front door. Trev's cobalt blue Dodge Ram was in the driveway. She watched Sam leap out of the passenger side of the cab, slam the door closed, and run to the house. She glimpsed a tearful, furious expression on the teenager's face.

Trev got out more slowly.

Kait turned as Sam strode into the house. She was very angry, and tears streaked her cheeks. "Sam, wait," Kait said automatically.

Sam turned, saw her, and her eyes widened in disbelief. "You! This is all your fault! I hate you!" She turned and ran up the stairs, disappearing.

Kait realized that Trev was standing in the doorway. She took one look at him and wanted to pull him into her arms. She didn't move.

His face was ravaged with conflicting emotions. He glanced grimly at her and started toward his study. Kait didn't hesitate; she followed. "What can I do to help?"

He went to his desk, but didn't sit. "Nothing."

"I'm sorry."

He stared at the papers scattered on the desktop.

"Is the gun hers?"

"I don't know." He looked up, meeting Kait's eyes. Agony was reflected all over his mobile face. "She said it was none of my business."

She couldn't stop herself. She went to him and slipped her hand around his neck. His eyes widened. "Can I try to talk to her?" she asked, trying not to notice how smooth the skin on his nape was; how soft the baby-fine hairs there.

"Actually, she said it was none of my *fucking* business."

Kate winced. She had never seen any man this upset.

"I hit her," he said.

She froze. "What?"

"I didn't mean to!" he cried. "But when she used that word, I smacked her." He sat down and cradled his face with his hands. "I love her, Lana. I love my little girl. I've never hit her before, not ever! It was a reflex! A goddamned terrible reflex!"

"I know how much you love her," Kait whispered. She rubbed his shoulder. "It will be all right."

"Will it be all right?" He looked at her with agonized eyes. "I hit my own daughter. I've never struck her, not ever. She'll never forgive me!"

"Yes, she will." Kait was firm. "Trev, focus. Sam may be in trouble. Stay focused on the fact that she had a gun in her possession."

He stared for another moment. "You're right. All right. Maybe you should try to talk to her—being as you are suddenly so wise." He gave her an odd look.

"Thanks," Kait said, looking away and not responding to the question in his words. "I'll let you know how it goes."

"You do that," he said, worry clear now on his features.

Kait patted his shoulder and walked out. But once she had her back to him, her reassuring demeanor changed. He had struck his daughter. That would not be easily overcome. And while there was no excuse, she understood. But she must stay focused, as well. Sam had had a lethal weapon in her possession, and Kait had to get to the bottom of whatever was going on.

Kait took the stairs very slowly, praying for more wisdom than she knew she possessed. As she went upstairs, it struck her that what Sam needed now more than a parent was a friend. Maybe, somehow, she could become that person.

Kait felt a flash of trepidation as she faced Sam's closed door. She knocked.

"Go away," Sam said hoarsely.

Kait hesitated. "Sam, please let me in."

"You! You're the last person I'd talk to now! Screw off!" The stereo went on, blasting at full volume.

Kait winced. Sam's door was probably locked. Still, she tested the knob. She had been right. "Sam, please. Your father loves you very much, and that is why he is so upset. He didn't mean to hit you. He's sick with guilt right now. I know how hurt you must be feeling. Why don't you let me in so we can talk about it? I'm actually a pretty good listener."

The only response Kait had was the stereo blasting some horrible, screeching rock band. She didn't know what to do.

"My dad never hit me," she finally said. How true that was—she had been the apple of his eye. But with Lana, the story had been quite different. "And I was a handful growing up, too," she said, referring to her twin now. "When I was your age I stayed out all night with my friends, with boys, and I went to wild parties." In reality, Lana had been uncontrollable, hadn't she? Their mother had died and their father hadn't known what to do. But he'd been grieving for his wife. He'd grieved for a long, long time. "I broke every rule my dad had—my mother died when I was thirteen—but he never hit me. He never did much, in fact, after my mother died. I guess his heart was broken and he never recovered, really." Kait paused, saddened by the memory of a man she had loved and admired. Then she heard a silence on the other side of the door—the stereo had been turned off. Sam was listening. "My father moved down to Miami to retire when I went to college. He died a few years ago. I wish now that he'd paid more attention when I was so young and so wild. Maybe if he'd cared a bit more he would have." Kait paused. "Your dad hit you because he cares so damn much, Sam."

A long moment passed. Sam pushed open her door. She had been crying—tears were drying on her smooth skin, and the tip of her nose was red. "Are you making that up?"

"No, I'm not. I was wild as a teen, and my dad was so lost in his grief he didn't notice and didn't care. Your father loves you very much, Sam," Kait said earnestly, "and I know you know that."

Sam wiped her eyes with her arm. She stepped away, but left the door open. Kait followed her in; Sam flopped stomach-first on the bed, her face in the pillow. Kait paused a few feet from the bed. "Trev is so worried about you," Kait said softly. "He's worried because you had the gun in your drawer."

Sam sat up. Her long, straight blond hair whipped about her face and shoulders. "He wouldn't have ever known if you hadn't been snooping in my room!" she cried angrily.

Kait said carefully, "I should have asked you about my clothes. You're right. My judgment was poor."

Sam blinked at her. "Damn right it was!"

"Do you have to curse?" Kait asked quietly.

Sam was incredulous. "Why shouldn't I? I hear you cursing all the time!"

Kait winced. "It's a terrible and unladylike habit," she finally said.

Sam blinked at her again, as if she had come down from the moon. Then, her shoulders up, she asked, "Aren't you going to say something about the sweaters and your jacket?"

So she had taken a jacket, too? "No. I think that's something we should talk about another time." Then, "I would gladly lend you anything in my wardrobe, Sam; I'd only appreciate it if you asked me first."

Sam stared, wide-eyed. "Anything?"

"Anything suitable for a girl your age."

Sam scowled. "Can I borrow that black lace dress for Gina's party?"

Kait knew the dress she was referring to, as it was an eye-catcher—very sheer and absolutely inappropriate for a girl Sam's age. "No. But you can borrow the black dress with the cap sleeves and the chain belt," she said. That was elegant but still sexy, only in a subtle way. In fact, on Sam, who was tall and leggy, it would look great.

Sam brightened. "Really? That's a Donna Karan!"

Kait smiled and dared to sit down on the edge of the bed. "I said it was fine."

Sam stared now with suspicion. "What do you want? You have to want something if you're being so nice to me."

That broke Kait's heart. She wanted to cup the girl's smooth cheek and then give her a quick hug. Of course, she did not. "I want to talk about the gun. Is it Gabe's?"

Sam gave her a disbelieving look. "No."

Kait had a strong feeling that she was telling the truth. "Why did you have a gun in your room?"

Sam didn't look up. "I had my reasons."

"Sam," Kait said gently. "What reason could you possibly have for having a gun?"

Sam stared at her feet, mute.

"Well, if it's not Gabe's, if you weren't keeping it for him, you must have a reason for having a gun."

"I do!" she cried defensively, more tears shimmering on her long lashes.

Kait couldn't imagine what excuse she would come up with now. "Go on."

Sam took a breath. "There are bad kids at school. From across the tracks. The factory side of town. They're a gang. They give all the kids a hard time," she said with stubborn determination. "Including me."

Kait blinked. How much was the truth—and how much was fabrication? "So what is the gun for? Are you planning to use it on one of these boys?"

Sam shrugged. "They're bullies. And mean. I need it to keep them away," she said fiercely.

"And how does Gabe fit into this? Is he a part of this gang?"

"No!" Sam cried, startled. "He's worked so hard to stay out of trouble, even though he lives right near them! They want him to join, but he won't! They even beat him up—" She stopped.

Kait was getting the picture. Maybe Trev was right. Maybe the gun belonged to Gabe and he had it for a good reason—such as to protect himself—or maybe not. But clearly, Sam was protecting him.

"Gabe's not bad! His dad's a drunk, but his mom is real good and hardworking; she works at the factory too! Gabe is an honor student! Did you know that? And they even asked him to play football—he's a great wide receiver—but he can't, because he works after school. My dad *hates* Gabe! Just because he doesn't have money like us! And he doesn't even know him!" Sam cried.

The words had tumbled out in such a rush that Kait knew Sam cared about this young man, that she was really worried about him and that she didn't have anyone to share her feelings with. Kait hesitated, touched her briefly, and said, "He sounds like a very special young man."

"He does?" Sam gaped.

Kait nodded.

Sam smiled a little. "Want to see some pictures?"

"Of course."

Sam dove beneath her bed and came up with a painted keepsake box. She opened it and handed Kait a dozen photos—of Gabe in baggy jeans and a baggier sweater, of Gabe in his McDonald's uniform, of Gabe behind the wheel of a beat-up station wagon, of her and Gabe, arm in arm, clearly in some tiny, do-it-yourself photo booth. He was dark-haired and fair-skinned, dimpled and handsome. In every photo he was grinning. He looked like a nice young man.

"He's very handsome," Kait said truthfully.

Sam grinned. "I know." Then her smile faded. "Aren't you going to yell at me?"

"No, I don't think yelling will accomplish anything. This sounds like a dangerous situation, Sam. Not just for you, but for everyone."

Sam stared, for a moment, appearing bewildered. "It is. Those guys are such bad news. Everybody's afraid of them—except for Gabe. He's not afraid." She was proud now. "He's told them to go F off."

That sounded brave, but not encouraging. Still, Kait had to admire Sam for being so loyal to Gabe Jenkins now. "Sam, you still shouldn't have had a gun. That is wrong."

Sam hesitated, glanced away.

Kait knew that she knew it was wrong. "Has anyone spoken to the principal about these kids?"

Sam looked up. "No."

"This is a matter for the principal, and maybe even the local police." She thought about Rafe Coleman then. "Have you discussed this with your uncle?"

"No." Sam looked sullen now. "I'm not stupid. I knew I'd

get in trouble for the gun. I just didn't expect anyone to go snooping in my room." She shot Kait a dark look.

Kait hesitated. "I knew you'd been taking my clothes. I'm sorry I didn't ask you about it. Even adults make mistakes." She was thoughtful. "I think it's time the principal was told about how upset all of you kids are about this gang."

Sam stared. "If I snitch, they'll come after me."

Kait stiffened. "You really are afraid of them?"

Sam hesitated, and tears filled her eyes. "The girls are especially afraid of them."

Kait stood. "Have they made improper advances?"

Sam also stood. She wrung her hands. "Sort of."

"Have they hurt any of you, Sam?" Kait had to take the girl's hands. "You have to tell me."

"Not really," she whispered, then, "just a little. You know. Copping a feel. That kind of thing."

Kait was appalled. "Your father has to know about this. And so does the principal—"

"No! If you tell my father anything, I won't ever speak to you again!" Sam shouted desperately.

Kait realized Sam was really afraid of the gang—or was she afraid of something else, something that had to do with Gabe Jenkins? Still, as much as she wanted Sam's trust, she knew Trev had to be told of the matter. Guns and gangs were far too dangerous for him not to be told what was happening.

And Sam saw her decision in her eyes. "You're going to Dad!"

"Sam—"

"Damn you! I trusted you!" Sam shouted furiously—tearfully.

"I don't want you or any of your friends getting hurt," Kait tried. "Please, Sam, this sounds too serious to be ignored."

"Get out!"

"Please, Sam. I'm worried about you."

"No! Marni was wrong," Sam said brokenly. "She was so wrong!"

Kait faltered.

"You're not different, not at all—you're exactly the same and I still hate you!"

Kait breathed. "I don't hate you. In fact, I care very much and I have to do what I think is right—and in your ultimate best interest."

"Get out!" Sam threw a magazine in her direction.

Kait left.

Rafe Coleman was coming to dinner.

Kait had told Trev what she had learned from Sam, and while she went to get Marni, he had called both the principal of Sam's school and his brother. Rafe, as it turned out, was in D.C. on police business, but they had spoken briefly and Rafe had said he would stop by around seven as soon as he got back into town. Well, it was almost seven. Marni had eaten and had her bath, and Kait was reading her a book.

"And Willy finally saw the error of his ways," Kait read. "So he picked a posie and went to Loulou, and Loulou was so happy to see him that they hugged and made up. And to this day, Willy the frog and Loulou Jones are the two very best friends."

"The end!" Marni clapped, beaming. "Hi, Daddy."

Kait shifted around from where she sat with her back to the door, and sure enough, Trev stood there, looking rather amazing in a turquoise turtleneck sweater and a pair of black trousers. He was wearing a black belt that looked expensive, his gold Rolex, and gleaming black loafers. He was staring at her through his sooty lashes with an odd expression, as if he simply didn't know her anymore.

Kait smiled warmly at him. It was hard to be so composed when her heart was doing so many wild flips and rolls. Tonight, Trev Coleman was sexier than she had ever seen him.

"Willy is the best frog," Marni said, leaping off the bed and running to him. He swung her up into his arms. "Can I have a frog?"

"No."

"But frogs are fun, Daddy!"

"You're getting a puppy, remember?" Trev said softly, his gaze straying to Kait.

Marni nodded as he set her down. He looked directly at Kait. "Rafe called. He'll be here in a few minutes." He hesitated. "Are you joining us?"

But he had already suggested that she join them—maybe he didn't remember. "Sure," she said, her pulse rioting madly. She was having dinner with Trev and his brother, and while she knew Trev wanted to talk about Sam, the gun, and the gang, she was thrilled to be included.

"Are you going to change?" he asked carefully.

Kait didn't hesitate. After picking Marni up at school, they had gone to the mall. Kait had bought three pairs of Levi's, plain old 501s, as well as several short-sleeved and long-sleeved cotton T-shirts. Then she had bought Marni two storybooks and a set of pj's covered with grinning panda bears. Kait was wearing a pale pink long-sleeved cotton crew neck with the sand-blasted Levi's, thick wool socks, and no makeup. Of course she would change for dinner, as Trev had clearly done so.

"I'll be five minutes," she said happily. "Marni, keep your dad company, okay?"

"Okay," Marni said, as chipper as Kait.

Kait ran to the bedroom and into the closet. She quickly chose a pair of black pants and a black-and-white blouse, not wanting to overdo it. A moment later she dropped the items on the floor. "What the heck!" She grabbed the Donna Karan dress she had offered to lend Sam. The black jersey dress was simple and elegant, but the fabric, which would cling, was so sexy—and she wanted to impress Trev tonight. Refusing to think about *that,* she stripped, shimmied into the soft jersey, failed to find any pantyhose, and, barelegged, stepped into a pair of high-heeled black pumps. In the bathroom she fluffed her hair, added mascara, and dabbed gloss on her lips. She paused to study herself, trying to be critical—she looked as excited as a girl on her first date. But there was nothing girlish about the dress, which slithered over her curves. It was ladylike; it was sensuous and alluring.

Kait reminded herself that this was not a date, that Lana was coming home after the weekend, and that she was merely a temporary substitute for her sister. Her excitement did not dim. It was simply wonderful to have somehow reached a truce with Trev Coleman, even if the circumstances were Sam's possession of a gun and the conflict he and his daughter were now embroiled in.

She was so happy to be able to help smooth things over.

Kait glanced at a malachite clock and saw that eight minutes had passed, not five. She ran out of the room and skidded down the hall. When she reached Marni's room, she saw that Elizabeth was there, tucking her into bed. Kait stumbled over to the bed, silently cursing the shoes she had picked. The heels were too narrow and too high. "Sleep tight, sweetie," she said, hugging the little girl hard.

"I love you, Mommy," Marni said sleepily.

"I love you, too," Kait said. She smiled at Elizabeth, who did not smile in return.

Once on the stairs, Kait clung to the railing, slowing. She could hear the men in the living room. Rafe Coleman's voice was about the same timbre as Trev's, but it was whiskey-rough, and he had a true Virginian's drawl.

She paused on the threshold, her heart skittering when her eyes landed smack on Trev's broad back. She reminded herself, very firmly, that this was *not* a date and that he *was* Lana's husband. Her heart laughed at her silently and reminded her that Lana was as hell-bent as he was on a divorce.

Rafe Coleman saw her. He wore his uniform—a slate blue shirt and his badge, navy blue pants, a gun and holster, but not the Western-style hat or the black bomber jacket. Now, his stance seemed to stiffen as he stared at her.

Some of her elation vanished, replaced by wariness. "Hi," she said, coming forward. "I didn't mean to keep you waiting."

Trev turned. His eyes swept over her. Kait managed a smile. She had never looked so alluring and she knew it, but she couldn't afford designer clothes in her own life, either. "You haven't kept us waiting," he said, smiling just a little.

Kait was still smiling at him when she began to cross the rug, hooking one stiletto heel into it. She cried out as the rug acted as a brake, causing her to trip and fall.

Trev leapt forward, catching her before she went down in a heap.

Kait clung to his shoulders—once again, his sweater was soft cashmere—then got her balance and straightened. She felt her cheeks flaming. "Caught a heel. Darn shoes," she said roughly.

He started to smile. "You love those shoes. Are you all right?"

He hadn't released her. That is, she was pretty much in his arms. Her breasts, which were braless due to the dress's deep V, were crushed against the hard planes of his chest. She looked up and somehow fixated on his chiseled mouth. Her heart lurched. The sensation went entirely through her. What would it be like to kiss this man? To be kissed by him? To have their mouths locked . . .

"Fine," she murmured as he released her. She glanced at Rafe, blushing now. "Hello. How was your trip?"

He folded his arms across his chest and eyed her. "Just fine, thank you," he said, his drawl oddly sarcastic.

She tensed.

Trev moved over to a bar cart with brass handles, a glass top, and brass wheels. He poured a bourbon and two scotches. He handed her one scotch, Rafe the bourbon, taking the other glass of scotch for himself. Kait did not drink hard liquor and she blinked at the bronze liquid in her glass. She would have loved a glass of wine.

"I started to fill Rafe in. But I didn't get very far," Trev said.

Kait nodded, nervous now and wishing that Lana had not alienated Trev's brother, too. Rafe's gaze was as cool as ice, and it remained unwavering upon her. He seemed fascinated by her hair or lack of makeup or both.

"Why don't you tell him what you found out?" Trev asked.

Kait nodded, setting her glass aside. She told him about the gang that appeared to be frightening Sam and the other children at school.

He said, "You never came down to the sheriff's office to make out a complaint."

Kait froze. She knew the opening thrust of an attack when she saw one. "I haven't had the time."

He nodded, skepticism all over his face.

Kait realized that her not filing a complaint looked bad—as if she had made up the entire story about being shot at while riding Pride.

"Do you have any names?" Rafe asked her, changing the subject entirely.

And now she was off balance. She knew he had done this deliberately. She cleared her throat. "Unfortunately, I never got that far. And Sam is afraid to speak about this to anyone, even to you. Apparently these kids are real bullies. I'm worried about her and her girlfriends, frankly."

"Really?" Rafe stared. "Since when?"

Kait stiffened, and fought to control her rising anger. "Yes, really. And since I found a gun in her room."

"And she spoke to you," Rafe murmured after a pause during which he sipped his Jack Daniel's.

"I beg your pardon?" Kait asked uneasily.

"I didn't realize you were Sam's confidante," he said, his green gaze unwavering. He had the same complexion as his brother, almost olive in tone. But as his hair was as dark as midnight, he somehow seemed darker, more dangerous and deadlier than Trev could ever be. The fact that he hadn't removed his gun added to the menacing effect.

This man would make a terrible enemy. But he was a cop. He was supposed to be on her side. However, he clearly was not.

She thought about Max Zara then. She had the urge to tell Trev all about him and his secret arsenal, but she decided not to share that information in front of his brother, whom she did not trust.

"I'm not usually her confidante," Kait said as firmly as possible. "As you both know. But serious situations call for serious measures, wouldn't you agree? And she needed a friend today," she added.

"So you played her and she decided to confide in you," Rafe said.

"No, I did not play her," Kait said, her tone rising. "As horrid as I am, I don't want to see some teenager shot or even mistakenly killed!" Clearly, her brother-in-law despised her. It felt like one more weight that she could not bear. "And she didn't just decide to confide in me. We had a long conversation. Girl to girl."

"Girl to girl," Rafe repeated, and then he cast a look at his brother.

"I hit her, Rafe," Trev said hoarsely. "When she told me the gun wasn't any of my business, I smacked her."

Rafe whirled. "You hit Sam?!" He was aghast.

"I will regret it until the day I die," Trev said grimly. "Sam still isn't speaking to me. But that's why Lana made headway with her, I think."

Rafe jerked his wide eyes back to Kait. Suspicion was etched all over his face.

Kait recoiled. "She needed a friend," Kait whispered.

"And you're her friend? Since when? Oh, wait, since you and Trev are weeks away from a permanent split!"

Kait was stunned that he would be so rude—that he would not make an attempt to hide his true feelings—that he would say exactly what he was thinking.

"Rafe, Lana tried to help," Trev said sharply. "In fact, she did help."

"Really?" Rafe looked furiously at him. His temper seemed about to explode—and he seemed to be struggling not to allow that. "Oh, yeah. Since you handed her divorce papers, she's had a personality change. Since then, she's decided to be a mother to Marni, to Sam—Jesus, to the entire world!?" He looked at Kait. "Forgive me, darlin', if I just don't buy the whole sweet, big-eyed act of wifely devotion and motherly love."

Kait was frozen with disbelief. Her mind had gone blank, except for one single thought—this man loathed her sister.

"This is uncalled for," Trev said, grasping his brother by the arm and whirling him around. "We're here to get Sam out of trouble—and to make sure she stays out of it!"

"And you're buying Lana's act, hook, line, and sinker," Rafe said, shaking him off. "Goddamn it, this is déjà vu!"

Trev hesitated. "This isn't an act. Sam's in trouble and Lana has been more than kind."

"This is exactly how she played you when she picked you up in New York!" Rafe cried. "She's been playing you ever since that day, and damn it, knowing all that you do, she is still playing you!"

Trev grabbed his brother by the shoulder and it turned out to be more of a push than anything else. Kait stiffened, horrified. "I asked you here tonight to talk about Sam—not about Lana," he said angrily.

"How can I not say something? Listen to yourself!" Rafe exclaimed. "She's got you by the balls, and I bet I know why." He gave Kait a look of disgust. Then he strode to her. She shrank back. "The day Trev made it clear he was taking you to the altar, no matter what I thought, was the day I shut up and did my best to tolerate a real bad situation. But he's handed you divorce papers, and Goddamn it, I am not going to let you bring him down again. *Do you hear me?*"

Kait was horrified. "It's not like that," she said weakly. But this was the second person who had stated that exact intention, and dear God, how could she have been so stupid as to not recall that Max Zara had uttered those exact same words?

Had Zara changed? He also wanted to destroy Lana—just as Rafe Coleman did.

"Cut it out." Trev seized Rafe from behind and whirled him around.

"How gullible can you be? After the past six years of lie after lie?" Rafe demanded.

Trev was angry, but he gave Kait a look that told her that he was being swayed by his brother. "Nothing's changed," he said. "Lana and I have agreed on a divorce. But this is about Sam, damn it! It's about my daughter—your niece. It's not about Lana and me."

"Yet somehow she's in the middle," Rafe said, more calmly.

Kait swallowed and sucked up her courage. "Sam needs a friend right now. She's only sixteen, and she's in trouble—or very close to it! If you cared about her, you'd be asking me about the gun and that gang—instead of hurling accusations when you don't know squat about me!" Kait cried, far more firmly now.

Rafe's hands found his hips. The fact that he wore a gun made him even more intimidating. "Trev gave me the gun. I'm running a check on it." His green eyes were cold. "*You* found the gun?"

She nodded. Now she had a very bad feeling, based on his inflection of the word "you."

"In Sam's room?"

"Yes, in a drawer with her underwear."

His mouth quirked, but with no humor. "Now why the hell would you be looking in my niece's bureau? That is something Trev didn't get around to explaining—as if he could."

"What?" She stiffened.

"I want to know what you were doing in my niece's bedroom, Lana. I mean, this is all a bit much for me."

"I was looking for a sweater Sam had borrowed," she managed.

Rafe's look was mocking and incredulous, all at once.

"Rafe, Lana is not on trial here," Trev said firmly. "Sam had a gun, and the reason seems to be to protect herself—or that Jenkins boy—from a gang of young thugs."

Rafe stared. "I just find it odd that Lana found the gun, putting her smack in the center of everything."

"I was looking for my sweater," Kait repeated. "Sam's been borrowing things, actually, and I felt certain that it was in her room."

His hand shot up. "So now you're calling Sam a thief?"

"I said 'borrowing,' not stealing!" Kait cried. Why was he so intent on backing her into a corner this way?

A long pause ensued. He finally smiled, with no mirth whatsoever. "It will be interesting to see how the gun checks out. Because, somehow, I know this isn't about Sam. This is about you."

ELEVEN

"What?" Kait gasped.

Trev set his scotch glass down. "What the hell are you saying?"

"I'm going to talk to Sam. She in her room?" he asked.

Trev's jaw was hard. "Yeah."

Rafe headed out of the living room. Trev quickly followed. Kait trailed after them, but did not cross the threshold. She watched Trev grip Rafe's arm. "What did that last comment mean?"

Rafe faced him. This meant that he faced Kait in the doorway—but he didn't look at her now, not even once, though he had to see her. "Am I a good cop?"

Trev didn't hesitate. "Yes. You should still be with D.C. Homicide and you know it."

Rafe made a self-deprecating sound. "My instincts are screaming at me, Trev."

Kait saw Trev's shoulders stiffen. "And that means?" he asked.

"It means don't be a sucker for a piece of pussy now."

Kait winced, hugging herself.

Trev hesitated and looked at Kait. Then he turned to his brother and said, "That was uncalled for. Lana found a gun in Sam's room, Rafe. Just how the hell does that make me a sucker?" he demanded.

"That's what *she* says," Rafe returned. "Have you gone

nuts? That woman has done nothing but lie to you from the day you met! Her schemes are so complicated that nobody, not even me, can figure them—or her—out! And suddenly she comes back from New York without her hair, without her red lipstick, suddenly she's wearing your shirts, suddenly she falls off a horse! And she *claims* someone shot at her. There was no trace of a gun having been fired out there, Trev. We combed the area. If someone shot at her, we would have come up with a casing, residue, something!"

So he had investigated the claim she had never made, Kait thought.

"Not necessarily," Trev said harshly, but uncertainly.

Kait couldn't move—but she wanted to flee. Her heart continued to sink, and it was hard to imagine it getting any lower. She would give anything if she could just up and leave, head back to New York.

"She said the bullet went past her ear, damn it! I had some buddies of mine in D.C. do a projection on their computers, Trev. We know where the shooter would have been, within a diameter of fifty feet. We have a wider radius for where the bullet must have landed, but a radius nonetheless. And we came up with nothing. Zip. Zero. *Nothing.*"

Trev stared at Rafe; he stared back. A long moment ensued. Kait turned and went back into the living room, sinking into her favorite chair. A heavy, unfamiliar weight had claimed her—the weight of depression. How much more of this could she take? Just when things were looking slightly better, along came Rafe Coleman. Trev's own brother was as suspicious of her as everyone else.

And he was the county sheriff. He should be on her—Lana's—side. He should be the one they turned to when the time came—if it ever did—to go to the police.

But he was the enemy, that is, because he hated Lana so, that made him Kait's enemy too.

"I can see it now—she's doing a number on you, isn't she? That cute little haircut, the natural girl-next-door look, tripping over her high heels. Please! . . . But mostly, the whole mother thing. She's not the motherly type. She hasn't changed. She's up to something. I can smell it, Trev. With my cop's nose."

"I hope you're wrong."

Rafe made a disparaging sound. "In fact, I *know* she's up to something."

"What are you saying?" Trev was asking quietly, dread seemingly in his rough tone.

"I know for a fact she's not being straight with you. But I can't say any more," Rafe said. And finally, he looked over—and directly—at Kait. "Not yet."

And Kait didn't move. She was sick inside, sick in every fiber of her being. She wanted to scream at them both; in that instant, she wanted to tell them the entire truth as she knew it. But that would be selfish. She could not get out now, not until this was entirely over and she knew for a fact that Marni and Lana would remain safe and sound, and that there was no more danger threatening either one of them.

"What the hell do you mean, you can't say anything?" Trev demanded.

"Don't trust her," Rafe said, clapping his hand on Trev's shoulder. Both men were the exact same height—an inch or two above six feet tall. "Fuck her brains out if you must, but do not trust her."

And Trev did hesitate. "I don't trust her. But—"

"No buts," Rafe said flatly. He gave Kait a quelling look, and turned away. "I'm going up to see Sam."

When he was gone, Trev turned around and looked right at her. For a long moment, he did not speak. Then he said, suddenly appearing weary, "I must be a fool. An idiot and a fool. Rafe's right. He was right from day one."

Kait came forward—and tripped on uneven planking in the wood floors. She recovered her balance and gripped his hands. "You're not a fool!" Still, she couldn't argue that Rafe wasn't right. "Trev, I promise you that I will not hurt Sam or Marni. I promise," she said harshly. And she wanted to add, I would never hurt you! But of course, she could not, she didn't dare.

And even as she begged him silently to trust her, she was

afraid that Lana would return and do precisely as Kait was now claiming she would never do.

Kait was afraid of what might happen when her sister returned.

He looked at her and she did not look away, partially because she could not, and partially because she so wanted him to trust her, Kait. She saw his eyes soften. Then his face tightened and he pulled away. "What is Rafe talking about, Lana? What is it that he knows about you—or thinks he knows—that he's not telling me?" he asked very quietly.

Kait sensed that she was at a crossroads with him, one that would never again reappear. She desperately wanted to tell him the truth—that her personality change wasn't that at all, because she wasn't his wife—but she simply could not, because of Marni.

She sensed that he was as desperate now—that he desperately wanted to hear a genuine explanation from her.

She took a deep breath. Her mind sped, raced. What if she told him a part of the truth? "Trev, Rafe is right. There is something important that I haven't told you."

"And just what the hell is that?"

Kait straightened. "I'm deeply in debt."

He didn't say a word.

"I owe a lot of money to . . . someone. Maybe, that person is after me now."

"What the hell are you pulling?" he asked slowly.

"I'm not pulling anything. You asked for the truth. I'm trying to fix things—really—but I can't tell you any more."

"I pay all your bills. You're pretty extravagant, and I've let you spend as you choose. We don't have any debt."

She stiffened. He was refusing to believe her, and she didn't know what to do now, because she couldn't tell him any details. "I'm telling you the truth," she whispered. "I'm afraid, Trev."

He started. Then, "Why are you doing this? Why are you lying to me about this?" he demanded.

Kait was dumbfounded. Her plan to give him a grain of

truth was backfiring. "I . . . I," she began nervously and with dismay.

He was staring into her eyes. "What are you covering up?"

"Nothing." She had to wet her lips again. She wanted to insist that she was telling him the truth, but suddenly, she could not get the words out.

"Why do I see fear—no—anxiety—in your eyes?" he asked. "And don't tell me you're afraid because you've been spending money you don't have! Why the hell are you behaving this way?" Suddenly he seemed furious. "Why the hell did you cut your hair, damn it? Where the hell is that lipstick you wore every single day? What is this sudden love of blue jeans? Explain this to me, Lana!" He was shouting.

She could only stare, speechless.

He threw both hands into the air, turning away, his entire body taut with tension.

"I can't," she heard herself whisper brokenly.

He faced her, grim. "You know what the worst part is?"

He paused; Kait shook her head fearfully, speechlessly.

"I *know* I shouldn't trust you—I think Rafe is right, and I have for some time—but I *want* to trust you," he said.

She could not be thrilled. She was too upset, too shaken. He spoke again, and he was harsh, his green eyes resigned. "Ever since you came back from New York, somehow different, and changed, as Marni keeps insisting you are, I've had the oddest urges toward you." He was quieter now. "But I am not going to trust you, Lana. I've had six years of bitter experience, and in all of those years, you have let me and the girls down, time and again. *I will not trust you.* No matter how that little body of yours may be screaming at me, tempting me, but I am not going to cave in, give in, trust you, all over again. It's simply *not going to happen."*

She heard herself say, "But you can trust me."

He walked away.

No one trusted her.

Lana had so many enemies and one of them was Trev's brother, the county sheriff.

Kait could deal with that. She had no choice. But what hurt was that Trev, who had been softening toward her, who wanted to trust her, refused to trust her and would not out of sheer determination and will.

How had their lives ever come to this? If only she knew what she and Lana were up against!

Kait wondered if he would ever come to trust her and believe in her once Lana returned, once he knew who she, Kait, really was—once he and Lana were divorced. She realized she badly wanted him to believe in her—to know who she really was, a woman with good family values, kindness, and consideration. Kait sighed, throwing in the towel. She sat in her favorite tweed chair in the living room, sipping scotch. Kait was furious with her sister.

Trev hadn't deserved her inconsideration and he certainly hadn't deserved to be a victim of her infidelity. And her behavior had affected the family—hurting Trev, Marni, and Sam. Lana should have gone for some kind of marital help years ago. Kait felt certain it was too late, not that her sister wanted to save her marriage. In fact, she didn't deserve Trev Coleman.

There, she had admitted it—Kait had taken sides.

Kait closed her eyes in real despair. The real problem was that no matter what Lana had done—and Kait hardly knew the extent of the trouble she was in—she was still Kait's twin sister and Kait did love her. Well, maybe everyone would find happiness after the divorce, even though it threatened to be a very bitter one.

On that extremely depressing note, footsteps sounded on the stairs. Kait opened her eyes and saw Rafe appear. Trev had been standing by the window, looking toward the rolling hills on the horizon, which was now purple and star-studded. His empty scotch glass was in hand. He, too, turned.

"Sam's plenty upset," he said, giving Kait a bleak glance—as if that were her fault. "But she gave me what I need as far as that gang goes. The leader is Ben Abbott, which is what I thought. He's been picked up a few times, mostly for drinking and rowdy behavior. It's a matter of time before he does something we can't let slide. I hate to see a kid his age go to Juvy." Rafe sighed. "He's tough and remorseless. He's trouble. I'll stop by his folks' house and then have a chat with Principal Greene. I'll have the boys keep a closer eye on him as well."

"What about Sam?" Trev asked.

"She claims the gun is hers." He hesitated.

"I don't like it, Trev. I think she's got a big thing for this Gabe Jenkins, but I also think she's telling the truth, and the gun is hers. Or, it's not his. She won't tell me how she got it."

"The gun can't be hers," Trev said. "Go speak to Jenkins. The kid and his father."

Rafe slapped his shoulder. "Read my mind. Look, I'll pass on dinner, make these calls instead." His gaze stayed on Trev, as if Kait were not even in the room.

Trev hesitated, and then glanced at Kait.

Kait stood. "No, stay." She couldn't smile, not if her life depended on it. "I'm exhausted. I'm calling it a night." She suddenly wanted to cry. She had, stupidly, looked forward to a pleasant evening spent with Trev and his brother. When was she going to face what had become inescapable? Lana had alienated everyone in this family, and there was no way Kait was going to get past that, no matter how hard she tried, not until Lana returned and they came forward together to explain their deception, and maybe even then it would remain an impossible task. "Enjoy supper," she managed through tears, and this was to Rafe. She hurried from the room.

She stumbled again in Lana's damned high heels. As she caught the banister, she finally heard Rafe say, quietly, "In a way, I don't blame you for falling for her all over again. Those big blue eyes are pretty hard to resist."

Trev didn't respond.

Kait halted, gripping the staircase.

"I never saw her cry before," Rafe said then.

Trev said, "Me neither."

• • •

Kait slowly came downstairs.

She was barefoot, but still in the Donna Karan dress. She had finished the scotch and had heard Rafe driving off. Just to be certain, she had rushed to a window in a guest bedroom, overlooking the front of the house. Sure enough, the black-and-white SUV had been driving away from the house. She was wildly relieved to have him gone.

She had waited a long time for Trev to come upstairs to the room he was using. But when he hadn't done so, she had decided not to wait any longer. She was a bit buzzed, very confused, extremely saddened, and quite famished.

Kait crept downstairs as quietly as possible, hoping Trev was in his study with the door closed. She wasn't up to being with him now—she was afraid of more questions, a confrontation, the look in his eyes—she did not have the strength to muster up another lie. Not tonight.

At least Rafe Coleman would now handle the situation with Sam, the gun she'd had, and that gang. Kait did feel that she could safely walk away from that one other burden, which she simply did not have the energy to bear.

Although the kitchen could be approached from the hall, the quickest way was to walk through the living and dining rooms. The moment Kait stepped into the living room, she sensed that she wasn't alone.

But all the lights were off.

She faltered, straining to see and to hear.

A shadow by a corner window turned. "What are you doing?"

Her vision adjusted to the darkness. The shadow emerged into a man—into Trev. He stood by the window, a glass in hand. Kait wished her heart wouldn't riot at the mere sound of his voice. She found a lamp on a table beside the couch and turned it on. "I'm hungry," she said.

His eyes slid over her, lingering on her bare toes with their pastel pink polished nails. "I'm sorry about the way the evening turned out."

She started. "Thank you." Oddly, in spite of everything,

he seemed sincere. If only Rafe hadn't been by that night. Kait had the feeling he would have softened even more toward her.

Trev continued to regard her. Kait realized that his glass was empty and that she could hear her racing heartbeat.

She swallowed uneasily. She wished it weren't so late. And she wished that they weren't alone. But that last wish was a halfhearted one. Because she wanted this moment of intimacy as much as she feared it—as much as she knew it was wrong. Because just standing there, yards away but alone with him, did terrible things to her body, her heart, her mind. Kait was yearning for what she could not—and should not—have.

"Drink?" he asked, moving to the bar cart.

Kait glanced at it, and saw that he had made quite a dent in the contents of the scotch decanter. It had been full a few hours ago—he must have had four stiff drinks since then.

Kait hesitated. She had to say no, and not because she was not a scotch drinker. But because it was late, because they were alone, and because she was hungry—and food was no longer the issue. Her heart was hungry now. She had become irrepressibly drawn to this man.

Trev walked over to the cart, filled a fresh glass, and then his own. He handed hers to her. "I must be drunk," he said, not sounding in the least inebriated. "Because I wish you and Rafe hadn't hit it off so badly all those years ago."

"I'm wishing that too," Kait whispered truthfully.

He started and their gazes met and locked.

Kait gripped her drink. It was so hard to think clearly when he was standing just inches away from her, looking impossibly sexy in that turquoise sweater, his gaze frankly speculative, impossibly male, upon hers. And what *was* wrong with her? Why did being around him make her insides melt, her loins throb, her mind spin forbidden fantasies?

Worse, why was she starting to *care?*

"I had better go," she said, and heard how rough her own tone sounded.

I don't love him. Lana's words echoed in her head.

"Why?" Trev asked, his voice as harsh as hers had been.

She froze, incapable of looking away from him.

"Maybe Rafe is right after all," he said, setting his scotch down without ever taking his eyes from her.

She knew exactly what he meant. "What?" *This could not be happening. . . .*

He took her glass from her hand. She let it go. "Maybe if I have you, I can get you out of my system, and think straight once again."

This was not a good idea. She had to tell him; she had to leave. Kait actually started to turn away, but her voice escaped her now.

His large palms caught her on each hip, dangerously low. She inhaled. "Trev—"

He swung her back around. "Don't," he said, clasping her buttocks firmly, intimately, and pulling her close.

Kait gasped as her pubis met his fully aroused loins.

"Don't ruin this. Don't talk." He held her tight, pressed against him. "I want you, Lana. I want you the way I did when we first met. No," he laughed derisively. "I want you a thousand times more." Something tender crept into his rough tone. "Have I told you that I love your hair?" he whispered.

She could barely think. His hands had easily clenched each cheek, his erection ground against her hip. "No," she meant to say, instead, she moaned.

"Don't move," he said harshly, and for one moment, as he slid down her body, Kait was startled and confused.

And then he was on his knees, his face pressed to her sex. Kait realized what was happening, in real shock—he was lifting her jersey dress, thumbing her through the cotton panties—and she cried out.

He slid the brief aside. His long fingers parted her private parts. "You are so wet," he said in real surprise. "You're already ready for me!"

Kait wanted to reply. There was one corner of her mind that was willing him to stop. But the rest of her mind was begging him to never stop touching her.

He slid his tongue around her and then he began a very skilled and sensual manipulation of her clitoris.

Her knees buckled.

She cried out.

Her fingers dug into his head, his hair.

As she fell, he caught her, never easing the delicate but insistent pressure of his mouth and tongue. Kait's mind spun. Her body arced. She vaguely felt him spread her thighs and then as he stroked an extremely sensitive area of her buttocks, still laving her, a zillion stars exploded overhead. She shouted, "Trev," bucking convulsively, rhythmically, spiraling up, up, and away.

Then she landed softly in clouds.

Kait regained a degree of mental coherence. She suddenly realized that she was flat on her back with her skirts thrown up to her waist, her panties gone—ripped off?—and Trev Coleman was on his belly, between her legs. Slowly, stunned, she opened her eyes and looked down at him.

In fact, Trev was not merely between her legs—he had his head propped up on his hands, and he was staring up at her, his expression strained with lust but thoroughly bewildered.

Kait opened her mouth to speak and no words came out. She thought, *Oh, my God.*

"What the hell was that?" he asked very quietly.

"Wh-what?" she stammered. She started to wiggle away. His hands grasped her bare hips and she realized she wasn't going anywhere. She began to blush and she felt it. "Please."

"You came in ten seconds flat."

"Were you timing me?"

"And I know you weren't faking it. You're soaking wet." He was grim.

Was this a bad thing? Kait didn't understand what he was thinking—but she knew one thing—this was not good, no matter how amazing their brief interlude had been, and she had to get up.

Because his breath was feathering her and she was swelling again.

Because desire was there, heavy and heated and demanding.

Gut constricting.

"You shouted my *name*."

Kait swallowed. "May I get up?" she asked, torn between tears and ecstasy.

"No. You shouted my *name*." He seemed angry.

She wet her lips. "Please let me up."

"I don't think so," he said, and suddenly he slid his hand over her sex, cupping her, hard. "You shout a lot of things—but not my name."

Oh, God, she thought, frightened.

Suddenly his fingers eased, stroked over her. Kait stiffened with a huge pang of desire and felt him shudder with the same feelings. She knew, in that moment, it was now or never.

If she didn't get up now, they were going to make love.

"Trev," she whispered.

His gaze shot to hers, unmasked, raw, and hungry.

Weakly, she said, "Someone might see."

"Let them," he said, and suddenly he was looming over her. He took her hand and pressed it over his erection; Kait inhaled sharply, loudly. He gave her an odd look, then unzipped his trousers. Only fine-spun cotton rested between her and him.

He lifted her up and nuzzled her neck.

Kait didn't mean to, but somehow her hands were slipping into his briefs. She caught his slick, heated length in her palm and thought she might die. *Trev Coleman was magnificent, and she had never wanted any man the way she wanted him. She had wanted him insanely from the moment she had first walked through the front door of Fox Hollow. But she had been pretending all along, pretending to herself, that he did not excite and arouse her.*

"Don't stop now, baby," he whispered.

Kait stiffened instinctively, hating being called "baby." She was about to tell him not to call her that when he shifted, ripping off his trousers and briefs. His knees moved her thighs apart; she looked up, ready to protest, but his eyes were tightly closed, as if in utter concentration, sweat beading his brow.

Her insides flipped with gut-wrenching urgency.

"Open, babe," he murmured roughly, "because I can't wait. I want *in*."

Kait felt him pressing his huge tip against her. She grabbed his shoulders, her intention, perhaps, to push him away, but she was shaking with excitement and she was so slick that the reverse occurred. She held him and her body arched uncontrollably toward him; he thrust deeply, irrevocably, into her.

Kait cried out. Not because he was huge, which he was, not because she wasn't exactly a sex machine—it had been a long, long time since her last boyfriend—but because nothing had ever felt so perfect, so deep, so right.

Trev froze.

She felt his utter surprise then, and their gazes clashed. His eyes were wide with shock.

He knew she wasn't Lana.

He stared at her.

He knew.

Kait tried to think. It was impossible with him throbbing inside her. "Trev," she began roughly.

His jaw flexed. He grabbed her by a hank of her short hair, anchoring her down. And just before he kissed her for the very first time, she met his eyes. Something was there, which she could not comprehend, much less describe—she understood the astonishment, the excitement, but not the layer of emotion beneath.

And then it simply didn't matter.

His mouth claimed hers. No soft, tentative brushing of his lips, but a greedy kiss, with him using his tongue, with him determined to somehow fuse their mouths as deeply as their bodies. As she tasted him, an emotion very much like love ballooned inside her. Bewildered, frightened, and on the brink of another explosive climax, she imagined that this was more than right—this was meant to be.

He moved, gasping with pleasure. Slowly, tentatively . . . long, giant thrusts. "Am I . . . hurting you . . . darling?"

"No, no," Kait whimpered, joy surging in her veins, joining the elation, the love, the pending ecstasy. *He had called her darling. . . .*

"Don't want . . . to go . . . too fast . . ." he panted, moving so slowly, with such exquisite control, that Kait simply couldn't stand it. "Don't want . . . to hurt you . . . now."

"Hurry," she whispered, all coherent thought leaving her now as heaven beckoned her once more.

And he began to move more swiftly, driving her across the floor, inch by inch, and Kait died then, thrown up into another universe, another reality, an even deeper, brighter galaxy, clinging to his broad shoulders, while he called her darling again, begging her to hang on, just a bit longer, and even longer yet. . . .

She held him as she floated back to earth and as he exploded, crying out hoarsely into the night, tears came to her eyes.

She held him tightly, never wanting to let go, fear flooding her—fear and guilt.

Kait was afraid that she was falling in love.

TWELVE

Trev Coleman moved off her.

Kait became acutely aware of the hard wood floor beneath her back—but she wasn't half as aware of that as she was of what she had just done and the man lying on the floor beside her.

She had never imagined that lovemaking could be like that.

Breathless and stunned, she tugged her dress down. An image of her sister seared her mind. Lana didn't deserve Trev Coleman, but guilt overcame her now. Lana was getting a divorce, but she hadn't gotten one yet. Lana did not want Trev Coleman, but he was her lawful husband. Worse—Trev thought he had just made love to his wife.

Kait began to tremble. Fear filled her, and it had nothing to do with Trev discovering the truth now. While they had been making love, an emotion that felt suspiciously like love had blossomed inside her. It had been joyous, tentative, huge, fearful, and potent. And it simmered within her even now.

Kait closed her eyes, desperately trying to rationalize away her feelings. Yes, she had come to care for Trev Coleman, because he was Marni's father, because he was her brother-in-law. Jesus. He was her brother-in-law.

What had she done?

You slept with him, that's what you have done.

But it was even worse than that, wasn't it?

He was the kind of man women dreamed of—handsome, wealthy, athletic, intelligent, successful, and charming. He was the kind of man she had always dreamed of. But so what? She was not falling in love with him—she simply didn't dare!

Kait suddenly realized that he had yet to move. She glanced at him anxiously. He lay on his back, eyes closed, his breathing normal, and Kait simply knew that his mind was racing. She could feel it.

Had Trev known the moment he entered her that she was not her sister? Kait thought she had seen the stark comprehension in his eyes.

She was stiff with fear now. It was all too much. Making love was bad enough—falling in love was simply unacceptable. In another second he might turn to her and demand to know who she was and what she was doing, in his house, in his bed, in his life. She had to run, escape. She'd had enough of the charade she wanted to blame Lana for, but she had agreed and been a willing partner to the scheme.

Kait was staring when his head began to turn. His eyes opened. She forgot to breathe and their eyes met.

He stared at her.

She couldn't move.

A dozen excuses tumbled to her mind, and one of them was the entire truth—a truth that included her forbidden feelings. Stricken, she watched him sit up, still in his turquoise sweater. He gave her a searing look, one she could not comprehend—was it bad? Good?—and he stepped into his briefs and trousers. Kait trembled. "Trev?"

He reached down and took her hand. "Ssh." His smile was brief, strained. "Let's go upstairs," he said, pulling her to her feet.

For one moment she did not understand. "What?"

And he reeled her into his arms. "I think I'm gonna make love to you all night."

Kait awoke and stretched deliciously—then stiffened. Reality paralyzed her.

She had no idea what time it was, but the sun was up, so it had to be seven or so. Trev's side of the bed was empty but warm. They had last made love a couple of hours ago, finishing with dawn coloring the night sky dove gray.

She sat up, clutching the covers to her bare breasts. In the light of day, last night seemed insane. It *was* insane. *What should she do now?*

She had slept with her sister's husband, never mind that they were getting a divorce, never mind that Lana had even insinuated she wouldn't care if Kait did such a thing, never mind that Lana had been the most faithless of wives. It was terribly wrong, and Kait wore the burden of guilt to prove it.

She shuddered.

Did last night mean he intended to reconcile with Lana?

Kait was afraid. Now, of course, she no longer wanted them to reconcile, in fact, a reconciliation would cause even more personal complications for everyone. Yet even if Trev had changed his mind about a divorce, Lana had been crystal clear the other night on the phone. Kait felt certain that she was not changing her mind, no matter what happened.

Was she falling in love and, if so, what should she do about it?

Kait attempted to explore her own feelings, but it was impossible—was so tense, she could hardly breathe. And maybe that was for the best. Because maybe she had been mistaken by her emotions last night, and maybe, given some time and distance—and the fact that Lana was returning after the weekend—she would return to being her usual, very moral and uncomplicated self.

Should she tell him the truth?

Trev clearly hadn't guessed the truth, or he would have accused her of her gross deception after their first round of lovemaking in the living room. He hadn't said a word all night, which meant that he thought she was his wife. Kait had clearly been wrong to think otherwise. But last night changed everything from Kait's point of view. Before, continuing her charade had been a matter of protecting both Lana and Marni. Now, to do so meant betraying Trev even more than she already had—and that was as unacceptable to her as jumping off the roof. He was a good man. He didn't deserve another betrayal.

Kait was desperately worried and desperately frightened. *Did she dare come forward with the truth of who she was?*

Kait tried to imagine his reaction. She tried to imagine him smiling in relief, pulling her into his arms, holding her tenderly and telling her that he loved her, Kait, and that he always would. In this scenario, he quickly divorced her sister and the two of them married, had more children, and lived happily ever after.

Kait was ready to throw up.

Who was she fooling? He was going to be very angry when he found out she was a little actress and a part of Lana's grander scheme. Kait backed up. No, Trev would be furious, enraged.

Kait knew him well enough to know that.

In fact, he was going to despise her, as much as he despised Lana; he might assume her to be exactly like her twin.

And would he be very wrong? Somehow, the attempt to help her sister in a dangerous time of need had seriously backfired. Originally, Kait had been afraid for Lana, and she had wanted to help in any way that she could—now, she wished she had never agreed to masquerade as her, she wished she could go back in time and relive the past. By agreeing to cover for Lana, she had fallen in love with Marni and maybe even Trev, and if Trev ever learned the truth, he was going to hate her.

If he ever learned the truth?

Kait realized she had grave reservations now about ever telling him what had happened. Now, she was terrified that he would hate her forever for her deception. Lana had blithely said that he would eventually forgive her, but Kait knew she had been merely placating her in order to have Kait remain in her place.

Kait felt trapped. She was trapped in Lana's lie, only now, it had become her own. And the lie had taken on a life of its own, becoming bigger, deadlier, a trap from which she could not escape. And Trev Coleman did not deserve any more lies.

She cringed inwardly. And she knew, without a doubt, that she had to tell him now, before the lie got out of hand. Before her life came to a place where she was knocking on his door and introducing herself for the very first time *after* his divorce. Before the lie became a secret that must never be revealed . . .

What if she lost him?

Kait was sick. She had already lost him, hadn't she? She should have told Trev last night who she really was, before they'd had full-fledged relations. Now, there was no way out. Now, he was going to hate her when he found out the truth— if he ever did. And if he didn't, she would live a lie for the rest of her life, and hate herself forever because of it.

He chose that moment to step out of the walk-in closet, in his jeans, paddock boots, and a black turtleneck sweater. His eyes moved instantly to her. They were hooded, wary, and cold.

Kait froze. This should be a lovers' morning, a time of warm smiles, kisses, touches, of shared glances and happiness. But she couldn't smile, and neither, it seemed, could he.

He nodded curtly and turned toward the door.

What was going on? "Trev!" Kait leapt from the bed. Too late, she realized she had nothing on, worse, she didn't know what she was doing, only that she had to speak with him now—after last night, she desperately wanted some kind of reassurance from him, which was foolish in itself.

He shifted, his eyes moving over her slim, nude body.

Kait whipped the quilt off the bed, no easy task as it was custom-made and very heavy. Too late, she knew that Lana would never be modest. But he didn't seem to notice her odd behavior. "Good morning," she whispered uneasily. The look in his eyes scared her now completely. Why was he so cold? As if last night meant nothing?

"Do you want to speak to me?" he asked, glancing at his watch, as if now that the spectacular and impossibly sensual night was over he had no time to waste on her.

And it hurt. It felt like an arrow to the heart, when it shouldn't—because he thought her to be Lana. "Have I done something?" she managed cautiously. Why was he behaving as if last night had never happened?

He glanced up, his gaze impossible to read. "I don't know. You tell me?"

She gripped the quilt so hard that her fingers ached. Was this a new game, of cat and mouse? Or was she reading something into his words out of her guilt and fear? "I thought—I thought that maybe, since last night, we . . ." She had to stop. "We" what? Lana had no intention of reconciling, and she no longer wanted her sister to do so either. But had he changed his mind about the divorce?

And surely, for now, there could be a truce, a partnership, even friendship.

His eyes widened mockingly. "You thought what? That we'd make up and live happily ever after? It was just sex, for God's sake. Good sex, I'll admit that, but let's not paint the kettle white, okay? I want to have breakfast with Marni." He turned, striding across the room.

Kait was stunned. And while she was relieved that his feelings for Lana hadn't changed, she was also dismayed. After all, she, Kait, had been in bed with him all night, worshiping his body, giving him every ounce of her love. She ran after him, dragging the huge quilt and stumbling over it. With one hand, she grabbed his wrist, with the other, she managed to keep the quilt covering the front of her body. "I can't believe you're behaving this way," she cried. Last night, he had touched and held her as if he actually loved her, too.

Or was she so inexperienced that she couldn't tell the difference between raw sex and lovemaking?

"What way? Oh, wait, you mean you can't believe you don't have your hooks in me? Well, think again, because you don't." His smile was mirthless.

Kait was speechless. She finally managed a coherent sentence. "No. I thought that maybe we could be friends now."

He stared grimly at her. It was a long moment before he

spoke. "We slept together. Big deal. It wasn't the first time and it probably won't be the last. I am not going to trust you—and since when did you decide you want to be my friend?"

Kait recoiled, blinking through her rising tears. Yes, the task ahead of her was now impossible. They would never be friends—or anything more. "I don't want to fight anymore," she whispered roughly. She found a core of inner strength then. "I will not fight with you, Trev."

"I don't want to fight anymore either. I only want to divorce." He stared coldly at her.

It hurt. Even if she wasn't Lana, because he was speaking to her, Kait, the woman he had just made love to all night. But it hadn't been lovemaking. He had said so himself. It had been sex. Good sex—not even great sex. "We have to talk," she said hoarsely.

"We do? Now what could you possibly have to say to me, now, after last night?" One dark brow lifted.

This was it. She simply had to tell him that she was Lana's twin and covering for her. It was that, or get in so deep that there was no way out, not ever. But what about Marni?

Hadn't she decided to continue her charade for Marni's ultimate protection?

And then it struck her, hard. He was going to hate her even more than he hated Lana for such a monstrous deception on her part.

"Let me guess. You've changed. You're no longer a calculating, selfish bitch. Six years of lies and adultery don't count. You've seen the light! Somehow, you've become a different woman—kind, vulnerable, honest. A woman who's been thoroughly miscast and is now being thoroughly misjudged?" His gaze narrowed. "How am I doing?"

Did he know after all? And was that why he was so angry with her? Kait stared, forgetting to breathe—he stared back, as motionless as she.

She finally said, unsteadily, "I hope I have changed. I think I have. I regret—"

"You know what?" he said sharply, cutting her off. "I am so tired of the bullshit, of the games. I am tired of *your* games. I have no idea why you started this one, but this time, I've really had it." He gripped the door and their gazes locked—and Kait knew she wasn't ever going to be able to tell him the truth. "Last night was good, but as far as I'm concerned, it was good-bye." He stalked out, slamming the door in her face.

He knows, a tiny voice whispered tauntingly in her head.

He can't know, because he would have said something, the different, stronger voice answered, more firmly.

Kait wasn't sure that it mattered. She had never felt so miserable, so crushed, and somehow she had gotten her heart broken after all.

By a man who hadn't ever loved her in the first place—by a man who didn't even know she existed.

Trev was not in the kitchen by the time Kait came downstairs, clad in her new faded Levi's, a baby-blue cotton pullover, and polished paddock boots. Sam was blending up one of her healthy drinks, this concoction pink. Marni was fooling around with Frosted Flakes, and Elizabeth stood by the sink, a piece of buttered toast in her hand. Marni shrieked with pleasure as Kait walked into the bright, airy kitchen. "Mommy, Mommy! You slept late! Like before! Daddy said not to disturb you," she cried.

Kait flushed, relieved that Trev was not present. She simply could not bear his hostility now. "Hi, sweetie," she said, hurrying over to kiss her niece's baby-soft cheek. She felt eyes upon her, and looked up to see Elizabeth's cool regard. Instantly, Kait knew that Elizabeth was fully aware of what had happened last night.

She felt her color increase. Had Elizabeth heard them in the living room? Or worse, had she heard them in the bedroom? And why the hell did she have to look so miffed and disapproving? What did it matter to her if Trev was sleeping with his wife?

Except, of course, Kait was not his wife.

Guilt and depression overcame her.

Kait forced a smile. "Good morning. It looks like snow."

"It never snows this early in the year. We're in Virginia—not Colorado," Elizabeth said, turning away.

Kait walked over to the coffeemaker. Sam had her back to her still, blending her drink yet again. She poured a coffee, added whole milk, and turned. "I am ready for a truce, Elizabeth," she said.

Elizabeth shut off the faucet, whirling. "I beg your pardon?"

"I want to lay the past to rest. I apologize for my sins—every single one of them. I want to start over."

Elizabeth stared.

Sam had turned off the blender. Clad in black leather pants, her black leather vest, and a white T-shirt, she turned and stared. She was wearing a rope cuff on one wrist, a beaded bracelet with a dangling cross on the other wrist. A huge silence fell over the room.

"What sins?" Marni demanded, sliding out of her chair. "Mommy, have you sinned?"

Kait smiled gently at her. "Honey, it's just a way of speaking. No, I haven't sinned. But I've made mistakes, and now I am apologizing—for every single one."

Elizabeth hadn't moved. She said, "You're still taking milk in your coffee. You're wearing jeans. And now this—this odd proposal." Clearly, she was almost but not quite speechless.

"Are you religious, Elizabeth?"

She started. "You know very well that I go to a Lutheran church every Sunday."

"Then you also know that it is hardly godly to refuse the kind of apology I've just made."

Elizabeth nodded stiffly. "You win, Lana."

"This isn't about winning. This is about forgiveness."

Elizabeth turned away.

Kait sipped her coffee and met Sam's baleful stare. "You're still angry with me?"

Sam nodded, but she seemed completely in control of her

anger. In fact, she seemed more wary than mad. "You told Dad, and Uncle Rafe."

"I did what I had to do, Sam. Your welfare is more important than keeping a secret—one which is illegal and wrong."

Sam folded her arms over her breasts. "My welfare," she said grimly. "Are you still going to lend me that dress?"

Kait hesitated. That dress was stained and it now needed a dry cleaning. "Yes. When do you need it by?"

"Saturday," she said. "Gina's party is Saturday."

Tomorrow was Saturday. "I'll take it to the cleaners when I drop Marni off at school." She would pay anything for overnight service.

Sam's tight expression eased. "Really? You're really going to lend it to me?"

Kait nodded. She felt her own face soften. "You will be beautiful in it. Wait till Trev sees." Then she felt ill all over again.

Sam became curt. "I don't care what he thinks." She grabbed her juice and strode away.

Kait stared after her. How long would it take Sam to forgive Trev for striking her?

Marni suddenly ran after her sister. "Sammy! Wait! You forgot to give me the Magic cards!"

When she was gone, Elizabeth spoke. "Why are you lending her that dress? Why did you apologize to me?"

Kait sighed. "She'll be lovely in that dress."

"I know what you're up to. Trev knows too. You think to change his mind about the divorce, don't you?"

"No, I don't." Kait walked over to the refrigerator.

Elizabeth followed. "Well, it won't work. This time, he's through."

"Great. I'm glad to see you're so happy that the man you consider a son is getting a divorce." She took out a jar of peanut butter and one of jam.

"You're the worst thing that ever happened to him, and I will do anything—*anything*—to make sure he is finally free of you."

Kait stiffened. There had been venom dripping in Elizabeth's tone. Slowly she turned to face her.

"I mean it," Elizabeth said.

And Kait wondered if Elizabeth hated Lana enough to want her dead.

Marni was in school, and the beautiful black Donna Karan dress was at the cleaners. Kait had gone to the grocery store, desperate for Pepperidge Farm Milano cookies, and then to a drugstore for some cosmetics—she wanted to buy her favorite Maybelline mascara and Pantene shampoo. After doing her errands, on impulse, she'd gone back to the mall. There, she had found Sam a beautiful patchwork leather jacket, one that seemed to suit her somewhat rebellious and bohemian style perfectly. It was now lunchtime—in another hour she could pick Marni up to bring her home.

Kait glanced around a food court, debating between McDonald's and pizza and wondering what she might buy Marni before leaving the mall. As it was Friday, the mall was rather busy, far more so than it had been the other day. Pizza Hut won, and she veered toward the counter.

Then she saw Sam.

Kait halted in her tracks, more than surprised, because she had assumed that Sam was in school all day. She stared, but there was no mistaking the tall, lanky blonde with the long, fine hair in the black leather pants and vest. It was Sam, all right, and she was with a boy.

Kait ducked behind a column.

They had their backs to her. They were standing between the Pizza Hut and McDonald's, chatting. Kait wanted to assume that the boy was Gabe Jenkins—his hair was dark, like Gabe's in the photographs—but it was hard to say. He was very tall for a sixteen-year-old—he was an inch or two shy of six feet, she supposed.

Sam half turned, but so did he. The boy grabbed her and they kissed. It quickly became a long and lingering embrace. Kait had to look away. Anyone who kissed like that could not be a virgin. She was more than uncomfortable—she was concerned.

She hoped they were using birth control.

"See ya!" Sam's happy voice rang out.

Kait peeked around the corner and saw Sam fully flushed and smiling and oh-so-happy. The boy—no, the young man—was definitely Gabe Jenkins. He was also smiling, and in person he had too much sex appeal for someone his age. But there was also something disturbing about him— something that she had not seen in the photos.

At first she couldn't define what was bothering her. But then she knew. It was trouble with a capital *T,* just as Trev had claimed.

Gabe's smile faded. He looked dark and sulky standing there, staring after Sam. He also looked too old for her— Kait had assumed they were the same age, but this boy had to be seventeen or eighteen.

Kait ducked back behind the pillar as Sam hurried past. Was she going back to school? Should Kait follow her—and ask her why she wasn't on campus? Or should she leave well enough alone?

Maybe she didn't have any more classes. It was Friday, after all.

The last thing Kait wished to do was violate Sam's trust again. Stumbling across her and Gabe had been a coincidence, but Sam might not see it that way.

Kait turned and saw Gabe disappearing behind the McDonald's counter and then duck into a back room. She hesitated, realizing he must work at McDonald's. A few moments later she saw him step out behind the counter, wearing an employee uniform.

Her mind raced. She did not want to cause any more discord, not in the family and not with Sam, but Sam had had a gun. That was serious business, indeed. This seemed to be a golden opportunity to check out Gabe, more subjectively than Trev ever had. And she was doing so only because she cared. She still thought that Sam had lied to protect Gabe and that the gun was really his, not hers. If Gabe was bad news, she wanted to find that out, and there was no time like the present.

She walked over to the counter.

He looked up, not smiling. He had fair skin and blue eyes. His hair was jet black and wavy and far too long for her personal taste. "Can I help—?" He stopped. "Get the hell away from me!"

Kait recoiled. "What?"

He leaned on the counter, his eyes wide, his cheeks flushed. "Get away from me—before Sam sees us!"

Kait was stunned. *"Us?"*

Anger distorted his handsome face. "I said get out of here, Mrs. Coleman." He spat out her name. She saw hatred in his eyes as well as rage. And something else: fear.

Lana knew Gabe Jenkins. What did this mean? What could it mean? "I need to talk to you," Kait said, as calmly as possible. But she was reeling. Surely "us" did not mean "us" in the biblical sense. After all, Gabe Jenkins was in high school. He wasn't a boy, but he wasn't a man either.

"Well, I'm not talking to you," he snarled.

"Sam's gone. Did she go back to school?"

He cursed. He looked around, said, "Cover for me," to another employee, and he pushed out through the swinging door of the counter. Kait wound up following him over to the column where she had been hiding. He faced her, hands on his hips, fists clenched. "I told you to never come near me again!" he cried.

It was hard to think, to breathe. "This is the last time," she assured him.

He looked as if he didn't believe her. "I'm working," he spat. "I'm not partying with you!"

Oh, dear God. Kait looked at him and was afraid of whatever truth he hid. It couldn't possibly be what she was thinking.

But Lana had done something to make this boy hate her—and fear her. Kait wet her lips. "This isn't about a party."

His face collapsed, flooding with relief.

It was hard to stand up straight, to remain calm, composed, assertive. "I found the gun, Gabe."

His head came up. His eyes were wild. "I know. Sam told me. She tells me everything."

"Do you love her?" The question was impulsive—this wasn't why she had approached him.

"Like you give a damn?" He was incredulous.

"I don't like her protecting you. I don't think much of a boy—a man—who hides behind a woman's skirts."

"I don't hide, not behind anyone, not from anyone," he said harshly. "What do you want? Why are you really here?" Fear flared in his blue eyes again.

"I want to know if the gun is yours," she said.

"Are you nuts? This is bullshit," he was shouting. Then he leaned close, and he was suddenly intimidating. "If you think you can lure me off somewhere and have some fun, you're wrong!"

Kait flinched. Was that what had happened? Surely Lana, her sister, hadn't seduced a seventeen- or eighteen-year-old boy?

"I've been sick for weeks," he said fiercely. "I hate myself more than I hate you! At first I tried blaming it on the beer and wine. But I've been drinking since I was twelve. I can hold my liquor! You're hot for an old woman, really hot, but I love Sam, and now you're going to hold this over my head forever! Aren't you?" he asked desperately. *"What do you really want?"*

Kait was ill. *Her sister had seduced Gabe Jenkins.* "I'm sorry," she whispered. "Is the gun yours?"

"No," he said. "And you know it. You know damn well whose gun it is, so I don't understand any of this. This is some kind of new game, isn't it? I have to go." He started to leave.

Kait gripped his arm. "What do you mean, I know whose gun it is?"

He gave her another incredulous look, yanked free, and rushed away.

Kait had a very bad feeling, worse, she remained ill at heart. Lana had seduced Sam's boyfriend. Why would she do such a thing? And how could she do such a thing? And in that moment, Kait was struck by a searing comprehension: Lana hadn't changed.

The teen who had stolen other girls' boyfriends and laughed about it had become a woman who took lovers as she chose—married, unmarried, boys as well as men. The teen who had lied to her parents in order to do as she chose now lied to her husband and family for the same selfish ends. Kait had spent her entire youth trying not to see the bad in Lana, trying to believe in what had to be good. Now, staring after Gabe Jenkins, after all that had happened at Fox Hollow, her belief in her sister collapsed.

It more than collapsed; it vanished into thin air.

She slowly bent and picked up the shopping bag filled with her Milanos, the drugstore items, and Sam's wild leather jacket. It was time to go get Marni.

It was déjà vu.

"Look, Mommy, the police are here!" Marni was delighted as Kait parked the Porsche. "Is it Uncle Rafe?"

Kait wet her lips, about to reply, when Trev and Rafe stepped out of the house and onto the veranda. Both men looked very grim. "Why, he's here," she said as gaily as possible. But she remained thoroughly shaken—and heartbroken. No amount of mental debate could convince her that her twin sister had any redeeming qualities. She had run out of excuses to make for Lana. She didn't even want to hear her side of the story.

Kait slowly got out of the car. Sadness and depression had made her feel old and heavy. Marni climbed eagerly out of her side and Kait reached into the back for her shopping bag. She realized she was also numb. Not turning, she heard Marni running up to the house, calling for Trev and her uncle, and a moment later she heard her happy squeals. Kait somehow slammed the driver's door closed—the effort to do so, huge—and turned, sick with trepidation.

Trev was saying, "Elizabeth just baked some brownies, sweetheart. Go inside."

Marni ran off. The two men were alone on the porch. And clearly, they were waiting for her. Her heart stopped. They were waiting for her for a reason. And whatever that reason was, it wasn't going to be pleasant. It wasn't going to be good news.

Kait was dry. She wished for a glass of water. She slowly started up the path and then up the house's front steps, filled with dread. She had reached her absolute limit—she knew she could not handle anything more.

Rafe was staring at her as if she were a convicted ax murderer. But it was Trev who made her stumble. His eyes were dark with anger.

"Trev?" she heard herself say, a whisper. What did he now think she had done?

He seized her wrist. "I told you this morning. *I've had it with your games.*"

He was furious. He was also upset. She looked from his eyes to Rafe's. His look was hardly any better. "Wh-what?" Had they figured out that she was Kait London after all?

Rafe stepped between them, forcing Trev to release her wrist. "Ran a check on Sam's gun," he remarked, with relish.

And Kait knew an ax was about to fall. She knew it was Lana's head that was supposed to roll. She knew her own head would roll instead.

"An' guess what I found? A Mrs. Trevor Coleman purchased the gun in Halifax—six years ago."

Kait reeled.

He shoved his face against hers. "You got a permit to carry a weapon . . . Mrs. Coleman?"

THIRTEEN

Kait felt weak in the knees. Rafe's words were like a severe blow, one knocking the air from her lungs. *The gun was Lana's.* Despite the fact that someone had threatened both Lana and Marni, Kait was stunned. Suddenly she recalled Sam's surprise when she'd been asking questions about the gun. And now Gabe's comment that she knew whose gun it was made sense. She realized that Sam must have taken the gun, the way she had taken the sweaters and the jacket.

But Lana had had the gun since early in her marriage. Why?

"How could you do this?"

Kait flinched and looked up at Trev.

"Bring a gun into the house, not telling me. And why?" He stared. "Why the hell would you buy a gun right after we were married?"

Kait was speechless. She simply had no idea.

People bought guns—kept guns—for a reason. The usual reason was for protection. Had Lana felt, even six years ago, that she needed protection? And why?

Kait didn't like her thoughts now.

"I can see you trying to come up with an answer," Trev snapped. *"Why the hell did you bring a gun into my home, Goddamn it? What the hell is going on?"*

He was furiously angry with her. Kait cringed. His reaction was out of proportion to her—Lana's—crime, and she didn't have to be a psychologist to know that he was using the gun as an excuse to express all of the anger he harbored against her. In fact, since they had spent the night together, he seemed angrier than ever. She had to think, and fast. But no coherent excuse came to mind. "Trev, it's not what you think. The gun was for self-protection." She touched his sleeve, quite certain he would never buy such a pathetic excuse.

He jerked away. His cold eyes held hers, however. "Why would you think you needed to protect yourself? We live in one of the safest counties in Virginia! The Skerrit County population is under five thousand, and we have one of the lowest violent crime rates in the country!"

She bit her lip, consumed with guilt for telling yet another lie. "It was for all those times when you travel, when I'm here alone with the girls."

"Half the time you come with me so you can show Pride," he said sharply. "In fact, now that I think about it, you're on the road more than I am. Can't you do better than that?" He was sarcastic now.

She shook her head in negation, suddenly so tired of all the lies and the accompanying burden of guilt. But if this man was furious over the deception of her having had a gun for so many years behind his back, he would be even more enraged over the real deception she was participating in— and over her posing as Lana even while he touched every inch of her body and made love to her. Kait wished her mind would stop wandering back to the events of last night. "Can't we let it go?"

His eyes narrowed. "Don't tell me you've run out of lies?"

Their gazes collided. She inhaled sharply. In that simple moment, she had the striking feeling that he knew she wasn't Lana and his words were about her masquerade. Suddenly she was cold—chilled to the bone. If this man already knew the truth, it would explain his fury and hatred.

Kait backed up, horrified. *But surely he hadn't made love to her all night while knowing she was someone other than his wife?* She could not meet his eyes now. It was only Friday—she had an entire weekend to survive. Kait didn't know if she could do it—not after last night. After being in his arms with such passion, she was no longer capable of parrying with him, or holding up her end of this terrible deception. Every time she met his gaze, inwardly she cringed. "I'm sorry about the gun. You're right. I should have asked your permission before buying it."

Somehow, he heard her. The look he gave her was a skeptical one. "Really? Since when do you ask my permission for anything?" Then he was looming over her. "Sam could have gotten in terrible trouble because of you and that gun. If something had happened to her, I would never forgive you."

Kait wouldn't have forgiven Lana—or herself—either.

Trev was now disgusted. He turned and slammed into the house.

Leaving her alone with Rafe Coleman. Kait slowly turned to face him, then looked away from his careful and searching look. "Are you going to arrest me?"

"Possession of a firearm without a permit is only a misdemeanor." He smiled, without any mirth whatsoever. "But selling or dealing arms to a minor is another thing, sweetheart."

"Dealing arms to a minor?" Kait gasped.

He was enjoying himself. "That's a felony."

"Sam took the gun without my knowledge and you know it!" Kait cried.

His put his hands on his hips. "You know what I think?" he asked, but it wasn't a question. "I think you'd better turn over a new leaf, and fast. But then again, that won't change the past, now, will it?"

Kait hugged herself. "What have I ever done to make you hate me so?" She dared to whisper, because she felt certain she knew. He had been another one of Lana's sexual targets, although she had no doubt that this man would have turned Lana down in one second flat or sooner.

But she was wrong.

He started. Then he was in her face. "Are you kidding

me? My brother comes home with the cheating bitch of the century, and you have to ask? You been fucking around behind his back for six years—no, in his face! Worse, you've done nothing but hurt him, Sam, and your own daughter! Do you think I'm some redneck oaf? I know the truth, baby, the entire truth." He was livid with his rage.

"I have to go," Kait cried, whirling—because she simply did not have the courage to hear any more.

He gripped her wrist and spun her back around. "We both know that this entire marriage was a setup."

"What?" she gasped.

"You married him for his money—his position—for legitimacy. This was a setup from the day you first appeared in his life. In fact, I get the feeling you knew where he'd be that day—and that you were there, waiting for him."

"No," she whispered, praying he was wrong.

Rafe gripped her chin and tilted it up, frightening her with the strength of his grip and the ugly look in his eyes. "I'm on the inside track, and I'm bringing you down, baby. You can count on it." He released her.

Kait backed away, breathless and trying not to tremble.

He saluted her with the tip of one finger to his wide-brimmed hat, and it was mocking. He strode out.

Kait stared. And when her brain began to function, she thought about the lunch Trev had never shown up to, the one six or seven years ago, the one where she'd planned to ask to use Fox Hollow for her client's charity event. But he had never shown up and they had never met.

Kait tried to think.

It had been so long ago.

When was the last time she and Lana had been in contact?

Kait was grim. By her best recollection, it had also been six or seven years ago, but whether it was six months or so before her marriage to Trev Coleman, she simply didn't know. But it might have been longer than that or less than that—she couldn't be certain. What she did recall was that Lana had been in New York and they'd actually had dinner together. It had been one of her brief, breezy, pop-in visits, with lots of charm and very little substance. At the time, Lana had been living in Miami. What Kait did remember was getting her call out of the blue and being thrilled to be able to see her sister.

That stopped her racing brain right in its tracks.

Hadn't it always been that way with her and her sister? Lana appearing at her bedroom door when they were kids, quite unexpectedly and with a grin, as if it were the most natural thing in the world, inviting her to the mall or for a pizza. But it wasn't natural, because Lana was always busy with her friends, with her sports, with boys.

And from the moment they had gone off to different colleges, it had been even more of the same thing. No word for months, and a sudden call or an out-of-the blue visit, with Kait experiencing sheer delight merely at being with her sister again, with Kait hanging on to every word and detail of her sister's exciting life.

Kait was grim. She suddenly felt so detached from the past, as if she were an observer watching those old memories on a played-back tape, and she felt sorry for herself.

Had she been that desperate for her twin's attention?

After the past few days at Fox Hollow, Kait no longer felt like the same person. In fact, she was sad, but wary and cautious now.

Kait was disturbed. She hoped Rafe Coleman was very wrong about Lana seeking Trev out after already knowing who he was. Instinct propelled her now. Kait decided she'd use Trev's desktop computer later and check her own on-line calendar. She was very organized, and she would find out the last time she had seen her sister in New York for that dinner. She also was curious about the exact date of the lunch Trev had never shown up for.

While she was at it, she would find out their wedding date, too.

She was persona non grata now. Kait was in disbelief. She stood in the living room, a scotch in hand—yes, a scotch—trying to stop shaking like a leaf. Trev had appeared in the foyer. As he wore a suit and tie, it was obvious that he was going out.

She closed her eyes, afraid of where he was going—and stunned that after the intimacy they had shared, he would not invite her to join him. But mostly, her mind had reduced itself to a single litany—what kind of trouble was Lana really in?

Rafe Coleman was a cop. Rafe Coleman was after her sister, big time. He looked like the kind of man who rarely failed at anything he set his mind to. To state that he intended to bring her sister down either meant that he intended to see her out of Fox Hollow on her ass, or it meant that he intended to send her to jail. Kait had the horrible feeling that he had meant the latter. He had also said that he knew the entire truth. Somehow, Kait felt certain he was not referring to the fact that she was Kait and not Lana.

So what had he meant? What did he know? Did he intend to send Lana to jail?

Rafe also claimed that Lana's marriage to Trev was a setup. What did that mean? A setup for what, exactly? A setup to become a rich and wealthy wife?

Kait didn't know what to think, except that the county sheriff was after her sister, and nothing would stop him, as far as she could see.

Her instincts warred with one another—she wanted to protect Lana from Rafe Coleman, but she also wanted to protect Trev and the girls from any fallout involving her sister and their deception.

And she finally came to one striking conclusion—Lana's life had not been ordinary, and whatever she was mixed up in, it wasn't simple or uncomplicated either. Kait was afraid, but she was also angry at her sister for inflicting her trouble on the family—and on her twin.

Kait realized that Trev's footsteps had stopped. She opened her eyes and found him regarding her, the tight, angry expression from earlier gone. And for one moment, as their gazes met, she saw confusion and bewilderment and something very, very serious there on his features, there in his eyes.

And the moment she met his gaze, his expression hardened, closed.

Clutching the scotch—which she truly hated, Kait came forward. "Out to dinner?" She tried to make her tone light, but it came out as a hoarse and undignified croak instead. She felt certain his intention was to now avoid her.

He nodded. "That's right."

Oh, how this was hurting her now—especially after last night. "Let me guess." She wanted to be pleasant—how bitter her tone sounded to her own ears, instead. "Alicia and John? Mitch and Sara?"

He eyed her. "Do you care?"

She cradled the scotch to her breasts. "Yes," she whispered, "I do."

She saw him start—she realized she had genuinely thrown him off balance. It crossed her mind that she did have, after all, some power over him—that she might try to use it, dissuade him from going, so they could spend the evening together.

Dangerous images flooded her mind.

In each and every one of them, they were passionately entwined.

How could she control her own sexual attraction for this man? And that was *all* it was. It was physical, nothing more.

He made a disparaging sound. "It's a little late for that, don't you think?"

She swallowed, turned, set the scotch down. Then she slowly—carefully, approached. "I am filled with regrets," she said unsteadily. "Trev . . . I am so sorry about everything."

He didn't move. Then, "Why are you even bothering?"

"Because I don't think it can ever be too late," she said, and as she spoke, a terrible plot appeared in her mind. He didn't ever have to know about the switch. Lana could return and divorce him, and later, when things had cooled down, she, Kait, could appear in his life. Kait was horrified with her own sudden urge to save herself as far as Trev Coleman was concerned. With her sudden urge to save them.

She reminded herself that there was no "them." And she was not a liar except in this one instance—lying was wrong. She hated lying, and she hated lying to him. Kait had to face the fact that after all was revealed, she would lose any chance of a friendship with this man. But he was going to have to learn about the switch. She wished she had never deceived him in the first place.

Trev seemed incapable of moving. "This is about last night, isn't it?"

She hesitated. He might believe her to be Lana, and she might be trapped for now in a lie that had become as much her own as her sister's, but she would be herself. She wouldn't even attempt to be like Lana now. "Yes . . . and no. It's about everything. But . . . last night was special."

And he threw back his head and laughed. "You can do better than that!" he exclaimed. Then he moved closer to her. She tensed as he said, "Last night meant nothing, Lana, nothing. It was raw sex, pure and simple. Do not keep throwing it in my face!"

She didn't move away from him, bewildered. Did he protest overmuch? She certainly wasn't throwing anything in his face. "If it wasn't special for you, it was for me. I've never been with anyone like that."

"Is this a bad joke?" he demanded.

She ignored that. "Why not spend the evening here?" The words just popped out. She held his gaze and he couldn't seem to look away. "I can whip up some gourmet sandwiches, or we can order a pizza and crack a great bottle of wine and . . . we can talk."

"Talk?" He was incredulous. "Since when have we ever talked, Lana? Our entire relationship was always about sex—sex and money. I'm late. Don't bother waiting up—not that you ever do." He walked out.

Kait had failed. Crushed, she moved to the window and watched him get into his Dodge.

"You really love him, don't you?" Sam said softly, with surprise.

Kait turned. "I . . . yes."

Sam stared. Then, hesitantly, "Thanks for the jacket. I . . . I really like it."

That lifted Kait's spirits. Sam hadn't been home earlier, and she had left the jacket in a gift box with a pretty card on her bed. "It so suits you."

"Why? Why are you acting this way?" Sam asked. She stood on the threshold, more in the foyer than the living room, and made no move to come any closer.

"People change," Kait said with a shrug. She had to glance wistfully out the window. The big Dodge was gone.

"I don't think so," Sam said.

Kait stiffened, glancing at her. "What do you mean?"

"Marni says you're a new mommy. I think she's right."

Kait managed a smile, while her heart began to beat hard. "I am a new mommy. I've changed. Call it an early midlife crisis if you will, but I woke up one morning and realized I didn't like myself."

Sam shook her head. "That's not it."

There was dread, fear. "It's not?"

"You're not her, are you? Lana never looked at my father the way that you do. You're not Lana. You're someone else," Sam said, pale.

Kait felt her knees buckle. Was she going to faint?

"Who are you?" Sam whispered, her eyes wide.

It was half past ten. Kait was not waiting for Trev to return—but she was sitting on the veranda outside, a coffee mug and a bag of Milanos by her side. The mug and the cookie bag were empty. It was a beautiful, star-studded night, but Kait couldn't appreciate it; and it was cold. Kait had borrowed one of Sam's jackets, a blue parka that she claimed she hated and never wore.

Kait knew why—it simply wasn't trendy or funky or chic.

She had insisted to Sam that she was Lana, that she'd had a huge awakening, that it was part of an early midlife crisis. But Sam hadn't said anything, and Kait knew she didn't believe her.

The clock was ticking now.

She had only been at Fox Hollow for five days, and both Sam and Marni knew she wasn't Lana. Sometimes, she thought that Trev knew it, too. At other times, like a few hours ago when he had been on his way out, she was certain that he didn't know. Besides, there was simply no reason for him not to demand what she was doing and who she was if he did know about her deception.

Kait's cell phone also lay by the bag of cookies. She glanced at it, but as she hadn't heard it ring, she knew there were no messages. She knew that she wouldn't hear from Lana until Lana was on her way back to Fox Hollow. *Had Lana done something illegal?*

The question haunted Kait. And so did another one. *Was she a conspirator now? An accomplice, an accessory, whatever the legal term was?*

How had she ever gotten into this mess?

This had been the one time in her life that Kait should have said no when Lana had asked her to cover for her. But it was too late for pity and regrets, and at least, thus far, no one had come forward to threaten Marni again.

Kait prayed that Lana was not using Marni to manipulate her. She hated even thinking it, but she had an awful feeling that Lana knew that Marni was her weakness, and that she would say anything to get Kait to remain in place.

Kait was angry, frustrated, and sad. She knew that Lana hadn't told her everything—but now she had the terrible idea that Lana was somehow lying to her as well as everyone else.

And if Rafe intended to put Lana in jail, could she wind up convicted in Lana's place?

Kait hugged her jeans-clad knees to her chest. She tried to reassure herself that this entire mess could be simply and easily straightened out. But her efforts failed, because until she knew everything, it was like being a blind man trapped in a house with a stalker.

Remembering her on-line calendar, Kait decided that this was as good a time as any to check it. She had hours in which to do so—it would only take a few minutes. She stood brushing off her jeans when a car's engine roared to life. Kait started and glanced automatically in the direction of the noise, which was the first big barn.

Which meant it was Max Zara's old Toyota.

Kait glanced at her watch. It was twenty to ten now. Where was Max going? And, more important, why?

The mystery of Max Zara had just deepened. Kait watched the Toyota reverse and turn in order to go down the driveway.

Then, on impulse, she leapt up and ran to the Porsche. She slid in, grabbed the keys, which were under the seat, and waited another moment for the Toyota to get farther away. She turned on the ignition, but not the headlights. She felt certain she could navigate the driveway without them now.

A moment later she was at the end of the drive, and she saw Max's taillights disappearing around a curve on the country road as it wound to the right, toward Three Falls. When he was gone, Kait flicked on her beams and turned right, following him.

It was time to get to the bottom of the question of who was Max Zara.

Kait parked on a side street that bisected the divided highway. A diner was on one side of the strip, the first in a short section of commercial stores. Vacant property was on the other side. As it was so late out, only the diner was open, and a dozen cars were in its parking lot. One of those cars was Max Zara's Toyota. A black-and-white Chevy Blazer was also in the lot.

Kait had turned off the ignition, and now she inhaled, certain that the police vehicle belonged to Rafe Coleman. It was just a gut feeling, but one she intended to quickly verify.

She stepped out of the Porsche, began to lock it, and operating on instinct, changed her mind. Zara hadn't realized he was being followed; she had kept such a distance between them that she had been lucky not to lose him. Twice, she had turned off her headlights the moment she turned a corner when she'd glimpsed his taillights ahead in the distance. Fortunately, Northwoods Road ended at the two-lane highway, and the strip began a mile later. It hadn't been hard to guess that he'd take the highway in the direction of Three Falls.

There was no traffic on the highway, much less the side street, and Kait brazenly crossed it. In the parking lot she slowed her pace, keeping close to a Ford pickup and a commercial hauler. The diner had a huge storefront window, and it was fully illuminated inside; Kait could see in as clearly as if it were day. It took her a few seconds to realize that Max Zara was sitting in a booth by the window—and that she had been right. The police car was Rafe Coleman's, because he sat opposite Zara.

She shrank against the side of the building, her heart now feeling as if it were wedged in her throat. What was going on? Why was Max Zara having coffee and pie with Rafe Coleman?

Max Zara was no ordinary citizen.

Jesus! Was Max Zara a cop?

Kait's mind spun; she didn't know what to think. But Rafe Coleman wasn't going to be palling around with a stable boy, now, was he? And they had both stated, independently, that they wished to bring Lana down. Kait began to shake. She peered around the corner of the tan brick wall, through the window, and back into the diner. Both men had coffees in front of them. Coleman was digging into a bowl of ice cream. If there was tension present, she couldn't discern it. Both men seemed relaxed and comfortable with one another. As they ate, they were talking. She ducked out of sight.

What the hell was going on?

Kait closed her eyes briefly, knowing beyond a doubt that she was way out of her league. Then she took another peek into the diner again.

Zara was leaning forward and speaking with urgency. Rafe was sitting almost slumped against his side of the both, listening. Eventually Rafe shook his head.

She shrank back against the wall. That did it. Kait felt certain that these men were working together. And that made Max a cop. Was he undercover? Had she watched too much

TV? It certainly seemed as if he were. In any case, this was a terrible turn of events as far as Lana was concerned.

She turned and stared grimly at Zara's pickup. Had he locked it?

Kait didn't bother to engage in a mental debate. He had parked almost in front of the diner's window, in the first line of spaces. Rafe had parked by the highway, in the last line of spots. One other line of cars took up the middle of the lot. There was nothing more to be gained by peering through the window at the two men. Kait ran past three cars and ducked down by Max Zara's pickup, right by the driver's side door.

She slithered up it, glanced at the diner's front window, but couldn't see their booth now. Which was just as well, she thought grimly. She tried the door—it was unlocked.

Kait dove over the driver's seat and seized the door of the dashboard compartment. It was locked. This time, she cursed aloud.

She climbed in, but the seats were immaculate except for a half-eaten Snickers bar. No papers, no clues, no nothing. She dug her hand into the pocket on the passenger door, and came up with nothing. In the pocket on the driver's door, she came up with a map of the state, and a smaller one of the county.

So Max did not know his way around. She filed that bit of information away.

Then she reached under his seat.

For the third time in as many days, her hands closed around cold, fatal steel.

He had another gun. This one under the seat of his truck. And Kait knew it wasn't the same gun, because it was twice the size.

Why did he feel the need to carry so much protection?

The answer was easy—he was a cop and the case he was on was a dangerous one.

Now Kait recalled him telling her to watch her own back. He had given her that bit of advice when he'd found her snooping in his suitcase. He had surprised her, because she had expected hostility from him and instead had received a warning meant to protect her.

If Zara knew she wasn't Lana, then Rafe Coleman knew it, too.

Kait slipped out of the cab and closed the door when she heard a man's voice.

She halted.

"Yeah, by tomorrow."

It was Rafe Coleman. Kait ducked low, her heart thundering now, having no doubt that he was with Max. Which meant that they were going to part ways and Max was going to come over to his truck and get into it. Except, she was crouched down by the door, so he was going to discover her there in sixty seconds—or less.

"All right. Thanks, Rafe," Max was saying, his voice far louder now, and too close for comfort. Kait could also hear gravel crunching under his feet.

She had no choice. She darted toward the back of his truck and then around the tailgate. Her own shoes made the same crunching noise—a dead giveaway.

But neither man commented on it.

And that was cause for alarm. Surely they had heard someone who they could not see moving about the cars in the lot? More specifically, moving about Max's truck?

Kait froze on the other side of his pickup. Her instinct was to run for freedom—Max could not see her from where he was now standing, and as he was going to his truck, he would never see her, not until he pulled out of the space he now occupied.

But Rafe had to cross the lot. If he did so, and if he looked back, she would be a sitting duck and right in his line of vision.

Sweat trickled from her brow and into her eyes.

Yet if she made a run for it, they might both see her, and right now, crouched as she was, she was, briefly, securely hidden.

She heard Max's car door opening. Why weren't they speaking?

And as she had the thought, Rafe said, "Been a long day. Beat. Let's touch base tomorrow."

"Sure," Max said. But he had spoken awfully lightly. Or had his tone been normal?

Kait couldn't seem to breathe. But if both men were now standing on the opposite side of the Toyota, she had to make a run for it.

Kait did.

She ran around the small Ford coupe parked beside the Toyota, and gravel spit and shrieked from beneath her paddock boots. She didn't stop. She didn't dare. She ran around the Ford's hood, and then raced down the line of cars to the street that bisected the highway.

Cars were parked there, too. Kait ducked behind one, panting, waiting. She couldn't move now, because if she dashed across the street to her Porsche, they would see her if they looked her way. On the other hand, the Porsche was safety now.

Kait ran.

Rafe Coleman shoved his hands in the pockets of his black sheriff's-issue jacket. Tonight he wore a black baseball cap with the word SHERIFF emblazoned upon it. He stared briefly out into the night, then turned to fully face Max Zara. "Well, well," he said softly, finally smiling.

"I told you I was followed," Zara returned, not smiling. "That her?"

"Oh, yeah."

Max did not look out across the parking lot. He leaned against the old Toyota, clad only in a flannel shirt. "She's on to us." He spoke in a matter-of-fact manner.

Rafe shrugged. His eyes gleamed. "Doesn't really matter, now, does it?"

Max sighed. "No. It doesn't."

Rafe scuffed the gravel with the toe of his boot reflectively. It was another moment before he spoke. "She'll hang herself. . . . They always do."

FOURTEEN

A car had appeared in her rearview mirror. Kait had just turned onto Northwoods Road, and as soon as she realized she wasn't alone, her grip on the steering wheel tightened. She told herself that she was not being followed by either Rafe Coleman or Max Zara, but the hollow feeling in her chest was proof that she did not believe her own rationalizations. It had been too easy escaping to her Porsche undetected. It did not seem right.

Kait stepped on the accelerator. Max was probably the one in the car behind her—as he had to return to Fox Hollow, just as she did. But why was he—or someone else—closing in on her, ever so steadily? Whoever was behind her was driving too fast for the winding country road.

She continued to perspire. Cop or thug or something in between? Who was Zara? And why were he and Rafe Coleman working together? Kait knew they both hated Lana and that they both wanted to bring her down, but she had to know why.

Kait's tension increased as she glanced in her mirror again—the car was only a few lengths behind her now. Maybe it was some reckless teen under the influence. It was time to pull over and let whoever it was go past her.

Kait hit her blinker, slowing, deciding she'd stop now, before turning the next corner.

The car behind did not decelerate.

She glanced back quickly, and thought, shocked, he was going to rear-end her. And the moment she had the thought, her little car was hit from behind, hard and fast.

As the Porsche shot off the road, Kait slammed on the brakes. The moment she did so, she knew it was the wrong action to take—the sports car whipped around, back end toward the front, dizzily. Branches snapped off as the car hit the trees in its path, its windshield cracked, the chassis jerking and bouncing, rocks flying from its wheels, until the rear end shuddered to an abrupt halt, slamming fully against the side of a pine tree. A huge noise filled the car. The air bag had inflated, jamming Kait back against her seat.

Oh, dear God.

Kait blinked and began to breathe. The car was still now. She was gripping the steering wheel as if her life depended on it, which maybe it had. Now she was facing the road in the direction she had just come from—the small car had spun an entire one hundred and eighty degrees. *Someone had rammed into her from behind.*

Had someone just tried to kill her?

Kait inhaled hard. She realized she was shaking uncontrollably. The car that had hit her had not stopped to see if she was alive or dead, injured or safe. And that in itself spoke volumes.

"Stay calm," she whispered aloud. Was she hurt? Kait realized that a shooting pain was going through her temple. She released the steering wheel and touched the area, and knew instantly that the sticky stuff there was blood. She took another deep breath—and decided she had no broken ribs. She wriggled her ankles, moved her legs, then her fingers, wrists, and arms. She was, thank God, intact.

Had someone meant to kill her? Or scare her? Did it matter? This had gone too far!

Kait choked back on a sob of fear and pushed at the air bag. When she got it out of the way, she stepped out of the car, leaving the door open. *Had Max Zara been the one to drive her off the road?*

Kait tried to think. Had the car that had hit her and then

continued to speed by been as large as a truck—or an SUV? Kait wanted to say yes. But the truth was, she had been trying to steer the Porsche as it flew through the woods and she simply wasn't certain what type of vehicle had whizzed by in the night.

Besides, Zara had had ample opportunity to harm her or kill her—she crossed him off the list. If he wanted her dead, she would not be alive now.

And she was also leaning toward the conclusion that he was a cop.

Kait inhaled deeply, willing the trembling in her limbs to cease. After all, she was fine. A bit shaken perhaps, a bit bloody, but fine. And maybe, just maybe, the hit-and-run had been an accident caused by a reckless teenager or a drunk.

In her heart, she knew it wasn't so. Kait knew that whatever trouble Lana was in, it had come home and reached her, Kait, at Fox Hollow.

In any event, she had to get going. She couldn't continue to stand around in the woods like a terrified fool. Kait looked around. She was about twenty feet from the road and the night was pitch black, except for a handful of stars overhead. There were no lights to be seen. That was hardly a surprise, as all of the homes on this road were estates set way back from it, and they were few and far between. Kait suddenly realized that she was in a dangerously deserted area. It became hard to breathe properly all over again.

She told herself that the worst was over. The hit-and-run driver was long since gone. He wasn't coming back.

But what if he did come back—to see if she were alive or dead?

She had to get out of there.

Kait turned and was about to jump into the Porsche when she realized that both front tires were flat. In disbelief, she stared.

Then she dove into the front seat, found her purse, fumbled for her cell phone. Everything but her phone came up in her hand—her wallet, her sunglasses, her lip gloss, and tissue case. Kait cursed savagely and turned the bag upside down, spilling everything out. The dashboard was illuminated so she saw the phone and seized it. The urge to call Trev was overwhelming.

Was he home? She dialed the house, begging the fates to have him there. She did not know his cell phone number—how stupid could she be? As she listened to the phone ring and ring, she glanced at the clock on the dash. It was midnight. Surely he was home by now.

"Hello?" Trev sounded irascible and sleepy, as if he had just been woken up.

"Trev! It's me—there's been an accident," Kait cried.

"Are you all right?" he asked instantly, no longer sounding the least bit hoarse or vague.

"I think so. I mean, yes. Someone hit me from behind and ran me off the road," she continued, aware that she was near tears and sounding hysterical. "I have two flat tires," she said with a sob.

"Where are you?"

She inhaled sharply. "About two miles from the highway."

"I'll be right there," he said.

Kait didn't hesitate. "Thank you," she whispered, deeply grateful. His only reply was a click of the line going dead.

She leaned against the hood of the car, hugging herself. If there was one person she could count on, she knew that it was Trev.

She hadn't really wondered, even for a moment, if Rafe Coleman had driven her off the road, had she?

Kait shuddered. The answer was a resounding yes and it didn't matter that he was a county sheriff. He loathed Lana, and with good cause. He loathed her for betraying, using, and hurting his brother.

He loathed Lana a zillion times more than Max Zara ever could.

Kait glanced down the road in the direction that the hit-and-run driver had disappeared. "Please hurry, Trev," she whispered. She almost expected that driver, whoever he was, to reappear. But she told herself that the headlights she would see next coming from that direction would belong to Trev.

She heard a car approaching. Not from the direction of Fox Hollow, but from the direction of town.

Kait turned to locate the vehicle and froze. The car had seen her—it was slowing.

Kait ducked into the Porsche and turned off the headlights, cursing herself for leaving them on. Just then, she did not want anyone to find her except for Trev Coleman.

She remained squatting beside the open door, silently willing the oncoming driver to speed up and go away. But she heard the car come to a stop. The engine didn't die, but after a pause, she heard a car door opening.

Kait cursed, but silently. She reached into the car's back space and seized the tire iron she'd left there the other day. She slowly straightened, hiding it behind her back. The moment she did so, she was bathed in the other vehicle's headlights.

"You okay?" a man called out.

"I'm fine," Kait managed to reply. "Just fine. My husband is on the way."

The man halted. As the headlights were behind him, Kait couldn't make out much more than a shadowy figure. "Lana? Is that you?"

Kait cursed under her breath. Who was this? By now, she doubted it was a friend. "Yes, it's me."

"It's John," he exclaimed, hurrying forward. "What happened? Are you all right? Did you call the police?"

Her mind wanted to go blank. Instead, as he emerged from the shadows into her focus, she fought for comprehension. *John.* Who was John? Was this Alicia's husband? Warily, Kait faced a husky man with an attractive face and thick, distinguished sideburns. In fact, he reminded her a bit of a middle-aged Sean Connery.

"I called Trev. He should be here any minute," she said, as John paused before her.

"You're bleeding!" he exclaimed, his eyes widening. "What happened?" Instantly, his arm went around her as if she needed his support to stand up.

Kait didn't like it. She jerked free. The moment she did

so, she felt his surprise. "I'm an idiot. I fell asleep at the wheel—can you believe it?"

For one moment, their eyes met. He looked astonished and Kait did not know why. Then he softened. "Thank God you're all right," he said. "But you're bleeding. And why are you holding that jack? Here." He pulled an old-fashioned handkerchief from the breast pocket of his navy blue blazer. "Let me." He smiled a bit at her.

Kait didn't move as he wiped her temple. She told herself that this was her best friend's husband, so it was hardly unusual for him to be so solicitous. And as he smiled again, Kait had a sinking feeling. There was no reason for it, but it had happened, and she pulled away. "Thank you," she managed, setting the jack down.

He folded the handkerchief neatly into a small square and pocketed it. "You told me you would call me the moment you got back from New York," he said, his dark gaze on her face.

Kait started. "What?" She was too tired for this.

"I don't understand why you didn't call me," he said, a nearly plaintive note in his tone. Then, "Alicia told me you cut your hair. God, you're so beautiful, Lana."

A chill went through her. She hoped desperately that she was not going to find out that Lana had been lovers with her best friend's husband. "I've been busy," she whispered. "And I had that fall."

"I know. I wanted to come charging right over, but I didn't dare. I sent Alicia instead. I miss you. I need to be with you, Lana," he added, watching her carefully.

That answered her question. In shock, Kait stared at him. *Did Alicia know that her best friend and husband were having an affair?*

Of course she didn't. Otherwise she would have behaved very differently the other day.

Carefully, Kait said, "I want to reconcile with Trev."

"What?!" he cried. Then, "You despise him! You told me so a dozen times! You told me you can't wait for the divorce, and that you can't wait to be free! You told me that Fox Hollow was a choker on your throat and that it was choking you to death!"

Kait stepped back. She shook her head, appalled that her sister had said those things—and had probably meant them. "No. Not anymore. I've had a change of heart," she said weakly. "I'm tired. I can't talk about this now."

"Then when are we going to talk?" he demanded. And he was angry now. "I've wanted you from the moment we first met, and it took me six years to finally get you. Are you jilting me now? Like all the others? Is that it?" His dark eyes flashed. "I *love* you. You're all I can think about."

"What about Alicia?" Kait had to ask.

"You know our marriage is one of suitability. She's a sweet girl and a good mother, but I would leave her for you. You know all this. I told you many times. Say the word and I'll leave her, sell the estate, and we'll go anywhere in the world, Lana. Anywhere. Just say the word."

At least her sister hadn't promised him that. "I have two flat tires," she managed. "I had better call Triple A."

"I'll call for road service. You're avoiding the question. How can you be thinking of staying with Trev? He doesn't love you. He despises you!"

"We have a child," Kait said slowly. "John, Trev is on his way. This discussion can wait."

"Can it?" He was angry again. "I haven't seen you in over a week! Are you playing games with me now?"

The night yawned about them. Crickets sang. Leaves rustled. The road was dark and deserted. John's face remained half in shadow, while the headlights of his sedan fully illuminated Kait. Where was Trev? Why wasn't he there yet? Kait had had enough of John Davison. She didn't want to spend another moment alone in the woods with him. "I'm not playing games. I'm hurt and tired. Exhausted, actually."

He stared, his expression changing to bewilderment. It was mild at first. "Lana?" He seemed puzzled now. "Are you sure you're all right? You're acting so differently. Maybe you hurt your head in the car accident."

Kait touched her temple. It was no longer bleeding, but

she seized on the excuse. "Maybe you're right. My head hurts terribly. Please. We can—and will—talk another time."

He stared, then took her hands in his. Kait tensed, but forced herself not to fight his grasp. "Just promise me this talk of staying with Coleman is just that, talk. Promise me we can decide our future together."

Their future? Had Lana been playing this man like a fisherman played a trout on his line? Dumbly, Kait nodded.

Relief covered his distinguished features. He smiled. "Come. Let's call Triple A. We can save Trev the call."

Kait slipped free of his grasp. "It would be great if you could do that," she said, wondering if he could read the relief in her expression.

His expression changed—it seemed to harden with mistrust—but then a car could be heard approaching and they both glanced toward the sound. It was coming from town. Dismayed, Kait thought that if it was Rafe Coleman, she might simply die. And sure enough, a moment later a flashing red light could be seen atop the approaching vehicle.

"Trev must have called the police," John said, watching the police car, a black-and-white Chevy Blazer, stopping behind John's sedan. The door opened and a tall, agile form emerged. Kait's heart sank like a rock. She knew it was Rafe—she recognized the almost indolent and leonine way in which he moved. Kait bent and picked up the jack, gripping it firmly in her right hand.

Rafe walked slowly to them. "John." He nodded at him, then turned to Kait and noticed her bloody temple. He lifted a walkie-talkie. "Get me an ambulance and a tow truck, Maggie," he said.

"Ten-four, boss," came the crackling female reply.

Then his arm shot out. Kait had no chance to recoil—he grasped her by the arm before she could move. Her gaze leapt to his and she was frantic with fear. His eyes narrowed but did not leave her face as he urged her to the hood of the car. Kait realized he wanted her to sit on it. "You can let go of that jack," he said matter-of-factly.

Kait looked into his fathomless green eyes and didn't

know what to think. She was shaking. For one moment, she had thought that he might strangle her, never mind that John had been present. "You hate me," she said weakly. But she dropped the jack.

"Yeah, I sure do. But you're hurt." He released her and folded his arms across his chest. "What happened here, Lana?"

"Someone hit me from behind," she said. "No, someone followed me from town and rammed me from behind." Too late, she realized what she had said. She stiffened, but if he had known she was spying on him and Zara in town, he gave no sign.

He said, "You get a look at the vehicle—the driver?"

Kait shook her head. "It happened too fast."

"Think he or she was drunk?"

Kait looked right into his eyes. "No."

"No?"

She didn't bother to tell him that the vehicle hadn't been weaving. Or that its speed hadn't varied. "I think it was someone who wants me dead," she said.

Trev arrived at the exact same moment as the fire department. He came striding forward, followed by two paramedics. Kait took one look at his expression—another police car had arrived and the entire scene was thoroughly illuminated by headlights—and knew he cared.

Concern was written all over his face. He paused, his eyes widening as he saw her temple. Kait hadn't bothered to look in a mirror, but she guessed she looked pretty bad. "I'm okay, really," she said softly.

He took her arm and with his other hand, turned her face to the side. "Glass?" His eyes went to the cracked windshield of the Porsche.

"I have no idea. But the air bag inflated, so what else could it be?"

For one moment, he did not speak. "What do you mean, someone ran you off the road?"

"Someone came up behind me and did not slow. Not even

a hair. I may have even been followed," Kait said in a low tone. The two paramedics now stood behind Trev, and she didn't want to be overheard. "I was rammed once from behind. The driver did not stop."

He stared. "Who would follow you, and why? And where were you tonight, anyway?"

Kait froze.

"Excuse me, sir, but we need to take a look at the lady," one of the firemen said.

Trev didn't move.

"Sir?"

Kait licked her lips. "I followed Max from the farm. It's a bit of a story, but I'll share it with you when they're through."

His jaw flexed and he gave her an enigmatic look. "That's a good idea." He stepped aside.

Kait was quickly examined by the first paramedic, who checked her vitals and pronounced her no worse for wear. He cleaned up her cut, informing her that it looked a lot worse than it was and he doubted it would scar. It had been caused by a piece of glass, as Trev had thought.

During the examination, Trev turned to view his brother. Rafe and another police officer stood in the road, which had been cordoned off with flares, examining what Kait supposed were marks left from the tires of the Porsche. Then he gave Kait a brief look and walked over to the pair. Kait wished she could overhear what they were saying, but there was not a chance in hell.

John Davison hadn't left. He remained standing by the hood of his sedan, and every now and then he would glance Kait's way. She wished he would get in his BMW and drive away.

"Well, that's that," the blond medic said cheerfully.

"Thanks," Kait said. A tow truck was finally pulling up behind the second police vehicle.

Trev remained in the road with Rafe and the other officer. John strode over, and as he approached, Kait flinched. "So, you are all right?" he asked.

Kait met a pair of dark, unwavering eyes. "Yes." She hesitated. "You certainly appeared in the nick of time."

"I certainly did," he agreed. Then, his voice dropping, "I heard what you told Trev. Why would anyone deliberately try and run you off the road? What is going on? Surely this was an accident."

"I don't know," Kait lied. "But I guess I've made a few enemies in the county." She watched him.

He glanced over his shoulder. Trev was watching them. John faced her, putting his back to her husband. "This is a small town. The women are all jealous of you, and you've certainly jilted a few of my friends, but no one would do something like this. That would be insane."

Kait shook her head. "I happen to agree with you—about the insane part."

Their eyes locked. For one moment he didn't move. Then he said, "When can we meet?"

"After the weekend," Kait said, pleased by her answer. For Lana would have returned and she would be Kait London again and she would not have to deal with this.

He seemed skeptical but he nodded. As he walked away, he came abreast of Trev. They exchanged words, but Kait could not overhear them. They seemed cordial and Kait knew that Trev had no idea that Lana was sleeping with his friend.

She had a headache now, and she doubted it was from the superficial cut on her head. Trev and Rafe approached. Rafe said, "Got a skid mark from the other vehicle. Looks like we got paint all over the back of the Porsche, too. Must have been a truck or SUV that rammed you—it sure wasn't bumper to bumper. We need to send everything to the city lab boys, but we'll see what we can come up with."

Kait nodded uneasily. Should she trust this man or not? Was he now trying to help her when a few hours ago he had promised to bring her down? How she wished that he really was on her side, that he was really going to find out who had done this.

"If you remember anything, give a holler," Rafe said. "Anything at all."

Trev took her arm. "Let's get you home," he said.

Kait hesitated. Rafe hadn't moved. "Rafe—thanks. Thanks a lot," she said.

His eyes narrowed. "I'm only doing my job," he said. But he was staring at her. Then, "This doesn't change a damn thing."

Kait walked into the kitchen, aware of Trev following her into the dining room but then veering aside. Lights had been left on. She sat down at the center island on a stool, untying and removing her boots. Fear claimed her and she began to tremble.

There was very little doubt in her mind now that she was a killer's target. Someone who was after Lana was out there, and believing her to be her sister, he was now after her. Kait couldn't take it anymore. As soon as Lana returned, she had to know everything and they had to go to the police for protection and help. For what if the would-be killer decided to target Marni next? And was the killer a thug, involved in whatever shady business Lana was into, or was it someone who hated Lana with a personal vengeance? And would Rafe Coleman honestly protect her when he was determined to "bring her down"? Kait couldn't be sure.

Trev appeared, two glasses of scotch in hand. Not speaking, his eyes on hers, he offered her a glass.

Kait stood. "No thanks." She walked grimly over to the freezer and withdrew a pint of Ben & Jerry's Chocolate Fudge Brownie, grabbed a teaspoon, popped the lid, and sat back down. Aware of his eyes upon her, she looked up almost defiantly—and very close to tears. She dug in.

Chocolate ice cream was her favorite version of chocolate, period. In general, it was heaven on earth. Then she assessed Trev as he silently sipped his scotch, while regarding her over its rim. No, Trev Coleman was heaven on earth, in just about every way, but Chocolate Fudge Brownie ran a distinct second. Tonight, however, it was not doing its job.

"Damn it." Kait had taken one bite and now she set the pint aside. Tears finally filled her eyes. She cradled her head in her hands.

"What is it?" Trev sat down on the other side of the island, facing her.

"Chocolate always calms me down. Makes me happy. You know. Best drug around. Tonight, I can't even taste it." She didn't look up.

He was thoughtful. "I never realized you were into chocolate of any kind, or Milanos, or pizza."

She slowly shifted so that their gazes met and held. Did she have to stay in character even now? It was simply too much. "I'm on a binge. Every woman has her day."

He set his scotch down and took her hand. Kait looked at their clasped palms in real surprise. Then she looked up into a pair of mesmerizing green eyes. "It was a drunk. I feel pretty certain, Lana."

"Someone's trying to kill me," she whispered. "I know it, Trev."

Trev hesitated. "There are a lot of people in this county who don't particularly like you. But to try to kill you? I can't grasp it."

"That's because you're sane," Kait whispered unsteadily. She looked up into his eyes. "I'm scared." She thought about the terrible lie she was engaged in. "I can't take it anymore."

Trev stood. And suddenly he was angry. "Why do you keep doing this? One minute, I look at you and I feel like you're the woman I should take into my arms. The next minute, I look at you and remember all the lies and all the other men."

She trembled—she felt ready to cry. "But I am scared. If someone rammed you from behind and drove you off the road, wrecking your car, you'd be scared too." She felt her chin tilt up. "And I'm sorry there are moments when you actually like me!"

He didn't move.

Determined not to cry, Kait reached for the ice cream and dug in. It tasted like sand. "We should record this moment," she muttered. "We can rename my favorite flavor Chocolate Cardboard."

Trev didn't answer. She felt a tear trickle down her cheek. She swiped at it and stood, not looking at him. She shoved the pint in the freezer. "Sorry to be a burden," she said. She finally looked at him and managed a bright, brittle smile. "Must be the monsters in the night. Tomorrow will be a whole new day. Yippee."

He was staring very grimly at her.

Kait was as tired of his internal battles as she was of everything else. She walked out.

Upstairs, she picked up the phone and dialed her own cell phone. When she got the voice mail, she said tersely, "I'm at the end of my rope. Someone tried to run me off the road tonight—I'm pretty sure someone is trying to kill me. We have to go to the police. If you can come back sooner than Monday, please, Lana, please do." She hesitated, but she was angry as well as fed up and didn't know what else to say. She hung up.

And she did not feel better. There was no relief. Because nothing had really changed—she remained in her charade, and Marni and Lana remained in danger, as she did, too.

In either case, her charade was almost over. Tomorrow was Saturday. She had two more days to get through.

And then on Monday Trev Coleman was about to be devastated. Would he hate her forever?

Kait thought so. But at least the temptation of never telling him the truth was finally gone. This was one lie she simply couldn't wait to get rid of. It had become an impossible burden.

She turned away from the phone, about to collapse into the bed. Trev stood in the doorway.

She froze. How much had he heard? Had she left the door wide open while calling her sister or had he opened it? She hadn't heard a thing. She stared, trying to read his expression. But it was impassive and she had not a clue as to what he was thinking—or if he had heard her phone call at all.

But even if he had, surely he hadn't understood—and she hadn't used Lana's name, had she?

"May I come in?" he asked quietly.

She realized he was holding a bowl of her chocolate ice cream in his hand. "Sure. It's your room." She tried to smile and failed. In fact, her heart was starting to beat a bit too fast.

He came in and handed her the bowl. "Try this."

She looked down and saw that a dark liquid had been dribbled heavily over the ice cream. She smiled. "Kahlúa?" How could she not love Trev Coleman?

Then her smile vanished. She was not allowed to let her thoughts go in that direction!

He smiled a bit in return. "One better. Godiva Chocolate Liqueur."

Her heart flipped, and not because of the alcohol-laced sundae he was handing her. But because of the thought behind it, because of his smile, because of the sincere way he was regarding her with his green bedroom eyes. "Why?" she asked helplessly, and that emotion she had tried to fight began to blow up inside her chest, powerful and potent, heady and exciting, and she felt herself sliding headlong past the crevice of infatuation and into the abyss of love.

"Because I can be a prick at times," he said. He dipped the spoon into the ice cream and then posed it before her lips.

Kait met his eyes as her insides tightened and her breath completely stopped.

His eyes changed, becoming emerald green.

She opened her lips and let him insert the spoon. The ice cream had flavor again—fantastically sweet, thickly chocolate, and spicy hot from the Godiva liqueur. Trev withdrew the silver spoon.

And she saw the heat in his eyes just before his thick black lashes lowered, shielding his gaze from hers. Kait didn't move. For one moment she could not, because her lower body had begun to throb in the most wild and insistent and primitive way.

She took the sterling spoon from his long, graceful fingers.

He glanced up.

She smiled a little and dug up some ice cream. "Your turn," she breathed.

"Is it good?" His tone had turned rough.

She nodded. "Very good."

His mouth quirked. He had the most beautiful, mobile mouth, and Kait wanted to run her tongue all over it. Instead, she lifted the spoon of ice cream and prodded his lips with it.

He slowly opened. She glimpsed his tongue as the ice cream disappeared. Their eyes met.

Locked.

He took the bowl from her hands. "I can think of a really good place for that ice cream."

She thought she might die. "So can I."

His lips lifted in a bare smile as they stared at each other.

Then he took her arms. Kait found herself on her back, beneath him, on the bed. His mouth took hers, and his chocolate-coated tongue thrust into her mouth. Kait slid her hands beneath his cashmere sweater, over the silken slabs of muscle that formed his back. He lifted her blouse, grasped both her breasts, kissing her almost desperately.

Kait managed to get his sweater off while their lips were locked. She dove for his belt, his fly. His mouth claimed one nipple. As he sucked, she freed him, grasped his fullness in her palm, and sighed.

"We're going too fast," he said, coming up for air. He tugged off her cotton pullover, unhooked and pulled off her bra.

"The door's open," Kait agreed.

Trev moaned and jumped from the bed, dropping trousers and briefs. As he slammed the door closed, Kait shimmied out of her own jeans and panties in record time. He dove onto the bed before she could remove her socks, and he was smiling as he pinned her flat on her back. "This *notion*," he murmured, flicking his thumb along her jaw, "has been torturing me all day."

"Bad, bad choice of words," Kait whispered, aware of his having spread her thighs impossibly wide—and of his man-

hood straining against her sex. "Because now you can torture me all night."

"That," he said, reaching over her body, "is a very agreeable prospect." He palmed her.

Kait gasped, as his hand was covered with cold gooey ice
cream. He grinned at her. "Oh," was all she could say.

Still grinning, he lowered his head.

"Damn," she managed, completely incoherent.

He added more ice cream.

Kait was dressing with extreme care for Parker's black-tie
party. As she surveyed herself in the mirror, she thought that
she had got it just right. She had opted for a knee-length
dress and sexy silver sandals, but as the dress was by Ungaro, it meant that that ultra-feminine lace-edged floral chiffon floated over her body with breathtaking sensuality. The
sheath had an uneven hem that was slit high up on one thigh,
lace cascading down one leg, and both shoulder straps were
for mere decoration, as they hung down over her shoulders
uselessly. Kait had added one of Lana's necklaces, a pearl
choker with a platinum heart clasp, studded with diamonds.
She had turned the clasp in front.

She had kept her makeup minimal—a dab of lavender
shimmer on her eyes, pink gloss on her lips. She stared at
her reflection. She had never looked prettier—she was radiant—and she knew why.

They had made love all night. And Trev might dare to
claim today that it had only been sex, but no man could touch
and hold a woman with such tenderness and affection and not
truly care. Of course, he had claimed no such thing. Trev had
spent most of the day at the barn or in his study, and he'd had
a lunch meeting in Three Falls. But the few times she had seen
him in passing, he had smiled at her—with his eyes.

He no longer hated her.

Kait knew it. She knew it the way she knew that she had to
inhale to breathe. She continued to stare at herself. For the
first time in her life, she was as beautiful as her sister, as alluring, as seductive, but there was also no mistaking the worry in

her eyes. She was in dangerous waters now. Trev had started to care about her, Kait, yet he thought she was Lana.

And she had fallen in love with him. She could no longer deny it.

Kait shivered, even though it was warm in the bathroom. She wanted a future with this man. She couldn't imagine not being a part of his life, a part of Fox Hollow. And after the past five days, she couldn't imagine not being his wife.

How much time did she have left?

It was Saturday night. Lana was due back on Monday. But Kait had left that damn message on her cell phone, begging her to return earlier. Now, Kait prayed that Lana had never gotten it, or that if she had she would ignore it.

Kait knew she was in over her head. Every free moment that she had was spent fantasizing. She would imagine herself explaining to Trev the reason for the switch. She would explain to him who she really was, how different she was from Lana. She would beg him to understand why she had done what she had done—how she had only wanted to protect her sister and have her back. That she had fallen in love with Marni at first sight, and from that moment only wanted to keep the child safe and sound. In her mind's eye and her mind's ear, every single explanation she made up, every excuse, failed to rationalize all that she had done, sounded absurd and hollow.

She didn't even bother hoping that Trev might accept her explanation and forgive her for her lies. He would throw her out of Fox Hollow. He would be more than furious. He would hate her more than he had ever hated Lana—Kait was certain of it.

The mere concept of a future without him and Marni and Sam hurt so much.

Kait heard the telephone ring.

She actually jumped.

Her heart raced.

Even though she knew that Lana would not call her at the house, that was how nervous she had become. It stopped ringing—meaning someone had picked it up.

Kait had chosen a velvet patchwork evening bag with long leather fringe for the affair, and with trembling hands she put her gloss and perfume inside. Ill, she reached for her cell phone and took out the battery, then put the dissembled unit in a vanity drawer as if that might delay the inevitable.

Kait worked on her breathing as she went downstairs. Somehow, she had to let go of her anxiety and fear, because these last few hours and days with Trev and his daughters were so precious to her.

Marni was with her father in his study. Already in her grinning panda pj's, she was earnestly studying a horse magazine. Trev was on the phone, clad in his tuxedo, his profile to Kait. She looked at him and lost her ability to breathe. She lost her ability to move, to think. She could only feel.

He married the wrong twin.

Lana's words echoed now. God, she was right. Trev had married the wrong sister.

How was she going to live the rest of her life without him?

"Mommy! You're so pretty!" Marni cried, jumping up and galloping toward her, her long, curly hair still damp from the shower.

Trev had half turned to smile at her. The look in his green eyes made her heart stop. And Kait recalled the fact that she hadn't yet checked her own calendar to satisfy her curiosity about when she had last seen her sister in New York City and if, just possibly, she had been working on the charity event that she had hoped to hold at Fox Hollow at that time. Now the idea seemed far-fetched, coincidental.

Kait couldn't quite smile back at him and she bent and hugged Marni. "I'm not half as pretty as you," she said huskily, wishing that Marni were her own daughter. The moment the terrible thought appeared, she tensed and straightened. Marni was *not* her daughter. She would never be her daughter. She was Lana's daughter, and after the divorce, Trev would have full custody. Kait no longer objected to that; in fact, he was right. As painful as the idea was, Lana had failed as a mother, and Marni would be better off living with her father.

Besides, if the cops were after her, then Lana had involved herself in something illegal.

The phone clicked as the receiver was laid down. Kait felt her cheeks heat and slowly she turned.

Trev was studying her, a gleam in his eyes.

She warmed beneath his regard. "I'm sorry if I'm running a bit late."

"We'll be fashionably late," he said with a smile and a shrug. His eyes slid over her from head to toe. "That's some dress. I haven't seen it before."

Kait felt herself flush, but now, with pleasure. "I was hoping you would like it," she said softly. She had raced that afternoon to Neiman Marcus, where she had bought it. For once, she wanted to wear something that didn't scream Lana. She had wanted to wear something that expressed her personality, that belonged to her, not her sister.

His green gaze locked with hers. And in that moment, she knew exactly what was on his mind, and she wondered why they didn't simply skip the party. "I'd like to take it right off," he said in a sexy murmur.

Kait heated, about to suggest they go upstairs, when she realized that Marni was standing right there beside her.

"But Daddy, the dress is soo pretty! Don't take it off," Marni cried in some alarm. "Mommy looks like a fairy princess!"

Trev flushed. "You're right, darling. Mommy looks exactly like a fairy princess. Daddy's mistake. Men can be such fools." He smiled at his daughter—but then he sent Kait such a potent look that her knees almost buckled.

How was she going to do this? How was she going to leave him and his daughters?

If only Lana wouldn't come back!

He swooped down on his daughter, lifting her into his arms, hugging and kissing her. "I'll come up to say good night when I get home, but I won't wake you up. We may be late."

Marni frowned, tugging at the wisp of sunstreaked hair that fell over one cheekbone. "Don't be late, Daddy."

"Why not?" He chuckled. "You won't know the difference, honey, you'll be sleeping."

"Because Mommy will sleep too late," Marni pouted. "And she promised to make me special waffles for breakfast tomorrow. If you ask, I know she'd make them for you, too, Daddy."

Kait laid her hand on her heart. It felt as if it were breaking. And she must never have that terrible thought again! Lana *would* return, only God knew what would happen when she did. She, Kait, was moving to Three Falls, but that was the only thing she was certain of.

"Honey? I won't sleep late," she said, and to her horror her tone was choked.

Trev looked at her. "What's wrong?" His tone was mild, his regard was not.

Now was the time to act. She smiled, brilliantly. "Nothing. We're late."

He eyed her for a moment and acquiesced. After hugging Marni again and shooing her off to the kitchen where Elizabeth was cleaning up, he moved toward her. Kait was motionless. He took her hand. "Something's wrong." It wasn't a question.

She wet her lips. "Not really. Do we have to go to Parker's gala?"

His eyes widened. "I have to go—even if just for an hour or two. You don't have to go, however—"

"No, that's fine, of course I'll come," Kait said, overcome with desperation and urgency.

He slid his arm around her. "It will be an endless evening, won't it?" he murmured, his breath feathering her cheek.

She was pressed to his side. She thought about how the evening would end—with her in his arms, in his bed. And in a few days, she would be packing up her office at work and her apartment in the city, sleeping alone.

"You seem sad tonight. Something's wrong. What is it?"

Trev turned her so that she was in his arms. Kait started,

because he was aroused. "I . . . I'm not sad. I'm . . . I'm tired . . . from last night."

His gaze was searching.

Kait had to avoid his eyes.

His thumb stroked over her jaw. "I wasn't kidding when I said it would be a long night," he murmured.

She gripped his lapels, thrilled and heartbroken all at once. His mouth covered hers.

Kait melted as he brushed her lips gently, sensually, again and again. She felt her mouth open, she felt him brush the inside with his tongue. Heat gathered in her loins, followed by moisture and need. His hand cupped one of her buttocks, and as the chiffon was so delicate, it was almost as if she were naked in his hand.

A cough sounded from the doorway.

Trev looked up and stiffened instantly, setting Kait away from him.

Had Lana returned?

Kait whirled in terror.

But it wasn't her twin standing in the doorway; it was Sam.

She was wearing the Donna Karan dress that Kait had lent her. She looked tall and elegant and twenty-one, not sulky and sixteen. And the several funky silver bracelets and dark rose lipstick simply couldn't detract from her beauty or elegance.

"Sam," Trev breathed in admiration.

"Oh, Sam," Kait heard herself cry. "That dress is so lovely on you!" Tears had come to her eyes. Kait rushed to her, hugging her. "You can have the dress, sweetie," she whispered, "because you look amazing in it, just amazing!"

Sam darted a glance at her father, then fully faced Kait. "Do you think?"

"Honey, you're stunning!" But Kait glanced back at Trev, and saw the disappointment on his face—Sam was still refusing to speak to her father.

"Is the lipstick too much?"

Kait hesitated. "Why don't we blot it and add some gloss?"

Sam bit her lip, then nodded. "Okay. Can I really have the dress?"

"Of course you can," Kait said. She extracted a tissue from her purse, dabbed off some of the lipstick, and handed Sam her gloss. As Sam was applying it, using a small compact from her own bag, Trev said, "Sam, you look just like your mother."

Sam stiffened. She snapped closed her compact and handed Kait the gloss. She did not look at her father. "Thanks."

Kait glanced worriedly at Trev. He was making a valiant effort to control his emotions, but she saw how hurt he was. "Honey, isn't it time for you and your father to bury the hatchet?"

Sam whirled to face her father. "No! And I don't look like Mom—she had dark hair—I look like you!"

"You look just like your mother did when she was your age, except for your hair," Trev said hoarsely.

"I don't care," Sam said rudely. "She's dead."

His expression hardened. "I expect you to come right home after Gina's party."

Sam glared. "We might want to go to the mall and get a pizza or something."

Trev's eyes darkened. "You mean, go see that Jenkins kid?"

"I can't help it if he works there!" Sam cried.

"I told you, I don't want you seeing him," Trev warned.

Kait stepped between them, but not before Sam said, "You can't tell me who to see and who not to see. I'm sixteen, not six." She turned and walked out.

Trev started after her; Kait grabbed his arm. "Let her go, Trev."

He turned to her with frustration. "At least she actually spoke to me."

"You're right. And that keeps the door open."

"She's going to go see Gabe Jenkins after the party—that

is, assuming he doesn't have off tonight and isn't taking her to the party!"

"You know, in a way, Sam is right. She's old enough to make most of her own decisions, even the bad ones."

"She had a gun!"

Kait winced. "One she took from me, not him."

That gave him a moment's pause. "He's a bad kid, and he hangs with bad kids—which is why she felt she wanted a gun in the first place."

"I don't think he's all bad," Kait said softly. Seeing his expression, she added, "I met him at the mall the other day, purely by chance. I'm not saying I approve of Sam's choice, either. I think it's too soon to deliver a verdict. But I have an idea."

He folded his arms across his chest. "And that is?"

"Why don't we invite him and his mother over for dinner tomorrow night? Sam would be thrilled, and it would give us—and you—a chance to really get to know him."

He stared at her for a long moment. And finally, he smiled, with a small shake of his head. "Why didn't I think of that?"

She smiled, looping her arm in his and tugging it off his chest. "Because you are too emotionally involved. Because she's your daughter. Because you love her so much."

He studied her. "You are really a different person, Lana," he finally said. "It's as if you *are* a different person, actually."

Kait had no response.

FIFTEEN

"You seem awfully quiet."

Kait glanced at Trev as a valet approached the Jaguar they were seated in. Kait had managed to keep a straight face when Trev had driven it out of the garage, as if she'd known he had another vehicle other than his truck. "Am I?"

He stared at her for a heartbeat. Only the dashboard lights illuminated the Jag's squeaky clean interior. "I can be a good listener," he said.

The valet was at the driver's side door. The big colonial home at the head of the drive was brilliantly lit from inside and the grounds were also illuminated; Kait could hear the strains of a band, and the din of conversation and laughter. "I'm really fine," Kait lied with a smile.

Trev seemed to accept that. They stepped out of the car, Trev coming round the Jag's front end to take her arm. The smile he gave her was an uncertain one. "Careful," he said. "Those heels were not made for walking."

Kait sent him a grateful smile as they crossed the drive and started up the brick walk to the big, stately manor. Azaleas lined the walk and rosebushes the veranda. A couple was entering through the front door ahead of them, the older woman in a long red evening gown, the man in a tuxedo like Trev. As the front door opened, the sounds of the party in progress intensified. Trev said, low, "You're not having second thoughts about last night, are you?"

Kait stumbled but he caught her. "No," she said fervently. "Absolutely not."

His expression softened. "Good," he said.

Kait felt as if she were drowning. What should she do now? Now that Trev had feelings for her, her charade was unfair, and somehow, more terrible, more immoral. And the repercussions would be even worse. God, she was deceiving the man she loved with her every single breath.

The treacherous thought she'd had earlier returned—if only Lana would not come back. Kait was furious with herself for entertaining it yet again. Not only was Lana returning, what did Kait hope to gain if she did not? To engage in a permanent lie for the rest of her life?

As they entered the house, Kait felt as if the place she was stuck in—between a rock and a hard place—had become even worse. Now her back was to a spiked wall, her front to an inescapable vise.

The front hall, which was large, was crowded with guests, and Kait suddenly blinked and realized that she had stepped into another world—a world of old money, Thoroughbred horses, and Southern charm. This mansion made Fox Hollow seem casual and cozy. The room might have been a showroom for Ralph Lauren. Understated elegance was in every architectural detail. The women all wore conservative but elegant and expensive designer gowns and equally conservative but equally expensive jewels; the men were resplendent in tuxedos, some even wore tails. Soft slurred consonants and dropped vowels washed over Kait like warm honey. She felt as if she were standing in a photo gallery for *Town & Country* magazine.

How had Lana ever fit into this life to begin with?

A pleasant-looking man in his fifties approached, beaming. "Trev! Can't believe it's that time of year again, can you?" He clasped Trev's hands.

Trev seemed to genuinely like their host. "No, Parker, but unfortunately, the older one gets, the faster time does fly," he said. "Big crowd tonight. Guess no one thought to miss the county's biggest fall ball."

"Not a single nay on our RSVPs." Parker nodded happily. Then, finally, he looked at Kait, his smile slipping. "Lana. As always, you are stunning and sans pareil tonight. What a sweet hairdo."

Kait was in no mood for games—or for picking up after her sister. "Thank you. The house is so lovely tonight. Everything is lovely." She meant her every word.

He started. "Thank you," he said. Then, "The only person I am not sure I may see tonight is Rafe."

Trev's expression became strangely blank. "Is that so?"

"He never responded to my invitation." Parker's expression had become oddly twisted—it was almost a grimace.

"He gets somewhat preoccupied with county affairs," Trev said.

Parker made a sound, nodded at Lana, then slapped Trev's back. "He should be more like you." He left.

Kait snatched a flute of champagne from a passing waiter. As she did, she realized that a tall elegant man with dark hair was staring at her. He smiled—she looked away, giving him her back. "What was that about?"

Trev hesitated. "Parker and his wife—his third wife— split up for a while. Rafe had an affair with her. Now Georgina's back."

"I see," Kait said, not surprised. She could imagine Rafe a ladies' man, unlike his brother.

"Let's mingle," Trev said, taking her arm. But he looked over her shoulder before they moved off.

Kait automatically did the same. The tall gentleman with gray eyes the color of his silver cummerbund continued to stare. When he saw them both regarding him, he lifted his flute in a sardonic salute, turned, and walked away. "Who is that?" Kait asked without thinking.

"Like you don't know?" Trev demanded harshly.

Kait jerked and saw that he was flushed with anger. Alarm bells went off.

"Let's go," he said firmly, and taking her arm, he guided her into the next room.

Kait dared to look back, but the gentleman in the black tuxedo with the silver cummerbund was gone.

An hour later, Kait made her way to a powder room, only to find it occupied. She'd had enough of Parker's party, although Trev seemed to be enjoying himself. He knew everybody and was extremely well liked. Maybe too well liked. Kait hadn't been imagining the fact that quite a few wives found him far too attractive for her taste. But she supposed they were drooling over him in their dreams. The county was too old-fashioned for the kind of affairs her sister was infamous for. Had they been single like Marni's schoolteacher, she would have been certain they were lining up to snag him after his divorce.

And everyone did stare, at them, at her. So Kait had clung to Trev's arm possessively, smiling eagerly at his every word.

Kait paused outside the powder room, no longer smiling. She was not having a good time. No one liked Lana and pretending to be her in this milieu was difficult and awkward, not to mention stressful. The women hated her, and Kait felt certain most were very jealous of her, although she could not fathom why. Most of the men eyed her with far too much appreciation and speculation. How had her sister lived this way?

Kait hated to think it, but she guessed that Lana had enjoyed the women's jealousy and the lust and admiration of the men.

"My, you are so happy tonight!"

Kait flinched and came face-to-face with Alicia and a tall, extremely beautiful willowy blonde. The pretty redhead wore a long, rather boring black evening gown, and even though it screamed designer, it made her look as matronly as Nancy Reagan. Now she hugged Kait hard. "I don't think I've ever seen Trev this happy," Alicia whispered, her eyes wide. "Not even on his wedding day!"

Kait managed to smile, thinking of her sister being lovers

with John and feeling sick about it. "Actually, I'm a bit tired. How are you?" she asked, refusing to get personal now.

"Just fine," Alicia beamed. "That dress is fantastic! You look like a gypsy! Where did you find it?" she asked eagerly.

"Neiman Marcus," Kait said.

The young blonde smiled at her. Her brilliant blue eyes were rather vacuous, and she wore the most dazzling emerald-and-diamond necklace that Kait had ever seen. It had to be worth a fortune. She said, "Are you and Trev back together? Alicia seems to think so. Wouldn't it be odd if the two of you reconciled—just like me and Parker?"

Kait realized she was Parker's third wife, Georgina. Kait wondered what her relationship with Lana had been. She smiled at Georgina. "Life is full of odder things," she said lightly. And she quickly changed the subject. "That is the most amazing necklace I have ever seen. The color matches your gown perfectly."

Georgina beamed. "Parker gave it to me, out of the blue, right after we got back together. Isn't it awesome? It's Bulgari. I found this dress in Neiman Marcus yesterday. Isn't that funny? We could have gone shopping together. Thank God they had a size four! It's Marie St. John. Doesn't it go with my necklace perfectly?"

Kait wondered if Georgina had any intelligence whatsoever. "Perfectly," she assured her. "Is there a bathroom upstairs? The one downstairs is occupied."

"Straight up and first door on your left," Georgina smiled. "I love your haircut, Lana. When I was a model, I almost cut all my hair off—can you believe it?"

"Thank God you didn't," Kait said. The woman had long blond hair that had obviously spent hours being colored and styled in a salon. Besides, clearly Kait's response was the one Georgina was looking for.

As Kait turned, Alicia touched her wrist. "The two of you have been acting like newlyweds. I'm so happy for you—if this is what you really want now."

Kait knew a question when she heard one. She turned. As Georgina hardly seemed interested in their conversation, she said, "What I don't want is for Trev to hate me. We share a child, Alicia. Don't you think it's long overdue that I started behaving with some dignity and respect?"

Alicia blinked. She began to flush. "Actually, I do. So will you stay together now?"

Kait hesitated. "I don't know." Then, "I really have to use the ladies' room." She smiled and squeezed her hand. "I'm sorry about the past, Alicia, I really am."

Alicia looked utterly confused. "Okay," she finally said. And as she spoke, Kait saw John drifting over to them.

"Hello, Lana," he said with a polite smile, taking his wife's arm.

"How are you?" Kait managed, flushing and wondering if she were beet red. She reminded herself that she had not slept with this man. Lana had been the one leading him on beneath her friend's very nose.

"What a wonderful dress," he said.

"Isn't it fantastic?" Alicia smiled. "She found it at Neiman Marcus."

"What a wonderful party," Kait returned.

"Need a rescue, Mrs. Coleman?" Suddenly an urbane Australian accent drifted whisper-soft over her, as a man paused to stand behind her.

John was saying something, his arm still around Alicia. Kait turned and collided with the man who had spoken, as he stood that close behind her. She tensed as he grabbed her arms, steadying her, and met a pair of startling gray eyes. The gentleman with the dark hair and silver cummerbund grinned at her. A dangerous and amused twinkle was in his eyes.

"Are you all right . . . Mrs. Coleman?" he asked as softly.

"Hello, Farrell," John growled, clearly dismayed.

"Colin," Alicia murmured.

Kait began to perspire. She didn't turn, mesmerized, not liking the way he continued to hold her or the way he looked so deeply into her eyes—as if he knew her very well—too well. Hadn't Alicia said something about a man named Farrell? Something that implied he was in love with Lana? "I'm fine. You can let me go now."

That seemed to amuse him even more, as he chuckled but obeyed. "Lovely gown," he said.

"I need a glass of champagne," Alicia said. "John?"

But John didn't move. "Lana? Would you like one as well?"

"No, thank you," Kait said uneasily.

John was clearly grim. And Alicia was looking from her husband to Kait to Farrell and back again.

Suddenly Kait had had enough. She shifted to look at Farrell. "I'll take that rescue effort now," she said firmly.

Colin Farrell laughed and took her arm in his, guiding her up the wide, sweeping staircase. Kait had to look back, and found Alicia leaving, while John stood in the hall, gazing up at her. Farrell murmured, "You've been home for an entire week. What have you been waiting for?"

Alarmed, Kait met his sparkling gaze and tried to pull free of him. "What?" she gasped. But she already sensed that this man was involved with her sister. He seemed exactly Lana's type—suave, confident, handsome.

"And you cut your hair," he said. He shook his head. "I know you must have had a good reason—it's cute—but it's not you. Not at all. What *could* have possessed you?"

She stared at him and he continued, in the same sexy murmur, "Did you *see* that necklace Parker bought for Georgina? I imagine he'd hit the roof if he knew she was still shagging our county sheriff."

Kait tugged on her arm. Speaking very firmly, she said, "Please let me go."

They paused on the landing. He looked closely at her, the laughter disappearing from his eyes. "Are you all right, love? You don't look like yourself at all. You are acting oddly."

"I'm fine! I just need a powder room," she said. And as she spoke, a door opened near them and an older woman stepped out. As the woman went downstairs, Kait didn't wait. She pulled free of Farrell and darted into the marble bathroom. She closed the door and breathed hard, overcome with relief.

But the door opened immediately and he stepped inside with her, closing the door behind them—and locking it.

For one moment, Kait was so stunned, she could only gape.

He grinned and pulled her into his embrace. "What new game is this? I've missed you."

Kait pushed at his chest. "What are you doing? Let me go! My God, are you insane! Get out of here!"

He stopped trying to kiss her and stared at her in real surprise. And this time, his gaze penetrated her eyes.

Kait was frantic. If Trev saw her like this, it was over. "Get out!" she said.

His regard remained deeply searching. "What is going on, Lana?" His tone had completely changed.

Clearly Lana had had another lover, but Kait had simply had enough. Still she fought for restraint. "I really do have to use the bathroom."

He simply stared at her, as if her words were incomprehensible. Then he said, slowly, "This is very odd, indeed. By now, you should be in my arms and I should have you up against the wall. It has been a week."

Kait said, "Please get out."

But he stared, and as if he had not heard her, he said, "I mean, in the ten years we have been together, you have never behaved this way. And you did not call me when you got back from New York. What is going on, Lana?"

She was sweating now. "Nothing is going on!" Lana and this man had been together for ten years? The concept was nearly incomprehensible. She swallowed. "Ten years is a long time. People change."

"Not you. Not us. Is this about Coleman? The divorce—the settlement we're after?"

Kait simply stared at him, horrified.

"Don't look at me as if I am a total stranger," he flashed. "For crissakes, we're far more than friends and far more than lovers. We're a team."

They were a team. "A team," Kait managed, reeling. And she wanted to ask just what kind of team they were. But somehow she knew. Because he and Lana were both after Trev's money—he had just said so.

Suddenly he took her hand and lifted it to his lips, pressing his mouth there. Kait froze. "I heard about that fall. I thought it was staged—as you always have a reason for everything you do. But it wasn't, was it? Did you hurt yourself? Is that why you're looking at me as if I am Jack the Ripper?" He smiled then. "Which we both know I am not."

She tried to tug her hand free and failed. "Farrell, let's talk outside." She no longer had to use the bathroom. Her heart beat hard and fast, almost choking her.

He looked hard into her eyes and opened the door. Together, they stepped outside. How did she question him now? She wanted to know who he was, when exactly he and Lana had first met, when they had become involved, and what kind of team they were. She started down the hall, when he grasped her wrist from behind.

She met his coolly amused stare again. "You're going the wrong way, love." His gaze remained searching, but his easy grin was back.

"Sorry." This man was going to guess the truth in another instant if she did not get her act together.

"Have you forgotten our business here tonight?" he asked, his face now impossible to read.

"Business?" she echoed. "No, of course not!" She smiled at him, and felt that it was strained.

He tucked her arm in his and they turned the opposite way. Kait could not imagine what he and Lana were involved in, but it sounded very much like Rafe Coleman had been right—that Lana had targeted Trev for his money, with this man at her side, as her partner. What did not make sense was waiting six years to file for a divorce. A gold digger might wait six months.

Farrell had released her arm, and Kait followed him warily down the hall, to its very end. Her heart was racing with alarm and she was filled with dread. She did not know what awaited her on the other side of the closed door that they faced, but she sensed she was about to witness something ghastly, appalling—something simply unthinkable.

He pushed open the door, ushered her in. As he closed the door, Kait started. "This is the master bedroom," she whispered uneasily.

"Really?" He seemed somewhat amused by her comment. Kait hugged herself, cold now, in spite of the sweat that drenched her body. He walked ever-so-nonchalantly over to a medium-sized portrait of a pretty blond woman in a ball gown, a woman Kait recognized as Mrs. Parker. He lifted the portrait up, taking it off the wall.

"What are you doing?" Kait cried.

A safe was on the wall. And the moment she saw it, she knew. Her eyes felt huge as she watched him smile charmingly at her and then place a small, palm-sized device on it. A second later there was a click, and Colin Farrell swung open the safe door.

"Stop," Kait cried, more firmly. She was in shock now.

He had taken something out of the safe; now he closed it. He held up his hand, showing her a huge yellow diamond ring. "This, love, is what we came for tonight."

Kait remained speechless.

He replaced the painting on the wall, over the safe.

Kait's mind came to life. She realized what was happening. Colin Farrell had just stolen a ring worth a small fortune. Colin Farrell was a thief.

And he was Lana's partner.

He was approaching her. Kait wanted to tell him to get away. But she couldn't get a word out and he was smiling at her, pressing something into her palm. No, not something— it was the stolen diamond ring.

It was burning her palm.

Kait blinked down at it and the yellow diamond swam before her eyes. "I don't want this!" she cried frantically, finally finding her voice.

He wrapped his arm around her, and before Kait could protest, he had hustled her back into the hall. "But you do. You always do. You have never said no to a job."

"A job?" Kait whispered, horrified.

He stared at her, brows drawn together, perplexed.

Voices sounded, approaching. Kait shoved the ring at him. "Take this and put it back!"

Farrell did grin. He folded her fingers over the ring, saying, "Smile, love, we have company."

Kait looked past him, down the hall, and saw, of all people, Georgina Parker and Rafe Coleman. Georgina and Rafe saw them at the exact same time, and they pulled up short. Kait couldn't think. She could only stare.

She had just helped steal a diamond ring and the county sheriff—who despised her—was on his way to the master bedroom for a lovers' tryst with the owner of that ring.

Could this really be happening?

And then she saw his expression, and it was one of outrage. "Well, well," he said softly. "Fancy seeing you here, Lana . . . Farrell."

Kait suddenly realized that Farrell had his arm around her as if they really were lovers—and she realized that it appeared that they had been using the master bedroom for the same reason Rafe was about to use it with their hostess. "Nothing happened," she heard herself whisper pathetically.

Farrell released her. "Nice party, mate," he said easily.

Kait shot a glance at him—he was enjoying himself. She was terrified—but he was enjoying himself! Colin Farrell was cooler than a block of ice.

"Rafe, uh, let's go downstairs. That, uh, antique I wanted to show you can wait." Georgina was flushing the color of beets. On a blonde, it wasn't particularly attractive.

"After you," Rafe said to Kait.

Kait inhaled, because the diamond ring remained hidden in her palm. She felt its heat and wondered why Rafe couldn't sense that she held it in her hand. She started past him, followed by Colin Farrell, making certain not to even brush his sleeve. Then she stumbled and stopped.

Trev stood on the top of the stairs.

Kait straightened, meeting his gaze.

His eyes dark with anger, he turned abruptly, going back downstairs.

"Trev!" Kait flew after him. It crossed her reeling mind that she still had the ring in her hand, but Rafe Coleman was behind Farrell, and she could feel his eyes boring holes into her back. She wanted to drop it on the floor, but was terrified Rafe would see. She caught up with Trev in the front hall. "Please, wait."

He whirled. "You told me the two of you were through!"

She gasped. So he knew about Lana and Farrell? "We are over," she cried. "I went upstairs to use a bathroom, and Farrell, damn him, followed me!"

Trev stared, and Kait knew he was deciding whether to believe her or not.

Farrell—damn him—paused beside them. Kait flinched, but was stunned to find not a trace of amusement in his expression or his eyes. He said, "She's right. I hounded her, Coleman." He turned to Kait and nodded in such a way that it was almost an old-world bow. "I apologize. My behavior was hardly that of a gentleman." He nodded grimly at Trev and walked away.

Kait realized then just how thoroughly Lana and Farrell were scamming Trev.

Not only that, they were thieves.

And from the look of things, professional ones.

Trev suddenly took her arm. "Don't lie to me now," he said heatedly. "I mean it, Lana."

Kait wet her lips. "Trev, after last night, how could I possibly ever look at another man the way I look at you?"

His eyes softened. And Kait knew he believed her—but then, her every word had been the truth, and spoken from the heart. "Let's get out of here," he said, taking her arm and pressing it against her side.

Kait glanced back. Rafe and Georgina stood a few feet away from them, Rafe watching her like a hawk. And was it her imagination, or was he eyeing her fisted hand?

And before Kait knew it, Trev had guided her out onto the veranda and down the front steps to where a valet was waiting. Kait tried to think. Should she just drop the ring? She was about to do so when a sixth sense made her glance back

again. Rafe Coleman had followed them outside. He stood
on the veranda, regarding them coolly, waiting for her to in-
criminate herself.

Kait faced forward, breathless with fear. Trev reached for
her hand. "The brown Jag," he said. As the valet hurried off
he looked at Kait. "What are you holding?"

Kait smiled brightly—sickly. "Lipstick," she said. She
tugged her fisted palm free, and with her other hand, opened
her evening bag. She held it carefully in front of her ab-
domen, so Rafe Coleman couldn't possibly see what she was
doing. And she dropped the diamond ring into her purse, instantly snapping it closed.

A moment later, they were in the Jag and on their way
back to Fox Hollow.

SIXTEEN

Trev lay on his stomach, his head turned toward her, and he was breathing softly. He was out like a light. Kait glanced away, at the illuminated dial of the small clock on her bedside table—it was three in the morning. She quietly slipped from the bed, nude.

On her way to the bathroom, she paused and bent to pick up her sandals, one by one, her Ungaro gown, a thong that she had recently purchased, and her evening bag. Her clothes had hastily been removed the moment they had stepped into the bedroom. In the walk-in closet, she hung up the dress and slid on one of his T-shirts, which happily reached her thighs. She dropped the sandals in a pile near her rows of carefully arranged shoes, then shook her head sadly.

No, those were not her shoes, just as the man in the bedroom was not her husband—they were Lana's shoes and Trev was Lana's husband and her sister was a thief.

She simply couldn't believe it.

But she had the proof.

Now she was only holding the evening bag with its long, cascading fringe. She opened it and instantly saw the big yellow diamond ring. Horrified, she snapped it shut.

When was Georgina Parker going to realize that her ring was gone—and how long would it take Rafe Coleman to recall that he had found her and Colin Farrell standing right outside the Parkers' bedroom door?

Sick with fear, Kait thought that once the ring was discovered missing, Rafe would take about two seconds flat to remember where he had found her and Farrell on the night of the gala.

She had to return the ring, before it was discovered missing.

Could she be charged with burglary?

How could this have happened? And just when Trev was falling for her. He might think she was Lana, but Kait knew now with all of her heart that he would never be behaving this way with her sister.

She heard his soft footsteps before she heard his equally soft, sleepy voice. Kait rearranged her expression as Trev paused on the threshold of the bathroom. "Hey," he said, with a soft smile. "What are you doing?"

Kait hesitated. "I can't sleep."

He rubbed his eyes, looking like a man who had just spent hours making love and who had just been earning his well-deserved rest, that is, he looked sexy and delicious and oh-so-impossibly good. "I haven't worn you out yet, have I?" he asked, his tone having changed into a sensuous rumble.

Kait met his green gaze and saw the seductive smile in his eyes. *On top of everything else, on top of her pretending to be his wife, he would find out now that Lana was a thief.* "Trev, you're naked," Kait finally said. She felt like melting into his arms and crumbling into tears at the exact same moment.

"And you are upset. Why?"

Kait shook her head, hugging herself. Did Farrell have the answers she needed? Good God, he had met Lana when she was twenty-two, ten years ago. Did that mean what Kait thought it meant?

Surely Lana and Farrell had broken up six years ago, Lana had met and fallen for Trev and married him, and then she had gotten back with Farrell.

Kait was ill and filled with dread. Because she knew with every fiber of her being that it hadn't been that way. She respected Trev enough now, and knew him well enough, to know he would not accuse her sister of targeting him for his money if it hadn't been the truth.

Had she and Farrell targeted Trev together? But why wait all these years to divorce? Had they decided to hide from the police for a while? Or had it been convenient to remain a wealthy woman—while they preyed upon their unsuspecting neighbors?

Trev disappeared and reappeared a second later, clad in his white Jockeys. "What's up, Lana?" he asked quietly, sitting down on the edge of the Jacuzzi bathtub not far from where she sat on the ottoman.

She met his gaze and saw so much concern there. Her heart turned over hard. This man would be devastated, not only when he learned of her charade, but when he learned the extent of Lana's treachery. Kait had to speak with Farrell, as soon as possible. And it was time, damn it, for Lana to come back. It was time for the truth.

"Let's go back to bed," Kait said, standing. His eyes followed her movement, ending at the hem of his T-shirt, where it brushed her upper thighs.

"Trying to distract me?" he asked, also rising.

"No." She did smile, because she knew she had distracted him.

He slid his arm around her, pulled her close, and kissed her on the mouth. "I'm going to check on Sam. What time is it?"

"It's past three," Kait said. Sam's curfew had been midnight. "I'm sure she's been back for hours, Trev."

"So am I, but I should have checked hours ago," he said.

Kait followed him. In the walk-in, he slipped on sweats and a T-shirt. As he left the bedroom, Kait paused by the bed. The lights were on now, and she gripped the footboard, feeling helpless and lost, but also becoming angry. What should she do now?

The urge to go the authorities had become overwhelming. Because the bottom line was that her sister was a criminal.

But Lana was her sister. Kait did not know if she had the strength to send her to prison. Kait was mentally and emotionally exhausted, but suddenly she realized that everything Lana had told her should be questioned. Lana had said she owed someone a tremendous sum of money, but why should Kait believe it? The only thing that seemed certain was that Lana's life was in danger, and Kait knew that for a fact because of the two attempts made to hurt or kill her there at Fox Hollow.

Before Kait could reflect any further, she heard Trev shout, followed by a female scream.

Kait yanked on a pair of jeans and ran down the hall and to Sam's room. The door was wide open, lights had been turned on. And Trev was shouting, "You goddamned little bastard, I am killing you!"

Kait dashed inside and the impossible tableau crystallized before her very eyes—Sam naked in bed, holding a sheet up over her breasts, and Trev, enraged, pinning a very naked Gabe Jenkins to the wall.

Gabe looked frightened and angry all at once. Trev jammed him against the wall. "It's not what you think!" Gabe shouted.

"Dad, stop!" Sam screamed.

Kait ran forward, grabbing Trev from behind. "Trev, stop. This isn't the solution," she cried.

He became still. But beneath her hands, his body was a rock of solid tension. "You're screwing my daughter," he snarled. "And if I'm not mistaken, you're eighteen and she's sixteen, which makes this rape."

"Ow," Gabe said. The side of his face was against the wall. "I love her!"

"Let him go!" Sam cried. "What difference does it make if we're sleeping together? I haven't been a virgin since I was fourteen."

Trev whirled, releasing Gabe. He stared at his daughter in

shock while Gabe ran to retrieve a pair of blue plaid boxers and hop wildly into them.

"It's true," Sam said defiantly, her face covered with tears.

"How could you do this?" Trev asked. "How, Sam? I mean, you were such a good, sweet kid and then . . ." He stopped.

"And then you married Lana and forgot all about me," Sam cried.

"I've never forgotten about you," Trev said. Gabe was now shrugging on an oversized button-down shirt. Trev glanced at him. "Freeze. I'm calling the cops."

"Trev, don't," Kait whispered.

"I hate you so much!" Sam shouted. New tears fell.

"It will be all right," Gabe told her.

"Like hell it will be," Trev spat. He crossed the room to use Sam's phone. Kait walked over to Sam and tried to take her hand, but she wouldn't release the sheet and she wouldn't look at her—she stared at her father's back with sheer hostility.

"Is he calling the cops or Rafe?" she asked fearfully.

Kait realized there was a difference. "I don't know. Honey, he'll calm down. He's in shock and upset." She hesitated. "Are you guys using condoms?"

Sam flushed. Gabe moved over to them. "Of course we are. I'd never be so stupid to get her pregnant."

Kait turned to look at him. He was wary now, and still frightened, but more in control of himself than he had been when Trev had had him up against the wall. "Condoms break, Gabe," she said quietly. "Accidents happen. It only takes one time. I happen to think that unless you're at that stage of life where you are ready to marry and have children, you shouldn't be sleeping around."

"I'd marry Sam in a heartbeat," Gabe said. Then he looked at Sam.

Kait watched them share a deep glance and she realized that they were deeply in love, never mind that they were kids going through life's roughest time—adolescence.

Trev slammed down the phone. "Rafe's on his way," he said, pointing at Gabe. "I *never* want you near my daughter again."

"Dad!" Sam cried. She leapt from the bed, sheet and all. Her face had turned spectacularly white.

"I mean it," Trev said. "Because if he comes around again, I'm pressing charges."

Gabe also turned white.

Kait winced, horrified. She knew Trev meant well. She knew he loved his daughter. And it wasn't exactly her place, but it seemed to her that he was doing everything wrong.

"You can't tell me who I can see and who I can't," Sam cried. "I'm sixteen, not six."

"And that makes you a minor living under my roof, so I can damn well tell you anything I want," Trev said harshly.

Gabe touched Sam. She glanced at him. Kait didn't know what the silent communication meant, but then Sam said, "Dad, if you send him to jail, I'm leaving. And you'll never see me again."

Trev paled.

To Kait, the waffles tasted like cardboard.

But Marni was clearly enjoying them. Kait had allowed her to cover them not just with syrup but with gobs of whipped cream and maraschino cherries. Fortunately, Elizabeth had left for church, so Kait didn't have to deal with her disapproval.

Trev pushed back his chair. His waffles were basically untouched. "Thanks," he said to Kait. "I'm going to school Charm today."

Kait happened to know that Charm was a young new stallion that he had recently purchased. "Okay." She shoved a piece of waffle around in the gooey maple syrup. Sam hadn't come downstairs. Kait had wanted to peek in on her, but her door was locked. She suspected that the teen was soundly asleep.

Last night, Rafe had taken Gabe home. Apparently, there

would be no charges pressed—the brothers had had a long and heated argument, with Rafe clearly winning the day—but he had promised Gabe that next time he would not be so lenient.

"Daddy, you never school on Sundays! You didn't read your newspaper!" Marni wailed.

Trev said, his tone affectionate in spite of the heavy and grim set of his mouth, "I know. But today's different. Do you mind, sweetheart? You can stay with Mommy."

Marni pouted.

Kait understood—Trev was more than upset, and he needed to work in order to distract himself. "Honey, why don't you help me do the dishes? I'll wash, you dry," Kait said.

A week ago, Trev would have stared at her in disbelief, as they both knew Lana did not do dishes. But that was a week ago—now, he smiled at her before grabbing a jacket from a wall peg and walking out. He had completely accepted the new and improved Lana.

Kait and Marni began clearing the table. Kait hesitated. "Marni? Do you think you could run up and see if Sam needs anything? I could bring her waffles in bed."

Marni beamed, agreed, and raced off. Kait was grim as she finished clearing the kitchen table. This was the last thing that anyone needed right now, a terrible teen situation. She felt terrible for Trev, for Sam, and even for Gabe Jenkins. She was incredibly relieved that Rafe had talked Trev out of pressing charges against him.

Marni came downstairs at a trot. "She said she's starving and if you bring her waffles, she'd eat them," she announced.

"Really?" Kait was thrilled. Ten minutes later she was carrying a tray upstairs. Sam's door was ajar. Kait glanced in. "Knock, knock," she said.

Sam sat in bed with two magazines, her headphones on, in jeans and a sweatshirt. She removed the headphones and looked at Kait, not smiling.

Her eyes were swollen and red.

Kait asked, "Can I come in?"

Sam nodded. "At least you ask," she said.

Kait walked in and laid the tray down on a cluttered bedside table. "Did you cry all night?"

Sam nodded.

"Your father isn't pressing charges," she said softly.

"He isn't?" Briefly, her face lit up. Then it fell. "That's only because of Uncle Rafe! My father sucks!"

"Actually, he's a wonderful man," Kait said. "Can I sit down?"

Sam nodded.

Kait sat down at the foot of her bed.

"You're only saying that because you're in love with him. You wouldn't say that if you were me."

"No, probably not, not now, not at your age. But Sam, remember the story I told you? You are so lucky to have a father who loves you and cares so much that he went berserk when he found you with your boyfriend."

Sam blinked. "I can't give up Gabe."

Kait sighed. "You had better cool it until Trev calms down. Look, we were planning to have Gabe and his mom for dinner tonight—until this happened."

Sam gaped. "You were? That must have been your idea!"

"It was. I thought it high time your dad meet Gabe—and see for himself who he is."

Sam almost smiled. She said, "You are a really nice lady. I don't know who you are and where that bitch is, but I hope she never comes back. Are you going to stay?"

Kait stared.

Kait had gone back to the kitchen, and was almost through with the dishes when she heard the front doorbell. She was tremendously preoccupied now. She could insist until she was blue that she was Lana, but she didn't even want to. She had merely told Sam that she was wrong, and she had promptly fled the room.

But Sam wasn't wrong—and how long would it be before she said something? Kait had no idea; because teenagers were simply too unpredictable and she didn't dare try to assume how Sam would think or act.

Marni was still in Sam's room, regaling her with the details of a story that had been read in her kindergarten class on Friday. Kait dried her hands on the daisy-dotted apron she was wearing and went to the front door. She opened it, and there was a grinning Colin Farrell.

She wanted to slam it closed in his face. Instead, she stared in disbelief. "You!"

His grin vanished. He took in every inch of her appearance—her bare feet with their sheer pink toenails, her low-rise jeans, the daisy-sprinkled apron, the lemon-yellow T-shirt, and the fact that she wore not one stitch of makeup, not even mascara.

Kait felt panic. "What are you doing here?" If Trev saw him, he would never believe that he and Lana were through. But did it matter? Because this was the end of the game; they had come to the end of the road.

With no sign of the abundant amusement Kait had witnessed the night before, he said, "Do relax. Coleman just drove off to town. And you're not her," he stated flatly. "You are not Lana, now, are you, love?"

Kait felt the floor tilt wildly beneath her feet. "Are you insane?" she gasped.

"Lana would never, ever, be caught dead in jeans and an apron and without her face on. Not ever," he stressed, his gray eyes wide and riveted upon her.

"Just get out," Kait said. Then she changed her mind and grabbed his arm, dragging him inside. "No—we have to talk!" She slammed the door and lowered her voice. "I want you to return that ring!"

"Like bloody hell," he said. He slowly circled her, studying every inch of her. Then he stopped short. "Good God— she told me so long ago that I'd completely forgotten. You're her twin!"

Kait inhaled. There was no escape hatch now.

His hands were on his hips. Today, he wore a navy blue sports jacket over tan slacks with a paler blue polo shirt be-

neath. "She told me once, shortly after we moved in together, that she had a twin. A physically identical carbon
copy of herself."

Her lips had turned into wood. "She told you?" Lana had
told this man, but no one else. She had told Colin Farrell, but
not her husband, Trev.

"She told me once, in passing. I do believe she mentioned
you were as different as night and day and that you spoke
rarely. And that was the end of that conversation." He was
suddenly reflective. "What the bloody hell is going on?
What is she up to?" Now he was grim and concerned.
"Where is she?"

In that moment, Kait instinctively knew she had an ally in
her quest for the truth, never mind that he was a thief. "I
don't know where she is," she said.

He gave her a long look. "You must tell me what's going
on," he said warningly.

Did she dare bargain? "Will you return the ring?"

He nodded.

"Lana asked me to cover for her so she could borrow or
raise the money she owes," she began.

He grabbed her arm. "Hold right there. The *money* she
owes?" He was incredulous.

Kait stared. But she had known since discovering that her
sister was a thief and a pro that her story was a lie.

"I'm going to throttle her," he said with a disbelieving
shake of his head.

Kait wondered if he meant it. He wasn't all that angry,
and he seemed somewhat amused. "So then why *did* she ask
me to come here and switch places with her?"

"You're a fool," he said with a laugh that wasn't humor-
ous. His gray gaze was direct. "Believing that rot. But what I
cannot believe is that she did not tell me what she was doing." He was finally annoyed. But he still didn't seem angry,
and Kait couldn't decide if he were a cool, cool cucumber or
a very good actor. It was probably a combination of both.

"What is going on?" Kait asked grimly. "Please, Colin.

Please. I have been going crazy pretending to be her—not to mention that someone shot at me—her—and also drove me off the road."

He studied her for a long moment. "She's conned you. Quite thoroughly, it seems." And he did smile, suddenly amused.

Kait felt like smacking the smile right off his handsome face. "It's hardly funny."

He gave her a look she could not decipher. "I find it rather amusing—she's even conned me. Not for the first time, I might add."

Kait stared. "So then why are you with her?" Her previous thoughts assailed her. "Did you guys break up when she married Trev?"

He eyed her. "Romantic, eh, love?"

"Yes," she said, and the single word hissed out on her breath.

"We've never broken up. I'm with her because she is the most exciting woman I have ever met. And we are partners. Neither one of us could survive without the other one."

Kait walked away to sit down. Her worst suspicions were right. "She never loved Trev." It wasn't a question.

"No. Although I do think he amused her for a while. You *are* romantic."

Kait didn't look up. "But what about Marni?" she whispered, finally meeting Farrell's gray eyes.

For the first time, Farrell hesitated. "Some women are better mothers than others," he said.

That was an understatement. "I need to know the whole . . ." She hesitated.

"Scam?" he supplied.

She nodded. "So she married him for his money?"

"My, you are a bit of a terrier." His white teeth flashed. "We were looking for a mark. A nice, rich chap with nice rich friends—and then Lana learned about Trev Coleman. She came to me one day extremely excited, because he was old money, recently widowed, with a daughter, and lots of old-world friends. We both felt that he'd be vulnerable and easy to manage. We were right. He fell for her like a sack of rocks."

Kait couldn't move. Her earlier suspicions returned. "How did she find out about Trev?" she managed.

"I have no idea. But she knew he'd be at a certain restaurant for a business meeting, and she intercepted him there." His expression changed. "What is it?"

And suddenly, Kait knew the truth.

"Tell me," Farrell said.

Kait looked up. "Lana had dinner with me. I was working on a charity event and I told her I wanted to hold it at Fox Hollow. I had a lunch meeting scheduled with Trev two weeks after. But he didn't show. When did they meet, Farrell?"

"May of 'ninety-seven. They were married the following September—Labor Day weekend, in fact."

"He was supposed to meet me. She fixed it so that she met him instead."

Both of Farrell's brows lifted. Then, "She's very good," he said suavely.

"She's horrible," Kait cried, standing.

"I begin to see. You are the moral sort, aren't you?"

Kait could imagine what Lana had done—call Trev, pretend to be Kait, change the time and place of their meeting, then waltz in and attract his attention. Kait London had never shown up. Lana had been there to pick up all the pieces.

Kait was furious.

"Oh, come, Kait. It's hardly the end of the world that Lana messed up your business meeting with Coleman. Oh, wait! I begin to see." He was wide-eyed now.

"There's nothing to see," Kait snapped. She hurried out of Trev Coleman's office with Farrell at her side.

"No? You've fallen hard for the fellow and you're thinking that if Lana hadn't interfered, right now, you'd be the proper mistress of Fox Hollow."

"That's not what I'm thinking," Kait lied. *But it was exactly what she was thinking.*

In the living room, Kait faced him, her arms folded across her chest. "I still don't understand why. Why con me into covering for her?"

Colin Farrell smiled. "Isn't it obvious? She wanted to pull off a job without me. Either that, or she's setting one up." He didn't seem angry, but he was no longer very amused. "She's never cut me out before. Where is she?"

"I have no idea."

"When did you last hear from her?"

Kait told him. "She intends to return on Monday. That's tomorrow," she added.

His gaze narrowed as he absorbed that. Suddenly he held out his hand. "I'll take that ring now," he said.

Kait couldn't wait to get rid of it. But she still had questions—lots of questions. "Not yet. What about Rafe Coleman? He knows, doesn't he, what Lana really is?" Now, his hostility and threats made sense. "And is Zara an undercover cop?"

Farrell laughed, but not with mirth. "Zara's a PI working for Trev."

"What?" Kait gasped, completely surprised.

"That's right—he's gathering dirt on Lana so he can divorce her without handing over the keys to the kingdom. As if she gives a damn about this place."

Kait sat down, in shock. *How much did Trev know?*

How long would it take for a good private investigator to discover that Lana had an identical twin?

"What does Rafe know?" she managed then.

"We don't know. I think he despises Lana for the obvious reasons, but she started worrying a few months ago that he was on to her—to us."

"He knows she's a thief," she said. "I'm certain of it." She stopped herself from adding a warning that he was pursuing Lana with a vengeance.

Kait stiffened. Which side was she now on?

She couldn't be on her sister's side, but Lana faced a serious indictment if caught, and hard jail time if convicted.

"Well, if that is so, this is the perfect time for Lana's divorce—and our departure from the area." He was impatient now. Clearly he was interested in leaving. "It was nice meeting you, Kait."

He was about to leave. "I'll get the ring," Kait cried.

His hand clamped down on her shoulder before she could rush for the stairs. "No need."

"What?" she gasped, meeting his eyes with a sinking sensation.

His smile was wide, his eyes sparkled. He leaned close. "Tell me. You just stole your first bauble, Kait. How does it feel?"

"I didn't steal anything!" she cried in a frantic whisper. "Now let me go so I can get that damn thing!"

He didn't release her. "No rush? No high?" He was now amused. "There is a rush, love. It's almost better than sex."

"Let go!"

He obeyed.

"You *are* taking the ring."

"No, actually, I'm not." He turned to leave.

She ran after him. "Are you nuts? I can't keep it! It needs to be returned. Immediately—Rafe saw us, Farrell!"

He paused at the front door. "You're keeping it. It's called insurance, love."

Kait felt her mouth drop open and hang there.

He flashed his brilliant smile and walked out.

SEVENTEEN

Kait stood in the doorway, staring after Farrell, when Marni came dashing out of the house. "Colin!" she squealed with delight.

Kait stiffened with amazement; Farrell turned, smiling, and the next thing Kait knew, Marni was high in his arms, being swung wildly around. "How's the most gorgeous girl on the planet?" Farrell asked, grinning, as he set her firmly but gently back down on the ground.

Marni's cheeks were bright red. "Mommy made waffles for breakfast! They were the best!"

"I'll bet they were," he said, tugging on a curl. "I have a surprise for you, sweetheart," he said.

"Is it a present?" she asked eagerly.

"Did I also say you were the cleverest girl on the planet?" He laughed.

Marni giggled, and glanced back at Kait. "What did he bring me today, Mommy?"

Kait was reeling. She prayed now, with all of her heart, that Marni was not Colin Farrell's child. She was so aghast that she could not speak.

Hand in hand, Farrell and Marni walked over to his big black Mercedes sedan. Kait closed her eyes, knowing how he could afford Mercedes's most expensive luxury car. She was going to have to return the ring herself.

Marni's squeals made her eyes fly open. "Look, Mommy, look, a real necklace!" she shouted.

"Hug first," Farrell said, squatting.

Marni obeyed and they hugged like dear old friends—or like an uncle and his niece—or a father and his daughter. Marni dashed back up the veranda, while Kait stood there like a statue. Farrell grinned at her and slid into the sedan. As he drove away, Marni showed her a small necklace with her name hanging on it. "It's beautiful," Kait said, hearing another car approaching. She tensed, afraid it was Trev. And if it was, he and Farrell would pass one another in the driveway.

But it wasn't a spanking-new oversized cobalt blue Dodge Ram, and it wasn't the trim, sexy tan Jaguar either. It was Elizabeth's dusty old Land Rover.

Kait and Marni walked into the house. "Does Farrell—Colin—give you lots of presents?"

"He never comes here without one," Marni announced. "He loves me. He told me so. He thinks of me like the daughter he doesn't have."

"I suppose he told you that?" Kait said, sickened.

Marni grinned and nodded. "Can I wear it? Please?"

Kait helped her put the necklace on, clasping it closed for her. The front door opened and closed. Kait did not want to deal with Elizabeth Dorentz now. She straightened and turned.

Elizabeth looked as if she'd swallowed a jug of turpentine, in spite of her navy blue Sunday church dress and peach lipstick. Had her expression been different, she would have been a very beautiful and elegant older woman.

"Good morning," Kait said with a big, false smile.

"I never thought to see Colin Farrell in this house again," she said.

So her sword was drawn. "It wasn't my idea," Kait said grimly.

"Mommy?" Marni asked in a small worried voice.

Kait bent, clasping her shoulder. "Why don't you go upstairs and show Sam that beautiful necklace?"

Marni grinned and ran off. Then she stopped. "But can we play with my horse models later?"

"We can do that, and more. Why don't we go see *Beauty and the Beast* again?" Kait smiled.

Marni agreed eagerly and dashed up the stairs. Kait faced Elizabeth, her hands on her hips. "As she is fond of Farrell, you shouldn't be speaking of him in that manner in front of her."

Elizabeth paled. "How dare you tell me how to behave in front of that child! I am more a mother to her than you will ever be!"

"You are not her mother," Kait spat. Fury enveloped her now—fury at Lana, fury at Farrell, fury at this woman and everyone else who hated Lana and had to have their fingers in the messy, carved-up pie that was Lana's life. She was even, dear God, angry at herself.

"And you are?"

Kait straightened. "What the hell does that mean?" Her ears rang. *Elizabeth knew she wasn't Lana.* And this woman couldn't be trusted with her secret—she would use it against her—Trev would never look at her again once Elizabeth got to him. Speech failed Kait.

Should she explain? Beg? Threaten? Cajole?

"We both know you came back here expecting divorce papers—and once you got them you decided to use Marni to protect yourself against Trev! If he hadn't decided to throw you out, you wouldn't be taking her to a movie this afternoon, now, would you, Mrs. Coleman?"

"You're wrong," Kait said.

"And to have that lover of yours here! Right under Trev's nose!" Elizabeth shouted. "He thinks it's over with you two, but I'm on to you, Mrs. Coleman!"

Kait looked up and saw hatred in her twisted expression and in her baleful eyes.

"I am not keeping your dirty secrets, Mrs. Coleman. It was different before he decided to divorce you, but now, I will do everything I can to help him stay to his course—as it is a course he should have taken years ago!"

Kait didn't respond—she was staring into the blond woman's blazing blue eyes. Did this woman own a gun? Could she have driven her off the road two nights ago? Was she capable of making such threats—or of really trying to take her life?

Kait was suddenly jolted into a very harsh and frightening reality. Her instincts said yes. In fact, they shouted at her now. She slowly stood. "You can tell Trev whatever you feel you must. Farrell came by of his own accord; I had nothing to do with it."

Elizabeth made an angry and disparaging sound and strode away, toward the stairs. Kait felt her knees weaken once the horrid housekeeper was gone. Trev would be furious about Farrell's visit. She did not know if she could talk her way out of it.

And what about the damned ring? Should she flush it down the toilet? Throw it in the lake? Or could she try to rectify a wrong and actually attempt to return it?

The answer was obvious, but Kait was afraid of being caught while attempting to return it to Georgina Parker. And if she did get back into the Parkers' house, where would she leave it? On a table downstairs? Or did she dare try to steal into the master bedroom, and leave it there, perhaps on the vanity in the bathroom? Clearly, Kait couldn't get it back into the safe.

Her temples throbbed. Damn Farrell and her sister for their reckless criminal escapades. And what about Lana?

She had never loved Trev Coleman. She didn't seem to really care about being a mother either. She had married Trev for his money, his position, his social set—so she and Farrell could steal from his friends.

It was stunning . . . unbelievable, but it was now a fact.

And Lana had found out about Trev Coleman from her, Kait, in the first place. She'd diverted him from his business meeting with Kait, and then strolled in to seduce him, con him, marry him herself.

Kait felt the loathing for her sister again.

She needed air. How could she hate her twin, no matter what she had done? Kait ran outside, and once strolling down the hill toward the stables, she fought for emotional control. Lana had done too many unconscionable things to count— Kait could not forgive her for using Trev or for being a thief— but she was her twin. Kait loved her. She had loved her all her life. And as hard as it was reconciling the woman Lana had become with the wild child and reckless teen she'd once been, Kait knew she had to do so. Something was terribly wrong with Lana, because Lana was a liar, a criminal, a cheat.

Kait reminded herself that she hadn't heard Lana's side of things. Surely Lana had a dozen excuses to make for her behavior. Then Kait gave up. She was only trying to fool herself. There were simply no excuses to make, not anymore, not now. Lana was sick.

But Kait knew Lana wasn't bad. She wasn't evil. She wasn't a killer. She was selfish, and she had somehow gone astray. Lana needed professional help.

Kait's emotions had calmed. She could not hate her sister for very long, thank God. Amazingly, for the first time in her life, she felt sorry for her twin. For the first time in her life, there was no more envy, and no admiration.

But nothing could change the feeling Kait had had for some time now, of being in deep and treacherous waters. No amount of effort or skill could keep her afloat for much longer.

What should she do now? And what was she going to do when Lana returned tomorrow?

Kait's steps suddenly slowed. Max Zara was standing outside the stable, leaning against the hood of his battered pickup truck. *He was a PI, hired by Trev, to get the dirt on Lana.* How much did he know?

He was sipping from a can of soda. Kait didn't veer away. His intent blue eyes settled on her. He tilted the can of Dr Pepper up and drank thirstily. When he was done, their gazes met, he crushed the can of soda with his fist, and tossed it into the back of the Toyota truck.

He was actually a good-looking man. He seemed to go out of his way to make himself look disreputable—he wasn't shaved, and he wore a blue chambray shirt that had had its sleeves ripped off, over a tissue-thin white T-shirt that showed off his body. Kait bet anything he drank too much, ate burgers and fries, but had quit smoking cigarettes. She'd bet anything that, shaved and in a suit and tie, he'd turn more than a few female heads.

At least she now knew that he had not tried to kill her. If he was a legitimate private investigator, working for Trev, then he was gathering information, and that was all.

Did he know she was Kait London? If so, Kait knew Trev also knew the truth. She shuddered to think that Trev had known who she really was for some time now and hadn't said a thing. The idea was frightening. She had to be the one to tell him the truth.

"Nice mornin'," he said.

"Have a little hangover?" she asked sweetly, noticing his red eyes.

"Just a teensy-weensy one. Nice visit from Farrell?"

She tensed. "Not really."

"No? That's a first." He appeared amused.

"I asked you this a few days ago, and now I'm asking again. What do you want from me, Zara?"

His regard moved over her slowly, but not insultingly. "Maybe not much."

Kait didn't like his answer. "A few days ago, you told me to watch my back."

"Still think you might want to do that," he said.

"Am I in trouble? In danger?"

"Gee, only if you think being shot at and driven off the road is fun."

He wasn't going to open up. "A few days ago, you told me you meant to bring me down." Her heart beat hard now. Surely he could see how frightened she was. "That's changed, hasn't it? Why?"

He lolled back against the truck, propping both elbows up behind him, on the hood. His biceps popped. "Has it changed . . . Mrs. Coleman? Now what makes you think that?"

She stared into his eyes. He stared back unwaveringly. He was impossible to read. "I know you were in New York when I was there last week."

"Bravo." He clapped his hands once, twice, three times. "I'm from Brooklyn, remember? I got a girl there."

"Liar," she said.

He started. "My, you've grown back your balls, Mrs. Coleman. Now why would I have been in the Big Apple if not to see my girl?"

She wet her lips. "You were following me."

He came close. "Do you have something to hide, Mrs. Coleman? Because you're sweating like a pig."

She meant to tell him that she had nothing to hide, but it was such a monstrous lie that no words came out.

He leaned back against the hood of the Toyota. "Thought so."

"How much do you know?" she whispered.

He smiled at her. "Do you really think I'd tell you . . . *Lana?*"

As he seemed intent on lolling against his beat-up pickup in the autumn sun, Kait escaped into the barn. It was empty, as all the horses had been turned out. The moment she was inside, she collapsed on a stall door, on the verge of tears. The way he had said her sister's name made her almost certain that he knew she wasn't Lana.

Why would Trev go along with her charade?

Kait knew why. The answer was glaringly simple. To see what she was up to.

And it meant that he was also in the throes of a theatrical performance—it meant he was pretending to have fallen in love with her.

Kait was ill. She flung open the stall door and went down on her knees, throwing up her meager breakfast. And when her retches became dry heaves, she remained there on her hands and knees. The tears fell profusely now.

She loved him so much, but their entire relationship was built on lie after lie. Maybe it was better that he knew the truth and was a liar too. Because maybe they would then have a chance: two liars together, instead of one.

But then he wouldn't be the man she had fallen in love with.

And they didn't have a chance. The moment Lana returned, it was over. Trev would never forgive her and he'd never even look at her again, much less speak to her.

A door slammed shut.

Kait didn't think about it, assuming it had been the wind. She sat back on her calves and wiped her eyes with her fingers, then brushed wisps of straw off her face. Maybe, just maybe, she was wrong and Zara didn't know anything incriminating yet.

Kait suddenly tensed, thinking she smelled smoke. She sniffed, felt reassured, and started to stand. But before she was even fully upright, the acrid odor returned, intensified.

Kait ran out of the stall, and saw smoke curling at the barn's far end, where she had recently come in. And as she stared, she saw a stall burst into flames.

And the door she had come through was closed—while the catty-corner door, through which all of the stables' vehicles entered and exited, remained closed as it had been before. Kait ran to the small side door and tugged on it to open it—but it refused to budge.

A huge whoosh sounded.

Kait jerked on the door again, but it was stuck and did not budge.

She turned.

In her corner of the barn were six stalls, three on each side of the corridor. Now all three stalls on the far side of the corridor were on fire. The entire barn was going to go up in flames.

Kait screamed and ran away from the fire and down the corridor toward the indoor arena, past another dozen stalls. As she did so, she heard the fire claiming stall after stall, racing after her, almost on her heels. For the first time since arriving at Fox Hollow, she saw that the door in the passageway leading to the indoor arena was also closed, and before she even tried to open it, she knew it was closed for a reason—she knew it was locked.

And that the fire was a trap.

A trap meant to kill.

But Kait tried the door anyway, to no avail. Smoke was infusing the air now, making it hard to breathe. Behind her, every single stall was engulfed in a raging inferno.

She glanced to her left, beginning to cough, where stairs led to Max Zara's apartment and the other, unused one. As she did, she heard her sister's name.

Kait froze. Had she imagined it?

"Lana!"

It was Trev. "Trev! Help! Trev!" she screamed. But the effort cost her dearly, and she had a fit of coughing. Kait tore off her T-shirt and used it to cover her mouth and nose. Sparks landed on the knee of her jeans.

Kait batted them out and dashed up the stairs. From the corner of her eye, she watched the fire overtake the door to the tack room. She burst into the unused apartment, going right to the window. And as she crossed its width, she could feel the heat of the fire under the soles of her shoes.

If she didn't get out now, she would die.

Kait reached the window and jerked on it; to her relief, it flew open. Smoke billowed into the room behind her; Kait didn't dare pause. She climbed over the ledge, releasing her T-shirt. The ground loomed up at her from one story below. "Trev!" she screamed. "Trev!"

She looked back. The fire had reached the landing in the hall and she saw the flames crackling along the floor there through the open doorway. There was only one way out.

Kait looked back down. She'd survive the jump, wouldn't she? She'd break a leg or two, but surely not her neck. She hesitated.

The fire roared loudly in the room behind her.

"Lana!"

Kait glanced back and saw Trev and Max in the field below. "The fire's in the apartment," she cried.

"Lana! Can you move? The gutter's about six feet to your left!" Trev called up to her. His tone was calm—his expression was not.

Kait glanced left and saw a gutter that ran down the side of the building. It seemed a zillion miles away.

"Lana, you can do it! But you have to hurry!" Trev said firmly.

She looked behind her. The fire was climbing along the door to the apartment and had crossed half the floor. Fortunately, the floor was oak, not a synthetic carpet, and there was only one area rug, which it hadn't yet reached. "I don't know," she cried. Her mind was telling her to jump, her body was resisting in fear, and she was afraid to try to navigate the ledge to the gutter—she was afraid of falling.

"Go, now!" Trev cried, frustration creeping into his tone.

Kait looked down and seemed to meet his gaze. This was it, then. It was get to the gutter and slide down it—or jump. She inhaled, beginning to shake. And keeping her hands flat on the building at her back, pressed up against it as hard as she could, she started to shuffle along the narrow ledge toward the gutter.

"That's it!" Trev cried.

Her foot shot out. Kait screamed and somehow shrank up against the building, her heart stopping with terror. She had almost fallen off the ledge.

"Lana—get going!" Trev shouted.

She blinked through sweat and tears. The wood siding had become so hot against her back that it felt as if it would burst into flames at any moment. Kait moved.

Recklessly, she dove at the gutter and the next thing she knew, it burned and tore at her hands and the flesh on her bare torso as she slid rapidly down it.

Seconds later, she felt Trev's hands on her feet, and a moment later, as his hands reached her hips, she let go. He caught her and held her hard, in his arms.

She began to cough, wildly, uncontrollably, as the sirens sounded in the not-so-far distance. He turned her to face him and she melted into his arms, against the wall of his solid body. Kait buried her face against his chest. "It's all right," he said softly, stroking her hair.

And Zara spoke. "We had better get out of here," he said. "And we had better get the horses out of the near paddocks."

"How bad is it?" Kait coughed.

"A little smoke inhalation. You'll be just fine," Mitch said soothingly, his smile gentle.

"No." She was hoarse. Her throat hurt. "The barn."

"They managed to save the indoor arena and the offices," Mitch said. "And the fire didn't spread to any of the other barns—and not a single horse was lost."

Kait nodded, and tears trickled down her cheeks.

Mitch took her hand. "Honey, it will be fine. Trev has this place insured, and he's got enough stalls and he didn't lose a single horse—and he didn't lose you."

Kait cried harder.

"What's wrong?"

"You would never understand," she managed. "But it's all my fault."

Mitch looked taken aback. "How could you possibly think that?"

"It wasn't an accident." She took a tissue from the box on her bedside table. "Someone locked me in. Someone wants me dead."

Mitch stared.

Kait leaned back against the pillows. "Is Rafe Coleman here?"

"The entire sheriff's department is here, and half the police department, not to mention the fire department and just about every one of your neighbors."

Kait nodded.

"You'll have a sore throat for a few days. Take some over-the-counter lozenges. But other than that, I'd say you are one lucky lady."

Kait couldn't smile.

"Chin up," Mitch said. He kissed her cheek. "Call me if you need me."

Kait watched him leave. The moment he was gone, she lifted the phone and dialed her cell phone, determined to confront her sister at long last. There was no answer, just her own voice mail.

Kait hung up, furious and frustrated. This had gone on long enough, and had she not had her wits about her, right now she might be dead. She tried to think, no easy task, as she was not just hurt but frightened and angry as well. The one person who might have an idea of where Lana was, was Farrell. Kait didn't have Farrell's number, but she intended to reach him next. Whatever he knew, he would spill, oh yes. Even if she had to go out, buy a gun, and use it. She was that frightened—and that mad.

Kait called information. Farrell was listed—she wrote down his address while she was at it—but he did not pick up the phone. Instead, she got his answering machine. Kait left a brief, terse message.

"We need to talk, Farrell. I need to find your partner. Call me at the house on her cell." She hung up, trembling, but more with anger now than anything else.

How could she have agreed to this deception in the first place? Without knowing any details, any facts? Had she been so utterly desperate for her sister's approval—and love? In hindsight, as incredible as it was, it certainly seemed that way.

And Lana had lied to her, Kait, as badly as she had to everyone else. She had used Kait in the same deliberate and remorseless manner. *Had she known that by switching places she was putting her own twin sister in terrible danger?*

Kait wanted to believe that the answer was no. She was afraid that it was yes.

An idea struck her. They had switched places. What if Lana was using her New York apartment? She was holed up somewhere—she was using Kait's identity—or so Kait assumed—and suddenly it seemed possible that she might be at Kait's condominium. Kait quickly lifted the receiver, dialing her own home breathlessly.

To her utter disbelief, no one answered the phone—and the machine did not pick up. Her telephone number was no longer in service.

What did that mean?

Kait leapt up from the bed, stunned. How could her telephone be out of service? She always paid her bills. She needed this like a hole in the head.

Kait dialed Verizon, her local carrier. After fifteen endless minutes, a customer-service representative came on the line and informed her that she, Kait London, had requested that her own service be terminated.

"What?" Kait gasped.

"Excuse me, ma'am, but you are Kait London?"

"I'm Kait London," Kait cried, perspiring now, her heart racing like a drum. Only one person could have known her Social Security number and have done this. And that was Lana.

But why?

Kait hung up in shock.

For one moment, she simply sat on the edge of the bed, reeling. And when some of the shock abated, she became aware of real and comprehensive dread.

Lana was up to something, but what?

Was she in New York?

Kait decided to dial a neighbor. Mrs. Grubbman answered on the first ring. "Ellen, it's me, Kait, how are you?" Kait cried.

"Kait? Kait London?" the older woman asked as if they hadn't been neighbors for eight years.

"Yes, Kait London!" She knew her tone was hysterical, so she took a deep calming breath. "I need to reach my sister, but oddly my phone service seems to have been interrupted. Could you go over there and see if she's in? And if she isn't, leave a note asking her to call me?" Ellen Grubbman knew Kait had a twin. But she had never met Lana.

"Kait, are you sure that's you?" Ellen Grubbman asked slowly, warily.

Kait stiffened. Slowly, she said, "Yes, Ellen, I am quite sure that this is me. Why?"

"Why? Because we spoke the other day, when you moved out."

Kait stiffened. *"What?!"*

"You told me that you were moving to the country and selling the apartment. In fact, that broker must have shown it a dozen times since we spoke. Is that where you are now? In some place in Virginia? Three Rivers?"

Kait had leapt to her feet; she sat down in shock. *"What? What are you talking about?"*

"What am I talking about? You've moved out and your apartment is for sale. Kait . . . are you all right?"

Kait was reeling. "No," she finally whispered, "no, I am not all right."

"I beg your pardon?"

"And it's Three Falls," Kait whispered, absolutely stunned. "Not Three Rivers, *Three Falls.*"

Mrs. Grubbman began to speak—Kait couldn't hear a word she said. She hung up.

Lana had disconnected her phone service. Lana put her apartment up for sale. Lana had told her neighbor that she was moving.

Lana was giving Kait's life away.

But why?

And then Kait knew. In fact, suddenly it became terribly, frighteningly obvious.

Lana wasn't coming back.

Which meant that Lana intended for Kait to remain at Fox Hollow—Lana intended for her to stay.

EIGHTEEN

Kait could barely think. One man's image came to mind—and it was Colin Farrell. She had to reach him, because if anyone had the answers, if anyone knew what Lana was up to, and where she was, it was he. Kait began to dial him again.

"What are you doing?"

She jerked, slamming the phone down at the sound of Trev's voice. He stood in the doorway, smudges of soot on his face and polo shirt, appearing weary and grim. Marni was clinging anxiously to his hand. Kait hadn't seen him since paramedics had begun attending her in the driveway outside of the barn, which was when he and Max had left to move the nearest horses farther from the fire. She hadn't seen Marni since breakfast—apparently Elizabeth had kept her preoccupied since the fire. Her heart tightened and melted all at once—Trev didn't deserve this. And neither did Marni or Sam. Not the fire, not Lana's scheme, not her lies . . . none of it. "I'm sorry," she whispered unsteadily. She needed to be in his arms now. She managed a small smile. "Marni, sweetie, I'm all right. Really. Come here."

Marni rushed forward, looking ready to cry. "Mommy, you got smoke from the fire! Daddy told me you got smoke in your lungs!"

Kait caught her in a huge bear hug as she leapt onto the bed. "That's right, but I'm fine."

Marni pulled back to search her face the way that children do when they are looking for the truth. Her pinched expression relaxed. "But your voice is all funny."

Kait stroked her hair. "And it will be funny for a few days. That's what smoke can do when you breathe too much of it in."

Marni suddenly hugged her again. "Can I sleep here tonight? Please?"

Kait started, and her eyes lifted to meet Trev's. He was staring at them both. "It would be all right with me," she said, aware of her throat catching on a sob. "But it's up to your father."

Trev's jaw flexed. "Mitch wants you to get a good night's rest but . . . I don't mind."

Marni beamed. "I'm going to go get my pj's," she declared, even though it was early in the afternoon. She jumped off the bed and ran off.

Kait felt herself break down; she wiped tears away. Somehow, Marni had become her daughter—and it seemed to be what Lana wanted. Then Kait reminded herself that she had no idea what Lana wanted—or intended. She should not make any assumptions about her sister now. She cautiously met Trev's gaze. "Thanks."

"For what?"

"Letting her sleep here tonight."

His jaw flexed again. He seemed to be conflicted over the subject—or over a different, nameless issue—which Kait bet she could name. "I'll sleep in a guest room. What are you sorry about, Lana?"

She shook her head, suddenly speechless. The conversation she'd just had with Ellen Grubbman came to mind. Was this really happening? How could Lana think to simply give her life away? The answer became a glaringly easy one—because she was in trouble and about to go on the run. An image of Georgina Parker's diamond ring came to mind. She had to return it before someone decided that she was the thief, which, in a way, she now was.

Kait looked up at Trev, aware of tears of fear and exhaustion forming in her eyes. It was as if her sister had thrown a gauntlet at her, daring her to do what was wrong. The temptation loomed before her. Trev thought she was Lana, and they were on good terms now. Or at least, Kait hoped that he remained ignorant of her charade. And if that was the case, if Lana were giving her life away, she, Kait, could stay at Fox Hollow exactly like this—and never leave.

But could she live this terrible lie for the rest of her life? When it was so completely wrong and so morally reprehensible, when she hated it and herself for continuing it? Could she lie to the man she loved—forever?

But she would lose him forever if she told him the truth.

"It's all my fault," Kait said hoarsely. "Everything is my fault. The fire. Everything."

"Why would you say that?" he asked gravely, moving forward but not sitting beside her on the bed. And he did not attempt to hold her, comfort her. It was almost as if they had suddenly become strangers.

She inhaled. "Don't you get it?"

"No, frankly, I don't." His green gaze held hers. "But I wouldn't mind some clarification."

Was this doublespeak? Was he asking her for the truth about who she really was? "Someone wants to kill me. Trev, how can you think anything else right now? Someone shot at me, drove me off the road, and now this."

He stared at her. It was hard to know what he was thinking and what he was feeling right then. He was impassive, calm, controlled. But Kait had a flashing image of his expression when he had stood in the pasture below the burning barn, when she had been ready to throw herself off the second-story ledge. He had been afraid for her. He had not been impassive then. *He had been there to save her life.*

Which meant that he couldn't know the truth—it meant he was really falling in love with her, his pretend wife.

"I'm beginning to think that you may be right. I'm beginning to think that a crazy killer is out there," Trev finally said.

Kait tensed impossibly. "Who could it be?"

"I don't know."

"Everyone hates me—and with good reason! Every woman at Parker's gala hates me, Trev, I saw it in their eyes. Then there are the men." Kait rushed on. "Elizabeth hates me. Your brother even hates me!" Her tone had turned bitter.

"I don't think anyone that you mentioned would set fire to my barn in order to kill you," he said sharply. "And Rafe has only been looking out for what he thinks are my best interests. And it's the same with Elizabeth, who I consider family."

"Someone set fire to the barn. Someone is out there, Trev, hunting me." *And Lana wanted to trade places forever.*

Which meant that if she stayed at Fox Hollow now, posing as her sister, she would remain a killer's target.

And Kait was struck with an even more brutal realization.

Rafe Coleman was after Lana, who was a professional thief. If she remained in her sister's place, she might very well hang for her sister's crimes.

Kait was frozen with disbelief, with comprehension, with the inkling of what the future might be.

Trev covered her hand with his. "Look, Rafe and I were already discussing exactly what you and I have just been discussing. There will be a preliminary investigation, and if this was arson, it will turn into a full-fledged criminal investigation. Whoever is out there, he will be caught."

"Before or after he strikes again?" Kait heard herself ask.

He hesitated. "I'm not going to let anything happen to you."

She could not look away. And even as she did, tears finally came. Trev had fallen in love with her, Kait, even if he believed her to be Lana. How could she walk away from him now? How could she not?

"Trev? Let's go away, far away, just you and me, maybe to some Caribbean island, just the two of us, as soon as possible, even tomorrow." She gripped his hand hard. She was aware of the note of hysteria that had crept into her tone.

He started. It was a moment before he spoke. "Is that what you want to do? Run away?" he asked, his eyes holding hers.

Not trusting herself to speak, she nodded.

Suddenly he seemed grim, and he did not meet her eyes. "When this is over, that's what we'll do. I have to get back to the barn. Get some rest."

Kait watched him walk out.

She stared, disbelieving, because she knew a pretense when she saw and heard one.

They weren't going anywhere. In spite of how it seemed, Kait had the worst and most certain feeling that Trev knew everything now, and that their days together were numbered.

The moment Marni had been dropped at school the following Monday morning, Kait was poring over a local map, looking for Park Lane, where Colin Farrell lived. When she had found it, she set the Jaguar in motion, and ten minutes later she was entering a gated and very new suburban community set just outside of town. The freshly engraved sign hanging over the open front gates impressively labeled the community GREENHILL EQUESTRIAN ESTATES.

Farrell's address was 201 Park Lane. Kait drove by a half a dozen brand-new beautiful million- and multimillion-dollar homes, each set gracefully back from the road behind iron gates and manicured lawns, boasting newly planted trees and perfectly groomed shrubs. She found it hard to imagine the suave and nearly single Farrell living in such a place. He seemed the urbane sort, but clearly he rode horses—she had passed a sign for Greenhill Stables, which she assumed to be a community facility—and it did not seem likely that he and Lana would have chosen Three Falls as their stomping grounds if he could not enter the horsy set as well. Still, she could imagine him with an apartment in D.C. or a home in Georgetown, but not there, on a dignified, stately, and horsy estate. But he was there and for a reason— he was there to be close to Lana and his daughter, Marni. If Marni really was his daughter. How well he and Lana must do, for him to have his elegant colonial-style home. Kait was more than angry, she was bitter now.

His gates were open and Kait drove up to the house, grim-

acing with determination. She had to make him talk and she
had to make him take back the ring. She did not fool herself—this man was out of her league. He was a professional
thief and con—she was now an amateur in both areas.

The garage door was closed and she saw no car in sight.
But it was only nine—surely he was in. Kait got out of the
Jag, more nervous than she wanted to be, imagining him in a
silk bathrobe and monogrammed slippers, reading the *Wall
Street Journal* and the *New York Times* while sipping a cup of
French roast coffee. She started up the front walk. She
would not leave without learning where Lana was. By now,
Farrell had to know.

She rang the doorbell, but there was no response.

Kait tried it again—and again. She rang it four times with
no result.

He wasn't home—and neither was a maid or housekeeper.

Meanwhile, the diamond ring was burning a hole in her
handbag.

There was no way she could risk trying to return it to the
Parkers. Kait didn't hesitate. Maybe the fact that Farrell was
not home was for the best. She'd placed the ring in one of
Lana's jeweler's boxes before leaving Fox Hollow. Now she
took the box and set it in a potted plant just off to the side of
the front door. Instantly she was flooded with relief.

After she drove away, it occurred to her that she could
have peeked into the garage to see if his Mercedes sedan
was there. But why wouldn't he have answered the door?
She debated turning back and decided against it, but just as
she was at the end of his driveway, she glanced in her
rearview mirror.

And for one moment, she thought she saw a woman
standing on Farrell's porch, gazing after her—a woman
identical to herself.

Kait cried out, as the Jaguar swerved dangerously close to
an elm tree. She corrected the motion, steering the car back
onto the driveway, this time halting it. She turned around
and looked back at the house.

The front porch was empty.

. . .

Kait walked into the kitchen and found Elizabeth and Trev in a hushed and urgent conversation. Trev was speaking when Kait walked in. They both looked at her, Trev halting in mid-sentence, causing Kait to stop awkwardly in her tracks. What were they whispering about? Clearly, she was interrupting. Were they discussing her?

Elizabeth straightened—she had been leaning on the center island, facing Trev. "As you seem to have such a hearty appetite these days, there are roast beef sandwiches in the refrigerator."

Kait looked from her stiff and pained expression to Trev's equally grave one. "My hearty appetite is gone," she said tersely. She suddenly realized she was barking up the wrong tree as far as Elizabeth Dorentz was concerned. This woman loved Trev Coleman. She might hate Kait enough to kill her, but she'd never burn down his barn and jeopardize his horses in order to do so. "Am I interrupting?" she asked, unable to even smile.

"No," Trev said abruptly. His gaze swept over her. "You look better today. How are you feeling?"

"Better."

He nodded, remaining grim. "Good."

Kait stared. Last night she hadn't seen hide nor hair of him. Yes, Marni had been sleeping in her bed, but he had made himself awfully scarce. And last night she had wanted nothing more than to cuddle in his arms.

"Brent Black called," Trev said. "He's the fire inspector. The number's on the fridge—he wants to speak with you ASAP. I'll see you later." He walked out.

Kait trembled. It wasn't her imagination, but Trev had become a bit distant since the fire. But why?

Kait's gut feeling that he knew she wasn't Lana remained, even though rationally she doubted that he did, because of his concern for her welfare. But there was simply no way to understand why he was distancing himself from her now—when she needed him, even if only briefly, more than ever.

"Alicia called," Elizabeth said coolly.

Kait turned to face her.

"Your dear friend seemed terribly worried about you. She wants you to call her back."

Kait nodded, having no intention of doing so. While Alicia seemed sweet, every time Kait thought of her now, she thought of Lana betraying her friend with John. She automatically retrieved the note placed on the refrigerator with a magnetic horseshoe, then she halted in her tracks.

Alicia was so nice to her, Kait. Everyone else despised Lana, but not her best friend.

Yet Lana was having an affair with her husband.

How could Alicia not know?

Kait knew she was a terrible actress in normal times. Yet in the current crisis, she had become worthy of an Oscar.

What if Alicia were as worthy?

Kait realized that Alicia Davison should be as high up on her list of suspects as anyone.

The phone rang. Kait was closest to it and she picked it up. "Hello?"

"Lana!" Sam screamed. "Gabe's been shot! Help!"

The closest hospital was Middleburg Memorial, which was where they went. Kait, Trev, and Elizabeth dashed into Emergency. Kait saw Sam instantly, sitting in a blue plastic chair, huddled over, and crying. They rushed to her.

Sam leapt up and into Kait's arms. "What if he dies?" she sobbed. "Oh, God, what if he dies? I can't live if he dies!"

Kait held her and stroked her long, tangled blond hair. "Where is he, honey?"

She blinked through her tears. "In surgery."

"What happened?" Trev asked.

Sam looked at her father. "He got into a fight with that ass, Ben Abbott! We were at the mall." She burst into tears again. "Ben was rude to me. Gabe tried to get him to apologize. Then Ben pulled the gun! Fuck him!"

Kait held her hard again, but her eyes met Trev's. What

felt like a silent understanding passed between them. She was about to suggest he ask a nurse or doctor where Gabe was, and how badly he was hurt. But she didn't have to.

Trev said, "I'll see if I can find out how Gabe is doing." He whirled and took off. Kait saw him grab the sleeve of a doctor in a blue medical coat, then she looked down at the sobbing teen in her arms. "Sam, I'm sorry," Kait said. "When did this happen?"

"I don't know," Sam cried, gulping air. She was shaking like a leaf. "We split from school for a pizza. What time is it?"

"It's one," Elizabeth said, laying her hand on Sam's shoulder. "This is a fine hospital, Sam. I feel certain that your young man will be all right."

Sam looked at her gratefully. "He was trying to defend my honor," she said. "Because that's the way Gabe is! Then they fought for the gun and it went off!" Tears began flowing again.

Kait espied a police officer in a navy blue uniform at the Emergency desk. Trev had seen him at the same time. As he hurried over, Kait said, "Hold on, Sam." She gave her hand a squeeze and rushed over to Trev and the officer.

The policeman was saying, "We have him in custody. He claims Jenkins started it and that the gun was Jenkins's."

Kait gasped. "Sam told me that the gun belonged to Ben Abbott."

"I took her statement," the officer said. "Unfortunately, there were no witnesses. The incident took place in the parking lot of the mall, but on the far side. We have one woman who heard the shot, and that's it. Looks like there will be an investigation. We'll find out who had the gun and who shot whom."

Kait snapped. "Gabe Jenkins has been shot, Officer. That is obvious."

The officer gave her an annoyed look and walked away. Kait turned to Trev. "Can you get Rafe here?"

"He's on his way," he said. "Jenkins was shot in the side. He's been in surgery for about forty-five minutes. I have no real news—and I won't until the surgery is complete." Suddenly he was agonized. "Jesus, I hope that kid survives."

She took his hand. "Let's pray Gabe is all right."

He gripped her palm in return. "Is Sam telling the truth? Or did Gabe start it?"

"I don't know, Trev, but right now your daughter needs you—I think you had better give her the benefit of the doubt," Kait said firmly.

Trev seemed to accept that. But he looked so stricken that Kait wanted to pull him into her arms and hold him as if he were a little boy.

Instead, Kait tugged on his hand. "C'mon." She pulled him back across the emergency room toward Sam and Elizabeth. The moment she did so, Sam flashed to her father, "Are you happy now?"

"No, Sam, I'm not happy," he said grimly. He laid his hand on her shoulder, but she jerked away.

"I don't believe you!" she cried. "You hate him—I bet you hope he dies!" She burst into fresh tears.

He reached for her. "Sam!"

She faced him, her expression turning ugly. "I hate you!"

Trev recoiled.

Kait bit off a cry. "Sam, honey, I know you don't mean that," she tried quickly.

"But I do," Sam snapped viciously.

Kait saw the anguish so clearly in Trev's eyes. But amazingly he held himself together, and spoke calmly and firmly. "I'm not happy that you've been sleeping with Jenkins, but I don't want him hurt, and if you think for a second, I'm sure you'll realize that."

"His name is Gabe, damn you!" Sam shouted. She started to run away, when she froze. "That's the doctor!" She pointed across the room with her trembling arm. And she lost the little coloring that she had.

Trev hurried over to a doctor in tortoiseshell glasses who looked a lot like a young George Clooney. Kait stepped over to Sam and hugged her to her side. "Your father is sick with worry for Gabe, sweetie."

"Don't," Sam said, choking. Her gaze never wavered from her father and the doctor.

Kait also looked that way, and a moment later Trev returned to them. Kait took one look at his expression and knew that Gabe was alive.

"He's okay," Trev announced, looking anxiously at his daughter.

Sam cried out.

"He's stable and in recovery," Trev said. He glanced grimly at Kait. "Dr. Travis says he has a good chance of pulling through. The bullet did some damage to his spleen," he cautioned. "But he's young and strong, and that's all on his side."

"Is he going to die?" Sam whispered, still against Kait's side.

Trev hesitated. "Travis says he has a seventy percent chance of making it."

Sam stared at her father. "Only seventy percent . . ."

"Sam—he's a strong boy—he'll make it."

She stared as if mute.

Kait spoke for her. "Can she see him?"

"In a bit. When he's out of recovery, in about an hour or so, we can all go up."

Sam whimpered and turned to Kait. Kait held her again.

Sam was sitting beside Gabe, who was conscious but so groggy from the anesthesia and painkillers that he could do no more than open his eyes to look at her and then close them again. She held his hand. Gabe's mother sat in a chair beside Sam, a brave smile fixed on her face. Every moment or so she would reach out and pat his knee. She was a plump, pretty woman in a waitress's uniform and Kait had taken one look at her and liked her. Now she stood beside Trev, holding his hand. Elizabeth had left to pick Marni up at school.

Someone came up behind them. Kait and Trev turned to face Rafe Coleman. He nodded at them and they stepped out with him into the hall. "How's Sam?" he asked quickly.

Trev grimaced. "Devastated."

Rafe glanced from his brother into the hospital room. Gabe remained as white as death, and as he had an intra-venous in one arm, and oxygen tubes in his nose, he looked very ill. "I spoke with Travis and Officer DeWitt. He's young, Trev. He'll make it."

Trev raised his eyebrows at him. "Don't patronize me now, Rafe, damn it!"

Rafe looked grim. "I'm sorry. You're right. It's serious. But the odds are in his favor, at least."

"Are they? You've seen this kind of shooting before? Is it seventy-thirty?" Trev asked.

"I'm not a doctor, Trev. I'm a cop. Look, as soon as Sam is up to it, I'd like to speak with her, find out what really happened, even though this police investigation is not in my jurisdiction."

There was a moment of silence. Kait knew they were all hoping now that Sam wasn't lying to protect Gabe and that Ben Abbott had owned the gun and had been to blame for the shooting. Finally Trev said, "She'll need some time. She's hysterical with fear."

Rafe glanced into the hospital room again. His entire face softened. "Poor Sammie," he said.

And in that moment, in spite of Lana and Farrell and the fact that she, Kait, had actually stolen a diamond ring, she liked Rafe Coleman. "It's going to be a long afternoon—and probably a long night." Kait didn't think Sam intended to leave the hospital. "I'm going to go down to the cafeteria and pick up some sandwiches and soda. Sam should get something into her system."

Trev looked at her, the light in his eyes softening. "Thanks."

Rafe gave her a grudging nod. "You okay today?"

She was stunned that he would ask. "Yes, thank you."

Rafe turned back to Trev. "C'mon. Let's pay our respects. Sam needs us in there with her."

Kait walked down the empty corridor as the two brothers disappeared into the ICU. A nurse's station was at the far end, not quite in sight. Elevators were there as well. She was suddenly exhausted. She felt as if her life had become an endless roller-coaster ride. They all desperately needed a break.

And surely Gabe Jenkins would survive.

Not just for Sam's sake, but for his own sake. He was only a boy.

A hand suddenly closed on Kait's shoulder from behind.

Kait had not heard anyone come up behind her, perhaps because she was so immersed in her thoughts. She started and it was a moment before she could react.

And that moment was enough. Before she could turn around, before she could do more than cry out, she was being pulled into a stairwell, the door to the corridor closing firmly shut behind her. Kait jerked free of her captor and whirled around. *What the hell was this?*

She expected to come face-to-face with the killer who was after her—perhaps down the barrel of his or her gun.

But it was Lana who stood there, leaning calmly against the door to the stairwell.

It was Lana who slowly smiled at her.

Lana, with all of her hair cut off.

"Hi, Kait," she said.

NINETEEN

Kait could not believe her eyes.

Lana said, "You look awful, Kait. Have you been ill?"

"Ill?" Kait echoed. She was about to tell her sister that she was ill—that she was sick at heart. But instead, she breathed. Hard, deep, fast. She needed her composure now. "So you came back after all," she managed.

"Don't panic," Lana said, with a rueful smile. "I'm not staying."

Kait stared, her mind racing. Lana had cut off her hair, and her short cut was almost identical to Kait's. No one looking at them now would be able to tell them apart, except for the fact that Lana was in a gray pantsuit and Kait wore jeans. "I'm not panicking," Kait lied.

Kait had to sit down. In fact, she could barely breathe, no matter how she tried, as if the small walls of the stairwell were closing in on her. She sat down hard on the cold concrete steps. "Did you get my message?"

"No. I can't retrieve your voice mail, remember?"

Kait stared.

"What's wrong, Kait? You seem upset and angry."

"What's wrong?" Kait gasped. She gestured around her. "This is wrong."

"But it's almost over, and I'm not staying. However, I think we both know that you are."

Kait simply looked at her, refusing to reply.

Lana sat down beside her. "You're really mad. I came to say good-bye."

Kait hugged herself and shifted so their bodies would not touch. "I don't understand you," she said. "I don't understand how you could use and hurt so many people."

Lana leapt up. "Don't you judge me, Kait! You've never walked in my shoes before now, so let's just leave it at that!"

Kait also stood, shivering now. Very slowly, she said, "Did you think that by moving all of my furniture and belongings out, by putting my apartment up for sale that I would accept your plans, and stay here, pretending to be you until I die?"

"I quit your job, too. Kait, we both know that Trev is your Prince Charming and that you want to stay. Colin told me the two of you are getting along fabulously. So why argue with that? I want out of my marriage. I'm giving it to you."

"Why not stay, and get a divorce?"

"It's easier this way."

"Like hell."

"What?"

"Rafe Coleman wants to hang you, Lana—upside down."

"He has nothing on me, nothing. I'm heading to Paris tonight, Kait. And I am not coming back. Rafe can't touch you. He may want to, but he can't. And with time, all of his suspicions will die down, now, won't they? The switch makes perfect sense. I get what I want, and you get what you want."

Kait was shaking now, with all the anger she didn't dare express.

Lana came to stand beside her, putting her arm around her. Kait flinched. "Kait, why are you doing this? We both know that you don't want to go back to being Kait London. We both know you want my life—every single part of it. You always have." She smiled.

Kait looked into her sister's eyes. They were the exact same shade of blue as her own, with the same thick black fringe of lashes, and they even shared the same slight lavender tone of flesh beneath. But they were so different, too, because Lana's eyes were flat, opaque. Kait had never realized it before. "Tell me one thing. How can you live with yourself if you walk out on Trev, Sam—and your own flesh and blood daughter, Marni?"

Lana seemed amused. "I stink as a mother. By now, you know that—don't you? And I'm a horrible wife. But you're a romantic, Kait, and you and Trev are exactly the same. I knew it the moment I met him. I cannot think of two people who deserve one another more. Look at it this way. I *know* you. You're my twin—the sister who grew up devouring romance novels while secretly waiting for her very own Prince Charming to one day walk through the door. Well, you have a prince now. He might not be quite as flawless as those hunks in those books you used to read, but I know you well enough to know you admire Trev as well as love him—you wouldn't have slept with him if you hadn't given him your heart and soul. He should have chosen you anyway, not me. So now let's just say a wrong has been righted and he's yours." She smiled.

Kait stood, and in the back of her mind, the possibility of doing as Lana asked lurked, the devil's own temptation. "It's not that simple. You're asking me to continue to live a terrible lie! It was easy at first, before I knew what was going on, but now it's almost impossible to get through a single minute, much less an hour or a day."

Lana's carefully groomed brows lifted. "Honey, if you tell him the truth, he will *never* forgive you. And your Prince Charming will be history."

Kait inhaled, hard. She already knew that. "Why, Lana? *Why?* And *how* could you do this? You set me up—from the very beginning, didn't you? You set me up, for this, switching places with you—forever. Just like you set up Trev. Farrell told me that the two of you have been together for ten years. That you married Trev for his money, his position. That he was a perfect mark. Is Marni even Trev's daughter?"

"You're upset," Lana said calmly. She sighed. "Marni is Trev's daughter. I'm not a fool, Kait. I had to have his child, just in case he became suspicious of me. She was my security, my leverage, in case he ever found out the truth about what Colin and I were doing. And it worked. Marni kept us together for all of these years."

Kait wanted to vomit. "She's your daughter! You don't deserve her!"

Lana shrugged. "No, I don't. But you do."

But you do. Lana's words echoed. Kait hugged herself, fighting them—fighting temptation. "Don't you have any conscience? You're standing there as cool as an ice cube. Why, Lana? Why are you so . . . immoral? How can you steal from your friends? How could you marry Trev while being Farrell's lover? How could you cheat on Trev!" *How could you not love him?*

Lana laughed. "Which question do you want me to answer first, Kait?"

"This isn't funny!" Kait shouted, forgetting that they might be overheard and that Rafe Coleman was only a few doors away. "No, answer this! You found out about Trev from me, didn't you? You called him pretending to be me, and changed the place of our meeting—and then went to meet him—and pick him up—yourself."

"Right," Lana said with a shrug. "Kait, you were pathetic. You had this business meeting with a complete stranger, and I could tell you had made up your mind to find him interesting—as if you were thirteen, not twenty-six. I didn't mean to hurt you, not in any way, but he was just the perfect mark—a golden opportunity I could not pass up. And he was so easy. He fell right into my lap. He was a very lonely man."

Kait felt hatred then. It blinded her with its force. *Lana had stolen Trev Coleman from her in the first place. He had married the wrong twin. He should have been with her from the start. And if they had met as they should have, they would have been, too.*

Then she leapt back, aghast with the depth of her loathing. She must not succumb to hatred now. She needed her wits about her, because a decision was looming, and it had to be a rational one, not an emotional one.

"Kait? Relax." Lana went to her and put her arm around her.

Kait was sweating. She managed to stand still, when what she wanted to do was push her sister far away.

Once she would have given anything for a single embrace. Now, she was repulsed by her own twin.

Lana looked surprised. "Honey, I am giving you the man of your dreams. Don't cry. Please. This will all work out for the best for everyone, actually." She was pleased. "Honey, you really don't have a choice, now, do you?"

"How can our relationship ever work out when it is built on this kind of lie?" Kait shot. And in that moment, she knew it never would work out for her and Trev—because of the lies. Not if she confessed, and not if she did not.

She was stuck between a rock and a hard place.

Then she realized she wasn't stuck at all, because Lana was right—she had no choice, not a single one.

"Are you about to faint?" Lana asked, gripping her arm. "You just lost all of your coloring."

Her ears were ringing. Kait pulled free. "No, I'm fine." She fought for composure now.

Lana regarded her through narrowed eyes.

Kait swallowed. "I want to help you. Lana, you need help."

Lana smiled, amused. "Want to know a secret?"

Kait shuddered. "Not really."

Lana ignored her response. "We'd been living together about six months and we'd just pulled our first job—I was a maid on Fifth Avenue"—Lana smiled at the memory—"and, boy, was my employer's wife the dumbest bimbo! It took her forever to realize she had a thief in her midst—but a bit afterwards, I went to a shrink. Yeah, that's right, a shrink. I found stealing from the bimbo who was signing my paychecks so exciting, yet I knew it was wrong. But I didn't have *any* guilt. So I saw this old fart . . . exactly twice. You know why I only saw him twice?"

Numb, Kait shook her head. It was hard to focus on Lana's words. *Could she really go through with this?*

"Because he said I was a sociopath. *A sociopath.* And he wouldn't see me again—because sociopaths are, apparently, not treatable."

Kait shivered. "What, exactly, is a sociopath?" Images of bloody serial killers danced through her mind.

Lana smiled. "Someone who understands society's rules—ethics—whatever—and breaks them with no remorse—and no guilt. I have no guilt, Kait. I just don't have any. Unlike you," she added.

Kait felt faint again. "I want you to get help. To stop this kind of life. Lana, you have the most wonderful daughter, and I love you, and together we can beat this thing."

Lana sighed. "Didn't you hear a word I said? I don't feel guilt! And I love what I do. Ever have an orgasm, Kait?"

Kait flushed. "Excuse me?"

"Well magnify the high a hundred times. That's what pulling a job off feels like." She smiled. "It is sweet."

"Please listen to me," Kait whispered.

"No, you listen to me—because I have to go. I am offering you my life, Kait. I am offering you the life you deserve! You don't have to stay. In fact, you can do whatever you want, Kait, but I am out of here tonight." Lana was unruffled. "I came back to say good-bye, Kait. To say good-bye to you and to see Marni one last time." She sighed then. Suddenly there was a sheen in her sister's eyes, as if she was overwrought and about to cry. "We're history, Kait. Colin and I are out of here in another moment—and we'll never cross paths again. You'll never see me again. So you can stay—and be me—and have everything you ever dreamed of having—or you can leave." She shrugged. "And we both know that Trev will never forgive you if he learns you are Kait London and not Lana Coleman."

Yes, Kait already knew that. "How can you leave this way? How can you leave Marni this way?" she asked in a ragged whisper.

"It's not as easy as I'm making it seem." She touched her.

Kait fought not to recoil. "But I'm no good for her, Kait, and you know it." She smiled then. "I saw the two of you together at her school this morning, Kait. She loves you so. It's as if you are really her mother."

Lana wasn't playing fair and Kait knew it. "Where are you going after Paris?" Her lips felt so stiff, like two small boards.

"Can't tell," Lana said with a smile. "Not even you. But I have a present for you." She opened her purse and as she did so, a small black object fell out. Lana blinked. Kait stared.

A gun lay at their feet.

"It's protection," Lana said by way of explanation. She finally bent to retrieve it and dropped it again.

Automatically, Kait picked it up and handed it to her. "You don't owe anyone any money, do you?"

"No. That was a big lie, to get you in the door here." Lana slipped the gun back into her purse.

"Someone is after you. Who is it?"

"I don't know," Lana said. "Are you sure you're not mistaken? Because until you arrived here, no one ever tried anything against me."

"I was shot at, run off the road, and yesterday someone set Trev's barn on fire—while I was locked in it."

Lana's eyes widened. Then, "Well, that is a legitimate mystery for the police. If I knew who it was, I would tell you, honey. I guess if you really want Trev and Marni, you'll have to take a risk, now, won't you? You can get police protection. It is all in the family." She grinned. "Here."

A small object was tucked into her hand. Kait recognized the feel instantly. She cried out, horrified, and saw Georgina Parker's diamond ring sitting in her palm. "I'm not taking this! I don't want it!"

"But it's my parting gift, Kait. It's worth about one-fifty. A nice little nest egg. Don't you think?" Lana was amused.

Kate's mind raced. Lana wasn't giving her a choice, not about anything. Slowly, she looked up into eyes that might have been her own—but weren't.

"My, my, so you're not quite the Goody Two-Shoes after

all," Lana said with some glee. She slipped the ring into Kait's purse.

Kait gripped her purse, almost panicking. *Could she really do this?* Her heart said no, her mind said yes.

"Are you going to cry?" Lana asked, amused.

Kait fought the tears. "Will I ever see you again?"

"I think not," Lana said calmly. "Kait—this is the deal. First, I trust you. I know you'd never hurt me, not in a million years. I know you'd never tell the police about me and Colin, besides—would they even believe you? So go home. Go back to Fox Hollow. Take care of Trev—and take care of Marni. Be the mother I can never be. Take your dream, Kait. It's all yours now. And I'll take freedom."

Kait began to shake all over again. It was hard to speak. She felt dazed, and she was blinded now by fear. *She wanted to tell Lana that it didn't have to be this way.* But she knew that it did, and she was crying now, so she simply could not speak.

Lana understood. She hugged her, hard. "I'll miss you. But I just can't go to jail and being as I can't quit, well . . ." She shrugged. "It's been too hot around here for a while. I'm pretty sure that PI Zara uncovered some stupid stuff I did when I was a kid, and Coleman's no dummy. I've had a feeling for a few months now that the two of them have figured me and Colin out. So I have to go." She kissed Kait's cheeks, her lips surprisingly cool. "Just lie low and things will cool down. I'm so happy for you, Kait," she said. "I know how much you love Trev and Marni."

Kait could no longer breathe. The stairwell had become boiling hot. She felt faint, and as if she was suffocating. But her decision had been made, and there was no turning back. Especially not with the stolen ring burning a hole in her handbag. Her eyes locked with her sister's.

Lana smiled.

Kait could not.

"Good-bye," Lana said.

Kait nodded. "Lana?"

Lana paused at the door.

"I love you," Kait said through stiff lips.

Kait looked into the hospital room where Gabe Jenkins lay unconscious. The tableau hadn't changed since she had left. Sam and his mother remained at his side, Trev and Rafe remained at the foot of the bed, talking quietly. Trev immediately sensed her presence, because he turned.

Kait couldn't move. Their eyes met and locked.

Kait licked her lips. "Rafe?"

Rafe also turned.

She cleared her throat. "May I speak with you—privately?" And she was dizzy, reeling. But she had made her decision five minutes ago on that cold iron gray stairwell with her sister offering Kait her marriage, her husband, her life.

Rafe and Trev exchanged a glance and Rafe left the room. "Let's go somewhere quiet," Kait said, her heart beating with alarming force now. She did not want Trev to overhear the conversation she intended to have.

Rafe followed her into a small and empty waiting area. "What is this about?"

Kait looked him in the eye. "My name is Kait London. I'm Lana Coleman's twin."

For one moment he did not even blink, and then he said, calmly, "Really."

"Yes, really," Kait said, not able to detach herself from all feeling. She hugged herself and felt the tears come to her eyes. "My sister is a criminal, but I think you already know that. Ten minutes ago she dragged me into a stairwell to tell me that I could have her life and that she was going on the run. She said she's on her way to Paris tonight, but I know that's bullshit. She's too smart to tell me the truth."

Rafe said, "Don't fucking move." And he took off.

Kait sank down in a chair, cradling her head on her arms, and she wept. She cried because the sister she had admired and loved her entire life had been an illusion and the more she recalled the past, the more certain she was that Lana had always lied to and cheated everyone. Her sister had had all the charisma, all the sex appeal, all the charm, but she had always done whatever she felt like, no matter whom she hurt, no matter the consequences.

Kait felt as if she had loved a lie her entire life, and maybe she had.

But it was over now. Lana was far more than an adultress, a con woman, and a professional thief; even she herself had admitted that she was a sociopath.

Kait wiped her eyes and leaned back in her chair, staring blindly at the ceiling. A sociopath was, apparently, someone who broke every rule and law known to mankind and didn't have one iota of remorse, one bit of guilt. Well, that was Lana, wasn't it?

Had she really thought Kait such a pushover that she would accept Lana's life, and live a lie for the rest of her own life? In the end, there had been no temptation at all.

Had she really thought Kait so weak that she would let her sister get away unpunished for all of her crimes? Turning her own sister in had required all the strength and moral fiber Kait had.

Oddly, Kait thought the biggest crime of all was the way Lana had emotionally betrayed her own family—Kait, Trev, Marni, and Sam. But that was a crime she would never pay for, and her family would be the ones to pay the price instead.

Kait was glad their parents weren't alive to see how Lana had turned out in the end.

And now, there would be some justice—because Kait had turned her own sister in.

Suddenly Rafe strode into the room, speaking into a walkie-talkie. "She can't have gotten far. Seal off the hospital, put up a roadblock at the exit. Check every car and every passenger, damn!" He clicked off just as someone said, "Ten-four," and stared at Kait.

Kait didn't like the way he was looking at her. She slowly stood up. "Maybe you should put up some more roadblocks, in case she's already off hospital grounds. I'd also get someone over to Farrell's—and have him followed."

"Impossible. Too many intersecting streets." But he lifted

the walkie-talkie to his mouth. "Send someone over to Far-rell's. Two-oh-one Park Lane. Surveillance. If he leaves, tail him, and whatever you do, don't lose him," he snapped. Then he turned his unwavering stare on her again.

She shifted uneasily. "I've hated every moment of this charade."

"Right." He was grim.

"She told me she was in danger; in fact, she made me be-lieve that Marni's life was in danger, too," Kait said hoarsely. "She didn't even give me a chance to object. I hadn't seen her in years—I didn't even know she was married. She ap-peared, told me she was in trouble, gave me a letter, and took off. I mean, it was like a five-minute broadside."

"You two switch places often?"

"No. Never. Not since we were eight or nine," Kait said. "You don't believe me."

"I don't know what to believe, but Max found out Lana had a twin a few days ago. Question is, which one are you?"

Kait shivered. "I'm Kait. Kait London. I've been working at a Madison Avenue publicity firm. Check it out. Check me out. I'm who I say I am."

He stared for a long moment. "What do you want . . . Kait? And why turn your own sister in now?"

Kait opened her purse and gave him the diamond ring. "Farrell stole this the night of Parker's gala." He stared at the ring, his expression inscrutable. "It's Georgina's," she added.

"I know."

Kait was grim. "I didn't know who Farrell was or that he and my sister have been partners—and lovers—for a dec-ade. They did set up Trev, by the way. She married him for his money and his social connections."

Rafe lifted his gaze to hers. "So you and Farrell stole this—or was it Farrell and your twin?"

She swallowed uneasily, aware of where he was heading now—that the confusion of which sister was who and who had really done what was more than confusion—it had be-come a web that might not even be unraveled correctly. "I was with Farrell. But I have never stolen anything in my life, and I watched him steal it—then he tried to give it to me. I gave it back the other day."

"To him. Not me, not the police." He was watching her very carefully now.

"I wasn't ready to turn my own sister in! To betray her—to send her to jail!" Kait cried, losing all of her composure.

"But now you're ready to do all that."

"Yes." She gritted her teeth. "Yes, I am. She just gave me the ring, as a little parting gift. While trying to convince me to stay in her lie forever." She turned away, closing her eyes tightly. "Don't tell Trev. Please. I'll tell him tonight, when we get home."

There was silence.

She felt his eyes boring into her back.

Slowly, she turned.

"I could arrest you on the spot."

"Good," Kait whispered. "Because that is what I want you to do."

And finally, he was surprised. "What?!"

"Arrest me, Rafe. Arrest me and make it headline news. It's what she wants. You see, Lana's plan isn't to give me her life; she wants me to take the fall for her."

Their gazes locked.

"You think your own sister wants you to go to jail in her place?"

Kait nodded, stabbed with heartache.

"If you are really who you say you are, then I'd be arresting the wrong person—at least as far as grand larceny is concerned."

Kait shook her head, not liking his implication about arresting her at some other time for fraud. "Don't you see? Once you arrest me—as Lana—she'll think she's free. And then you can bring her to justice," Kait said.

Somehow, it was almost eleven o'clock at night. Kait hardly knew where the day had gone; spent as it was at the hospital, it had passed in an odd and surreal blur. Had it only been six, seven, or eight hours ago that she had finally come face-to-face with her sister in the stairwell of the hospital? Had it only been hours ago that she had turned her own sister in to the authorities? It felt as if it had been a lifetime ago. Kait had somehow gone through all the right motions, bringing sandwiches, cookies, soda, and water back to Gabe's room. Holding Sam's hand, then holding Trev's. Mitch had come by to oversee Gabe's care, and to try to sedate Sam and get her home. Sam would have none of it; it was Kait who had finally convinced Sam to go home and take a Valium, and Kait couldn't remember how she had done it or a single word that she had said.

Now, Trev stood on the threshold of Sam's room, his arms folded across his chest, not moving. He seemed so tired. Sam was in bed, still in her jeans and a T-shirt, soundly asleep. She'd finally taken the Valium Mitch had prescribed, just a few moments ago, and the moment her head had touched the pillow, she'd gone out like a light. Gabe remained in satisfactory condition in ICU and Ben Abbott had been released on bail.

Kait remained numb, and she supposed it was an effect of shock. She carefully pulled off Sam's boots and then her socks, concentrating very hard on what she was doing—as if that would block out her memory of her confrontation with Lana and her conversation with Rafe Coleman. She knew he wanted to apprehend her sister and Farrell at Reagan International; she also knew he'd never catch them so easily. If Lana said she was on her way to Paris tonight, she'd probably be heading for Singapore tomorrow instead.

Kait was numb with exhaustion and despondency. She had been fighting her terrible memories all day while trying to act normal—whatever that now meant. She was also aware of Trev watching her from the doorway. She had been acutely, painfully, aware of him all day. The moment of truth had come, and there was no more escaping it. If she didn't tell him, Rafe Coleman would. He'd said he would give her until midnight.

It was damn close to midnight now.

Kait covered Sam with the quilt, tucking it up under her chin. Then she fussed with the covers, avoiding what she must say and do. She checked and saw that the glass of water on the bed stand was full, and with stirrings of full-fledged dread, she straightened and ever so slowly turned.

It was the first time she had been able to feel anything at all since seeing Lana and betraying her to Rafe. Her gaze locked with Trev's.

"Thank you," he said, staring oddly at her.

She couldn't speak. He wasn't going to be thankful or anything else in another moment or so, except, of course, for angry. In another few moments he would, undoubtedly, never look at her with love or affection again.

"Do you want a drink?" he asked, not moving.

The numbness continued to lift. A sick feeling formed in the pit of her stomach. "No." If she ingested anything, even whiskey, she would vomit.

"Are you okay?" he asked warily.

"No."

His jaw flexed. "You've been acting odd all day."

He would never hold her again. They would never make love again. Their eyes would never again meet in silent communication, with a small, shared smile following. "We have to talk."

He stared.

"Please." She hesitated, still frozen by Sam's bed. "Privately."

"I don't like the sound of this," he said, the mask she hated coming down, first over his eyes and then over the rest of his features until he seemed more like a statue than a flesh and blood man.

"You shouldn't. I have something to say. . . . You won't like it."

He remained still, wariness entering his eyes.

Kait tried to breathe deeply, but it was simply impossible, as her breathing was rapid and shallow. She managed to move, and she walked past him, knowing now how it felt to walk to one's own execution. She heard and then felt Trev following her. She chose not to go a few steps down the hall to their bedroom, but downstairs, to the living room, territory that felt neutral.

Once there, he walked right past her to pour himself a large scotch.

"I'm not Lana," she said. And the moment she spoke, words she never intended to utter so abruptly, her heart exploded in a fearful frenzy within her chest.

Trev had just turned to face her, the scotch in hand. He did not lift it, and if he was stunned, he did not show it.

And it was Kait who was stunned. Disbelieving in spite of her earlier suspicions, she thought, *He knew*. "I'm her twin sister. My name is Kait. Kait London."

He set the scotch down, untouched. She saw that his hand trembled ever so slightly. "I know."

She stared, his words a nearly fatal blow. "Since when?" It never crossed her mind that Rafe had told him.

His face tightened. "Since we slept together."

Another blow. It was hard to breathe, to stand up, to think. *"Why?"*

His mouth twisted bitterly. "Why? Isn't that the question I should be asking you?"

She had to speak. "If you knew, why didn't you say something?"

"Why? I decided to play the game by your rules . . . Kait," he said coolly.

She didn't, couldn't, understand. Except of course she understood. Every moment they had shared had been a lie on his part as well as hers. Except his lies seemed worse now, because they were lies of the heart. "So this reconciliation of ours . . ."

"Two can play the same game, Kait." His nostrils flared. She saw the beginning of dark anger in his eyes. "Just like you, I can act when I have to."

She didn't want to feel, but pain joined the medley of impossibly hurtful emotions afflicting her now. "Do you have any real feelings for me?"

And now, he was startled. "No."

She somehow remained upright. "Everything was an act. Every moment—every caress—every kiss."

"Yes." His regard intensified. "So now it's my turn. Why? Why the charade . . . Kait?"

She thought she would swoon. He didn't love her, he never had. She wanted to tell him how she felt. She was terrified of exposing herself. "I had no choice."

"No choice?" Suddenly he strode toward her. Kait cringed. "Everyone has choices, Kait."

"I can explain, give me a moment. . . . I can't breathe," she gasped, and it was the truth. The room was graying before her very eyes, and she was afraid now that she would faint.

"No, I can explain." Now the hardness covered his face. And with it, there was disgust and revulsion, bitter and sharp. "The apple doesn't fall far from the tree—not ever— now, does it, Kait? You and Lana are two of a kind!"

"No! We're completely different people!" Kait cried. Fear and panic washed over her with the force of a tidal wave. But this was what she had expected. She had expected nothing less. Still, her heart had hoped for understanding, for forgiveness and a future of love.

"And I have another question for you," he said, his face creased in lines of loathing. "How many times did the two of you switch places? How often have you done this?"

"Never!" she cried. "I mean, when we were really little kids we'd swap places. . . . This was the only time—I didn't even know that Lana was married until she went to New York City to see me last week!"

"Really?" He was trembling now, mockery inflaming his tone. "Like hell. Because I remember your name. Kait London. It has a ring. A nice sound. *Kait London*. We had a meeting years ago, and you didn't show up—you had Lana show up instead!"

"No! Lana set me up, Trev, just the way she set you up," Kait cried, very close to tears.

"I think the two of you are a team," Trev said furiously.

Kait shook her head wildly. "Please listen to me! Lana and I were never close, not even growing up! She was always the wild one, the popular one! She was the extrovert and the thrill-seeker, she had all the boys, while I was always at home studying or at the stables hiding behind horses. We weren't even friends as children, and I hadn't seen her in six or seven years until last week! I had no idea she'd married you and I had no idea she had a child—none! Her call came out of the blue," Kait cried.

"If you are such an honest person, then you would have never agreed to walk into her life, pretending to be her, duping not just me, but my children!"

Kait jumped back—away from him. "She said she was in trouble, that she needed help! I was so happy to see her again, I was so happy to have my twin sister back that I would have jumped off the roof of the Empire State Building if she had asked."

He had become still. For one moment, Kait thought she had somehow, miraculously, gotten through to him, until he spoke. And when he spoke, she knew her fate was sealed. "Fuck with me," he said softly, "but never with my children." And before she could blink, in an act of rage, he flung his glass of scotch across the room.

Kait jumped as the glass shattered behind her, scotch spraying her back and shoulders.

And then he was looming over her. His hands closed over her throat. Kait gasped, meeting the most livid gaze she had ever imagined. And she realized the one thing she hadn't thought of was that he might wish to kill her—or that he might be so enraged that he would actually do so. Their eyes met and locked.

But his hands did not tighten on her neck. He released her, but did not move his body away, blocking her against the wall.

"You walked into my life—Sam's life—Marni's life!" He gritted. "Pretending to be my wife! Don't you dare tell me you are different from her!" He shook her once. "She's a whore, Kait, and so are you. A lousy, lying whore."

How his words hurt. Kait heard herself whimper, but the pain was in her heart, not from his grasp on her shoulders.

He paled, leaving two bright splotches of pink on his cheeks, and he pushed her away. Then he clasped his head, turning away, and she thought she heard him moan.

She fell hard against the wall. She somehow wound up on the floor, a crumpled heap. "I was trying to help my twin sister," she begged. "She told me she owed all this money to a loan shark and stupidly I believed her. She said he'd kill her, or Marni, and I believed her. She said I only had to cover for her for a few days, and I believed her. I had no idea she was setting me up to take her place here."

He whirled. "For all I know, you knew the whole game, and decided it was your turn to help yourself to the cushy life I could give you!"

"No! I came to help Lana, and then I fell in love with Marni, and Sam. . . ." *And you,* she wanted to add. But she didn't dare. She felt tears streaking down her face.

"You love yourself!" he shouted at her. "Don't you dare, ever, tell me that you love Marni or Sam."

"I do love Marni!" she managed to shout back.

He grabbed her and dragged her to her feet before she could continue. "Stop it!" he roared, shaking her. "Shut up, before I lose what little control I do have! You don't love us! You've used us, just like that bitch of a sister of yours! That's what the two of you are, a pair of beautiful manipulating bitches."

Kait clung to him. "I only told you one lie," she whispered hoarsely, "and that one lie was who I am. Everything else was the truth."

"I don't want to hear any more," he cried, and he threw her away. He started for the door.

She crashed against the wall, caught herself somehow, and hung on. "Trev, wait, please!"

He didn't pause, and he didn't stop.

Kait watched him disappear, and she slid down the wall, hugging herself, weeping. How quickly, then, she had lost him.

Except she had never had him. He had known the truth from the moment they'd made love.

She wept harder.

"Here."

At the sound of Max Zara's voice, Kait froze. She looked up to see him offering her a tissue. His blue eyes were soft and kind. "I really love him," she said.

"I know you do."

TWENTY

Kait hadn't been able to sleep. She had spent most of the night tossing and turning, her heart broken, wrapping her body around her pillow. Trev's side of the bed had remained empty.

Now the raucous cries of blue jays awoke her and she realized she had managed, at long last, to doze off for an hour or so. An unfocused glance across the bedroom showed her that dawn had grayed the morning sky but that the sun wasn't up yet. She didn't move, images of Trev, Marni, and Sam assailing her. How every single memory hurt.

She also thought about her sister and her heart lurched with dread. Where was she now? There had been no phone call in the middle of the night from the police, so Kait knew they hadn't caught her. Kait thought about all that she had done and she closed her eyes tightly, against more tears, more pain. She hugged her pillow more closely, then felt a soft downy limb against the back of her hand.

Kait moved the pillow and saw Marni sleeping peacefully beside her, a squishy teddy bear in her arms. Tears fell. She tossed the pillow onto the floor and pulled Lana's daughter into her arms.

She had the strength to leave Fox Hollow, to leave Trev. But how would she find the strength to leave Marni?

Marni's eyes fluttered open. She smiled beatifically and

yawned. Kait stroked her hair. "I see I had a little visitor last night," she whispered unsteadily.

"I had a bad dream," Marni said, snuggling closer. "I dreamed you went away!"

Kait couldn't speak. She stared into her niece's eyes and thought about how Lana wanted her to stay and take care of her daughter. Of course, Lana had never counted on Kait's need to turn her sister in or the fact that Trev might be a step ahead of them both.

"I'm here," she said hoarsely. "Go back to sleep. It's only six. I'll wake you at seven, sweetie."

Marni nodded, hugging her teddy bear more tightly, her eyes drifting closed. Kait stroked her hair for a moment, until she was soundly asleep. Then she got up.

It crossed her mind to call Rafe Coleman, but she decided against it.

Kait washed up and slipped on her Levi's and T-shirt. But autumn had taken a turn for the worse; it was a cold morning. She grabbed Trev's old gray sweatshirt and donned that, then went into the hall in a pair of fleece-lined leather slippers.

At Sam's door, she paused. Concern filled her and it was a godsend, briefly chasing away her own worries. Kait carefully opened the door, not wanting to awaken her if she was still sleeping. Sam hadn't even changed position from the night before; she remained dead to the world, on her back, the covers pulled up under her chin and tucked in tightly around her body like a straitjacket.

Kait backed out. Sam was exhausted, and with good cause. She continued downstairs. On the threshold of the kitchen she faltered. She had expected to be alone at this early hour and she was very wrong.

Trev and Elizabeth sat at the kitchen table with mugs of coffee. Trev looked as if he had had a sleepless night as well. He was unshaved, with circles under his eyes, his hair finger-combed. From Elizabeth's long and concerned expression, and the way she had been leaning toward him, Kait had no doubt that they had been up for hours and that Elizabeth now knew the full extent of Kait's treachery.

She looked up first. Anger, horror, and outrage mingled; it was hard to tell which emotion was predominant.

"Good morning," Kait managed, and then ignored her. She was looking directly at Trev.

He shifted and raised his eyes to hers. He didn't speak.

Elizabeth stood. "You've done enough here. You're not wanted here. When are you leaving?"

Kait squared her shoulders. "I'll pack after breakfast," she said, trying to hide her own emotions now. But her tone had sounded hoarse and broken to her own ears. She glanced at Trev again. Their gazes locked this time, very carefully.

It was Kait who quickly looked away, her heart racing. She wondered if he knew more than he had let on last night.

"I'll see if the papers arrived." Elizabeth stood, anger in her rigid shoulders and abrupt motions.

Kait poured herself a cup of coffee, aware of the way her hands trembled and that she was helpless to control it. She could not bear Trev's hatred. Yet this was what she had expected. She had known that if he ever learned the truth about her deception, he would reject her out of hand.

But her heart clearly had harbored such foolish hopes and dreams, and somehow, still did.

How could she have done what she had?

Could she ever forgive herself?

Kait looked at Trev again. He was staring at his coffee as if it were a vile poison, and as if she were not even in the room. She didn't dare sit down at the table, so she stood with her mug in hand, her hip against the counter. There was no mistaking that she was an intruder now.

Suddenly he stood up. "Where is she?"

Kait froze. She did not have to ask whom he referred to. "I don't know. But she said she's not coming back."

He stared at her. "That," he finally said, "is good riddance in my book." His eyes blazed as he grabbed his fleece-lined windbreaker.

A siren sounded once, twice, cut off abruptly, a warning blast.

Kait stiffened at the sound, trepidation filling her. Everything she had done since yesterday slammed over her like a runaway train. And she couldn't help it—her game was a dangerous one and she was scared.

The siren sounded again—and this time it was one short staccato blast.

Was this what she thought it was? She had meant it when she had told Rafe to arrest her. Once Kait was in jail and everyone believed that Lana had been caught, Lana would think her setup had worked, and she would let her guard down. She would become careless, reckless, and eventually she would be caught. Or so Kait hoped. It was, Kait thought, their only chance to catch her before she vanished without a trace into another wealthy community.

Trev glanced out the window. "It's Rafe," he said tersely, "and two other cars." He gave Kait a puzzled look and hurried from the room.

Kait remained in the kitchen, not moving. She now understood what fight or flight meant. Her body had become as taut as a bowstring, as if she somehow knew that nothing was going to go the way she had planned and that she should make a run for it.

But that was her nerves talking. She was not running. She had survived all of her sister's lies, and now it was Lana's turn to do the running.

Footsteps sounded. Kait somehow moved cautiously, warily, forward, reminding herself to be brave, reminding herself that she had told the truth, and that she was innocent, that Farrell had stolen the ring, and as she stepped into the hall, the front door flew open. Rafe entered. He was in full uniform, including his Western-style hat and his dark, impenetrable sunglasses. He had never looked more intimidating. "Morning, Trev, Elizabeth," he said. Two officers stood behind him, as menacing in appearance and intent.

"What's going on, Rafe?" Trev demanded darkly.

"Lookin' for a thief." Rafe removed his sunglasses and

turned his green stare on Kait. "Parker was hit recently. Maybe even the night of the fall ball. Took a Harry Winston diamond ring. I'd say it was an inside job. Wouldn't you?"

She began to tremble. She was innocent, but she wished now that Rafe were not so intimidating. "You didn't find her?"

"You mean, did I find your twin? Nope. We had the D.C. police on it, and we checked every flight bound for Paris, and every possible connection out of Reagan last night. Afraid your little tip didn't work, *sister*." He reached into the interior pocket of his bomber jacket and withdrew a folded document as Kait shrank with growing dread. This was an act on his part—wasn't it?

"Gotta warrant to search the house," he said, his regard unwavering on Kait.

Kait did not move. She had one coherent thought. *Rafe wasn't really arresting her—was he? This was all a part of Kait's plan!*

"A warrant?" Trev echoed as if he did not understand English.

Rafe didn't look away from Kait, but he nodded at his men. They took off toward the stairs. "Try the master bedroom first," he said. He added, "Inside tip." He looked at Kait directly again.

"I told you she wouldn't be on that flight," Kait managed.

"Yeah, guess you did. An' I got another warrant, signed about a half an hour ago." Rafe almost smiled. "This one's a warrant for your arrest."

Kait felt her knees buckle. This was it, then. *But this was her plan, wasn't it?*

Except that Rafe Coleman seemed to be truly enjoying himself.

"You have the right to remain silent," Rafe said, coming toward her. He jerked her hands behind her. "Anything you say can and will be held against you."

For one moment, Kait closed her eyes, steadying herself. Everything was going to be all right, she told herself. The papers would broadcast the news of Lana's arrest, and her sister would think she had a free pass to go anywhere in the world. She'd be careless. She'd be caught.

Kait's eyes flew open as Rafe snapped one handcuff closed. The cold metal gleamed on her wrist. Panic consumed Kait.

She struggled against it and failed. She turned desperately to Trev.

He was staring, eyes horrified—mesmerized.

The other cuff snapped closed. "You have the right to an attorney. If you cannot afford one, one will be appointed for you."

There were other deputies present. Kait wanted to scream that she wasn't Lana. That Lana and Farrell stole that ring, that they'd been stealing together for years. She said, "This is a mistake. I'm innocent. I didn't steal anything." She was perspiring—she told herself to stay calm no matter what it cost.

Rafe Coleman smirked at her.

"Hey, boss, look at this!"

Kait twisted so she could see one of the officers pounding downstairs, holding up a plastic bag. The movement caused the manacles to chafe her wrists, but she ignored it. Then she saw what the bag contained.

Kait cried out.

It was impossible.

It contained Georgina Parker's yellow diamond ring.

"You are under arrest," Rafe Coleman said.

Kait did not see Rafe Coleman again until they had arrived at the county jail. It was a long brick building, one story high, set behind the separate redbrick building that housed the sheriff's offices and the county recorder. A long paved walkway was between them. The entire compound was new, neat and clean, with manicured lawns surrounding the buildings and tall, stately trees lining the parking lot.

An officer unlocked the back door of his SUV and reached in for Kait. Kait let him pull her out, as she did not have the use of her hands, her eyes on Rafe as he approached from his own police car. He was wearing his sunglasses again. The lenses were reflective so she couldn't see past the silver coating on them. He had planted Georgina Parker's stolen diamond ring in her bedroom, the oldest trick in the book. But surely he had only done so to make her phony arrest look real. Hadn't he?

"Rafe. We have to talk."

"It's Sheriff to you and unless you intend to make a full confession, I suggest you wait to speak to your lawyer," he said. He jerked his head and the officer pulled Kait toward the walkway.

She tripped on the curb and the officer helped her to recover her balance. She tried to grab Rafe's arm but he easily moved out of the way of her manacled hands. If this was theatrics on his part, then he deserved an Academy Award. "I'm Kait London and you know it! You even told me that you knew Lana had a twin. What is this? What is going on?"

"You have the right to make a single call and I'd call that lawyer if I were you," Rafe remarked, not looking back at her as he led the way toward the front door of the second building. Engraved in the concrete stone above the door were the ominous words SKERRIT COUNTY JAIL. "I'd also shut up for now. Anything you say can and will be held against you. I'd save it for your lawyer, Lana."

Panic claimed her all over again. *This could not be happening.* . . . She wet her lips. "Kait. The name is Kait. We have to talk! Privately? Please," she added with desperation.

This time he didn't even bother to answer her.

Kait was aghast. Had she made the mistake of her life trusting him? Surely he was not going to pin Lana's rap on her? After all, he had spent all of last night looking for her sister—Kait had overheard a deputy talking about it. Apparently the Washington, D.C., police had also been involved.

But he hadn't found Lana. And now there was only Kait.

Kait's fear escalated. "Rafe, stop! Just for a minute. I'm not Lana. I'm not Trev's wife! We switched places—she's the thief," Kait pleaded to his broad back.

"Yeah, right. You're her twin. How convenient." He finally looked back at her as he pushed open the door. "Hey, fellas. Looks like we got ourselves a little cat burglar here. Jimbo, get the DA on the line."

Kait swallowed hard and reminded herself to stay calm. She reminded herself that she was not going to prison for her sister's crimes because she was not Lana and she had told Rafe and Trev the truth. But she was becoming afraid. The police hadn't found Lana. Why should they believe anything she said?

Why should Rafe or Trev believe anything she said—after all she had done?

Was her own plan to entrap her sister about to backfire?

Was Lana's plan to set up Kait going to succeed?

Kait felt faint now. Now, she thought about Rafe planting the stolen ring on her. God, she could go to jail for a long, long time. . . .

"I didn't steal that ring," Kait whispered. "Farrell stole it, and Lana gave it to me yesterday and I turned it over to you." She grabbed Rafe's arm so that he turned, forcing him to look down at her. "Damn it! Please don't do this!"

He looked at her with a cool, even smug smile. "I don't know and I don't care whether you are Kait or Lana or Anna Banana." His eyes blazed. "You know what I do know, sister? What I do know is that you are here, living with my brother, as his wife. What I do know is that about a year after you turned up in Trev's life a string of thefts began. In fact, it was like two heists the first year and then three and then four. . . . Yeah, so innocuous that at first no one even figured it out—then one day, it was like, geez, there's been a dozen burglaries in this county, all with the same MO—an easy safe crack from the inside and very valuable missing jewels. So what's your story? Oh, yeah. You're not the woman my brother married six years ago. You're her twin. You just showed up in town—conveniently switching places with your sister, who's the real thief. And that this other woman is where? On her way to Paris? You know what I do know?" He didn't wait for a response. "If you do have a twin, an identical twin, who's to say that you're not the thief and she's not the honest, hardworking, law-abiding one?"

Kait recoiled. Suddenly she realized just how much Rafe Coleman hated Lana. She could not move. *He hated her with a vengeance.* Enough to frame her for what he couldn't prove, enough to shoot her with the intent to kill, enough to drive her off the road with the same murderous intention, and to set fire to his own brother's barn.

She wasn't Lana, but he didn't know that.

"The day you conned my brother into believing that you loved him was the day you made your first mistake, baby, and the day you married him was your second," Rafe Coleman said, his green eyes blazing.

Oh, God, she had made a terrible miscalculation. Rafe Coleman was the enemy. How had she ever thought, for an instant, to trust him?

"We lifted half a dozen sets of prints from the Parkers' bedroom," Rafe said flatly. "They got two housemaids and then there's Parker and Georgie. How much you want to bet your prints are all over that room, Lana . . . Ms. London—or whoever you really are?"

Kait didn't move. Farrell had worn gloves when he'd cracked the safe. She hadn't worn any gloves, as the thought hadn't even occurred to her. She had, at least, touched the door or doorknob. Her prints would be in that room. And Rafe Coleman had planted the ring.

She was doomed.

"Book her," he said with disgust.

Kait sat on her bunk, her hands in her lap, unmoving. There was one other inmate in the jail, a young man who was badly battered and appeared to be sleeping off an excess of alcohol. His cell was across the corridor and at the end of it, and for that small amount of privacy, Kait was grateful. How long would she be imprisoned like this? And where were Lana and Farrell right now? She was in the throes of despair. Right now, the police should be chasing Lana down. But now

Kait knew that Rafe Coleman hadn't believed a word she had said to him.

She heard the door at the front of the corridor opening. Kait stiffened, as footsteps sounded, approaching. She did not stand up.

An officer was approaching. "You got visitors," he said.

Kait saw Sam behind him—and Trev standing in the doorway that they had just come through. She leapt up. "Trev." Her voice was a barely audible whisper.

His jaw tightened and he halted, standing there staring at her.

"Trev!" she cried, gripping the iron bars of her cell. "Please, I'm not Lana! I'm her twin! I'm Kait! I told you last night—you have to convince Rafe! Otherwise she will get away. . . ." She trailed off. "Please help me," she begged.

He whirled and walked out.

Had Kait not been gripping the bars of her cell, she would have collapsed. He had been her last hope.

"You got a few minutes. Boss says five."

Kait realized the guard was unlocking her cell to allow Sam in. Sam was ashen.

"Go tell your boss to jump in the lake," Kait whispered.

The officer shook his head, allowing Sam to walk inside, locking the cell door behind them.

"Clearly he doesn't think me a murderer," Kait said, as he walked away. "Otherwise he wouldn't let Sam in to visit me!"

There was no answer except for the sound of the door at the end of the hall as it closed.

"Damn you!" Kait cried. Then Sam touched her arm. Kait started, turning to face her.

Sam looked frightened. The next thing Kait knew, they were hugging one another hard.

"Don't worry," Kait whispered roughly. "Everything will be fine, just fine."

Sam pulled away. "The sirens woke me up. I thought Ben Abbott had lied and they were coming for me! I went to the window and saw them taking you instead. I had to come see you."

"Thank you," Kait whispered, touched. She thought about Trev, who would not talk to her now, who was in another room, only a few doors away. "How is Gabe today?"

Sam seemed surprised by her question. "If he continues the way he is, they're moving him out of ICU this afternoon," she said.

"That's great!" Kait was thrilled. "I'm so glad, Sam."

Sam hugged her, and this time, she clung. It was a moment before she pulled away. "How could anyone think you're her?"

Kait hesitated. "I'm her twin. I switched places with her, Sam, and what I did was very wrong."

Sam regarded her. "Dad said she lied to you just the way she lied to all of us. He said you thought she was in trouble, and you switched places only to try to help her—not to hurt us."

Kait almost swooned with relief. "He said that?"

Sam nodded, smiling a little. "Yeah, he did. Your name is Kait?"

Kait nodded, flooded with another wave of relief. Trev had defended her behavior to his own daughter. Did that give them a chance?

But why did he doubt her identity now?

"That's a nice name. It suits you . . . Kait."

Kait smiled back and sat down on the bunk. Sam sat beside her. "Why aren't you angry about my lie, Sam? I know you know that what I did was wrong. The end doesn't justify the means."

Sam shook her head stubbornly. "I'm glad you lied! I'm glad you came into our lives the way that you did! And Marni's glad, too!"

Kait tensed. "Does she know?"

"No. She's at school. I guess Dad will tell her what he told me."

"Are you and Trev talking now?"

Sam hesitated. "Sort of. I guess."

"Don't blame him for loving you so much," Kait said softly.

Tears filled Sam's eyes. "See? That is why I'm glad you lied and pretended to be her! Can't you stay, Kait? I mean, after you get out of jail? I know it's odd, but we want you to stay." She was vehement in spite of her tears.

Kait wet her lips. "I want nothing more," she whispered unsteadily. "But I can't. I hurt your father—he deserves so much more, Sam."

"He loves you."

Kait started. "How can you say that?"

She shrugged, smiling slightly. "It's, like, obvious."

Kait didn't correct her and tell her that she was wrong. "He won't talk to me."

"He's upset. When Dad's upset, he can get pretty cold. And he's *really* upset." Sam's hazel eyes held hers. "But he'll come around. He always does." She hesitated. "He never loved her the way he loves you."

Kait jumped to her feet. She didn't dare have any hope. Sam was only sixteen, and believing what she wanted to believe. At her age, she couldn't fathom loving someone and being so betrayed that walking away forever was the only adult choice.

"Don't be sad," Sam whispered, reaching for her hand as she also stood up. "I know you're innocent. Soon everyone will figure that out. Dad included. He'll take you back, Kait. I know he will."

Kait had to hug her, hard. How she had come to love this confused teenager. "Sam? I do need your help."

"Anything," Sam said cockily.

"I need a lawyer. A really good criminal lawyer."

Sam nodded grimly. "Don't worry. I'll get you one. I'll start making calls the minute I get home."

The door at the end of the corridor opened. Kait stiffened, turning; Sam said, "D.C., right? There should be plenty of really good lawyers there."

The deputy was strolling in with another woman. "Got visitors lined up to see you, Mrs. Coleman," he said.

And the moment he spoke, they had come close enough for Kait to realize that it was Alicia. She gripped the bars. It seared her mind that whoever had shot at her and run her off the road and then set fire to the barn was still out there, and word had just gone out that Lana had been arrested. Alicia was smiling. Kait's grip on the bars increased.

She told herself that she was safe because she was in jail.

The rationalization was not reassuring.

"Time's up, Sam," the deputy said, unlocking Kait's cell door.

Kait met Alicia's eyes. Sam stepped out. "Don't worry," she said to Kait.

Kait couldn't nod. Alicia stepped into the cell, the door closing behind them. Kait faced her warily as Sam and the deputy left. The door at the end of the corridor closed resoundingly. Alicia said, "Finally. You're finally getting all that you deserve."

She lifted her hand; Kait shrank back, for one heart-stopping moment thinking she held a gun.

Instead, the redhead's palm struck Kait with a loud crack across the face.

TWENTY-ONE

Two days later

It was only noon. Sarah Selman sighed with annoyance, having checked her watch for the hundredth time as she stood behind the Delta counter at Reagan National Airport. She was a newlywed; in fact, she had been married exactly three days. She could not wait to get home to her husband, and the mere thought "husband" made her break into a grin. Home was Three Falls, Virginia. She had grown up there, and Jason had instantly fallen in love with the small, quaint town, so that was where they had decided to live. Jason ran a small business on the Internet, so he could live anywhere.

They were going on their honeymoon in June. They had decided on Paris, the most romantic city in the world.

"Excuse me, I would like to check in. I do have a flight to catch," a woman said.

Sarah realized that she had been daydreaming. She smiled at her customer, accepting her ticket and passport, and then she did a double take.

The beautiful brunette waiting for Sarah to check her in was immediately familiar—her photograph had been on the front page of the tiny local newspaper, the *Three Falls Sentinel*, two days in a row. Jason read the *Wall Street Journal*, the *Washington Post*, and the *New York Times*—Sarah read the *Sentinel* front to back every day.

"You're staring," the woman said, still smiling a bit curiously now.

"Oh!" Sarah started, feeling herself flush. "I love your haircut. Who did it?" she asked quickly, but even as she spoke, even as she looked at the woman's ticket—her destination was Mexico City—all she could think of was that this woman looked exactly like Lana Coleman, a burglar who had finally been caught by the police after preying upon Skerrit County for six years. But the name on the ticket was Kait London. Clearly, Lana Coleman had escaped, and she was using an alias!

"I had it done in New York," the brunette said patiently.

Sarah was sweating. "Would you like a window seat?" Oh, God, she was face-to-face with an actual thief—and an escaped felon!

"No, aisle, thank you."

Sarah gave her an aisle seat, telling herself to breathe, and praying her hands would not shake. "Two bags?" she asked, glancing at her customer's baggage.

"Yes, and one carry-on," the woman smiled warmly.

She seemed like a nice lady—hardly like a conscienceless thief. Sarah looped the baggage claim tickets on the bags and hefted them onto the conveyor belt. She handed the woman her tickets with another smile. "Enjoy your flight. The gate is to your right," she said.

"Thank you." The woman smiled, picked up her carry-on, and left.

Sarah finally was able to breathe. Gulping down air, she ignored her next customer, slapping a CLOSED sign on her countertop, and dashed into the back room, where she called the police.

Lana flipped through a fashion magazine, admiring first a Dolce & Gabbana dress that would be perfect for Puerto de Raya, her final destination that day. She was smiling, an image of herself and Colin on the beach, sipping celebratory frozen drinks coming to mind. God, no one looked better than Farrell in his tight little Speedo swimsuit. Other images came, of her and Colin in bed in their bungalow, tearing each other's bathing suits off.

It had been so easy.

Not that she wished a prison term upon her sister. Truly, Lana didn't. But there was no way she was ever going to jail, just as there was no way she would give up the life she now lived. The tiny beach community where they would briefly linger was only their first stop in a series of small, desolate Caribbean communities. By the New Year, they would be in Rio de Janeiro, and if all went well, it would become their new home for years and years to come.

Kait was so naïve. And so desperate. Lana loved her, but she also felt sorry for her. Any woman who could fall in love with a man so quickly was hopeless. And as for the fall she would take, she would get a good five years, but then there would be parole. It wasn't that bad, and as Kait had always had it so easy, Lana felt that the time she spent behind bars would be good for her. It would give her some character.

Lana had the oddest feeling that Trev Coleman would wait for her, too.

Annoyed now, she slapped her magazine closed. She told herself not to be annoyed, because they were perfect for one another, but she couldn't help it—in a way, it was unfair. She didn't love Trev and she never had, but Kait was always the favorite with everyone. Her mother had held Kait's hands and told her how proud she was of her when she lay dying, but her words to thirteen-year-old Lana had been quite different. She hadn't been proud of Lana, not at all. She hadn't told her what a wonderful student she was, or how kind she was, or anything like that. She hadn't even told her how beautiful she was. Instead, she had chastised her for her latest sport, motocross, and then she had begged her to stay home more, to help more, to be with Kait more. She hadn't even told her that she loved her, but she had managed to tell that to Kait.

Kait had been their father's favorite, too. After their mother had died, Lana had always felt like an outsider in her own home, a home that belonged to the two of them. It had always been Kait and Dad in the kitchen preparing supper, or working together in the yard. And all through high school, every single teacher had doted on Kait, the perfect student and class valedictorian.

Lana had had any boy she wanted, but secretly they had all been in love with Kait, and what they had done with Lana hadn't had anything to do with love.

But who cared? Lana stood and stretched lazily, instantly aware of a dozen pairs of male eyes veering toward her, especially as her sheath dress rode high up on her thighs. She smiled then. She was insane to be even slightly jealous of her meek and mild sister. She was wearing a pale blue sleeveless dress that clung to her curves and was several inches above her perfect knees, and she knew that every man at her gate wanted her.

She looked carefully at them all.

A muscular blond who was not even twenty-five caught her eye and gave her a suggestive look.

Lana smiled back, because the flight would be a long one and she was bored and she particularly enjoyed the mile-high club.

Besides, it would be another full day before she met up with Colin at Puerto de Raya.

And then instinct made Lana stiffen.

She quickly turned.

Two men were approaching on the other side of the gate. They were wearing business suits, but Lana knew they were cops.

She told herself to remain calm. They could not be after her. No one knew where she was, except for Colin, and even if he had been caught, he would never betray her, not in a million years—just as she would never betray him. She picked up her purse and carry-on, then glanced carefully up at them again. They were entering the gate.

Her gaze took in the entire area, and she saw two policemen in uniform several paces behind the undercover cops. *There was no way she could make a run for it.*

Kait.

Lana blinked and thought about how willingly Kait had agreed to remain at Fox Hollow as her twin, about how easily she had accepted the ring. She thought about the newspaper headlines in Three Falls, baldly announcing Lana's arrest. Comprehension flooded her, and with it came sheer disbelief.

Her sister had done this? Weak, naïve, hopelessly vulnerable Kait? She had been outwitted by Kait?

Then she began to laugh. This was a joke!

The two plainclothesmen stopped before her. "Lana Coleman?"

She smiled seductively at them. "I'm afraid you are mistaken," she said. "My name is Kait London."

"You'll have to come with us," the younger one said. His expression was ice cold and he gripped her arm firmly. Instantly Lana knew he was indifferent to her as a woman.

"Would you care to see my ID?" she asked sweetly.

"We know you're carrying Kait London's ID," the older, portly detective said. He wore a wedding ring. "I'm afraid you will have to come with us." He gave her a kind smile. Lana's heartbeat quickened when he glanced down at her bare thighs.

"What have I done?" Lana asked as if surprised as she was escorted from the gate area. "This has to be a mistake! I'm not Lana—she's my twin! I'm Kait London and I can prove it."

The older detective met her gaze. "We really don't know what this is about, but there is an APB out for Lana Coleman. Just relax. We'll sort all of this out when we get to the precinct."

Lana smiled gratefully at him.

There was no way that Kait was going to win.

Kait heard the door at the end of the hall opening. She leapt to her feet and ran to the edge of her cell, gripping the bars. Her heart felt as if it were wedged in her throat. Hope renewed itself, but the fear of never getting out of jail remained. The past two days had been the longest of her life.

And being accused by Alicia of stealing her husband hadn't helped.

But that was all that she had done, other than to strike Kait once across the face. And she had been as stunned as Kait by the blow. She had then choked out how much she hated her and, sobbing, she had left.

The only bright side to the two days she had spent in jail was that Alicia had not returned and that Sam had found her a top criminal lawyer. They'd spoken twice on the phone and were meeting first thing tomorrow there at the county jail. Kait could hardly believe that she needed a lawyer to defend her against the charges that should be leveled against Lana. She could hardly believe that this was really happening after all . . .

Kait pressed her face to the bars. *If only Lana had been arrested,* she thought wildly. And then she realized that it was Rafe Coleman sauntering down the corridor toward her. Kait tensed, rigid with sudden, real hope. And even before he paused at her cell, their gazes locked.

Kait wet her lips. "What's happened?"

His expression was mild. And then he smiled. "Your sister was caught at Reagan National just before boarding a flight to Mexico. I don't know the details yet. Your plan worked."

Kait almost collapsed. Instead, she backed up and sat down on her cot, breathing hard. *She had done it.* Lana had intended to set her up to take a very hard fall for her criminal ways, but she, Kait, had figured it out and she had actually outwitted her sister.

There was no glee. There was relief, and there was regret. "Farrell?" Kait asked harshly.

"She was traveling alone. Unless she talks, I think he's already out of the country. I don't think we're going to grab him."

Kait simply looked at him, unable to move or speak or even think clearly. She was in the throes of exhaustion now.

He unlocked her cell door. "You okay . . . Kait?"

She met his oddly neutral expression now. "No. No, I'm not."

He hesitated, standing in her cell doorway. "You did the right thing."

Kait spoke, but her mouth barely moved. "I know. But that doesn't change the fact that she's my twin. She's twisted and ill, but she's my sister. Nothing will ever change that."

"She brought you down here to take the fall for her," he remarked flatly. "It was her or you. Don't be too hard on yourself."

She finally met his eyes. "Does this mean that you don't hate me?"

He started. "I don't know how I feel about you. You lied to my brother, Sam, and Marni, but without your help, we wouldn't have brought Lana down. I've done a bit of checking. You're as well liked in New York as Lana was disliked down here."

Kait got to her feet, weary in every fiber of her being. "What I did was wrong. And the more I fell for Marni, Sam, and Trev, the harder it was to justify what I was doing and to continue the lie. She told me Marni's life was in danger. That was a crock, wasn't it?"

"She played you," he said softly. "But she's good at playing her cons, now, isn't she? That's what she does. She knows how to find a man's—or woman's—weakness, and then she goes for the jugular, all with an easy smile on her face."

Kait stepped out of the cell. "Why do you hate her so much? Did she try to seduce you?"

He laughed briefly, without any mirth. "She was too smart to ever try to put me in her sights. I hated her from the day Trev brought her home, because I could read her like a book. I know a con when I see one, Kait. But she'd gotten Trev good and he refused to even speak about her with me." He was grim. "We didn't speak for six months after the wedding, actually. It was pretty bad."

"I'm sorry," Kait said, meaning it. "I know how much you love him and your nieces."

He didn't respond. But he stared at her oddly.

Kait knew what he was thinking. "I am different. I'm not her. We only look alike."

"Actually, you don't look alike, not at all. Your eyes are different from hers. Gentle. There's a smile there, even now. I never saw a smile in Lana's eyes, not once in six years."

They walked down the corridor slowly. Each step felt like a vast effort for Kait now. "You were so convincing that I was afraid *you* had set *me* up, Rafe," she said, searching his face.

"I believed you—but not completely. I had some doubt. I mean, after all, why should I trust you? You could have been the one robbing us all of these years. She could have been the honest one. I figured we'd bring her in and then sort it out. But Sam claims you are who you say you are—and most importantly, Trev seems able to tell the difference between the two of you with his eyes closed."

Kait flushed. She hoped Rafe didn't mean what he had said literally, but he was precisely right. "I've been really scared," Kait said. "I was scared you'd never find her and I'd go to jail in her place."

"Trev wouldn't let that happen," Rafe said. "And I was pretty sure you were who you said you were—I had to overdo the theatrics so no one would ever think we had concocted up such a crazy scheme in order to apprehend Lana."

Kait halted and gripped his arm. "Really? Trev wouldn't let me go to jail? How can you say that? Did he say something?"

He smiled in that slight, understated way she was becoming familiar with. "Why don't you go home and find out?"

"Home?" She didn't have a home. Not in New York, and not in Skerrit County.

"And let go of the guilt. This is a case where you are only guilty of being easily manipulated by your sister, and having some pretty bad judgment—nothing more."

She *was* guilty. "Is it so obvious?" she whispered.

He finally smiled. "A man can read your eyes, Kait, and that's the biggest difference between you and her."

"Truce?" she asked softly.

"Truce?" He was startled, a rare moment for Rafe Coleman. He hesitated, then held out his hand. "Yeah, we have a truce."

Kait shook his hand. His grasp was hard and strong and very much like his brother's. She thought about losing Trev and the girls, and tears clouded her vision. But at least she had done the right thing. At least Lana was in jail.

"Look, you're exhausted—and probably more so emotionally than anything else. Go home and get some rest. You'll feel better in a couple of days."

She stared at him. "I don't have a home."

He returned her stare. "I think you do, but, then, last time I meddled in my brother's affairs he ignored my advice completely. In any case, two of my favorite girls are waiting to see you." He pushed open the corridor door.

Kait could not imagine facing Trev. She was filled with dread.

"You're right," she finally said, because there was no avoiding it now. She had to pack, and she had to say goodbye.

An officer gave her a ride back to Fox Hollow. Kait thanked him, and as he drove away, she looked up at the front door of the big house, her heart sinking. *She didn't want to leave.* But she was unwanted now, and she didn't have any choice.

Kait slowly started up the front steps. The door flew open, Marni dashing out, screaming, "Mommy, Mommy!"

Kait stooped and caught Marni as she ran directly into her arms. She stood, the child in her embrace, holding on to her for her dear life, her sanity, her future.

"Mommy, I've missed you! You went away!" Marni cried in protest.

"I'm so sorry," Kait returned, finally setting her down. "I had to go away, but just for a few days." Then her heart sank. She had to be very careful about what she said now, and how she said it.

"But you didn't say good-bye and you didn't tell me where you were going!" Marni wailed, clinging to her hand. Then utter determination covered her tiny face. "You are not going away again."

Kait somehow smiled, but it was wooden. "Sit down with

me, honey," she said, and they sat down on the front steps of the house, hand in hand. Her heart was already broken, so how could it be breaking again, but this time into a thousand shards, each one more painful than the one before?

"You're not going away," Marni stated stubbornly.

"What did Daddy tell you?" Kait asked carefully.

"He said it was an emergency and that you had to go, and that when you came back, he would explain everything," she said. She stared at Kait. Kait heard a sound behind them and stiffened, knowing it was Trev. "I know he knows now, Mommy, that you're a new mommy."

Kait felt Trev's eyes on her back. "Yes, he does." She slowly shifted and met his green gaze. She didn't know what she expected to see when she finally looked at him, but to her amazement, she saw sadness. She started, realizing that his heart was broken too.

"Hello, Kait," he said softly.

She had seen hurt and pain in his eyes before, but never like this. She stood up. "I . . . I was just going to explain everything to Marni."

He nodded, walking over to his daughter and cupping her head. He seemed incapable of speech.

Kait wished desperately that he would forgive her so they could rekindle the love they had briefly found. But she knew her wish was a flight of pure fantasy. "Honey? I have a story to tell you, a story about sisters," she said to Marni.

"A story?" Marni began to relax, although she darted another suspicious glance between Kait and Trev.

"Sit down," Kait said, and they both sank back down on the front steps of the veranda. Trev moved to lean against a column. Kait glanced at him and their eyes briefly met. Quickly, they both looked away from one another.

"There were twin sisters, Marni, two little girls who looked exactly alike," Kait began nervously. "But these little girls weren't alike at all. One was shy, a bit afraid of her life, even afraid to have friends, and she spent all of her time reading books or working at the stable so she could ride a pony there. The other twin wasn't shy at all. She had lots of friends, especially boys, she was always laughing, running, jumping. She never studied and she almost failed all her classes, while the shy twin always got the highest grades." Kait had Lana on her mind now, and it more than hurt. She felt a tear rolling down her cheek.

"What were their names?" Marni asked with avid interest.

"Lana and Kait."

Marni stared, no longer smiling. "My other mommy was named Lana. My mommy who went away."

Kait stroked her hair. "I know. The twins lost their mommy like you. She died of cancer when they were thirteen. Their daddy was so sad, his heart broken, that it was hard for him to be a good daddy afterwards, like Trev. The twins had never been like other sisters, and now they grew even further apart. Lana had a lot of boyfriends, she skipped school, she bought a motorcycle, and she went to wild parties. Kait studied hard. Kait dreamed of having one boyfriend, just one. And then one day, after they went to different colleges, Lana just never came home."

Marni was wide-eyed. "Never?"

"Never," Kait said, feeling another tear. She didn't dare look at Trev now, for she might lose it. "So the twins, who were never like real sisters to begin with, were apart for many years. Kait thought it was sad, and she missed her sister so much—and then she saw her sister once or twice— Lana would suddenly come to Kait's town, and they'd have lunch or dinner. And then she was gone again. Kait never understood what she had done wrong, so that her own twin sister didn't love her." She had to stop. Marni patted her knee. It was hard to see.

"Don't cry, Mommy," Marni whispered.

Kait nodded, fighting the need to choke out a sob. A handkerchief was dangled in front of her. She looked up and met Trev's pain-filled expression, accepted the handkerchief, and dabbed her eyes. "But one day," she choked, "Lana came home. And she said she was in trouble, and she begged Kait to do a terrible thing."

"To change places?" Marni asked.

"Yes." Kait nodded. "Lana asked Kait to go to her home, and pretend to be her. I was so happy to see her again, so desperately happy, that I couldn't refuse. You see, I'm Kait, honey. I'm your mother's twin sister."

"But you're my mommy now!" Marni cried, on her feet like a shot.

Kait stood, shaking. "I'm your aunt, but I love you as much as if you were really my own daughter," she whispered.

"No!" Marni stomped her foot. "You are my new mommy now and I won't let you go!"

Trev took his daughter's hand. "Sweetie, Kait has to go. She has another life in New York."

"I won't let her leave," Marni shouted, pulling away from her father. "Daddy, don't let her go!"

Kait stared at father and daughter, Marni furious and frightened and beginning to cry, Trev with tears welling in his eyes. She silently begged him to ask her to stay.

He did not. "Kait has to go back to New York." He was hoarse but firm.

Marni whirled. "Don't go!"

Kait felt as if the words were a robotic fist, somehow striking right through her chest and body, splitting her flesh apart. Her soul crumbled in its wake. "I did a terrible thing, lying to you and Sam and your father about who I really am," she said.

"Mommy asked you to do it! It's not your fault!" Marni screamed.

Kait heard the front door open and close; she glanced back, it was an ashen Sam. "Lying was my fault, honey. It was wrong. Can you understand that?"

Marni nodded, remaining fiercely determined. "But you're not lying now! So now you can stay!"

Kait was completely broken now. She looked up at Trev.

"Elizabeth already packed your bags," he said to her. "If she missed something, we can send it to you."

He was really going to do this. He was really going to forget everything they had shared, and let her go.

"I'll go call a cab," she said hoarsely.

Trev nodded, not offering to drive her the hour it would take to get to Reagan National.

"Dad!" Sam cried. "Don't let her go!"

Trev didn't answer.

Kait knew that if she didn't leave immediately, she wasn't ever going to make it out of Fox Hollow in one manageable piece. She walked past Sam, incapable of sending her the faintest smile of reassurance, and reached for the door.

"How can you do this?" Sam screamed at her father.

Kait glanced back.

"Mommy!" Marni wailed, in panic. *"Mommy!"*

Kait couldn't move.

"Ssh, ssh," Trev soothed, taking her into his arms.

Marni kicked and punched him, wildly, desperately; Kait closed her eyes and somehow made it inside.

And she heard Sam shouting at Trev, "You suck!"

"Señor? I am leaving now. Do you want anything else?"

Colin Farrell came out of the bungalow's single bedroom, his cotton short-sleeved shirt completely unbuttoned, several days' growth of beard upon his face. The cleaning girl that had been hired by the Realtor from the local village stood in the bungalow's single room, a combination of living room, kitchen, and dining area. The bungalow was spanking clean and as neat as a pin. The refrigerator was fully stocked. A fan slowly whirled overhead. All of the villa's windows were wide open, all thanks to the slender Mexican woman standing near the rattan couch. And just past Rosita's head, Colin could see the wide brilliantly white expanse of beach and the sparkling azure of the Caribbean Sea. "No, *gracias*," he said.

She smiled at him, her big brown eyes flickering over his chest and torso. "I am pleased to stay, señor," she said softly, meeting his eyes.

He had no time for this. He knew what she wanted and was not interested at all. "I will see you tomorrow, Rosita. *Mañana. Hasta luego, gracias*," he said firmly.

She pouted but smiled once more before she left, leaving the front door wide open, the better to catch a breeze.

Colin walked to the fridge and took out a bottle of ice-cold beer, which he popped. He drank thirstily, then walked to the front door and stared out of it, first north and then south and then north again. Not a single vehicle could be seen. And there was one pedestrian, Rosita, walking slowly toward the village that was three kilometers away, her fine gauze skirts swinging about her swaying hips.

His heart lurched. *Where was Lana?* She had been due hours ago, and soon the sun would set.

He swigged and reversed direction, crossing the too neat and so empty bungalow, and finally halting on the veranda outside. A path led from it the short distance to the beach. He leaned against the porch's post, staring out to sea.

She had not been caught. Lana was the smartest and most resourceful woman he knew. No, she had *not* been caught, but clearly she had experienced a delay, or she had missed her flight. He had been waiting for her arrival all day.

But he would not worry. Not about Lana. She could take care of herself.

But he was worried. Because she had his number, and she had not called him on his cell phone. He was sick with worry now.

Suddenly he heard the most welcome and miraculous noise—that of an approaching vehicle. Colin dashed inside and to the front door. He ran into the driveway. A large vehicle—a bus, a van, or a lorry—was coming down the road at a snail's pace, and it was coming from the north.

His heart skipped and then beat hard. He tossed the beer into the shrubs and hurried to the mailbox, shielding his eyes and gazing into the sun.

Lana was on that bus. He knew it.

An eternity passed as the van approached. When it was but yards away, he saw that it was filled with passengers, but other than two boys riding the sidesteps, hanging on to the windows, he could not make out the identity of anyone in the old beat-up Chevy. He waited for the Chevy van to begin to slow down and then stop, so as to discharge Lana.

But it did not slow down.

In disbelief, he watched it creep by him.

And then it was going past him, not even stopping.

"Hey!" he shouted. He ran after the van. "Hey! You! Señor! Stop the van! *Detenga el carro! Quiero hablar contigo!*"

The van slowed and Colin ran after it, finally reaching the driver's window. *"Un Americana,"* he panted. *"¿Donde l'americana?"*

The driver looked at him as if he was crazy. In perfect English, he said, "There are no Americans here. Do you want a ride, señor?"

Colin stared at the sweating Mexican in disbelief. He finally shook his head. The van rolled forward and Colin leapt away to avoid having his foot run over by a back wheel. The two boys hanging on to the side of the car laughed at him, pointing and jeering.

He began to slump. Why wasn't Lana on that bus? He dug into the back pocket of his cotton chinos for the hundredth time that day. There was no message icon on his cell phone. Colin returned to the bungalow, grabbed another beer, and this time, he walked down the grassy, palm-shaded path to the beach. He was not going to worry. Lana was going to appear at any moment, like the mirage of an oasis in the desert, only she would not be a mirage.

And then he squinted down the beach, directly into the setting sun.

A figure appeared to be approaching.

He stared, willing the figure to be real and not a figment of his imagination.

The figure *was* real. His heart began to pump with insistence, with the seeds of joy.

He wet his lips, starting forward. Jesus Christ—the approaching person was a woman! She was too distant for him to make out her features, but she had dark brown hair that glinted with reddish tones in the sun, and she was Lana's height. He began to run.

Smiling.

The woman became clearer. A long, graceful step, a bright white bikini, no top. Brilliantly white breasts. Hair that was shoulder-length . . .

Colin stopped.

Lana had cut her hair a week ago, and the woman's face and body were suntanned.

He stared in dismay.

She smiled at him, a local girl with the high cheekbones of the native Indians.

Colin dropped his beer as she walked past.

She sent him another smile, this time over her shoulder, and he saw that her bikini was a thong. He turned away.

She was coming. He knew it. She had not been caught. It was simply impossible.

He made his way slowly back to the bungalow and then outside. There was a big white rock by the end of the drive where the rotting mailbox was. Now the unmarked two-lane highway was empty as far as the eye could see. Colin sat down on the rock and sipped his beer, staring north. He would wait until she came.

And if she didn't come today, then she would come tomorrow, or the day after that, or the day afterwards.

He would not leave Puerto de Raya until Lana arrived.

He would wait days, months, years.

TWENTY-TWO

He glanced into the rearview mirror as the unmarked sedan crept north on the freeway. The traffic was extremely heavy, as it was almost five P.M. and everyone who worked in D.C. was on their way home. And the prisoner seemed troubled and sad.

But it was not his business. It was not his business that she claimed she was Kait London, that she looked exactly like the photograph on her driver's license, and that she had spouted off enough information about her identity and her life to fill two novels. They were merely transporting her back to Skeritt County, from whence she came.

She met his glance in the rearview mirror and smiled gently.

Automatically, he smiled back.

Bill, who had recently become his partner and who was driving, immediately noticed. "Cut it out," he said, looking at the rearview mirror and speaking to Lana Coleman/Kait London.

She said softly, "I have to use a rest room."

Bill ignored that.

Dan turned. "We'll be back in Three Falls in about an hour. Surely you can wait?"

She recrossed her long legs, her blue dress riding higher on her thighs. It was impossible not to look, because she was the most beautiful woman he had ever seen in person. Not that it mattered. He'd been happily married twenty-eight years and he had two kids and two grandkids, not to mention a wife who hadn't left him in spite of the job. He *loved* Mary. She was plump now, and short-tempered, but she was still a beautiful woman and the best wife a man could have, to his way of thinking. Still, the woman in the backseat was the kind of woman men had fantasies about, and he'd had quite a few in the past six hours since picking her up at the airport.

Not that he would ever cheat. Never had and never would. But there was nothing wrong with a good, hot, triple X–rated fantasy, now, was there?

Tonight he would make love to his wife, all right. He was already hard thinking about it.

"It will be two or three hours at this rate," she protested softly. "I have handcuffs on. You can leave them on. Or you can come into the bathroom with me." She smiled a little. "I trust you not to look."

Their eyes met. He thought, *She knew.* She knew that he had the hots for her and if he wanted it, he could have it. Christ. For one moment, the temptation was so overwhelming, he actually considered it. Then he turned to his new partner. "Pull over at that Texaco, Bill."

Bill snorted. "She has to piss like I'm a fairy."

"Just pull over. Where's she going to go?"

Bill swerved hard into another lane, cutting off the car behind them, causing horns to blare and someone to curse through a rolled-down window. Bill slapped their siren on top of the car and turned it on. He gave the driver behind them an "I'm gonna break your balls" look followed by the finger and shoved through the next lane and onto the shoulder of the highway. Using that, he drove the next mile to the exit.

The Texaco had five cars at the three islands. Bill halted the sedan by the side of the minimart. "I'll check it out," Dan said, climbing out of the car. He smiled at the woman in the backseat. "One moment. You okay?"

She nodded. "Thank you."

He went into the store and was told by a young Hispanic man with a goatee and acne that the bathrooms were in the back. Bill walked down an aisle filled with chips and candy, grabbing a bag of Fritos as he did. He opened the door to the ladies' room. There was a toilet and a sink with a mirror over it, a garbage can, the paper towel dispenser and the hot-air dryer. God, Bill was such a dick. Shaking his head, he walked back outside, tossing the Fritos on the counter as he did so, intending to pay for them later.

"No problem," he announced to his partner. "No window, nothing."

Bill grunted, leaned back in his seat, and closed his eyes, apparently taking a nap.

Dan opened the back door, helping Lana out. Their eyes met. She didn't say a word, but she looked at him as if he were twenty-five and all muscle again. He shouldn't take the cuffs off, but where would she go? And more important, how? There was simply no way for her to escape.

He unlocked the cuffs and tossed them on the backseat, slamming the door closed and taking her soft, slender arm. "This way."

"Your partner could use a lesson in how to be a gentleman from you," she said as they entered the store.

He flushed with pleasure, leading her to the back. "Yeah?"

"Yes." Her look was direct. "I never forget a kindness."

"I'm married," he blurted, and felt himself turn red.

She laughed softly. "I know." She glanced down at his simple wedding band. "I need to buy some Tampax."

He knew he turned redder. "Okay."

She seemed grateful. He watched her choose a box and handed her a fiver to pay for it. Then he escorted her to the bathroom, where she promised to hurry. "Don't rush," he said, still blushing. "The traffic stinks."

She laughed and disappeared inside the bathroom, and he heard her lock the door.

He didn't care. She wasn't going anywhere, and he leaned against the door, imagining her dropping her panties.

They'd be lace and sheer. No, she'd wear a wisp of a thong. The setting changed. She pulled off her dress. They were in a hotel room. Her breasts were big and white. He already knew she wasn't wearing a bra. Now, she had no underwear either, not even a thong. Smiling, she got down on her knees, unzipping him. She sucked him down her throat.

He started, wishing he'd had his jacket on. He paced, shaking himself free of the extremely graphic and vivid fantasy he'd succumbed to. God, he'd actually felt her lips. . . .

He glanced at his wristwatch. How long had she been in there? Two minutes? Five? He had no idea now. Couldn't be more than five. He'd give her five more, then politely knock.

An image of her naked and spread wide for him on a bed assailed his mind. He shoved it away, and thought about how it would be a good four or five hours before he got home tonight to his wife.

When five minutes had passed, Dan said, awkwardly, "Kait? I mean, Ms. London? Er . . . Mrs. Coleman?"

There was no answer.

He knocked on the door, deciding to use the name she claimed was her genuine one. "Ms. London? You all right in there?"

No answer.

His blood rushed. He reminded himself that there was no window and no possible way for her to get out. He knocked again, this time forcefully. "Ms. London? Time to go. You all right in there?"

There was still no answer, and the silence was resounding now.

Dan rushed to the pimply-faced cashier, showing his badge and demanding a key. He was sick now, sick in his gut, but he kept reminding himself that the woman could not have escaped. Had she passed out? With the curious cashier on his heels, he raced to the back of the store and unlocked the door.

The bathroom was empty.

The garbage can was upside down and on top of the toilet, which had its lid closed. The bottle of soap had been taken from the dispenser, and was lying on the floor, where it had been dropped. In horror, Dan looked up at the ceiling.

There was a grille above the toilet. It had been pushed up and away, and a square black hole gaped down at him.

He stared in disbelief. *She had escaped.*

He whirled, gun in hand. "Where the fuck does that vent go?"

"Like, how the hell would I know?" the young man said, amused.

"Did you see her go out of the store?"

"No," he said, as if Dan were a moron.

Dan dashed into the store, but there were no dislodged ventilation units in any part of the ceiling there. Was she still in the crawl space above?

"Hey, there's a storeroom in the back. Maybe she's in there?" the cashier suggested with growing enthusiasm.

They raced to a door that was not locked, but which had a sign on it telling customers that entry was forbidden. The cashier pushed it open and Dan walked in as the young man hit the light. The small storeroom instantly became illuminated, and the first thing Dan saw was the wide-open door and through it, the parking lot at the back of the store.

"Hey, she must have dropped down in here." The cashier glanced up at the ceiling above their heads.

So did Dan. Another square hole grinned mockingly at him.

Dan ran outside. A block away was the freeway, lined with cars, and damn it, the traffic was moving now at a nice forty-five or fifty miles an hour.

"Guess she got a ride." The cashier grinned. "She a murderer or something?"

Dan knew his career was over. "Or something," he said grimly.

Sam was beside herself. She stood in the foyer, where two suitcases and a garment bag had been ominously placed. Her father had retreated to his study and Kait had gone upstairs.

Sam imagined that she would shower and change for her trip back to New York.

She swiped at the tears on her face, dashing up the stairs, taking them two at a time. Her huge chunky heels got in the way and she fell. She launched herself upright and ran down the corridor and into the master bedroom, not knocking. She halted breathlessly there.

Kait stood in the center of the room in a pale beige pantsuit, staring either at the bed or out the window beyond it. She turned.

"I can't let you go. We love you, Kait! Even Dad loves you."

Kait smiled sadly. "Your father may or may not love me, Sam, but I did something that he will never forget, and more importantly, will never forgive."

Sam couldn't breathe. First her father had hit her, then Gabe had been shot, and now this. "I don't get it. You and Dad—you're both hypocrites!"

Kait walked over to her and laid her hand on her shoulder. "Life is hard and it isn't fair," she said softly. Her blue eyes were swimming with tears.

"But you guys love each other!" Sam protested, her stomach sickening.

"I love him . . . and I always will." She sighed, and choked on a sob. "I had better go. While I am still capable of walking away on my own two feet."

Sam caught her elbow from behind. "No! Dad has always talked about forgiveness, about saying I'm sorry, about how important forgiving and letting go is! I've heard him lecture a million times! But when it's his life, now he can just refuse to forgive? Like, I should forgive him for hitting me and for hating Gabe, but he can't forgive you for coming here to help your sister?"

Kait shook her head wordlessly. Then she pulled Sam into her arms. "I love you and you can call me anytime," she said. Then she straightened, uncertain. "If your father allows it."

"This is shit!" Sam cried.

Kait gave her a tearful look and hurried from the room, her shoulders squared.

Panic overcame Sam. *Kait was their mother now! She couldn't leave them like this so suddenly, so abruptly—just like Mom had one day left them, when she had died. It wasn't fair!* It was happening all over again. Sam ran after her. "Kait! Please don't go! We love you! We'll be good—I'll apologize to Dad—I won't see Gabe—I'll do anything you want—please!"

Kait whirled and embraced her. "Oh, Sam! I'd stay if I could—if he'd let me!" She chucked up her chin. "Honey, you don't have to do anything differently. I love you just the way you are."

Sam wept.

Kait continued down the stairs; Sam couldn't move. She found herself sitting on a step, thinking that she could run away to New York to live with Kait. But what about Marni? She couldn't leave her little sister behind. And she wasn't so selfish as to steal her away from their father. Besides, that was probably illegal—it was probably kidnapping, and she and Gabe were already in enough trouble.

She heard the front door open and slam closed; she heard Elizabeth speaking and Kait replying. Sam leapt up and ran down the rest of the stairs, and when she reached the front hall, she saw Elizabeth's Land Rover pulling away, with Kait in the front seat beside the housekeeper. For one moment, she was frozen, and then she brushed her soaking-wet face with her sleeve and ran frantically into her father's study.

He sat at his desk, but his head was on his arms, his eyes closed, as if he were asleep. "Dad!"

He slowly straightened. "What is it?"

"You love her! You have to forgive her and you have to get her back!" Sam shouted.

Trev stared at her. "You don't understand."

"I do understand!" Sam came closer. "You love her, I love her, and Marni loves her! And we need her, Dad! And why do you get to get off on all the forgiveness stuff you always preach to me?"

Trev stared, looking odd and ill all at once. "I'm afraid."

Sam blinked. "But she's not like that bitch. She's nice and kind. And she loves us! She loves you! You're breaking her heart, Dad!"

"Sam, you're too young to understand." He stood.

"No, I do understand! I understand that you're nothing but a coward, Dad!" Sam ran out.

"Whoa," Rafe said from the doorway, catching Sam by the shoulders.

Sam glared at him. "He's so stupid and I'm going to go to New York City to live with Kait!" She flung a furious and tearful look at her father, jerked free of her uncle's grasp, and ran off.

Trev stared at his brother. Rafe stared back. Then he knocked on the open door. "Gotta moment?"

"Not really. Not if you came to harp on me."

Rafe smiled grudgingly. "Been a while since I saw you cry. In fact, I think the last time was the day Mariah died."

Trev felt the pain then, all the way to his heart. But it wasn't the pain of the wife he'd loved who had died seven years before; it was the pain of losing the woman he'd so recently come to love, it was the pain of losing Kait. He'd been trying desperately to keep it at bay all day. "That's a low blow. And uncalled for."

"Do you love her?"

Trev gave him a dark look and paced to a window, refusing to answer.

"Stupid question, being as I know the answer. You know I'm a pretty good judge of character. As much as I'd like not to like Kait, I do. I think she's as different from Lana as a sister can be, and I know she's head over heels for you."

Trev turned to look at him, shaking. Was she in love with him? He desperately wanted to believe so. And in a way, he did. But if so, how could she have done what she had? What if she was like her sister?

But she wasn't anything like Lana! He knew that with every fiber of his being even if he was afraid to take another chance, even if he was afraid to trust what his heart was telling him.

"Life isn't always about second chances," he said gruffly, aware that he sounded like a jerk. But wasn't he being a jerk?

After all, he had played her game too. He had known the moment he moved inside her that she wasn't Lana. In that instant, he'd recalled what Zara had recently learned, that Lana had an identical twin. In that instant, he'd known the woman in his bed, whom he was buried so perfectly in, was his wife's twin.

He had been relieved, he had been thrilled, and he had chosen to enjoy every stolen moment that he could, until the game had to end.

Because he'd wanted to be with her desperately. Because he'd been falling in love with her foolishly and helplessly. Because he'd been selfish enough to want the charade to go on forever if it could.

Before they'd both have to face a reality neither of them had chosen and neither of them wanted.

"Really?" Rafe laughed mirthlessly at him. "While there's life, there's hope—and that means there's a zillion chances, buddy."

"Damn it, Rafe! How the hell did you get on her side?" Trev asked furiously, and he was as furious as he was heartbroken, because the entire time he'd pretended not to know who she was, he'd always known that one day they would confront one another and their love affair would be over. And in a way, he was as angry with himself as he was with her—no, more so. He felt angry and frustrated and trapped by his own code of ethics, of justice. And oddly, the only person who didn't seem to matter anymore was Lana herself.

Somehow, being with Kait had exorcised his anger with Lana completely.

"I'm on your side, and don't ever forget it," Rafe said. "So let me say what I came to say. She's one brave woman.

Can't have been easy, turning your own twin sister in. Never mind Lana's a thief, a bitch, and a whore. Betcha she'll live with guilt for a long time, maybe forever. But in the end, she did what was right. I'd say she was a victim of Lana's, just like you, just like the girls, the Parkers, and half of Skerrit County."

"Damn it," Trev breathed. "You're not telling me anything new!"

"Then why are you letting her go?"

Trev met his gaze. It was a damn good question, and suddenly he didn't have a damn good answer. He was in love, he was afraid, and he was angry, mostly with himself. Now he knew he should have called her on her deception the moment they'd made love. How easy it was to see, in hindsight. And while his head told him that no couple could start a life together this way, his heart told him he was a coward and a fool.

"Do you love her?" Rafe asked pointedly.

"Yes."

Rafe smiled, satisfied.

Kait stared out her window as Elizabeth drove in silence toward the highway. Her heart was so broken that she had become numb. She couldn't think and she couldn't seem to feel, which was good, because if she dared to feel anything now, she would break down completely. The woods were a blur as they drove past.

Elizabeth suddenly slowed the Land Rover.

Kait wondered what she was doing but was too grief-stricken to care. She reminded herself that she was going to have to thank Elizabeth for offering her a ride to the airport; still, she would have preferred a taxi. But Elizabeth had canceled the taxi without asking her what she wanted to do. Kait sighed and heard herself choke on a sob instead.

Elizabeth braked and came to a stop on the side of the road.

Kait closed her eyes, thinking, *Now what?* She could not deal with another argument, confrontation, or debate. She couldn't remember now if she had apologized to the house-keeper or not, but she had no apologies left inside her now.

"Get out of the car," Elizabeth said grimly.

Kait turned and became rigid. The black barrel of a gun was pointed right at her nose.

"Get out of the car, you little whore," Elizabeth said.

"Wh—" Kait couldn't speak. Her mind came to life. *Elizabeth? Elizabeth was the one trying to kill her sister? But, she had set fire to Trev's barn!* "I'm not Lana," she managed.

"Get out!" Elizabeth cried.

Kait pushed open her door and leapt out of the Land Rover. She tripped and fell, and for one moment, the earth damp and moist beneath her fingers and palms, she heard Elizabeth climbing out of the car on her side. Elizabeth was trying to kill her sister. Elizabeth was the one. Kait leapt up and started to run.

A shot rang out.

Kait dove behind a wide oak tree, huddling at its base.

"I should have done this a long time ago," Elizabeth said.

Kait leaned hard into the tree. "I'm not Lana! Please! Elizabeth—don't do this!"

"I know who you are!" Elizabeth exclaimed. "There are two of you, dear God, two of you, and this time is worse than before! You have him wrapped around your finger—but, so did she. Still, it was only lust then, Trev has fallen in love with you. I will not let him go through this all over again! Get up!"

Kait didn't move. "Please, Elizabeth, think about what you are doing! I'm not Lana. I love Trev! I'd never hurt him—"

Elizabeth cut her off. "She used him from the first day he set eyes on her. When she came back from New York and started using Marni too, I knew what I had to do! But I failed! Now, thank God, she's in jail—where she belongs! But I will not allow Trev to destroy himself and his children by taking up with you! *Do you hear me?*"

The bark was scraping her cheek raw. Kait flailed wildly around, but nothing faced her except trees and more trees.

There was nowhere to run and nowhere to hide. Then she heard Elizabeth's footsteps approaching. "But you burned down his barn! You love him! How could you? And his horses—he could have lost five or six horses," she cried, panting.

"I thought the fire was foolproof. I thought I'd get you. I did what I had to do. Do you think I wanted to kill his horses? Get up, Kait."

Kait shifted and dared to peek around the trunk of the tree. Elizabeth's gaze locked with hers. And she fired.

Kait jerked back as the bullet slammed into the tree trunk an inch from her head. She couldn't breathe. *Elizabeth was a crack shot.*

"Trev doesn't love me," she gasped. "He's sent me away. Why are you doing this? Lana's in jail and we're not going to be together! Please, Elizabeth, stop and think!"

Another shot rang out. Kait felt the vibration of the bullet in the tree right behind her head. She inhaled, shaking. Somehow she was gong to have to make a run for it, but how? And to where?

She glanced desperately around, but nothing had changed, the woods were thick, but there was no place to hide.

Then she saw the tree lying down on its side and rotting. It was twenty yards away. But it provided a much better barrier than the upright oak she was crouched behind now.

A car door slammed. "Elizabeth? Kait? Are you all right?" Trev called.

For one moment, Kait was in disbelief. She shifted and saw Trev standing by the hood of the Land Rover on the side of the road, silhouetted by the setting sun, his blue pickup parked just in front of the SUV. Elizabeth had turned at the sound of his voice as well. Kait saw the moment Trev saw her gun. He paled.

"Trev! She's the one!" Kait cried.

His eyes were wide, stunned—horrified.

"Trev, I am protecting you. Go home. No one will ever know," Elizabeth said firmly.

Trev didn't move. His gaze went past Elizabeth and met Kait's. "Kait? Are you all right?"

"Yes," Kait cried.

Trev held her eyes for one more moment, then turned on Elizabeth. "Give me the gun."

Elizabeth faltered. "Trev, I have to protect you and the girls. I can't live with myself, watching you fall for her all over again."

"That's my choice. Give me the gun," he said firmly.

Kait got on her hands and knees. Elizabeth's back was to her and twenty feet separated them.

"Don't you see? She's playing you all over again!"

"You burned down my barn," Trev said. Then, agonized, "This isn't the way."

Kait leapt up and rushed Elizabeth from behind.

Elizabeth turned, firing directly at her.

"Kait, no!" Trev screamed.

Kait felt the bullet whiz by her head, impossibly close, just an instant before she landed on Elizabeth. Then she and the older woman went down in a heap, with Kait on top and Elizabeth on her back. The gun flew several feet away.

Trev pulled Kait into his arms. "Are you all right?"

Kait met his wide green eyes and collapsed against his chest, beginning to shake uncontrollably. "Yes."

He held her hard and tight. "I was coming to tell you that I love you and to ask you not to go," he whispered roughly.

She stiffened with disbelief—and slowly looked up. "You were?"

He nodded, and then they both looked at Elizabeth, who was sitting up.

He wet his lips. "Are you all right, Elizabeth?"

She started to cry. "I was only trying to protect you, Trev. You know that."

Trev stood, helping Kait to her feet. He released her, but not before giving her a reassuring look. He held his hand out to Elizabeth. She took it and he also helped her up. "I know," he said, attempting a smile, which failed miserably. "I know how much you love me and the girls."

"Do you?" she cried. "I'd give my life for all of you, you do know that, don't you?"

Kait slipped off her jacket and used it to pick up the gun, careful not to get her own fingerprints on it. She felt a tear sliding down her face. She could imagine how Trev must be feeling now. Elizabeth was family. Trev knew he considered her to be the aunt he had never had.

Trev had come for her. Trev hadn't let her go.

She smiled in spite of her tears. Out of the ashes might come real happiness—a bright and glorious future.

"I know that, Elizabeth," Trev said quietly—sadly.

Kait turned at the sound of another approaching car. When she had left the house to go to the airport, Rafe had been there with Trev. Now she watched his black-and-white Chevy Blazer cruise up to the scene. She glanced at Trev and their eyes met.

The police vehicle halted and Rafe got out, leaving the engine running. "What's going on, here?" he asked, his eyes taking in the scene.

Trev was silent. Kait walked the short distance to the road, and handed him her jacket containing the gun. He opened it, then slowly looked up.

"I had no choice!" Elizabeth cried. "Rafe, you couldn't possibly arrest me! I know you hate her, too! Someone had to do something!"

Rafe had the oddest expression on his face. Kait could feel his bewilderment—it was that of a small boy.

She moved closer to Trev. He put his arm around her and held her close, and she knew everything would be all right.

"Lana escaped," Rafe said.

The moment they walked through the front door of Fox Hollow, Sam came pounding down the stairs. Trev and Kait were arm in arm, and Kait sensed he was feeling the way she was—that he was almost afraid after all that had happened to let her go. Rafe had recovered from his absolute bewilderment and surprise and had taken Elizabeth to the county jail. Kait knew Trev was in shock over what had happened—and

so was she. Not just because Elizabeth Dorentz had been trying to kill her, but because Lana had somehow escaped.

And if she had escaped, Kait knew she wasn't going to
get caught again.

"You're back!" Sam cried, amazed.

"I'm back," Kait said, smiling.

Sam glanced at Trev. "Dad, you did it. You went after her.
You really did it!"

"Yes, I did," Trev said, one arm still around Kait. "You
were right, honey, and when she drove off with Elizabeth, I
just couldn't let her go."

Kait touched his hand and their eyes locked in silent understanding. Kait wondered what would happen next. Lana
would somehow leave the country undetected, but would
Elizabeth face charges? Surely she needed a psychiatric
evaluation.

"Are you all right?" Kait asked Trev softly.

He hesitated. "I need some time to come to grips with
what's happened," he said as softly. He turned her to face
him. "So much has happened that I may have forgotten to
tell you why I couldn't let you go. Did I tell you that I am in
love with you?" He smiled a little, his green gaze intense but
questioning.

Kait smiled back, forgetting that Sam was even present.
"No. Did I tell you that I fell in love with you the moment
you walked into the front hall in those faded jeans and that
cashmere sweater?"

He pulled her close. "That's nice to know, Kait."

Sam coughed but was ignored.

"You know what's eating at me? If Lana hadn't switched
our business meeting, we would have met six years ago,
Kait, and I would have married you in the first place."

Kait was thrilled. "That little notion had occurred to me,
too," she said softly. And it struck her then how easy it had
been to simply cross to the other side of the chasm of deception with this man. And on the other side lay the foundation
upon which to build a lifetime—a foundation of respect and
friendship, honesty and love, and passion.

Trev smiled at her and took her into his arms. Kait smiled back, her heart singing, and lifted her face for his kiss. It was finally occurring to her that the impossible was really happening—Trev had forgiven her and she wasn't ever going to leave Fox Hollow.

Sam coughed more insistently. "Hello! I'm still here," she said with laughter in her tone.

Kait inhaled, stepping back. "How is Gabe, Sam?"

Sam brightened. "They moved him out of ICU. They said he's out of danger and he'll be able to go home in a few days. But no school for a while."

Kait slipped free of Trev and walked over to Sam and took her into her arms. "I'm so glad, honey," she whispered.

Sam pulled back to study her face. "I won't see Gabe anymore. I promised you I wouldn't if you stayed."

Before Kait could respond, Trev came forward. "Sam, Gabe needs you now. Who will help him keep up with his schoolwork if not you?"

Sam was wide-eyed. "Really?"

"Really." He cleared his throat. "It's hard for me to see you with a young man, because to me you're my little girl, and I don't think that will ever change. But I am going to try to be a bit more thoughtful and a bit less selfish where you and Gabe are concerned."

"Dad," Sam gasped, clearly at a loss for words.

"I want you to be happy, Sam. It's what I've always wanted," Trev said softly.

Sam stared. Kait tugged her on the shoulder. Sam flushed and walked over to her father and they embraced. "Dad . . . thanks," she said huskily.

"Sam, I love you."

"I love you too," she managed, pulling away. She brushed away several tears and then smiled at Kait.

Kait smiled back. "Is Marni in her room?"

"She's with Max, down at the stable." Sam headed back upstairs to her room. "See you guys later," she cried happily.

Kait found herself back in Trev's arms. "How are you going to manage with what Elizabeth tried to do?"

He stroked her hair. "I don't know. I honestly don't know. I'm very sad, Kait. How do you feel about Lana escaping the police?"

Kait hesitated. "I don't know. I'm sad, I guess, but I'm not angry anymore. I just want to go forward now—with you and the girls."

"Can I second that motion?" Trev asked.

No charges were pressed against Elizabeth, and she remained at the New Haven Hospital in a psychiatric ward. Lana had not been found. Kait wondered where she had gone, and somehow felt that she had vanished somewhere in South America. It was just an instinct, but it was strong.

Kait refused to dwell on the past. She immersed herself in all of her new duties and responsibilities. Elizabeth had run Fox Hollow, and now Kait found herself doing so. She had grounds to keep up, a household to run, books to keep. She took Marni back and forth to school every day, began seriously training with Jim, and was given a gorgeous gray hunter from a grinning Trev. She bought Sam and Marni new school clothes, Trev a winter jacket, and she packed up all of Lana's things—and stored them in the attic. She made breakfast every morning and supper every night—with Sam an eager helper. Several times a week Rafe joined them for dinner.

She went with Sam every day to visit Gabe in the hospital, and called on him and his mother several times at home. They were invited to Sunday dinner. It was a huge success.

And she and Trev couldn't seem to keep their hands off each other. The other day Jim had caught them in the hay room of the barn. They had both turned red like misbehaving teenagers. But they had christened his Dodge Ram, the kitchen, his study, and the bathroom. Now Kait lay in his arms in the huge four-poster bed in the master bedroom.

Trev stroked her hair and kissed her temple. "I don't think I've ever been happier, Kait."

Kait smiled at him. "These past few days, I've never been happier, Trev. With every day that goes by, it gets easier and easier to let the past slip away." She wasn't thinking just

·about her charade as Lana, but the fact that Lana had once been Trev's wife and the fact that she had disappeared without a trace.

"I know," he said, with a smile. "Sometimes I find it hard to believe that I was ever with anyone other than you." He sobered.

Kait sensed he was thinking about his first wife, Mariah, whom she knew he had loved. "You deserve happiness in the present, Trev."

Their hands found each other. "So do you."

"I didn't know her, but I've seen her picture and I know Mariah would be happy for you, too."

"Yes, she would." He smiled and kissed her temple.

"I think I was afraid," Kait said slowly, finally voicing feelings she hadn't wanted to admit, not even to herself. "I think I was afraid that this wouldn't work."

"That we wouldn't work?" Trev echoed, propping himself up on one elbow.

She cupped his cheek. "I said 'was.' " She searched for the right words. "I think I was afraid that the past would haunt us. But these past few weeks have been seamless. It's been so easy to slide into your life. Sometimes I forget there was ever a time when I wasn't here and we weren't together," Kait said earnestly. "And one day, maybe yesterday, maybe the day before, I woke up and there was no fear; there was only happiness."

He kissed her nose. "I was worried about the past too—until the day I went after you and brought you back. On that day, Kait, I closed the door on any fear. But I'm glad you've let go."

Their gazes held. Kait thought about Lana then. "Let's make a pact. This is the last time we will ever talk about the past—and about Lana."

"I can agree with that." He sat up against the pillows. So did Kait. "We won't ever see her again. I'm certain of it."

"Yes, I can actually feel it."

He took her hand. "We may have to wait a long time before we can legally marry."

Kait blinked. She was breathless. "Is that a marriage proposal?"

"I think I can do a bit better than that!" He was teasing. Then he sobered. "I already consider you my wife, Kait. That's how much I love you."

Kait wiped away tears. "I already consider you my husband, Trev."

He stared at her. Then, "Would you ever consider having my child?"

Kait gasped. "I would like nothing more!"

He softened; he looked ridiculously pleased; he pulled her close again, and murmured, "Soon?"

She felt herself smile. "There is nothing I want more, other than to spend the rest of my life here with you and the girls, Trev—and to have your children."

"Children? As in more than one?" He tilted up her face so he could look right into her eyes.

"I'm only thirty-two. I mean, we could have a couple of children—if you want."

He embraced her fiercely. "God, Kait, yes, I want! You have made me so happy these past few weeks."

She pulled back. "So don't strangle me! You're only happy because we're as insatiable as fifteen-year-olds," she teased.

He kissed her cheek. "Well, there's that, too."

Kait smiled and sank deeper into his arms. "Let's work on that baby, darling," she said.

"I think that can be arranged . . . sweetheart."

EPILOGUE

Seven Years Later

Their wedding guests were dancing to a seventies rock 'n' roll tune on the stone patio they had added to the back of the house several years before. The band was live. The dancing was beneath a mostly full and grinning moon on a hot July night. Waiters in white coats passed champagne and pieces of wedding cake. Kait was in her wedding gown, a simple but stunning strapless lace sheath. Trev remained the most handsome man she had ever seen, especially now in his tuxedo and dancing with Sam. At twenty-three, she was a tall, slim, and beautiful young woman. She was working for her Ph.D. in psychology at Princeton and she had come home on Friday for the wedding with a boyfriend Kait did not know. She and Gabe had broken up years ago, when she had gone off for her freshman year at Wesleyan.

Trev was not dancing alone with Sam—not exactly. Dancing with their father and their sister were dark-haired Josh and blond Lacy. Josh was five, Lacy two. They both had Trev's green eyes and olive complexion. Josh was doing his best to imitate his father, and Lacy was trying to swing her hips like Sam and almost tumbling over in the process.

Kait bit off a laugh and her gaze moved past her immediate family to where Rafe was slow-dancing with his wife amidst the wildly gyrating guests. Six years and they were still behaving like newlyweds. Anna Leigh's wild red hair was hanging almost to her waist, and she seemed to be trying to disappear into her husband's body in spite of her huge watermelon-sized stomach. The baby was due any day now, but they seemed about to make love on the dance floor.

Kait smiled at the sight of the somehow still skinny redhead and then saw Max Zara sneaking off into the gardens with Canada Jones, the most beautiful woman in America, or so *People* magazine had once claimed. Love was most definitely in the air. Funny, how they had seemed to hate each other at first sight. The tabloids had had a field day with that marriage too—a down-and-out PI and one of Hollywood's most infamous actresses.

Kait's smile disappeared. Speaking of family, where was Marni?

She glanced carefully at the two dozen dancing guests—they had decided to keep the wedding small and intimate. But her twelve-year-old daughter was nowhere to be seen.

Kait could imagine what she was up to, and worried, she hurried into the house. In amazement she halted in the living room, where their wedding gifts had been piled on the couch. Marni was with thirteen-year-old Blake, just as she had suspected, but they were not on the couch groping with their recently discovered adolescent hormones. Her beautiful daughter, who looked exactly like Kait except for her green eyes and olive skin, was arm wrestling the boy, and from the look of things, poor Blake was about to lose. But, then, Marni was already five foot four and a hundred pounds, while Blake hadn't even started to grow yet.

Marni said, "Take that, sucker," and she jammed his skinny arm down on the table and let out a satisfied and "in your face" whoop.

Blake flushed. "You might as well be a boy," he said, leaping to his feet. "Bet you're going to *like* girls when you grow up! Betcha you'll *never* have a boyfriend, weirdo!"

"You're just jealous because I'm stronger and faster than you," Marni said, making a face. In her sapphire blue dress and with a touch of lip gloss, she was so pretty and feminine—except for the childish face she'd just made and the fighting words she'd just uttered.

"At least I really am a boy—and not pretending like you to be one!" Blake ran out in disgust.

Marni said, "Sore loser!"

Kait bit back a smile. Marni had all of Lana's courage, recklessness, and athleticism. But unlike her biological mother, she could not tell a lie—no one was more sincere and honest. And except for Blake, whom Kait knew she had a huge crush on—when she was ten she had stated she would marry him when she grew up—she was kind and generous. But when Blake was around, she became her most tomboyish and insulting self.

"Oh, hi, Mom," Marni said, standing and looking impossibly beautiful in her simple sleeveless dress. Her feet were bare. A pair of low-heeled black-patent pumps lay discarded by the small table where she and Blake had been arm wrestling. Marni was scowling now.

"You might try losing next time—if you want Blake to remain a friend."

Marni said, "He thinks I'm a boy."

"I don't think so. I feel quite certain he sees you as the beautiful girl that you are."

Tears rose. "But he hasn't kissed me!"

"Marni!" Kait was aghast. "You're twelve!"

"But Kendra's been kissed five times already," Marni said grimly. "I am never going to be kissed. I'll die without ever being kissed."

Kait hid a smile. "I doubt it."

Marni started forward, barefoot. "I'm going to ask that stupid Paul Silva to dance." She stuck her chin in the air.

She didn't mean to be a matchmaker, but knowing where Marni's heart lay, she said softly, "You could ask Blake."

"Never!" Marni cried, flushing, and she started to race to the patio doors. Then she whirled and ran to Kait and hugged her. "I forgot to say congratulations, Mom. You're so beautiful tonight."

Kait smiled at her daughter. "Not half as beautiful as you."

The flattery seemed to go right over Marni's head. "Do you think I'm ready for a motocross bike?"

Kait sighed. Even Marni, who did not have a selfish bone in her body, knew how to manipulate. "No."

"But why not?" she wailed. "I won't break my neck! I'll be really careful! Please!"

"I'll think about it."

Marni grinned and hugged her again. "You're the best." She ran outside. "Hey, Dad! Mom's inside!"

As Kait watched Trev cross the patio, their eyes met and her heart tightened. *God, they were now man and wife.* They had waited seven years for Lana to be declared officially missing and dead. Seven long, long years, and now it was official at last.

She had married the man of her dreams, her very own Prince Charming.

He quietly strode across the room. "What are you doing?" He slipped his arm around her. "Are you crying?"

"I thought I might find Marni in here making out with Blake." She sniffled. "I'm so happy."

"I know. No such luck?" He was amused.

"She whipped him in arm wrestling."

Trev chuckled. "Poor Blake. Or should I say, poor Marni? She's so besotted! If she weren't such a tomboy, I'd be worried."

"She thinks she'll die without ever being kissed."

Trev chuckled again and reeled Kait in. "I'll settle for sixteen."

They kissed and groped for a long time. Finally Trev whispered, "Let's go upstairs."

"But we have guests."

"They won't care," Trev murmured. "But I do."

Kait knew he did, so she touched him. "Insatiable."

"Only for you."

They started for the stairs when Trev halted her. Kait blinked. "What is it?"

He sent her a smile and, without a word of warning, lifted

her into his arms. Kait cried out, then was deliriously thrilled. "Silly man," she chided.

"I've waited seven years to be able to do this," he declared, carrying her up the stairs.

Kait looked at his face. "Good God. You're not even huffing!"

"I have the kind of wife that keeps me in shape," he said smoothly.

She tickled his neck.

He burst out laughing. "That may backfire, wife! I may drop you!"

Kait ceased her antics and Trev paused on the threshold of their bedroom. Years ago Kait had redone it—the walls were a warm yellow now, the bed a pale but rich pine, the coverings and upholstery all shades of orange and gold. Kait clung to his neck and Trev stepped inside. "I love you, Kait Coleman," he said.

"I love you," Kait began, and then she saw the box wrapped in brown postal paper on the bed. "Trev, what's that?"

She expected him to grin secretively, but he was as confused as she. "I have no idea," he said, setting her down.

"You didn't put that there?"

"José told me we had a package this afternoon, but in the rush of getting ready for the wedding, I guess I forgot. He must have decided to bring it upstairs," Trev said.

Kait went over to the bed. The package was addressed to her—Mrs. Kait Coleman. "It's for me. It's not a wedding gift." She looked at the return address. There was no name—just an address. "It's from Rio de Janeiro," she said, puzzled. "I don't know anyone in Rio." And she became utterly still.

There had not been a single word or note from her twin, not in all this time. Kait had refused to believe that she was dead, but there had always been some doubt. Now Kait stared at the package and she knew.

Trev looked at her with wide eyes and she glanced up at him, too. "Maybe you do know someone in Rio," he said. "Maybe we do." Clearly, he was on her wavelength, too.

Kait breathed. Then she tore open the brown paper and opened the medium-sized box. Inside was white tissue paper, and for one moment she thought that was all. But then she found a small, flat black jeweler's box. "Oh, my God," she said, not touching it. Her heart seemed to have stopped. "It's from Lana."

Trev was silent for a moment. Then he said, "Open it."

Kait wet her lips and reached down and opened the small, flat box. She did not gasp. Inside there lay a magnificent diamond necklace. A tier of pear-shaped diamonds dangled from end to end, forming a glittering collar. It was clearly worth a fortune.

She looked up at her husband.

"She's alive," Trev murmured, meeting her gaze. "And up to her old tricks from the look of it. There's a card."

Kait was filled with relief then. After all of these years she now knew where Lana was and that she was, after all, alive. Suddenly Kait could picture her on a beach in front of a five-star hotel in Rio, sipping a piña colada, Colin Farrell at her side. She inhaled and set the necklace down. Her name had been scripted on the white envelope in handwriting that Kait recognized. Inside the envelope was an equally plain white card.

"Well?" Trev asked, hushed. "What does it say?"

Kait took his hand. " 'Congratulations,' " she said. "That's what it says. It says 'Congratulations.' "